*The Collected Short Novels*

PAUL THEROUX

# THE COLLECTED SHORT NOVELS

HAMISH HAMILTON · LONDON

HAMISH HAMILTON LTD
Published by the Penguin Group
Penguin Books Ltd, 27 Wrights Lane, London w8 5TZ, England
Penguin Books USA Inc., 375 Hudson Street, New York, New York 10014, USA
Penguin Books Australia Ltd, Ringwood, Victoria, Australia
Penguin Books Canada Ltd, 10 Alcorn Avenue, Toronto, Ontario, Canada M4V 3B2
Penguin Books (NZ) Ltd, 182–190 Wairau Road, Auckland 10, New Zealand

Penguin Books Ltd, Registered Offices: Harmondsworth, Middlesex, England

Phototypeset in Sabon 12/14.5 pt by Intype London Ltd
Printed in Great Britain by
Clays Ltd, St Ives, plc

A CIP catalogue record for this book is available from the British Library

ISBN 0-241-13568-0

# Contents

# Introduction

Though I hardly bought a book until I was in college, I was a greedy and indiscriminate reader and I haunted libraries, especially the mansion-like main library in my home town of Medford. I sidled along the open stacks, snatching at books with promising titles, then stood there sampling them. At *Generation of Vipers* or *The Naked and the Dead* or *'Tis Pity She's a Whore*, my hand leaped to the shelf. *Up from the Ape*, by Professor Carleton Coon, gave me a taste for reading about Early Man, his scary faces, his clumsy tools. If a book was condemned or denounced or listed on the Catholic Index of Banned Books, I sought it out. I had almost no guidance, except of the internal sort, as when Baudelaire praised Edgar Allen Poe, or Camus praised Faulkner, or Samuel Beckett recommended Leopardi. That was my literary vein. I also devoured books about travel ordeals, cannibalism, and strange customs in distant countries. Long before I began seriously to write, before I dared even wonder what my own writing might be, I read books out of an abiding hunger for stimulation and pleasure. This activity was both precious and monkey-like, but in this way I learned to read.

Among so many shelves in the open stacks of a library I was constantly aware of the physical nature of books – their assorted shapes, their bulgy lettered spines and different typefaces, the age and authority of a leather binding; gold leaf, scribbled margins, the frontispiece, the smell of mildewed pages, the foxed cover, or simply the fatness of a book. This is how I came to discover the novella, which jammed among bigger books was to me something elegant in shape and size, something I reached for. Slipping it off the shelf from the narrow space between two big-shouldered volumes gave me the thrill of discovery, that I was liberating the book and myself at the same time. Such a book was for me both a physical object and an intellectual pleasure. I liked the dimensions, the fact that it could be read at one long sitting. I was pleased by the look of it – the slimness of the volume, and the undoubted power that such a book, a very stiletto, could have. Almost the first one I read was Nathanael West's *Miss Lonelyhearts* – a dark, remorseless satire that exactly reflected my mood, which was both rebellious and eager to please – helpfully conflictive, striking sparks.

*Heart of Darkness* came later, with James Purdy's excursion into American gothic, *63: Dream Palace*, and *The Old Man and the Sea* and *Death in Venice* and *Daisy Miller*. Henry James, who called this form 'our ideal – the beautiful and blest *nouvelle*,' produced some other masterpieces of the sort, with *The Aspern Papers* and *The Turn of the Screw*. I remained attracted to this form that allowed some elbow-room while still remaining compressed, neither a novel nor a short story, but rather something in between, loosely called a novella (though in Italian *novella* means 'short story'; 'novel' is *romanzo*). Such books exerted a profound influence on me, though I did not become a writer until I shook off that influence and wrote from my own life. The length of the short novel continued to fascinate me.

This collection represents both my earliest and latest short novels. Thirty years separate them. I wrote *Murder in Mount Holly* in Uganda in 1966. It was published by Alan Ross in England in a small edition now prized by book collectors, because it was never reprinted and never published in the United States – its scarcity grotesquely inflated its value. *Bottom Feeders* was published in 1996, also in England, in the magazine *Granta*. Readers of my novel *Kowloon Tong* will recognize the Singapore-based American attorney, Hoyt Maybry, and will see how he came to have his unlikely passport.

*The Greenest Island* I wrote in London in 1975 in a period of disruption, moving from one house to another. I wrote the first draft quickly and then carried it around, rewriting and correcting. That is another pleasure of the short novel: it is portable. This sad story is also about the writing ambition. The title is from a poem by Wallace Stevens.

An English television director asked me to consider writing a story about London which revealed the complexity and the contradictions of the city. At the time I happened to be reading Henry James's *A London Life* – another wonderful *nouvelle* – and had been thinking of a London story that got to the heart of the city I knew. London society, all those layers, is almost impossible to gain access to – or, let's say, you might penetrate one layer but fail at another. Writers got nowhere. Americans were at a certain advantage. It seemed to me that an American call-girl, especially an ambiguous more presentable 'escort,' had access everywhere. I wrote *Doctor Slaughter* off my own bat, but when I showed it to the director he was deeply shocked and said it was too scandalous to be televised. Soon after that, it was bought by a movie producer and made into the film *Half Moon Street*.

*Doctor DeMarr* had an odd history. It began with my desire to write a story about twins, a simple plot: one twin dies mysteriously; the other twin assumes his brother's identity and solves the crime, by dying in the same way – revelation and death come at the same moment. (A related idea gave me the inspiration for my novel *Chicago Loop*.) Sometime after *Doctor DeMarr* appeared (in a volume with *Doctor Slaughter*) I reread it and was dissatisfied with it. Pretending that the published story was a rough draft, I rewrote it, and published it on its own. Literary history shows that writers from large families in which there is intense sibling rivalry (the Wildes, the Jameses, the Manns, the Joyces, the Stracheys, and others) frequently write about wicked twins.

Early in 1990, after almost eighteen years of being a resident alien there, I left Britain for good. I travelled in the Pacific,

INTRODUCTION

carrying a short novel with me (*Lady Max*, I worked on it in New Guinea and Tonga – it was to become part of the novel *My Other Life*). At last, I came to rest in Hawaii. *The Rat Room* is my first attempt at using Hawaii as a fictional setting.

Apart from their length, a common feature of these short novels is that they are intentionally disturbing. They are the sort of stories I looked for as a young prowler on the shelves of my local library.

# Murder in Mount Holly

# Prologue

A decent interval after his father died, about a month or so, Herbie Gneiss bought the *Mount Holly Chickadee*, studied the classified ads and said, 'Hee-hee-hee.'

Late the same evening he picked up the newspaper again, ripped out a little section and laughed again. His laughter came in bursts, like a tire-pump being plunged very quickly.

The next day he stood in a phone booth and dialed a number. Although he frowned several times while he was speaking on the phone, he smiled when he left the booth.

Mr Gibbon squinted at the grey specks moving towards him. Soon he made out the distinctive shape of a Patton tank leading a convoy of supply trucks. Jeeps loaded with troops followed the trucks. Far behind were the soldiers, thousands of troops wearing field packs, carrying the wounded, staggering, pushing towards Mr Gibbon who stood at attention in his starched uniform. Far to the rear were the guided missiles on flat-cars, the big bombers overhead, crates and crates of ammo stenciled with the familiar battalion insignia (a jackdaw with a worm in its beak; the motto *Pro Futuro Aedificamus*). Mr Gibbon's heart skipped slightly as he raised his hand and waved the convoy past him. He saluted the big brass in the jeeps, the old man himself, tough, steely, sitting there with a bottle of bourbon clenched between his knees. He nodded to the foot-soldiers.

Everything was okay.

'Roger,' said Mr Gibbon. He licked his pencil and made a notation on a clip-board.

In the cloakroom of the Mount Holly Kindergarten Miss Ball counted coins from a jam jar into a dark hand. When she had counted all the coins she gestured for them to be put back into the jar. The counting started again.

The coins had been counted four times when Miss Ball turned the jam jar over and tapped on the bottom. Then she shook it. There was no sound.

The dark hand closed on the coins.

'Mucho, mucho,' Miss Ball said. Then she said, 'Better hurry off pronto.'

# *Part One*

Herbie had no choice. He had to get a job, for his mother's sake anyway. They weren't dirt-poor and chewing their nails, but his father's death insurance did not cover everything. At his mother's request he had to quit college and come home. His mother now thought she would starve. Herbie would have to work to support his mother; she was a very fat lady.

'I eat like a bird, but everything I eat turns to fat,' was Mrs Gneiss's explanation as she stared wide-eyed at her enormous knees.

Herbie imagined everything she ate adhering to the inside of her skin, inflating her. Nothing ever left his mother's body. Everything stuck.

'I've raised you good,' she would say in her suety voice, her lips never touching. 'And I think it's high time you made things a little easier for me. I haven't got long and I want it to be sweet.'

Herbie had entered college happily. He had been told dozens of times that he was not, as they say, 'college material,' but from what he could gather neither were any of the other 30,000 students college material. And if they were, and if the cross notes from the professors had any truth in them, then (*a*) it either took a long time to find the slobs, separate the wheat from the chaff or (*b*) any college worth its salt could tolerate a few ignoramuses or, as Herbie pictured himself, late-bloomers. He had planned on staying.

Once when he went home – it was Easter – he noticed that his father's processes seemed to be slowing down. A visit home after being away for more than a month made it clear to him that his father was slowly dying. Things were stopping in him, like lights being switched off in different parts of a city as you watch from a hill.

When Herbie got the news that it was all over he stomped his new waste-basket flat. Then he went home, rented a black suit, went to his father's funeral, was consoled by some people he didn't know, and before he knew it was back at college.

Almost as soon as he got off the bus after returning to college Herbie had trouble calling up the image of his father's face. He wished that his father had had a craggy face, an awful grin or a bald head, if only to remember him by. But Herbie could not remember what his father looked like. His father had no evidence of his having passed through and on, no evidence except some unpaid bills in the bottom bureau drawer and a bowling ball in the closet with under-sized finger-holes. It was his father's pride and joy. He had it specially made for his small hands. Mrs Gneiss discovered to her horror that, because of the holes, it was nearly unpawnable.

Fearing the worst, death by starvation, Mrs Gneiss ate everything there was to eat in the house the evening Mr Gneiss died. For a month this went on. She ran up bills and stocked the house with food, bought more and ran up more bills. Any hour of the day Mrs Gneiss could be seen in front of the television set licking her fingers.

One day Herbie got the letter he had been expecting:

Dear Herbert,

I think it's finally coming. Death, I mean. But that's okay. You go on with your studies and you study hard like you always meant to and someday you'll know what it's like to be a parent who is dying and has only a few moments to live (I wonder if I'll even have time to sign this letter?????). You be an awfully good boy and 'brace up' and remember to send your kids to college like I worked and slaved to. Teach them never to be 'ungrateful' and 'smart-alecky' and not to smoke in bed. I better stop now because my eyes are all sandy and tearing from crying and I need more light. Guess this is it. Oops, another pain. In the chest this time. Hope you're getting all 'A's' in all your subjects. Guess this is 'Goodbye' like they say. If you need anything just ask for it I'll be glad to do anything you want for you you only have to ask I'm always here.

So long from,
Your Sick 'Mom'.

He left the next day. When he arrived home his mother met him on the porch. She greeted him with a heavy and prolonged belch. She thumped her chest and reminded Herbie that that's where the pains were. Right (urp) there.

'Hello, ma.'

'I'm dying, Herbie.'

'I know.'

'This time it's for real.'

'I got your letter.'

Mrs Gneiss returned to where she had been sitting. A bowl of ice-cream, half-full, rested on the coffee table. Nearby there was a bag of potato chips. Mrs Gneiss cradled the bowl in her lap and picked up the potato chip bag and placed it next to her on the sofa. Then she dunked a potato chip into the ice-cream, scooped up some ice-cream and tossed the whole mess into her mouth. She licked and chewed and nodded for Herbie to speak.

Herbie couldn't think of anything to say.

'A mother's got rights,' Mrs Gneiss said thickly. Her next potato chip scoop broke under the strain of so much ice-cream. 'What ever happened to those man-sized chips?' she asked, glancing around the room.

'What do you want me to do?'

'You see any?'

'Any what?'

'Man-sized chips for the ice-cream dip.'

Herbie stood up and went to the far corner of the room. Then, at a safe distance, he shouted: 'Look, I don't mind getting your lousy letters and I don't mind coming back to this stinking house, but I do mind leaving college for good, moving out of the dorm, selling my bike . . .'

'Your gorgeous bike,' Herbie's mother mocked.

' . . . I said to myself, What's a semester? I said to myself . . .'

'You're going to give your mother a semester to die in?'

' . . . I thought you were lonely. I thought you needed someone around the house. I thought you were in trouble, sick or something . . .'

'I *am* sick.'

'You don't look sick to me.'

'The sickest people in the world don't look sick. I'm sick at heart. Heart-sick, that's what I am. And afraid.'

'You said you were *dying* in the letter.'

'Of course I'm dying. What do you expect? You think I'm going to live for ever?'

'I mean now. You said you were dying now.'

'You mean this semester?' Mrs Gneiss chewed.

'I don't know what I mean. I only thought that it was urgent. Now I get here and it doesn't look so urgent.'

Mrs Gneiss continued mumbling: 'I wouldn't have gotten you away from your precious books if I didn't think it was urgent.' She finished quickly. 'Now I'm sick and that's all there is to it.'

Herbie started to say something.

'I know what you're going to say. *You don't look sick.* [She mimicked him perfectly.] Well, for your information, I *am* sick. Seriously ill, as they say. I say I'm sick, and if I say I'm sick that should be good enough for you. If it's not . . .' Mrs Gneiss thought a moment. 'If it's not, well, tough taffy, you're home and you're staying home until I drop. You've got to like it or lump it. You've got to *learn* to like it – as we used to say back at *college*!' This sent Mrs Gneiss into torrents of creamy laughter.

With only his mother's death on his mind, Herbie said, 'Okay.'

'It won't be so bad.'

'No.'

'Course, you might have to get a job, and all that.'

*A job?* The word had almost no meaning for Herbie. He was one of those people who had escaped the tedium of paper-routes and had dodged what other more enterprising adolescents had got: selling glow-in-the-dark Krismiss Kards, foot balm, tins of greasy unguent – all in return for B-B guns and autographed catchers' mitts. Herbie had never worked a day in his life. There was simply no need to work. He liked to read and had started smoking at an early age. So why should he have had to work (of all things) to kill time? There were thousands of ways to kill time without working. And besides, his father was always there, *had been* at least. A very little man, very generous, very hard to remember; one of those faces that no one can describe – probably a perfect criminal's face. Herbie had gotten money out of him. Now Herbie missed him, for the first time in his life.

Herbie sighed.

'It won't be for long,' said Herbie's mother. Then she added, 'Although the longer the better, if you can see this from my point of view.'

Herbie looked at his mother. She was still eating away happily, shoveling in the ice-cream on potato chips. One thing about his mother: she wasn't a show-off. She didn't try to pretend she was thin. She knew she was fat. She looked fat. She had no time for girdles; she never used make-up, had never had her face lifted. Her one extravagance had been painting her toe-nails, but this was now virtually impossible. She would have had to learn to be a contortionist, and she knew there were no fat contortionists. Her wish now was to sit, to be left alone with a lot of food, and to spread in all directions under her kimono. There are two ways to die, Herbie thought: one, you don't eat enough and you starve to death; two, you stuff yourself and collapse with a belch. No, he didn't hate her. But if she had to go it might as well happen along the starchy street she had been traveling all along. It was her wish.

'When do I start?'

'Very soon.'

'All right, I'll just unpack . . .'

'Don't bother,' said Herbie's mother.

'Don't bother? I thought you said you wanted me around?'

'I do,' she said, shushing him. 'I want you around here so bad I could yell, but there are no jobs hereabouts, so you'll have to live near where you work . . .'

Herbie's mother summed up the job situation. There were too many Puerto Ricans from God knows where working for a song. They took all the jobs there were to take. It was the way of these Puerto Rican people. They really didn't want the jobs. What they really wanted was a lot of bananas. But their senses told them: move in and take the jobs. They didn't know what to do with the jobs once they got them, but there were a lot of Puerto Ricans and only a few good honest hard-working kids like Herbie in Holly Heights.

Holly Heights was a suburb of Holly. There were also Lower Holly, Mount Holly, Holly-on-the-Ivy (a creek), East, West, North and South Holly, Holly Junction, Holly Falls, Holly Rapids, Hollyville, Hollypool, Hollyminster, Holly Springs and a dozen others, including, yes, Hollywood. This covered an area of about two hundred square miles.

If Herbie moved into Holly proper, or in the adjoining burg of Mount Holly, he would have a better chance. There were lots of jobs going begging.

'I've never begged in my life,' said Herbie.

'Oh, tons of jobs,' Herbie's mother said. 'Just remember, there are bills to pay. Medicine, your father's medicine. It seems a downright shame to have to pay for medicine now that he's dead. It's seems crazy. I mean, why did we buy the medicine in the first place? And the embalmer's fees, the flowers and the headstone. Well, that's a break – you won't have to get another headstone for

me, although you'll have to have my name chiseled on the stone.
Extra with the initial. And there's always my food. Food is just
like medicine to me.' Mrs Gneiss stopped talking as soon as
she remembered what she had said about her dead husband's
medicine.

'A job.'

'When we get some cash you'll be free and clear. So will I. I'll
be able to rest easy.' *Rest easy*, Mrs Gneiss thought; that's a slip
of the tongue. 'Just try not to think about it,' she went on. 'Do
your work and send home some cash every week. I'll send you
fried chicken in the mail, and letters too. Like always.' Then, for
no reason at all, she said, 'It'll be like old times.'

'I was doing pretty good at college, you know.'

'You'll be able to go back,' said Herbie's mother. 'After.'

'Mmmm.'

'Do this for me, Herbie. Just this once.'

Herbie promised that he would. His mother really wasn't so
bad. Just fat was all. He would go to Mount Holly and make
good. There were lots of jobs there; lots of factories were crying
to get people.

'Kant-Brake,' said Herbie's mother. 'They need people real
bad.'

'Well, maybe I'll look them up.'

'You will.'

'I will?'

'Yes, I've written a letter to the owner. Used to know your
father,' said Mrs Gneiss, handing her son the letter. 'You've just
got to look neat as a pin and they'll hire you. And give them the
letter.'

'What the hell,' Herbie said. 'Might as well be there as any
other place. What did you say they made there?'

'Toys. You know, toys? Those little . . .'

'Oh, toys.'

Mrs Gneiss was through with her explanation. She turned
back to the T V. She champed her ice-cream sullenly. After a few

moments a fearful burp trembled through her body, crinkling her kimono and making her shake her head. It sent Herbie out of the room and into bed.

The next day Herbie kissed his mother goodbye and took the bus to Holly Heights. When he arrived he bought a newspaper. First a room, then a job, he thought. His eye was caught by an ad for a room. He called the number. A woman answered and, though her voice was a trifle shrill, seemed nice. She said he'd have to come over. Herbie agreed. Herbie mentioned Kant-Brake Toys. She said she had another boarder at Kant-Brake Toys. Herbie said that sounded just fine. He went right over.

## 2

Mr Gibbon was a fuddy-duddy, not a geezer, but he was old, chewed his lips, dressed horribly and so often he was taken for a geezer. He lived in Miss Ball's house, on the second floor.

He had few possessions. Each possession had a special significance. There was his comb. It was *part* of a comb, about five plastic teeth at various distances apart on a bitten spine. Mr Gibbon had used that same comb since boot camp. It was the last thing his Aunt gave him. In fact, it was the last thing his Aunt gave anybody, since she died on the railroad platform waving goodbye to the seventeen-year-old Charlie Gibbon as his train pulled away bound for New Jersey. So the comb was special. He used the comb often. The strange and even sick part of it all was that he used it without a mirror. He would stand, one arm crooked over his head, his eyes on an object so distant that it had no name, and he would scrape away at his scalp with those five plastic teeth.

Like most old men he wore his watch to bed. He had forgotten the last time it was off his wrist. But he remembered distinctly the time he got it, a bargain at the Fort Sam Baker P X in Missouri, two dollars and sixty cents. It was a huge watch and ticked very loudly. The chrome had flaked off and revealed brass underneath. The watch was so big that even Mr Gibbon could wind it. And Mr Gibbon had very thick fingers.

Mr Gibbon's other valuable possessions were his .45 calibre pistol (he had killed a man with it, he said), his canteen with the bullet hole through the side (it had foiled the killing of Mr Gibbon), a picture of his wife and two daughters in a bamboo frame he had bought somewhere near the Equator somewhere on an island somewhere, also his army discharge papers, his khakis, his clips of bullets, his hunting knife ('A man should own enough knife to protect himself with,' he said), his neatly made bed, his paper bags and his tennis shoes.

Of these last two items the bags were the most important; the tennis shoes were more of a sentimental thing. Mr Gibbon made it a practice to carry paper bags wherever he went, wrinkled brown-paper bags. It was hard to tell what was in the bags since they were not bulky enough to show the outlines of any distinguishable object. Even if they did contain a large object they were wrinkled enough to conceal the object's identity. Often the paper bags contained nothing more than many carefully folded paper bags. Mr Gibbon enjoyed the stares of people who were perplexed by a particularly huge brown-paper bag he had carried into town one day. He did not take the bus that day. Instead he walked all the way home, past all the eyes of most of his neighbors. What was in the bag? More bags. Mr Gibbon smiled and tucked his secret under his arm. Many times he hailed and hooted a good morning to another old man merely because the other man was also carrying a bag. He imagined a fraternity of old men carrying armloads of wrinkled bags. He saw them all the time.

The tennis shoes replaced his army boots, which he saved for special occasions (riding in a car, resting, cleaning his pistol). They were black basket-ball sneakers – the kind that a high school student wears after school. The canvas was black, the rubber was white. In spite of the thick rubber soles they added no spring to his step. He walked along the sidewalk with a pflap-pflip-pflap-pflip of the canvas and rubber, the long lacings trailing several inches behind. Over the ankle-bone there was a round label which read:

OFFICIAL TENNIES
'The Choice of Major Leaguers!'

He wore no socks. Usually his trousers were baggy and long enough to conceal the fact, but sometimes his white ankle flesh could be seen over the black tennis shoes as he walked along the sidewalk looking very much like a little wooden man marching down a plank, weaving from side to side.

What nearly everyone noticed first about Mr Gibbon were his eyes. They were cloudy, pearly and ill-looking. It was his eyes that got him discharged from the army and not the fact that he was at retirement age. He had changed his age several times on his file-card to make absolutely sure that he would die in the army. There was no way to disperse the fog in his eyes. He could see all right, his eyes were 'damn good' and he had never been sick a day in his life. Yet his eyes looked wrong. They were the wrong color. Indeed, there seemed to be something seriously wrong with those eyes. They were the color of non-fat milk.

Mr Gibbon's nose was sharp, as was his chin and the ridge of his head where the skull-sutures pushed against the skin. His neck was a collection of wattles, folds and very thin wrinkles. The base of his neck seemed small, bird-like, as if it had been choked thin by a tight collar for many years.

And his mouth. 'I've got fifteen teeth,' Mr Gibbon was fond of saying. The teeth were not visible. They were somewhere within the shapeless lips which stretched and chewed even when Mr Gibbon was not eating. It was the kind of mouth that caused people to think that he was a nasty man.

From the rear he looked like nearly every other man his age. His head was wide at the top, not a dome, but a wedge. The back of his skinny neck was an old unhappy face of wrinkles. There was even a wrinkle the size of a small mouth, frowning from the back of Mr Gibbon's neck. His ears stuck out, his shoulders were bony and rounded, his spine protruded. He was vaguely bucket-assed, but not so much bucket-like as edgy, a flat bottom that is known as starchy, as if it contained a large piece of cardboard.

'You can't rile me,' Mr Gibbon said. It was mostly true. He stayed calm most of the time, and when he was angry did not speak: instead he wheezed, he puffed, he blew, he sighed, he groaned. And maybe he would mumble an obscenity or two.

His favorite song was the National Anthem, and the less violins, the more brass, the better. An old song, he said, but a good solid one. You'd be proud to get up on your hind legs and be counted when it played – it was that kind of song, a patriotic song. 'If you wanna name names, I'm a patriot,' said Mr Gibbon. He liked the anonymity of citizenship and patriotism. He wanted to be in that great bunch of great people that listened, that saluted, that obeyed the country's command whether at home or abroad, whether down at the pool hall or far afield, at work or at play. The song ran through him and charged his whole body and made it tingle. Mr Gibbon wheezed and spat when he was angry, but he also wheezed and spat when he was emotionally involved; he got choked up. Something of a patriotic nature always brought rheum to his eyes: hearing the Anthem, seeing the Flag or his army buddies. Or just the thought of them.

He had resigned himself to being out of the army as much as he could. You couldn't do it completely. He knew that. It was in the blood. It was something that wouldn't leave you for all your born days. Something you wouldn't want to leave even if it were possible. Something great and good. Something powerful.

It was a sad day when the army doctor took a last look at Mr Gibbon's cloudy eyes and said, 'There's something sick about them eyes. I don't know what medical science would say, but I don't like the looks of them . . .'

That was all there was to it. In a few days Mr Gibbon was out of the army. He had been in for thirty-eight years. 'That's a lifetime for some people, thirty-eight years,' he would say. And when he was feeling very low he would say, 'That was my lifetime, thirty-eight years in Uncle Sam's army. Just hanging on now for dear life, and I don't know whether I'm coming or going.'

Mr Gibbon was smart enough to know that things were different in the army. Life was better, if not richer. There was good company, a nice bunch of kids. Raw kids, greenhorns, but they learned in the long run. They learned to pitch-in and fall-to. Life in the army was a constant reward. It was Mr Gibbon's first real haircut, grammar school, a trip to the zoo. For a man who had never had a youth that he remembered, and who could not remember whether (or not) he had passed through puberty, the army was a tremendously satisfying experience. Not really the romance of the recruiting poster, although there was more of that in it than people ordinarily thought. In the army you were someone, a man in khakis, a full-time threat to the enemy; Mr Gibbon was 'Pop' to a lot of young kids and a buddy to a lot of the others. Need a little advice on VD, a needle and thread, some notepaper, card tricks, funny stories? Want to know what the Jerries were really like? Ask Pop Gibbon.

Now he was out of the army and it pained. Maybe it was the weather, but the weather had never caused him to pain before. Pain in his back, his neck, his finger joints. Or his clothes were damp. His clothes had never been damp before. And when he did not pain he felt sticky, or maybe one of his teeth would be giving him a time. In the army he never had a sick day, although the Doc and others examined his eyes now and then and pre-scribed 'rest, lots and lots of rest for them eyes,' or 'try a little epsom salts, Charlie, bathe them and then get some rest, lots of . . .' Worse than all the civilian aches and pains was the one thought that occurred to him over and over again, the thought which zipped into his mind one morning and which stayed there, for good it seemed. Mr Gibbon had been on his way to take a bath and did not feel a need to take the precaution of wearing a robe (besides, nakedness always reminded Mr Gibbon pleasantly of the army). He was padding along the hall placidly, with a towel over his arm and his comb in his hand, and wearing his tennis shoes for slippers, and he passed one of the bedrooms and caught a glimpse of someone moving. He stopped and peeked through the door. He was right. In the full-length mirror he saw an old man, almost totally bald, carrying a broken comb and a tattered towel and wearing a suit of shrivelled fat.

It brought Mr Gibbon up short. He tried to cover himself with the towel, but to no avail. The towel was too small and too shredded. Mr Gibbon spilled over into the mirror. When he turned away from the mirror he got the most revolting view of all, a rear view, dying flesh retreating, and it was not starchy at all. It was just awful.

He could not forget the old man in the fat suit walking stupidly, awkwardly away from the full-length mirror. It had not been like that in the army. He had been a big strong man in the army. The army had promised to train Mr Gibbon. They had kept their promise. They had trained him to check the firing-pins on various large caliber shells; they had trained him to cook boiled cabbage and greens for upwards of 300 hungry, dog-faced foot-soldiers; they taught him to weld canteens, shout marching orders, cure rot, detect clap and execute a nearly perfect about-face. These trades had kept Mr Gibbon wise, his muscles in tune. In his thirty-eight army years Mr Gibbon learned many trades up and down.

When he was discharged he found that army trades were not exactly civilian trades, although there were some similarities.

At first Mr Gibbon did not try to get a job, but as he said, he had always been 'on the go.' It was the army's way to be always on the go. So twiddling his thumbs did not appeal to him. He was not a man of leisure. He took pride in making and doing a little each day. He had some money and a little pension, but it was not a question of money. Raising chickens was out, so was drinking coffee with unshaven men in the automat, watching people go by, remembering number plates, spotting cars and playing cards. Mr Gibbon was a little foolish, but he was not stupid and, perhaps worst of all, he had not yet been blessed with the time-consuming affliction of senility. He was in the still-awake period of dusk which exists for old people in retirement between the last job and the first trembling signals of crotchety old age and near madness. Still lucid.

He could be useful. To himself and his country. But he was worried when he thought of his training; the army had trained him well, but what use is a firing-pin fixer, rot curer, cabbage boiler and canteen welder in the civilian world? What good? No good, Mr Gibbon concluded. He took odd jobs at first, and even saw the humor in this. Gibbon, the taker of odd jobs. That's what it had come to.

His first odd job was with the Municipal Council of Lower Holly, directing a road-fixing crew. But the workers would not be threatened with demerits and they did not have the respect (and fear) that recruits generally had for Mr Gibbon. If Mr Gibbon gave an order they paused, shuffled their feet, and from the middle of the group of workers another order would be shouted back: 'Go back to the old folks' home, Grandpa!' Once a man told him to go suck his thumb.

His next jobs were as an usher in the movies, a special policeman at the Holly Junction bathing beach and as a cab-driver on the late shift of the We-Drive-U-Kwik Cab Company. It was not long before Mr Gibbon retired his flashlight and braided usher's cap, his badge and night-stick. The odd job with the cab company bore some fruit, killed some time, and it even showed signs of speeding Mr Gibbon right into his grave with no stop-over at senility or madness.

It was his third week on the job that finished him. The week of the teeth. Mr Gibbon had just gotten an upper plate of new false teeth.

'New false teeth,' Mr Gibbon had said to the dispatcher. '*New* false teeth. False and new. It sounds crazy, doesn't it?'

The cab dispatcher said that he had known a lot of people that had new false teeth. They liked them, the new false teeth. So why should Mr Gibbon think they were so crazy?

'I didn't say I *thought* they were crazy,' Mr Gibbon corrected. 'I said new false teeth *sounded* crazy. Like new used cars sounds crazy.'

The cab dispatcher did not see Mr Gibbon's point at all.

The teeth, both new and false, did not fit well. Or maybe it was Mr Gibbon's gums that did not fit. Whatever it was, it made his mouth pain, and Mr Gibbon said he'd have to get his gums in shape before he could stand them a full day. It was towards the end of the third week that the accident happened. The teeth were resting on the seat beside Mr Gibbon as he drove down the Main Street late one night. Then he heard the familiar squawk from the sidewalk and whipped the cab over to the customer. The customer got in and sat on the front seat; Mr Gibbon said, 'Where to, Johnny?'

But when he said it he realized that his teeth were under the man. He reached for them. The man, far from indignant, took Mr Gibbon's arm and happily guided it. The two-way radio crackled. Mr Gibbon gasped and struggled with the giggling man for full possession of his hand, his teeth, his wits. The car veered sharply and tore down the wrong lane of Holly Boulevard with the two reaching men, one grasping and wheezing, one delighted, in the front seat. The cab dispatcher back at the We-Drive-U-Kwik office listened to the wheezing and giggling. The cab dispatcher yelled into the microphone. Mr Gibbon lunged for the radio. In doing so he lost control of the car completely and rammed a utility pole. Two voices – one from the radio, one from the seat next to him – sassed him, told him he was a useless old fool, a flop, and a tease.

The door slammed and the radio went dead. Mr Gibbon left the We-Drive-U-Kwik Cab Company that same night. His sat-on teeth were broken, his pride had been toyed with, his age mocked once again, and for the first time in his life Mr Gibbon had been chewed out. In a matter of minutes his job was taken from him. And it was a long time before he found another one.

Six months later Mr Gibbon became a quality control inspector in the military department of the Kant-Brake Toy Factory. And, like all the other workers in the same department, he wore a uniform showing his rank and months of service. Medals were given for safety, punctuality and high bowling scores. Mr Gibbon was in heaven.

It was the logical place to go, but somehow the thought had not even occurred to Mr Gibbon. Why not a toy factory? It was the only place outside of the army itself that made murderous weapons a speciality. Kant-Brake manufactured soldiers, millions of planes, gunboats, bombers, bullets, sub-machine guns, tents, tanks, Jeeps, and even little officer's quarters right down, as the catalogue said, 'to the geraniums on the general's lawn.' Every weapon of war, murder, spying or sabotage could be found under the Kant-Brake roof. Some designs which were under construction had only just appeared on the drawing boards in the Pentagon. The Kant-Brake Company bragged that it turned out more planes, more ships and more tanks 'than all the world's man-sized factories put together!' They made a nuclear sub that could fire sixteen high-powered missiles. The missiles alone that appeared at Kant-Brake were so many that they were equal in number 'to all the bombs dropped by both sides during World War II.'

The emphasis was on realism, on craftsmanship. Now the toy soldiers could be wounded, bandaged, cared for. 'They bleed real blood!' the ads ran. And everything they said was true – you could hardly tell it from the 'real thing.' Each item was perfectly formed, expertly detailed; the colonels frowned, the captains were grim, the faces of the foot-soldiers were twisted in fear, pain, anxiety. Midget canteens held real water. The bombs fumed, the tanks groaned, the rockets were guaranteed to light up any child's play-room in a red glare.

Mr Gibbon was good with his hands, and his memory for army details was infallible. He could spot an imperfect M-1 several feet away. He studied rocketry in the evenings, and he had plans for complicated war games that he hoped would be accepted by the Games Department. Kids nowadays, he said, didn't give a hoot for Chinese Checkers and Old Maid. Kids had a vital interest in the world. War toys stimulated kids to keep up with current events. War toys were good for kids; a well-armed kid could work out all his aggressions in a single Christmas morning.

The director of Kant-Brake also held surprise inspections. The company picnics were called 'maneuvers.' The annual convention in West Holly was called a 'bivouac.' The company prospered.

Mr Gibbon stood at attention near the conveyor belt and squinted at the grey specks moving toward him. As they passed he gave a snappy salute, made a notation on his clip-board and said 'Roger.' Mr Gibbon watched the parade of toys pass.

## 3

Miss Ball taught kindergarten, loved her country and things with catchy names. Her house was full of things with catchy names: Stay-Kleen, Brasso, Reck-Itch, Keen-tone, Kem-Thrill, Kwickee-Treets and Frosty-Smaks. At school she had Ed-U-Kards in her Ed-U-Kit, Erase-Eez and all the Skool-Way products. She also had a Snooz-Alarm Clock (' . . . It lets you sleep') and hundreds of other things with catchy names. They kept her in the swim, she said.

She knew the value of a dollar, and even though she always

bought things 'on time' she paid her bills. It was not that she owed no man. She owed everyone. But she always paid up.

And so when her lover, Juan, the school janitor, needed a few extra two-bits, she always paid. She called it 'pin-money.' Juan's demands became more and more, and still Miss Ball paid or promised to pay. She had no intention of dropping Juan just because there wasn't enough money in the jam jar. When Juan grew impatient and muttered in the broom closet, Miss Ball had the presence of mind to take a day off from school.

It took a whole afternoon in the wing-chair to come up with the solution. When it finally occurred to her she jumped up from the chair, said 'Happy days,' and then smugly announced: 'I'll advertise.'

She did just that. She had plenty of room in the house. Why not take in another boarder? She decided to place an ad in the *Mount Holly Chickadee*. Her ad in the classified section of the paper was characteristic of her sweet disposition.

### COMFY ROOM FOR PEANUTS

Large homey room, warm, for single male, hooked rug, big quilt, just perfect for student who wants all the comforts and doesn't mind sharing 'boy's room.' Kitchen priv., tender loving care. Can't miss. Cheap. Nice. Call after 6. Tel. 65355.

She just couldn't keep it down to twenty-five words. It would have been a crying shame to do that.

She knew that it would click, too. Just as the ad which had fascinated Mr Gibbon had clicked. But still she ran the ad for three days 'just,' as she said to Mr Gibbon, 'for the sheer heck of it.'

Mr Gibbon grunted something in return (he was out of sorts) and went on with his paper bags. He was now used to Miss Ball, and on top of it had been in the army. Miss Ball's fling with Juan came as no great surprise. Things like that happened every day when you were in the army. Like when you find out your best buddy is a crumby stooge, or the C. O. is a pansy, or your best girl ran off with your best friend and never wrote back except to say, Dearest, I'm going to make a clean breast of it. It was all in the army, all in the game. As for Miss Ball and Juan, that dago bastard, Mr Gibbon really didn't give a rat's ass what happened.

He knew that she, Miss Ball, had just had that thing, that operation that women had sometimes. He couldn't blame her. Women always did screwy things like making their hair navy blue (Miss Ball's was 'Starry Silver'), or putting lard on their faces, or even running off with the crazy Puerto Rican janitor at the school. He was an army man through and through, and understood these things like other people couldn't understand them, since they had never had the privilege of going out and fighting, really fighting, with their guts, for their country. How could they know? But Mr Gibbon knew damn well what was going on in Miss Ball's mind. She was having her fling. He had seen a lot of folks come over the hill in his time, a damn sight more than a lot of people he knew that were always shooting their mouths off about human nature and such and such. He had seen people lose their marbles, too. Right in the same foxhole Mr Gibbon had seen a man lose nearly every one of his marbles. But Mr Gibbon had not done a damn thing because he had seen a lot of people come over the hill. He had seen guys on leave. Guys that had been in the trenches for days, months even. They had to get it out of their system.

Miss Ball? She had to get it out of her system too. So what if she was near sixty? Did that mean she didn't have anything in her system maybe? Like hell. Gibbon could testify to the exact opposite of that little theory. You could bet your furlough on that. What made people think that young folks were different from old folks? That was something Mr Gibbon could not understand.

What went for Mr Gibbon went for Miss Ball. They were friends, comrades. Mr Gibbon said nothing and that was good enough for Miss Ball. If Mr Gibbon had told her one time he had told her a hundred: *You're young at heart.*

'You're young *too*,' Miss Ball cheeped, when Mr Gibbon gave his consent to the unsavory business with Juan.

'Not me, Toots,' Mr Gibbon said gruffly.

Miss Ball had said he could have it his way. And he did have it his way. He could see what was going on in Miss Ball's head, thinking all those crazy things. But still, he knew she was in no danger. It was her way. She *was* young at heart; why else did she stay up late reading all those movie magazines? But you'd never catch Mr Gibbon making a damn fool out of himself with any two-bit big-assed movie queen (both Miss Ball and the magazines called them 'starlets').

Miss Ball believed that she was a starlet, although a little older than most of the other starlets. After her hysterectomy she believed it even more. And that was when Juan came on stage and left his broom behind. A few months later she placed the ad. It was all nice.

The ad clicked, as Miss Ball had predicted to Mr Gibbon.

After one day the phone rang.

The voice was young. A young gentleman. Perfect.

'Herbie what?' Miss Ball asked.

'Gneiss,' said Herbie. He spelled it out and then pronounced it.

This bewildered Miss Ball. She asked him his nationality.

'American, I guess.'

'You guess?'

'American.'

'We're all Americans in this house,' said Miss Ball triumphantly. 'Me and Mr Gibbon – he's the most American one of all. You'll like him lots.'

'I'm sure I will,' said Herbie.

Herbie went on to inquire about the 'boy's room' that was mentioned in the ad. What exactly was the boy's room and who would he have to share it with?

'I should have explained,' said Miss Ball. 'I'm a *teacher*. I teach kindergarten in the basement of Mount Holly High. We call the boy's room the boy's room. I should have explained. How silly of me!' She giggled.

'Oh,' said Herbie.

'What do you do?'

'Well, I'm not working at present. But I think I'll be working at Kant-Brake. The toy factory.'

'Holy mackerel! That's where Mr Gibbon works! What a co-*in*-cidence!'

'Fabulous,' said Herbie dryly.

'Why, you can't turn me down *now*!' Miss Ball said with glee. 'Mr Gibbon'll be sore as a boil if you don't come.'

'I see,' said Herbie.

'We've got something in *com*-mon!' exclaimed Miss Ball as if she had found her son, lost these many years.

'So we do,' said Herbie.

'I'll expect you for supper. At six. Don't be a minute late, Mr Gibbon doesn't like cold greens.'

'Who is this Mr Gibbon?' Herbie asked. But Miss Ball had already hung up.

A new tenant! It was like a gift from above. *He will provide.* That was Miss Ball's motto. He always provided. First the oper-ation, then Juan, then Herbie, who worked at the very same place as Mr Gibbon! Wonders never did cease as long as He provided in the moment of need. He could positively move mountains. Good Old Providence.

In Miss Ball's case He had moved something considerably more spherical than a mountain. He did just that from His Dwelling Place Up There where things were white mostly, soft, and didn't cost a cent. It really was as simple as all that. If only people knew what the very simple secret was: make yourself like a little child. You had to make yourself tiny and really believe in that Big Man Up There. Making herself like a starlet was, in her mind, the same thing as making herself like a little child, pleasing and fresh as a daisy to The Big Fellow In The Sky. And why not a starlet? Especially since she had a natural bent in that

THE COLLECTED SHORT NOVELS

direction, a gift, so to speak. It was all the same. He knew what was in your heart. You couldn't fool Him.

So Miss Ball got a new tenant, Herbie, and she was able to raise Juan's allowance, and she found that she was better natured to her kindergarten. Everything was rosy. All the money that Herbie would pay for room and board Miss Ball would turn over to Juan. It all came out in the end. She was no Jew. Why should she try to make a buck on a kid that didn't have beans to start with? That wasn't her way. Not Miss Ball. Maybe *some* people, but not Miss Ball.

# 4

'So what, he's nice,' Mr Gibbon said. Herbie had not come at six. Mr Gibbon had his cold greens and grumbled about them, and now, at breakfast, he was still grumbling. Herbie had arrived late and Mr Gibbon had heard the racket. He was awakened from a vicious dream: a Dark Stranger was trying to steal his paper bags. The Dark Stranger had snatched nearly every one of them. It was a Negro, a tall one, who wanted the bags to put watermelons in. Mr Gibbon had fought with him, and during the fight woke to the noise of Herbie banging the bureau drawers in the next room.

'That's his name.' Miss Ball spelled it out and pronounced it. 'Gneiss.'

'It sounds Jewish if you ask me.'

'Everything sounds Jewish if you say it a certain way,' said Miss Ball, trying for a little wisdom. 'But he's not. He's not Jewish.'

'Probably changed it.'

'He said he's American.'

'All Jews think they're Americans. Everybody does. That's the only fault I can find with this country. Everybody thinks they're so damn big. Like this Gneiss.'

'Don't be so cranky. You don't even know him.'

'You're the one who's cranky.'

'He's okay. He looks tip-top. Very clean-looking.'

'That's not like you, Miss Ball. Sticking up for a Jew.'

'I'm not sticking up for a Jew. I'm sticking up for my new boarder.'

'He's a Jew.'

'He's not. He's a fine young man with a remarkably small nose.'

'What's the difference. They'll take over the country, like everyone else, I suppose. They'll come.' Mr Gibbon heaved a sigh. 'But I hope to God they don't come in my lifetime.'

'Shush,' said Miss Ball. 'You're big and strong. You've got a lot of time left.'

'I hate that expression *you've got a lot of time left*. Like you're waiting to punch the time-clock and drop dead.'

'He must be dead tired. He came by bus all the way from Holly Heights.'

'Used to have a guy in the platoon named Gnefsky, or something like that. He was a Jew.'

'He's not a Jew.'

'Don't tell me! He was in my platoon, not yours. I should know.'

'I mean Herbie, the new boy.'

Mr Gibbon muttered. He couldn't grit his teeth. He didn't have enough of them to grit.

'He wanted to know what the boy's room was. Isn't that *precious*?'

'In the army we used to call it the crapper. He probably doesn't know what *that* means either.'

'Now you just be careful what you say,' said Miss Ball. She clapped her hands and then said, 'Oh, I'm so excited! It's like opening night!'

'He probably smokes in bed.'

'It reminds me of the day I saw the playback of my movie. That was in . . . let's see . . .'

For the next few minutes Miss Ball relived a story she had told so many times that Mr Gibbon was actually interested to see what changes she had made since the last time he heard it. There she was, Miss Ball in her first starring role, madly in love with the dashing special agent. He was an undercover man but, unlike most undercover men, everyone knew him and feared him. He was big and strong, liked good wine and luscious women and was always forking over money to flocks of ragged stool-pigeons who tipped him off. He dressed fit to kill and was very well-mannered. And when the spying was over for the day he came back to his sumptuous apartment and slapped Miss Ball around. When he got tired of slapping her around he nuzzled her, and bit her on the neck, and then threw her a gold *lamé* dress and they went out on the town where, in the middle of their expensive dinner, they were set upon by the squat shaven-headed crooks. Her under-cover agent boyfriend was a real bastard, but you couldn't help liking the guy. In the end he ran out on Miss Ball. To do good.

'Here he comes now,' said Miss Ball to Mr Gibbon.

Mr Gibbon turned away and began staring at the loudspeaker of the radio.

'Good morning.' It was Herbie.

'You're early,' said Miss Ball. 'You're an early bird.'

'*Shh.*' Mr Gibbon did not turn. He seemed to be shushing the radio.

'I try,' Herbie whispered.

'That's what counts.'

'Shut up,' said Mr Gibbon. He still did not turn away from the radio, and the radio happened to be playing the National Anthem. As soon as he said it the Anthem ended, and the effect was quite incongruous. *Shut up* and then the end of that glorious song.

'Your first breakfast,' said Miss Ball.

'Yes,' said Herbie. 'My first breakfast.'

'Did you ever shoot a machine-gun?' Miss Ball leaned toward Herbie.

'Beg pardon?'

'A machine-gun.' She chewed her toast. 'Did you ever shoot one?'

'No. Why?' Herbie twitched.

'Just asking, that's all.'

'Did *you* ever shoot a machine-gun?'

'No.'

'But you'd *like* to shoot one. Is that it?'

'No.' Miss Ball laughed. 'Really no.'

'You're interested in guns? You collect them or . . .'

'Gosh,' said Miss Ball, 'I didn't mean to start anything. I was just wondering out loud, just making conversation. Idle conversation I guess you'd call it.'

'That's what I call it,' Mr Gibbon said, turning full face upon Miss Ball.

My Gibbon's face was a study in hardened stupidity. It had an old hungry look about it.

Mr Gibbon's lips kept moving, as if he were silently cursing Miss Ball's idle conversation or finishing his egg. This made his nose – which was pointed and hooked – move also. Mr Gibbon was wearing a khaki tie, a gray shirt – a sort of uniform.

'I'm not talking to *you*,' Miss Ball said petulantly.

'I'm talking to you,' said Mr Gibbon. 'I went through three wars just so's I could sit here in peace and quiet and listen to my favorite song. And with you blathering I can't hear myself think, let alone listen to my favorite . . .'

'We have a new boarder.'

' . . . song,' Mr Gibbon finished. He recovered and said to Herbie, 'You been in the army?'

'No.'

'No what?'

'*What?*'

'I said, no what?'

'No what?' Herbie shook his head. 'What what?'

'*You* haven't been in no army,' Mr Gibbon roared.

29

'I didn't say I had, did I?'

'Didn't have to.'

'Why?'

'Why what?'

'Why,' Herbie caught on, '*sir*?'

' 'S'better. Sounds a hell of a lot better too. Reminds me of a fella we had in basic. A buddy of mine. He caught on. Didn't sir nobody.'

'What happened to him?'

'He learned how.'

'How did he learn,' said Herbie, 'sir?'

'They fixed him up real good. Then he learned.'

'Fixed him up?' asked Miss Ball, suddenly becoming involved in the conversation.

'Beat the living stuffings out of him.'

'That will be just about enough of that,' said Miss Ball.

Mr Gibbon had gone on eating, however, and did not hear. He chewed slowly, his fork upraised, his eyes vacant, but staring in the general direction of Herbie, as if he had just missed a good chance to beat the living stuffings out of Herbie.

'*Well!*' Miss Ball said, folding her hands and grinning into Herbie's face. 'You come from Holly Heights?'

'Yes.'

'I've never been there myself, but they say it's nice.'

'It's very nice. Like a lot of nice places it's very, very nice.'

'You look like a reader.'

'I like to read very much.'

'I was never a great reader,' Mr Gibbon offered, in order to signal that he was no longer interested in beating up Herbie.

'What does your daddy do?'

Herbie cringed. He had forgotten for a while that he had a daddy – a father, that is. He thought of the man and then said, 'My daddy – my father – was in tools.'

'*Was* in tools?'

'He used to make them. He's dead now, so he doesn't make them any more.'

'There's good money in tools,' said Mr Gibbon. 'And there's still a bundle to be made in tools.'

'I was never interested in tools myself,' said Herbie. 'People say I don't take after my father. Maybe they're right. I don't care about tools, although I realize they're important in their own way – just like people are . . .'

'*Hell* of a lot of money to be made in tools. Specially in machine tools.'

'It's almost time for school,' said Miss Ball, looking at her Snooz-Alarm which she carried around with her in the house.

'Your old man make machine tools?'

'Nearly time, I said,' Miss Ball announced again.

'You don't mind interrupting an intelligent conversation, do you?' Mr Gibbon was angry at Miss Ball. He had the habit of never saying anyone's name. He glared in the proper direction instead, to identify the person.

Miss Ball faced him. Then she patted Herbie on the arm and said, 'Don't you worry about old grumpy here. That's his way of making friends.'

'If I feel like grousing, I grouse,' said Mr Gibbon truculently. 'I don't care what people think. I been through three wars.'

'Which three?' Herbie asked.

'*Which three!*' Mr Gibbon almost choked. 'You hear that?' Mr Gibbon faced Miss Ball. 'That's a laugh.' He laughed and then turned back to his breakfast and muttered once again, 'Which three. For cry-eye.'

'I'd like to talk to you some time about war,' said Herbie.

'Any time,' said Mr Gibbon. 'I'm always prepared.'

'He'll talk your ear off,' said Miss Ball.

'I don't think it's a good idea, frankly.'

'He always does it. It's his way.' Miss Ball spoke as if Mr Gibbon were not at the table. But he was at the table, studying the horror-mask cut-out on the back of the cereal box.

'I mean war,' said Herbie.

'So does he,' said Miss Ball, amused.

Mr Gibbon grunted.

'But you'll get used to it. We all do. He's not so bad. Just in the mornings he's a little grumpy. Isn't that right, Grumpy?'

'You're going to be late for school.'

'Imagine,' said Miss Ball. 'You both work at the same factory. Isn't that *some*thing?'

Herbie admitted that it was something, and then he saw Mr Gibbon rise, click his heels and march out the door. Herbie gulped his milk and followed.

## 5

Herbie trotted, skipped and hopped after Mr Gibbon, who was striding grimly down the sidewalk to the Kant-Brake Toy Factory. At first Herbie held the letter in his hand, but when he noticed that the envelope was getting sweaty and wrinkled he stuffed it into his pocket. Herbie had asked Mr Gibbon who the man was whose name was on the envelope (a certain Mr D. Soulless). 'The old man himself,' Mr Gibbon had answered, without breaking his stride.

At the front gate there was a sentry-box, striped with red and white, and in front of it, at attention, was a militarily dressed (V. F. W. blue cap, braids, puttees, combat boots, breeches, assorted stained medals and insignia) though very old sentry. The sentry held a thick M-1 rifle (obs.) in place.

Mr Gibbon snapped the sentry a salute and started through the gate with Herbie. 'He's okay,' said Mr Gibbon to the sentry, jerking his thumb in Herbie's direction. 'Gonna see the old man. Business.'

But the sentry came forward. Herbie saw that he was about

ninety. He levelled his rifle at Herbie. The rifle shook and then inscribed an oval on Herbie's chest.

'Don't you move,' the sentry said threateningly.

'He's okay,' Mr Gibbon said. But he did not insist.

'Can't let him through without no authorization from the old man hisself.'

'He's new,' said Mr Gibbon, but Mr Gibbon's heart was not in it. Rules were rules. He knew better than to ask the sentry to do something which was not allowed. He knew the sentry well. Skeeter, the guys called him. He had towed targets during one of the wars.

'I got my orders,' said the sentry. His rifle was still weaving at Herbie and once it even stabbed Herbie's shirt.

Herbie tried to shrug, but he was afraid to shrug too hard. He thought it might make the gun go off. He imagined a fist-sized slug bursting through his chest.

'I'll call the C.O.,' said Mr Gibbon. 'I'll clear it through him.'

'How am I supposed to know who you are? Every man's a Red until he can show me different,' the sentry said. Mr Gibbon walked up the road to the main office. Apparently the sentry saw no point in talking to Herbie. He stopped. Perhaps he was out of breath.

'Lots of security around here,' said Herbie, hoping to calm the man down.

'Maybe,' was the cryptic reply.

'I mean, for a toy factory. Most toy factories don't have this much security, do they?'

'Do they? I don't know,' the sentry said coldly. 'I never been in *most* toy factories. Just this one is all.'

'Just asking.'

'I heard you.'

'A toy factory with a guard,' Herbie said to himself, and started to shake his head and smile.

'You think it's funny?'

'Yes,' said Herbie. 'No.'

'Pretty funny for a wise-guy, aren't you?'

'You think so?' It came out in the wrong tone of voice: an unintentional, but very distinct, rasp.

'I think so.'

'I was thinking,' said Herbie. 'With you standing there with that loaded gun, waving it at people like me and getting mad . . .' Herbie's voice trailed off, then started up again. 'I was thinking, someone might get hurt. . . .'

'Like you.'

Herbie nodded. 'Like me. Exactly.'

'I got a job to do.'

'That's what I was saying. A toy factory with a guard.'

'I'd shoot you down as look at you. I used to tow targets.'

'I wouldn't doubt it.'

'I seen action. Lots of it.'

Herbie noticed that although the sentry's body was faced in his direction and the sentry's rifle was still pointed in the general area of Herbie's chest, the sentry's eyes were glazed, his mind was somewhere else. Perhaps on some of the action he had seen.

'Damn right,' said the sentry. 'Plug you right there, if I had a mind to. I plugged lots of guys before. Wise-guys, just like you, mostly. We had more trouble with the wise-guys than the Jerries. So we plugged the wise-guys. It was war. You can't have wise-guys in a war, or smart-alecs either. I plugged my best friend. He used to wise around the place all the time. Had to give him the pay-off. Sure, I hated to do it – he was my buddy, but that's the way you lose wars. The wise-guys lose them for you.'

Herbie looked at the rifle riding up and down his torso. It had one eye.

'I got my orders. I wouldn't care. I'd just *shoot*!' The last word flew out angrily with a fine spray of spit.

Herbie backed toward the gate and the safety of the sidewalk. The guard still aimed his rifle where Herbie had been. Just as Herbie was thinking seriously about running back to Miss Ball's house Mr Gibbon appeared.

34

'You been cleared,' he shouted to Herbie. 'It's okay, Skeeter. He's been cleared by the old man.'

Skeeter, the sentry, wheeled around and jerked his rifle at the sky. Both Mr Gibbon and Herbie flattened themselves on the driveway. Herbie waited for the explosion, numbness, death. But there was no explosion.

'I woulda shot,' said Skeeter, the sentry.

'I don't blame you,' said Mr Gibbon. He understood security.

Herbie said nothing.

Mr Gibbon took Herbie to the Main Office and said, 'You're on your own now, sojer.'

On the door to the main office was a plaque which read, GEN'L DIGBY SOULLESS, UNITED STATES ARMY (Ret'd.).

'Come in!' bellowed a voice from inside.

Herbie nodded to the bellow and went into the office of the retired general. Inside he said good morning and started to sit down in a large chair.

'Don't bother to sit down,' said the man. He was, like Skeeter at the gate, wearing a fancy uniform. Very authentic-looking. 'You won't be here long.'

Herbie remembered the letter. He pulled it out and handed it across the desk.

The man with the fancy uniform read the letter quickly, then looked up. 'So,' he said. He fixed his eyes on Herbie, wet his lips, and began to croak affectionately. He had known Herbie's father damn well, about as well as one person can know another one. At least, the man qualified, these days. They had bowled together, had dime-beers together, grabbed ass together and been in tools together. Oh, it was all right in tools with the elder Gneiss, but he – after his retirement from the army – had moved up the ladder and built Kant-Brake from willing men and muscle, real pioneers, men with dreams and a lot of dough. Herbie's father had gotten married and stayed in tools. General Soulless couldn't stand tools himself. That is, tools *as* tools. He wanted to make something useful. He had a dream, too, if that didn't sound like bullshit. He went into war toys.

But he still had a hell of a lot of respect for Herbie's old man. They had done a lot of things together when they were young. He could write a book about all those crazy adventures. He could write twenty books. How they used to go swimming in the raw, fishing in the lake. Times had changed, but he still couldn't forget Herbie's father, a scrappier little guy there never was.

Herbie stood on one leg and then on the other. He agreed that his father certainly was a scrappy little guy. Herbie said that, of course, was before he was his father.

The man laughed. 'I'll say!' he croaked. 'You scrappy like your dad?'

'I guess so,' said Herbie, 'yes.' But all that Herbie could remember about his scrappy old dad was the large bowling ball with the undersized finger-holes.

'Them were the days,' the man said. He went on. He could – no he *should* – write a book about those days. It'd be a goddamned funny book, too. He said that some day he would write it. A big fat book. He'd put everything in it that had ever happened to Herbie's scrappy dad and him. All the rough-necks and shit-heads, all the skinny girls with flat chests and freckles, and that hungry rougey old bag they met one night. Did Herbie know about that? Probably not. But the retired general wouldn't leave out a single word. He'd get it all down on paper when he had the chance. It wouldn't be any sissy novel either. It would be a big lusty novel, sad sometimes, with all a kid's important memories of growing up. The way kids see things, since kids really knew what was going on. That's why the retired general was in that business, he said. He liked kids.

Herbie wished the man luck with the novel. Then for no reason at all he thought of his mother. There was a novel, or maybe a folk opera: jazzy tunes, honky-tonk, the swish of brushes on drums as his mother gobbles sadly in front of the T. V., a blue tube lighting up her bowls of ice-cream. And then, mountainous, glutinous, and jiggling with the rhythm of the tunes, she slides out of the house, down the street to the brink of her open grave and then flops ever so quietly into it.

'So you want a job, eh?'

'Yessir.'

'Like the place?'

'Very much.'

'It's not just any old toy factory, y'understan',' said the man. 'We got style – that's what counts nowadays. I mean, saleswise. You can't fool kids. Kids are the darnedest little critics of things. They know when you're putting the screws to them.'

'Sure do,' said Herbie.

The man continued. Kids were funny. They knew what they wanted, a certain color, size, shape, etc. They got books out of the library and studied about war and crap. They knew what was going on. If the retired general had his way he'd hire young kids, real young, impressionable, scrappy little bastards, instead of old men. But he'd get arrested, wouldn't he?

After saying this, the man laboriously got up out of his chair, walked around the desk to Herbie, and then skidded his fist over Herbie's chin in what was meant as a playful gesture of affection that old men become incapable of and, often, arrested for. The man went back to his chair heavily and repeated that he liked kids a lot.

Herbie said that if it weren't for kids where would they be? Then he thought of what he said and licked his lips.

Just the same, the man agreed.

Herbie said that he was absolutely right.

'You're a lot like your old man.' The man wiped his mouth with a chevroned sleeve.

Herbie tried to look as scrappy as possible. He looked at the twenty dollars' worth of ribbons and string on the retired general's chest. He tried to forget that his father was a runt and hoped that the retired general would forget it too.

'You got yourself a job, son.'

The man then introduced himself as General Digby Soulless, Retired, and took Herbie down into the workshops. Herbie would be in the motor pool with Mr Gibbon. Herbie would have to know the ropes. He was issued with a uniform, shoes, and a rucksack. He put on the uniform and worked for the rest of the day in silence. The rest of the men were good to him, told him dirty jokes and took him into their confidence. They saw that the old man himself had brought Herbie down and introduced him. So this is the army, Herbie thought throughout the day. At the end of the day Herbie went out through the main gate with the rest of the men. And when Skeeter, the sentry, saw Herbie approaching in uniform, he saluted grandly and nearly dropped his rifle.

## 6

Work at Kant-Brake went on. Millions of tanks, jeeps and rockets rolled off the assembly line without a hitch. Herbie got to enjoy working once he learned the routine. He sent money home, got an occasional note from his mother saying that she was keeping alive and well. Life at Miss Ball's was fairly pleasant. Mr Gibbon grumbled, barked a lot, but did not bite. Miss Ball was a sympathetic person, although she wore very heavy make-up. Herbie did not expect a woman with a perfectly white face, a little greasy red bow for lips, and hair that was sometimes blue, sometimes as silver as one of Kant-Brake's fuselages, and always tight with hard little curls, to be a nice lady. But she was kind and tolerant. She said she owed all her tolerance to her membership in the D.A.R.

Herbie talked to Miss Ball about many things. She knew the movements of any actor, actress or starlet he could name: who was queer, who was in Italy, who was really seventy and said he was forty-four. And late one evening, when they were talking about marriages, Herbie asked Miss Ball if she had ever been married. Juan was taken for granted. He was just one of the hired help and didn't count.

'Sure,' said Miss Ball, 'I've been married.'

'No kidding?'

'Wouldn't think so, would you?'

'Why not?'

'Maybe I'm not the type.'

'What's *the type*?'

'With a flowered apron, hamburgers sizzling on the griddle, with shiny teeth and bouncy hair. My hair's all dull and streaky.'

'That's the *type*?' Herbie thought only of his mother. She hadn't had any of the things Miss Ball mentioned. All she had, as a married woman, was a scrappy little runt of a husband.

'That's what they say.'

'I never heard it.'

'But,' Miss Ball smiled, 'did you put your thinking-cap on?'

'Well, what about him?'

'Him? You mean my *hus*band?' A laugh did not quite make it out of Miss Ball's throat, although there were signs of it approaching. It never came.

'Yes,' said Herbie. 'Your husband. The man you married.'

'Whatever became of him,' sighed Miss Ball. 'What shall I say? Shall I say we loved and then were, as they say, estranged? Or shall I tell you he was a big producer who did me dirt? Or shall I tell you he was a poor boy, a very mixed up young man that I found committing highly unnatural acts in the summer-house with another twisted little fellow? Shall I tell you he was a bald-faced liar? Yes, that's what he was, a liar.'

Miss Ball tried to flutter her hand to her lips. But it was late in the evening and her hand never got beyond her left breast.

' . . . he *did* do me wrong. Very, very wrong. But I'm not him, thank God. I am not that man and I don't have to live with his terrible conscience – I'd hate to be in his shoes right now.'

'Where is he?'

'He's dead.'

'I wouldn't like to be in his shoes either,' said Herbie.

'There was a bit of the Irish in him, you know,' said Miss Ball, abandoning the dramatic-hysteric role and lapsing into what she intended to be a brogue. 'A bit of the oold sahd . . .' She stopped and then went on. 'Full o' blarney, he was.' Miss Ball just could not get a twinkle out of her heavily made-up eyes. Her eyelids kept sticking. 'The sonofabitch.'

Venom frothed and boiled out of some hidden nodes in Miss Ball's body, surprising Herbie. Miss Ball cracked all her make-up to flakes in her rage. She was such a nice old lady, Herbie thought. And now Herbie didn't know her.

'The no-good sonofabitch. Want to know what he used to do? Hated me so much he used to get up early in the morning, before me. Then he'd sit down – it was four in the morning – and just eat his Jungle Oats as nice as you please. Then coffee. Had to have his coffee. Then, when he finished, he'd take the coffee-maker, the electric coffee-maker, and pull the screws out and screw the top off and wind the friction-tape off the plug I had to fix about ten times because he was too lazy. Then he'd fill the sink with hot soapy water and dunk the coffee-maker into the water and leave it in the suds.'

'And where were you?'

'I was in bed! That's where you belong at four in the morning – not taking coffee-pots apart so your wife can't have her coffee. But it doesn't stop there,' said Miss Ball. 'Not by a long shot it doesn't stop there.'

'He does sound like a skunk,' Herbie offered.

'He was a regular S.O.B.,' said Miss Ball. 'And I hope you know what that means.'

'I guess . . .'

'But that wasn't all, because then he had to yell in my room at the top of his lungs.'

'He *had* to?'

'That was part of the thing, the act he did. He always did the same thing every morning.'

'So what did he yell?'

Miss Ball stood up from her wing-chair and cupped her hand to her mouth like an umpire. She even raised her other arm as if she were signaling a safe catch. She twisted her mouth and shouted in an ear-splitting voice, '*When your ole lady died and went straight to hell she should have taken you with her and such and such and so and so!*' Miss Ball recovered, stared wide-eyed and said, 'I wouldn't repeat some of the things he said to me those times.'

'Then he left.'

'Then he left,' said Miss Ball. 'But he came back.'

'Really?' Herbie steadied himself for another blast. He was getting worried.

'He left in the morning. In the night he came back. He went to church and work in between.'

'Church. Which church?'

'The stupid Irish church, that's which church. He was what you might call a Catholic. He had to go to church.'

'I thought they just had to go on Sunday.'

'They don't.'

'That's not what I thought.'

'Not on Lent they don't.'

'But Lent is only a month or two in the winter, isn't it?'

'Don't ask me,' said Miss Ball. 'It was always Lent in our house. Lent and hate.'

'Maybe marriages can be based on hate instead of love,' Herbie said.

'Ours was. The girls down at the D.A.R. said to stay away from Catholics if you want to stay tolerant. But I wouldn't listen. Sure, he wasn't all bad – he used to pick up stray cats and stuff. The girls said that's a sign of loneliness. He was probably lonely.'

'It was his way,' said Herbie. He had been waiting for a good chance to say it.

41

'Maybe that's it. He was good about cats. And I really couldn't divorce him for taking the coffee-maker apart. You don't walk into a court and say, I want a divorce – my husband takes the coffee-pot apart before church every morning. It doesn't sound right. It wouldn't even sound right in a movie if Ava Gardner said it. Besides, who else is there? There aren't that many people in the world that you can just start tossing them away left and right just because they have a certain way about them. That's what love is – sticking with the guy even though he has creepy habits. It's learning to love the creepy habits so you can sleep in the same bed without killing the sonofabitch.'

'I thought I'd hate this job at Kant-Brake, but now I like it.'

Miss Ball turned all her face on Herbie. 'Of course you'll like it. It'll be fun. You'll learn to get the hang of it. Sure, you hated it at first, but every dog has his day. That's part of living.'

'My mother needs the money. She's getting along, getting old.'

'I'm getting along myself,' said Miss Ball.

'She's all alone now,' said Herbie. 'My father's gone. It's the least I can do.'

'I could have been in the movies. Don't think I didn't have lots of chances. But I sacrificed and here I am.'

'My mother just can't stop eating because my father died. Life goes on. You've got to keep eating no matter what happens.'

'My husband. He kept me going, I guess.'

'If it wasn't for her I wouldn't be here.' Herbie thought for a moment. 'Who knows where I'd be? Maybe in the real army.'

'He could laugh. You should have heard him laugh,' said Miss Ball. 'Like a barrel of monkeys.'

'My mother laughs all the time. She laughs at everything.'

'He taught me how to laugh, the old fool.'

'People don't laugh enough these days. It's good medicine,' said Herbie. 'Isn't it? I mean, if you don't laugh you'll go crazy.'

'I still haven't forgotten how.'

'Neither have I. Neither has my mother.'

'You've got to learn to laugh,' said Miss Ball. And to prove it she emitted a little bark, learned undoubtedly from the husband who rose so early in the morning. She laughed wildly, yelping, looking around the room, her eyes darting from object to object, her laughter growing with each object. It was not continuous, but a series of yelps, wet boffoes and barks. She showed no signs of tiring.

Herbie joined her, slowly at first. Then it was a duet.

## 7

'You gotta know which side of the bed your brother's on,' Mr Gibbon shouted to Herbie over the roar of the machines. But Herbie did not hear. No one heard anyone else at Kant-Brake. That did not stop the employees from talking. It encouraged them. There were no disagreements, no arguments, no harsh words, and still everyone talked nearly all the time. None of that impatient waiting until the other person finished to add your two cents' worth. And since most of the employees had been through many campaigns there were millions of little stories to tell. Happily, each man got a chance to tell them. So when Mr Gibbon offered his homily to Herbie, Herbie answered by saying that his tooth hurt. And then Mr Gibbon said that he liked spunky women and asked Herbie if his mother was spunky.

At noon sharp the machines were shut off. The scream of voices persisted for a few moments after the machines were silenced, then, when everyone heard his own voice, the sounds quickly hushed, as if the human voice were something to be avoided.

Mr Gibbon came over to Herbie and pointed to a bench. They sat on the bench and opened their paper lunch-bags (there was a mess hall, but Mr Gibbon had said that he could never stand mess halls, even though he was once a cook and could make enough cabbage for, let's face it, an army). They took out their sandwiches and hard-boiled eggs and began whispering. Everyone else at Kant-Brake was whispering as well. They always whispered at lunch-hour. Mr Gibbon asked Herbie about his family. They continued their lunch, whispering between bites.

Herbie said his mother was his family.

'No kin?'

'Nope.'

'Friends of the family?'

'Couple.'

'No brothers?'

'Uh-unh.'

'Ants?'

'No kin. None.'

'Girlfriends, though.'

'Used to.'

' 'Smatter now?'

'Nothing.'

'Get one.'

'Got one.'

'What's your mother like?'

'Okay. Still alive. Pretty strong woman.'

'Spunky?'

'You might say so.'

'Your old man's . . . ah . . .'

'Dead.'

'Passed away, huh?'

'That's what the man said.'

'What man? You pullin' my leg? You shouldn't fool with things like that.'

'Things like what?'

'Like saying your old man's dead.'

'My old man's dead. Dead and [bite] gone [swallow].'

'Stop that.'

'Tell *him* that.'

'Wait'll you get my age.'

'I'm waiting.'

'You'll see.'

'Sure.'

'It's a crime to talk about your old man like that. You should *never* fool with things like that. They should horsewhip everyone under a certain age once a week.'

'Who should?'

'The government should.'

'Who's gonna buy the whips? Who's gonna do the whipping?'

'Simple. The police. They should do it in public.'

'They should kill old men and old ladies. How'd you like that?'

'Don't like it.'

'Now you know how I feel.'

'Your poor mother. I feel for her, I really do.'

'I'm the one that's supporting her.'

'That's the least you can do. The very least.'

'She's not so poor. She gets enough to eat.'

'So you get enough to eat and you're not poor. You got a lot to learn about people, sonny.'

'You got a lot to learn about my mother.'

'Mothers got hearts. Hearts got to be fed, too.'

'With love. Ha-ha.'

'With love.'

'I can't swallow that.'

'Food isn't enough. You'll learn.'

'Don't tell me about my own mother, okay? I like her a lot. Maybe more than your mother.'

'You don't even know my mother.'

'But you meet her and then decide. She raised me, okay. Never hit me once. Now she goes and makes me get this job. She doesn't have it so bad and certainly isn't poor.'

'I'll be the judge of that.'

'She likes to eat. She eats like a hog.'

'What's wrong with eating?'

'No one said anything's wrong with eating.'

'I'm an old man. Ate my way through three wars.'

'It's some people's hobby. It's her job.'

'I'm partial to eating myself,' said Mr Gibbon after a pause. And they both went on eating.

After work Mr Gibbon said, 'I'd like to meet your mother. Bet she's a fine woman.'

Herbie thought a moment. He had told his mother that he would come home once in a while. The weekend was coming and if Mr Gibbon came Herbie wouldn't have to explain the Kant-Brake operation to her. Mr Gibbon would do all the talking. Herbie wouldn't have to say a word.

'I'm going home on Friday. You can come along if you want.'

'Well,' said Mr Gibbon, 'I'd like that fine. There's not a hell of a lot to do on the weekend you know. Just my paper bags and cleaning my brass and such. And Miss Ball's got that gentleman friend that usually drops in.'

Herbie felt foolish. There he was, walking down the street with an old man. But not just any old man. No, this old man was a real fuddy-duddy. There was something queer about it. Mr Gibbon was taller than Herbie, like a big bear, a bear with a cardboard rump ambling next to a little monkey of a boy. It was Herbie and not Mr Gibbon that had simian features.

It looked as though there should be a leash between them. One of them should have had a collar on, but it was a toss-up as to which one should be holding the leash.

Herbie had never walked so close to an old man before. Or an old lady, either. That included his mother. Herbie's mother didn't get out much. So when she opened the door to greet them her complexion was the color of newsprint, the kind of skin color that one would expect of a person who lived in a living-room, slept on a sofa and ate chocolates with the shades drawn. To Herbie she looked disturbingly well.

She motioned for them to sit down. The TV show wasn't over

yet. She kept her eyes fixed on the blue tube and shook a fistful of chocolates at some chairs. The screen jaggered and the picture went to pieces. Herbie got up to adjust the set. Mrs Gneiss waved him back to his seat. Then she stomped on the carpet with her foot. Her shapeless felt slipper came off, but her bare foot raised itself for another go. The TV snapped back to life, the picture composed itself on the command of Mrs Gneiss's big foot.

The show went on for several hours. First there was a newsreel, then something entitled 'Irregularity and You,' then a half-hour of folk songs which concerned themselves with bombs and deformed babies, then a documentary about the human scalp, a dance show complete with disc jockey showed teen-aged girls and boys bumping themselves against each other, and finally a panel of Negroes and Mexicans discussed who had been abused the most seriously. When they started feverishly stripping off their shirts to show their wounds and scars, Mrs Gneiss stomped on the floor again and the TV shut itself off.

'Television,' Mr Gibbon said. And that was all he said.

Mrs Gneiss looked at him. She chewed at him.

'Mr Gibbon,' Herbie said, 'this is my mother.'

'Well, any friend of Herbie's,' said Mrs Gneiss. Then she picked up a large piece of chocolate. It was an odd shape, perhaps in the shape of a fish. She threw it into her mouth, and once her mouth was filled she said, 'Can I offer you something to eat?'

Herbie swallowed, determined not to vomit.

'Say,' said Mr Gibbon, 'is that an Eskimo Pie?'

'Thipth,' said Mrs Gneiss. But she could not speak. She wagged her finger negatively.

'Looks like one,' said Mr Gibbon. 'Years ago we used to have them. My buddies used to eat 'em like candy.'

'They *were* candy, weren't they?' said Mrs Gneiss, once she had swallowed most of the chocolate.

'You got something there,' said Mr Gibbon.

'Mr Gibbon was in three wars,' said Herbie.

'What ever happened to Eskimo Pies,' said Herbie's mother.

'That's what I say,' said Mr Gibbon brightening.

'Even if they did have them today they'd be little dinky things.'

'That's the God's truth,' said Mr Gibbon. 'Years ago the Hershey Bars were the big things.'

'Nowadays they're a gyp,' said Mrs Gneiss. 'I try to tell Herbie how much he's being gypped nowadays, but he never listens. He just laps up all those lies.'

'Big ideas!' Mr Gibbon started. He crept over to the sofa and sat next to Mrs Gneiss. When he got there he was almost out of breath. 'Big ideas,' he finally said again. 'I think years ago people were smarter than they are now, but they didn't have any smart ideas like people do now.'

'Right!' said Herbie's mother. 'I knew a lot of people in my day, but I never met one with any smart ideas. Boy, I remember those big Hershies!'

'Trollies, too,' said Mr Gibbon. 'Years ago we used to hitch rides on 'em. Loads of fun, believe me. But today? I'd like to see you try that today?'

'Try *what* today?' asked Herbie.

'Hitchin' a trolley-bus,' said Mr Gibbon.

'You mean riding?'

'No, I mean *hitching*. You crawl on the back of the thing and hold on with your fingernails. Doesn't cost a penny. Nowadays you'd get killed on a bus. You could do it easy then.'

'What for?' Herbie asked. But no one answered.

Herbie's mother and Mr Gibbon continued to talk excitedly of the past. They talked of penny candy, nickel ice-creams and dime novels. Mr Gibbon said that he had once bought a whole box of stale White Owl cigars for five cents and then smoked the whole boxfull under his front steps. He had been violently ill.

'The things you could do with a nickel,' Herbie's mother said nostalgically.

'Remember Hoot Gibson?'

'Whatever became of Hoot Gibson?'

'The old story.'

'Isn't it always the way.'

'No one cares.'

They talked next of Marx and Lincoln. Not the famous German economist and the Great Emancipator, but Groucho and Elmo. Mr Gibbon went on to tell how he had run away from school at a very early age. He said that kids nowadays didn't have the guts to do that. How he used to go fishing with a bent pin and a bamboo pole, how he had joined the army at a very early age. No fancy ideas. Nowadays it was the fancy ideas that were ruining people.

'I don't have any fancy ideas,' said Herbie.

'You *do*, and you know it,' said his mother silencing him.

'Years ago,' said Mr Gibbon, 'good food, clean living, nice kids.'

'Nowadays,' said Mrs Gneiss, 'I don't know how I stand it.'

Mr Gibbon said that he had known a girl in his youth that looked just the way Herbie's mother must have looked. Full of freckles and vanilla ice-cream, plump, but not fat. Just the prettiest little thing on earth!

'You'll stay, of course,' said Mrs Gneiss.

'Course,' said Mr Gibbon. 'Us old folks got a lot of things to talk about.'

'Sure do,' said Mrs Gneiss.

'Probably wouldn't interest the youngster,' said Mr Gibbon. 'Now if I'm imposing you just tell me scoot the blazes out of here.'

'*Imposing!* I should say not. We'll just pop a couple of TV dinners in the oven. No trouble *ay-tall*! Unless you mind instant coffee.'

'Drink it all the time. Makes me big and strong,' said Mr Gibbon, his eyes glinting, his lips wet and pink.

'You're a card,' said Mrs Gneiss.

'Not so bad yourself, Grandma!'

'Ha-ha-ha,' said Mrs Gneiss.

'So's your ole man,' said Mr Gibbon.

'I'm tired,' said Herbie. 'I think I'll go to bed.' He took ten dollars out of his pay envelope and gave his mother the remainder. She thanked him. Herbie stared at the money on his mother's lap. Then he went to bed.

Just before he got into bed he heard Mr Gibbon say, 'They had all-day suckers then. You never see an all-day sucker nowadays. Not one.'

Throughout the night Herbie was awakened by wheezing and groaning and the creaking of springs. That was that. He tried to prevent his mind from making a picture of it, but the more he tried the sharper the picture became. He switched on the radio to keep his mind off the noise in the next room. The news was on. The President had just had his kidney stone and gall-bladder removed. The commentator said, 'The stone had the appearance of an irregular gold nugget or arrowhead. The opened gall bladder was reddish brown and the greenish half-inch gall-stone which infected it was visible in the lower left fold near the cystic duct . . .' After this the President himself came on and said that he just had to get out of the hospital and do his work, even if it meant further infection. There was a war on and that had to be tended to.

With the radio buzzing about the movements of troops, Herbie went softly to sleep.

## 8

Mr Gibbon became a frequent visitor to Herbie's house.

Herbie stopped going home altogether. Instead, he went for walks around Mount Holly, met a girl and took her to bed. The first time they went to bed the girl said, 'New, new, new!' which struck Herbie as odd. But they made love just the same. Afterwards, when Herbie offered the girl a cigarette, she said simply, 'New, thank you.' Like Herbie the girl had no plans, and Herbie had no plans for her.

Herbie's mother became more hostile, but also less demanding. Herbie sent her less and less money each week. She did not mention this in her letters. Instead she sent more letters and started using phrases like, 'Life is just beginning for me,' 'a big new world is opening up,' 'Charlie has taught me how to live and love,' 'old people have feelings too,' 'the sky's the limit' and 'dawn is breaking.' They were very uncharacteristic phrases. Mr Gibbon had apparently kindled a flame inside his mother, Herbie thought.

Indeed, Mr Gibbon had done just that. Mrs Gneiss, Mr Gibbon and Miss Ball had started an outing club to get fresh air. They walked, brought cold lunches, ate devilled eggs, and listened to their transistor radio. Some color – not much, but *some* – came into Mrs Gneiss's face. It would be rash to say she had a ruddy complexion, but it certainly wasn't chalky. It was lemony after a few picnics, and then it took on a slightly veined pinkish hue. The outings were doing her good. The walking increased her appetite, which Mr Gibbon was now paying for. She gained weight, but the new bulk was not perceptible. Only other really fat people notice changes in a fat person. Mrs Gneiss was not embarrassed by the added weight. She repeated that everything she ate turned to fat. There was no question that she was coming alive. She had started wearing dresses and muu-muus and had burned her tattered kimono. She took to walking and sweating. Firmness came into her hams and trotters just as color came into her jowls.

One Sunday the outing was held at the Mount Holly Botanical Gardens. Mr Gibbon, as usual with map and compass, had led the way. They spread their blanket under a tree and ate, then turned on the radio and listened to news of the President's kidneys and gall-stones and negotiations with what Mr Gibbon called 'The Yellow Peril,' and then lolled about on the grass. The sky was filled with clouds that kept getting in the way of the sun. This irritated Mr Gibbon. He said so. 'Those clouds aggravate me,' was what he said. Lots of things galled him, he said, but life was still worth living. He said that he owed a great deal to Mrs Gneiss. He had thought that his life was over, but Mrs Gneiss had convinced him that he could move on. 'If an old battle axe like me and an old biddy like you can fall in love,' he said, 'then anything is possible.' He had wondered about this before. Now he knew it for sure.

'Charlie,' said Mrs Gneiss, 'you're the sweetest man in the world.' Without pausing she added, 'Pass the salad, Miss Ball.'

'Just because you're a certain age,' said Miss Ball, passing the salad to Mrs Gneiss, 'doesn't mean there's anything you can't do. Why, it should be easier when you're old because you know more, but no one tries. That's the fly in the ointment really.'

'Sure is,' said Mr Gibbon. 'Sure is. Why, look at us. Three folks with lots of spunk left.'

'Oodles of spunk left,' Miss Ball interjected. 'Oodles.'

'And it's all going to waste. We're just wasting away,' said Mrs Gneiss, her mouth dripping mayonnaise.

Mr Gibbon smacked his lips in disgust. 'That greenhorn doctor had the nerve to boot me out of the army. Why, I was old enough to be his father! If I had stayed in they wouldn't be having so much trouble with their wars. Send me in! Give me fifteen men of my own choosing and we'll blast all those yellow bastards to Kingdom Come! I been in three wars and I won all three. Give me another one, that's what *I* say!'

'Oh Charlie, you're a real campaigner,' said the delighted Mrs Gneiss.

'Why not victory?' said Mr Gibbon. 'Just send me over!'

Miss Ball had been shaking her head. 'I'm a Daughter of the American Revolution,' she said, 'and I've seen a lot of our boys murdered in cold blood by the Communists. The real problem is right here in our midst: the You-Know-Whos. If we didn't have so many of them – and they're all as Red as they are black, as I'm sure you know – this country would be ours again and we could put a big fence around it. We could start life all over again in our own backyard. You don't have to scurry all over the world with your planes and such to find the enemy. Not when he's there, smack in Mount Holly, emptying your trash-can, shining your shoes, cleaning your car, grinning at you, lying in his teeth, taking food out of your mouth and money out of your pocket!'

'That's it in a nut-cake!' said Mr Gibbon, jumping to his feet. 'The problem is right here. We can't ignore it. And I say the best fertilizer for a piece of land is the footprints of its owner!'

Saying this Mr Gibbon looked across the grass, past the bunches of flowers, through the trees to the clouds – those fickle things that kept getting themselves in the way of the sun. He frowned at the clouds as if the clouds represented everything foul, all the You-Know-Whos that kept trying to prevent decent folk from having sunny days.

'So we sit here blabbing about it,' said Mrs Gneiss. 'Why don't we *do* something about it?'

'What can we do?' asked Mr Gibbon. 'Oh, I know. It's coming all right. Hate and bitterness.'

'I hate bitterness,' said Miss Ball.

'It wouldn't be so bad,' said Mr Gibbon, 'if they were just shining your shoes and emptying your trash-cans. That wouldn't be so bad. But did you ever see the beat of it when every You-Know-Who in the damn country decides to get uppity? You looked at any movies lately? They're up there doing a soft-shoe with our womenfolk. Been in any drug stores the last year or two? There they are, sucking up cokes. Been in a bank lately ["A *bank*!" Mrs Gneiss gasped] – like that bank in town maybe? There they are, putting their crumby fingers over all the money. I tell you, it makes my blood boil! Why, I was in that bank cashing my pension check just the other day. Stood in line. There's one behind the counter. Went to another counter. *Another* one in front of me and one in back. Complain, I says to myself. Do something. Decided to have a word in private with the manager. Waited in line outside his office. Finally went in. You guessed it! A coon in the chair! What could I do? I still haven't cashed the damn pension check.'

53

'It's too much,' said Miss Ball.

'Something should be done about it,' said Mr Gibbon.

Miss Ball tapped Mr Gibbon on the shoulder, narrowed her eyes and said, 'Sonny, you can do anything you want if you just get the bee in your bonnet.'

They returned to Mount Holly to find Herbie slumped dejectedly in Miss Ball's wing-chair. He was surprised to see his mother. He couldn't remember having seen her out of the house for years. But he soon recaptured his dejection. There was a slip of yellow paper in his hand. A draft notice. Herbie was to report for his physical the next day. The country was at war.

# Part Two

## 9

They finally settled on a bank robbery. 'It's the logical thing to do when you stop and consider that I can't even cash my U.S. Army pension check, the place is so loaded with coons and commies,' Mr Gibbon explained. It would take some planning, but they would be able to do it. The robbery of a communist bank would prove to the world that old folks still had a lot of spunk left.

The robbery became all the more important after Herbie passed his army physical. He was due to leave for boot camp in four days.

'You're a very lucky man,' Mr Gibbon said to Herbie.

Herbie thought otherwise. He didn't want to go. But he didn't know why he didn't want to go. At first he thought of Kant-Brake. The place was full of soldiers. They weren't bad. But there was something missing, and when Herbie finally thought of what was missing, a chill shot through the holes in his bones. Death was missing from Kant-Brake. That's what the army made him think of: death.

'This is a time for courage. This is a time when men of all races and creeds must join hands and make the world a safe place. This is not a time for us to waver. This is not a time for us to lose our nerve. This is a time for us to be strong,' the President had said in his now-legendary 'This is a Time' speech to Congress. Charlie Gibbon had wept.

For Herbie this was not a time to go into the army. Be strong? He had seen all those people carrying signs; the boys with the bushy hair and the woollen shirts; the girls with no make-up and necklaces made out of macaroni. They didn't want war. Herbie had seen them dragged, kicking and screaming, into police vans. They didn't think that this was a time to be strong. But when they mentioned God, Herbie thought of nothing. He just didn't want to go. He had no reason for refusing. He would have felt foolish with a sign. A beard would have made his face pimply.

And then, the day before he was to go to boot camp, he thought of his reason for not wanting to go into the army. I'm afraid, he thought: I don't want to die, I don't want to throw bombs at people and shoot guns, I don't want to sleep in the jungle, march around in the mud and get shot at. Herbie remembered how quickly the sweet old Miss Ball had turned into an angry, cursing old bag. There was Mr Gibbon's buddy that didn't say 'sir' and got the living stuffings beaten out of him. There was Skeeter's pal, the wise-guy, that had to be shot because wise-guys lose wars for you.

Dying is easy, Herbie thought. So I go and get killed. My mother watches television. Mr Gibbon crawls all over her, folds his paper bags in peace. Miss Ball and Juan have their jollies without the Secret Police breaking down the door. I die and life goes on in Mount Holly.

Herbie didn't hate anyone. He had even stopped wishing for his mother's death. Mr Gibbon was in charge now. The care and feeding of Herbie's mother was in Mr Gibbon's hands. Herbie could stay at Kant-Brake a while longer and make a few extra dollars. But the thought of going into the army scared him limp. Still, he knew that he would be laughed at if he said that his reason for not wanting to go in was strictly that he was chicken-livered. Not even the bushy people that carried the signs on the sidewalk would listen to him. The soldiers certainly wouldn't listen. Herbie pictured himself going up to a General and saying, 'I can't fight, sir. I'm scared.' The picture faded. A boy with a sign and hair curling all over his horn-rimmed glasses like weeds appeared. Herbie said to the boy, 'I don't want to go into the army either. I'm scared.' Laughter from the General behind the desk and the boy on the sidewalk spattered Herbie. If you were scared you were no good.

So he did not say he was scared. He told no one. He merely sat around the house thinking, my death will keep that television going. If I don't die and someone else dies I'll come back and watch it. At least I have a home to come back to.

The Kant-Brake employees gave Herbie a knife ('Get a few for us, Herbie') and a Kant-Brake Front Lines First Aid Kit, every detail done in perfect scale. A memento. General Digby Soulless slapped Herbie on the back and said that he had gone into the army when he was half Herbie's age. He added, 'This is the real thing, boy. Get the lead out of your pants.'

On the day Herbie left for boot camp Mr Gibbon told him how much he envied him. Beans tasted so good cooked in a foxhole. He told him how to creep under barbed wire and bursting guns, how to clean his mess kit while on bivouac (with sand), how to cure rot and so forth. He presented Herbie with a new comb and told Herbie about his aunt. He told Herbie, in a whisper, not to worry about his mom. Mr Gibbon would take care of her. 'Confidentially, she's fat and sassy, and that's just the way I like 'em.'

Miss Ball said it thrilled her to know that Herbie was actually going to war. She had read about so many of 'our boys' going off, never to be heard from again. Now she could say that she knew one.

Everyone was happy for Herbie and wished him well. His mother was on the verge of tears. She stayed on the verge. She told Herbie very calmly to be a good boy and mind his manners when he got to the war.

Herbie, numb with fear, promised he would. He noticed at the railroad station that their cab held four suitcases instead of two.

'Half the luggage is mine,' Mrs Gneiss said.

'Are you coming along?'

'Goodness, no!' said Mrs Gneiss. 'I'm moving into your room

at Miss Ball's. I can be near Charlie that way. I just sold the house.'

Herbie nodded goodbye, had his picture taken with the rest of the Mount Holly draftees and the chairman of the Mount Holly Draft Board, and then joined the mob of boys in the car reserved for them. Herbie sat next to the window and looked at the three old people on the platform waving their hankies.

'Smile, Herbie,' his mother said.

'He looks scared to death,' Mr Gibbon said.

'It takes all kinds,' Miss Ball said.

## *10*

A dusty twenty-five-watt bulb flickered in Miss Ball's dining-room. The less light the better, they had all decided. The three of them sat around the large mahogany table. Mr Gibbon was wearing his khakis. His pistol was strapped on. In the dim light of the room the faces of the three people looked even older than they were, bloodless, almost ghoulish. Mr Gibbon was doing all the talking. Only a few of his fifteen teeth were visible and his mouth seemed latched like a dummy's. His whole chin gabbled up and down.

'It's all relative,' he was saying. 'Even though it doesn't look on the up and up if you say, we gotta rob a bank and we may have to shoot somebody to do it right, it's okay in this case. The country is at stake, and we're the only ones that realize it. Herbie's gone now to do his bit. It's up to us to do our bit even if the only place we can do it is right here in Mount Holly. It's the enemy within we're after. The ones right here grinning at us in our own backyard, as Miss Ball rightly said. It's all relative. Why, I know what it's like to be an American. You take your average American. He can't find his ass with both hands, can he? Bet your life he can't. It's all relative. A commie bank is right here in our midst picking our pockets. And what do we do? We rob that bank right down to the last cent, and if we get any lip from the You-Know-Whos we blast 'em.'

Mrs Gneiss interrupted. 'I hate to mention this,' she said, 'but won't it be against the law to do this? I agree with you one hundred per cent that something's got to be done – why, if the communists ran this country we'd starve in two days. But there's the law to think about . . .'

'Let me remind you, Toots, that the law you're so worried about is the law that's made *by* the You-Know-Whos *for* the You-Know-Whos. It's not made for decent people like us. The law is made by coons. You got any objections against breaking the coon law? You don't think decent folk should break the coon law? When we rob this bank we'll be heroes. People will be brought to their senses. We'll be doing our country a turn and making the world safe for good government, small government. Now anybody knows that it's not legal to rob a bank. But is it legal for some bastard with dark skin and a Party Card, all niggered-up with fancy clothes, to walk into *your own bank* and put his fingers all over your money? If that's legal, then what do you call it when decent people want to set an example for their country? Okay, call it illegal if you want. It's all relative. But I'll tell you something: it broke my heart to fight the Germans. I was in that war and, Goddamit, I couldn't help but think that they knew what they were doing all along. I knew it in my heart. I said to myself, Charlie, it's all relative. . . .'

'I'm not being an old sceptic,' said Miss Ball, 'but when we get the money, what do we do with it? I mean, it won't be ours, now will it?'

Mr Gibbon shook his head in impatience. He had the feeling he wasn't being understood. 'We're not going to *steal* the damn money. We're just going to *transfer* it. I suppose we could give it to our favorite charities. Personally, I'd like to see a company like Kant-Brake, a company that's got a heart and thinks about the country, get a little of the dough. I'd like to see the V.F.W. get a

little, the Boy Scouts a little, the White Citizens Council a little
– spread it around, you see? Lots of people are entitled to it.
We'll be fair . . .'

'I'd like to see the D.A.R. get a little bit. They deserve it.
They're dedicated.'

Mrs Gneiss did not name her favorite charity. She had some
reservations about the robbery. It sounded like a lot of work.
Give the You-Know-Whos a few swift kicks. They'd learn. Why
rob a bank? And, if they went through with it, it seemed only
fair that they themselves should be entitled to some of the cash.
She thought of truck-loads of Hershey bars, gallons of vanilla
ice-cream, a new television and, in general, goodies in return for
their pains. But she kept silent.

'So it's settled. We knock off the bank and in the process we
might have to break a few eggs – that's how you make omelettes,
eh? I've got my old trusty .45.'

'You mean you might shoot your gun?' Miss Ball asked, her
eyebrows popping up.

'Right,' said Mr Gibbon. 'How do you like *them* apples?'

Information was needed. Plans had to be made. The next two
months were spent poring over detective novels and thrillers,
watching spy movies, preparing disguises, masks, and learning
to pick up items without leaving finger-prints. Miss Ball was in
charge of disguises, Mr Gibbon had the novels, Mrs Gneiss had
television robbery-movies. Mrs Gneiss watched all the programs
on TV just the same, so it was no extra trouble. It just meant
changing channels once in a while. When a detective story was
over on one channel, another was starting on another channel.
She flicked the knob and settled back with her food.

Mr Gibbon continued working at Kant-Brake. He was excited
about the robbery – it compared favorably with his best experiences in the army. He read the pulp thrillers during the lunch-
hour and earned the title of 'professor' for doing so. The other
employees credited the reading and contentment to 'Charlie's
new lady-friend.'

At the end of two months they met again, and this time used the stump of a candle for light. They had a map of Mount Holly in front of them. The Mount Holly Trust Company was marked with an X, and an escape route plotted out on it with one of Miss Ball's E-Z Mark crayons, which she had cleverly snatched from the kindergarten.

Plans were going well, said Mr Gibbon. They had picked the masks they were going to use, the gloves and special shoes. And they had the escape route decided in advance. There was only one problem. They didn't know where the safe was. They had no floor plan of the bank.

'Oh, shucks!' said Miss Ball. 'How can we rob a bank if we don't know where the money is?'

'But the employees know,' said Mr Gibbon.

'A lot of good *that* does us,' Mrs Gneiss said.

'Now just keep your shirts on,' said Mr Gibbon. He explained his plan. What they would do was kidnap one of the bank guards, a white one, and beat the stuffings out of him unless he told them where the safe was. First, of course, they would divulge their plan. But if he didn't want to co-operate they would have to beat him up. He would be able to tell them where the safe was, the strongboxes, the money, the keys, the emergency alarms. 'We'll have to kidnap him. It's the only way.'

'It's for the good of the country,' said Mrs Gneiss.

Mr Gibbon said that it wouldn't be too much trouble to get one of the guards. They could lure him to Miss Ball's house. The only thing they needed was a decoy. They had to find a decoy . . .

Her face chalky with make-up, her cheeks rouged with circles, her lips gleaming with the scarlet goo of nearly one whole tube of lipstick, her hair a stiff mass of tight curls, her round body solid with corsets and fixtures, Miss Ball waddled to the back door of the Mount Holly Trust Company and looked for a bank guard to lure.

It was the middle of the afternoon and the sun was very hot.

This caused the make-up to run a bit and get very sticky. Beads of perspiration appeared at Miss Ball's hair-line, behind her ears and on her neck.

There seemed to be no one to lure. She could see people walking back and forth inside the bank, accountants and tellers. They had little or nothing to do with the storing of money. They just collected it. But no one came out of the back door.

Miss Ball rather enjoyed standing there. Like a siren, she could lure anyone. It gave her a feeling of power. She knew the attraction that a woman's flesh had for men. They couldn't resist it. How many times had Juan, on the pretext of checking the cans of floor wax, covered her with rancid kisses in the broom closet? He couldn't stand it any longer. She understood the urge and let him paw her and grunt. Duty meant nothing. History was full of the stories of men who had given in to the low murmur of beckoning flesh. Fortunes, whole countries had been lost, careers ruined for a few minutes of pleasure in the bed of a beautiful woman.

And then she thought, when you're a decoy you've got to have something to decoy. There was nothing in the back of the Mount Holly Trust Company to lure. A dog sniffed at the hem of her dress and scuttered away, two little boys meandered by throwing spit-balls at each other, and once someone peered from the second storey of the bank. Miss Ball had glanced up, but before she regained presence of mind enough to wink at the person (one never knew what floor plan he had in *his* pocket) he turned away.

A full hour passed. Miss Ball was tired; her get-up was a wreck. Her handbag felt like a large stone. She knew she didn't look as crisp as she had when she arrived. A man likes freshness and vitality in a woman. If much more time passed Miss Ball knew that she would be able to offer none of these.

Then a man appeared at the back door. Miss Ball pressed her lips together. She trembled. The man was white, wearing a blue suit with a matching cap, rimless glasses and a badge. He looked like a bus conductor. But he was a bank guard, and he certainly had a dozen more rolls in the hay left in him. He shuffled out the door with a shopping bag, then went inside and got another bundle and put that beside the shopping bag. After one more trip inside he deposited an umbrella and a pair of rubbers beside the other bundles.

Miss Ball took one step toward the man. She eyed him, fluttered her eyelashes, and said hoarsely, 'That's an awful lot of gear for a little man.'

'Par' me?' said the man. He squinted through his glasses and coughed. Miss Ball corrected her false impression: the man did not have a dozen rolls in the hay left in him. He had one perhaps, at the most two. Also he was down at the heel and out at the elbow. But it made no difference. He knew the bank inside out. He had the information they wanted.

'Give you a hand?'

The man took another look at Miss Ball. The look cost the man a great effort. He shrugged.

Miss Ball smiled, took the shopping bag and umbrella and led the way. The man picked up the other bundles and the rubbers and followed. *Success*, thought Miss Ball.

They walked along Mount Holly Boulevard and attracted considerable attention.

The man glanced at her once or twice, then cleared his throat and asked her if she minded carrying the bag.

Miss Ball said that she didn't mind doing anything. She winked again.

The man said that he lived across town. Miss Ball said she knew a short cut. She walked along as briskly as her little legs would move her and finally got to her house. With a sigh she dropped the bags and said that she could go no further.

'That's okay,' said the man. 'I'll carry the stuff. I was planning to anyways.'

Then Miss Ball shrieked. The man dropped what he was carrying.

'For golly sake!' she said. 'Look where we are!'

The man said he didn't recognize the place.

'It's my house! Well, isn't that the limit! God help us – it's a miracle.'

The man said that he had to be going. He had the week's shopping in the bags, not to mention his wife's umbrella (he called it a bumbershoot).

'You just take your brolly and your shopping and come in. We'll have a little tea. I'm weak. I don't think I can make it into the house.'

The man tried to carry Miss Ball into the house. He struggled and panted. Miss Ball remarked that he must have been a very strong man in his youth. The man said he was.

Miss Ball poured a large tumbler full of whisky and handed it to the man. The man drank it and wiped his mouth with his sleeve. 'Red-eye,' he said.

'Oo! You like your tea, don't you now?'

The man said he didn't mind a spot now and then. He put his arm around Miss Ball and began pinching her breast.

'Not here, darling,' said Miss Ball. She tossed her head in the direction of upstairs. Then she stood up and took his hand and pulled him upstairs.

Mr Gibbon and Mrs Gneiss tip-toed out of the kitchen and upstairs after them. They listened, their ears against the door.

Inside the room bodies fell, groans resounded, flesh met flesh with slaps and shrieks. Miss Ball squealed, the man roared. Furniture fell and glass broke.

'Lotta spunk left in *her*!' Mr Gibbon whispered.

'They're having *fun*!' Mrs Gneiss said. She squeezed Mr Gibbon's knee.

'Clever little woman,' Mr Gibbon said. 'See, she must have learned that in one of the books. She'll get him naked and helpless and then turn on the heat. She'll get him talking about the bank and find out. The man goes away happy and doesn't suspect a thing. Nice as you please.'

But there was no talking. The noise had ceased, and now Miss

64

Ball could be heard crying softly. Mr Gibbon wanted to go right in, but he waited five minutes, and when nothing had changed (the only sound was Miss Ball sniffing) he drew out his pistol and broke the door down.

The room was covered with blood. Sheets and curtains were torn and hanging in shreds, the mirror was shattered, and on the floor lay the bank guard, a large knife-handle sticking out of his back. Bloody hand-prints were smeared all over the walls and floor. In the corner, a murderous look in his eye, was Juan. His shirt was torn and bloody, his hair bristled. He glowered.

'Dobble-cross me! Dat agli gringo bestid don't know what heet heem. I been seeing that share for two jowers.'

'Warren!' screamed Miss Ball. He turned. Mr Gibbon took aim and fired. The impact sent Juan into the wall like a swatted fly. Then he fell, his head making a loud bump on the floor.

'There's two commies out of the way,' said Mr Gibbon. 'Get a mop! See if anyone heard! Lock the front door! This is it, boys! It's war! We won a battle but we haven't won the war yet! Fall to, get this mess cleaned up, load the guns!'

Neither Miss Ball nor Mrs Gneiss moved a muscle. They looked at Mr Gibbon with horror.

'Hurry up!' said Mr Gibbon. 'You all *deef*?'


## II

Mrs Gneiss's empty suitcases came in handy for storing the dismembered bodies of Juan and the bank guard. At first, Mrs Gneiss was all in favor of getting the bank guard's finger-prints on the gun and calling the police. They would tell the police that there had been a terrible fight between the two men. Juan had stabbed the guard and then the guard had shot Juan for stabbing him. Tit for tat, so to speak. It made some sense. But Mr Gibbon saw that if the guard had been stabbed he wouldn't have been able to shoot Juan. Or if Juan were shot the guard would have survived. The murder was without precedent if it was to be believed. They gloomily hacked up the bodies with Mr Gibbon's hunting knife, stuffed them into Mrs Gneiss's suitcases and put the suitcases and the clothes into the attic. Miss Ball's Stay-Kleen and Surfy Suds took care of the gore on the rug.

Good Old Providence had done them a turn. The neighbors had miraculously not heard 'The Fracas,' as Miss Ball called the double murder. The three comrades had stayed up all night keeping a vigil over the bodies in case the police should come. Then they would have said, yes, we killed the lousy commies. But the police never came. And just as well, the two ladies thought. Mr Gibbon thought differently: he was convinced that Juan and the bank guard were 'in cahoots' (the bank guard more than anyone was a stoolie and a cheat, working for coons as he did). Mr Gibbon was, as he put it, 'pleased as Punch' to have plugged Juan, a man he suspected to have been spying on him for nearly a year.

But they had to make short-range plans. The morning after the fracas the three sat around the table (the news was on, but spoke only of the gall-stones and the war, both with fervor; the disappearance of a certain bank guard was not mentioned). They looked haggard and mussed, having stayed up all night keeping their vigil. They tried to think of a way to cover up the murder for the time being. They knew that afterward, when the truth about the Mount Holly Trust Company was known (a Communist Front Organization filled with black pinkoes), the murder would be laughed off and their fortune would be secure. Meanwhile, they would have to think of a way to pacify the bank guard's wife. Unless he had been lying when he told Miss Ball that he had to take the groceries home to his wife; maybe he didn't have a wife at all. But how could they find out?

It was Miss Ball that came up with the solution. Without a word she darted upstairs to the suitcases. She came back almost immediately, seated herself as before and dropped a blood-stained wallet on the table. Gingerly – because the plastic wallet was still sticky with the gentleman's blood – Miss Ball picked through it. Out tumbled membership cards, wedding pictures, snapshots of little kids with beach pails, and finally the prize: a picture of the man himself and a woman – obviously his wife; she looked grim and stood apart from him – who was leaning on the very same umbrella that was now resting against the wall upstairs in Miss Ball's attic. On the back of the photograph was printed: 'Benny's Fotoshop – Close To You in the Lobby of the Barracuda Beach Hotel,' and under that in ball-point: 'Baracuta Beach, 1962.' There was also an identification card which read:

Harold Potts, Jr
1217 Palm Drive
Mount Holly
*In case of accident please notify a priest and*
Mrs Ethel Potts
(address as above)

Harold's blood-type, a little ragged card with a picture of Jesus on the front and a prayer on the back, and a relic of a tiny piece of cloth that had 'touched a piece of the True Cross' sealed in plastic, were also among the valuables. Mr Gibbon searched in vain for a Party Card. He came up with a few suspicious-looking documents, but remarked, 'He'd be a fool if he carried the thing around with him.'

Miss Ball paid no attention to Mr Gibbon's investigation. She had found what she wanted.

Dear Ethel (Miss Ball wrote),
I wonder if you remember me? We spent those lovely days together at the Barracuda Beach Hotel back in '62. We met briefly during a bridge game. (I can't remember if we were playing, watching, or just passing by the bridge tables – goodness how the memory starts playing tricks as the years go by!)

To make a long story short I met dear old Harold just yesterday at the Mount Holly Trust Company – well, I tell you Harold just couldn't stop talking! We came to my house for tea and just talked and talked and talked of the wonderful days we spent at the Barracuda Beach Hotel back in '62. Harold said he had a touch of gastritis and wanted to go straight to bed, couldn't walk so he said. Well, here it is 10 in the AM and he's still sleeping like a baby! I called the bank and told them he wouldn't be in this morning. I think his tummy needs a rest, frankly Ethel, and I just hate the thought of waking him up, so peaceful he looks. I think he should be improving in the next few days and I'll be sure to have him call you when he wakes up.

I just wanted to let you know that he's safe in the hands of an old friend and that there's no need to get all flustered and call the Missing Persons Bureau! Ha-ha! And that I look forward to more happy days like the ones we spent at the Barracuda Beach Hotel back in '62.

Your old friend,
Nettie

'Perfect,' was all Mr Gibbon said.

'I feel as if I know her,' Miss Ball said.

The letter was sent Special Delivery ('What's thirty cents,' Mrs Gneiss said), without a return address, in a plain envelope. Mr Gibbon estimated that it would be in Ethel Potts's hands before noon.

'What about Warren's nearest of kin,' Mrs Gneiss asked.

'His nearest of kin? Well, that's *me*, I guess, and *I* know where he is!' Miss Ball said. She did not say it with regret; but there was no joy in her voice either. Miss Ball did not quite know what to think about Juan's death. He had been very pleasant – if a bit jumpy – at first. Only lately had he been asking for more pin-money. He had also recently demanded to move in with Miss Ball, but she had discouraged that. He had a good heart. He had bought things for Miss Ball. He was constantly surprising her with little mementos like the framed picture of Clark Gable or the doilies – he adored doilies for a reason Miss Ball could not even guess at. He had 'been with' Miss Ball for about ten months and had never once shown the sort of jealous rage that had prompted him to stab Harold Potts to death.

Juan would have died violently sooner or later. It's in the blood. Better he died in the privacy of Miss Ball's own home than in the gutter. And then maybe Mr Gibbon was right: maybe Juan *was* a communist. He was certainly dark, a Puerto Rican, there was no denying that! Mr Gibbon was more familiar with the You-Know-Whos than Miss Ball. She knew that. He knew what he was doing. So goodbye, Juan, *hasta luego* and sleep well, Miss Ball thought.

Meanwhile, Mr Gibbon was getting impatient. 'An itchy trigger-finger,' he said. Sooner or later Ethel Potts would start wondering who in Sam Hill was Nettie and might turn the letter over to the police. This would ruin Mr Gibbon's timing. Floor plan or no floor plan, they would have to rob the bank quickly – at least in the next week or so. Here Herbie was out of boot camp, on his way to the front lines – probably he had nailed a few dozen commies already. A greenhorn! And here was Mr Gibbon with only these two rather unimportant Fellow Travellers to his credit.

Mrs Gneiss agreed. She said she was getting edgy. She didn't enjoy getting edgy. If the robbery was to be done, it should be done as speedily as possible, so that they could all relax and enjoy the rewards and fame the robbery would bring them. She for one didn't want Ethel Potts going haywire and accusing them of killing her husband. But as usual she said nothing more. Charlie knew best. She would wait until he gave the word. The whole thing was his idea, he was the brains and should make the decisions.

'I'd just like to have a look around the bank tomorrow before we go ahead with it,' Mr Gibbon said. Miss Ball should not come along. They didn't want to arouse any suspicions. He and Mrs Gneiss would just sort of mosey around the bank, seeing what they could see and getting the general layout of the place and, in short, 'casing the joint.'

Miss Ball said that suited her fine. They sat around the house reading and puttering around for the rest of the afternoon. Mr Gibbon attended to his long-neglected paper bags; Mrs Gneiss watched TV. But Miss Ball sat and scowled. Her brow grew more and more furrowed as the afternoon wore on. By five o'clock she was genuinely distressed. Something had just occurred to her. No one took any notice of her, not even when she scribbled a little reminder on the notepad which she always carried in her apron.

## 12

Miss Ball kept looking into store windows. Before each one she paused, touched at her hair, pressed her lips together and, reasonably satisfied with the reflection that stared out at her from the foundation garments or baked goods, she walked on toward the doctor's office.

She had begun to worry. She had read of a man who woke up one morning with the beginnings of a sixth finger; she had heard of a lung ballooning to twice its normal size when it had to do the work of two. And there were tonsils, adenoids and the appendix which often grew back if they were not watched properly and nipped, so to speak, in the bud. It was her operation that was making her jittery. How could she be sure that her insides wouldn't grow back when so many other things grew back?

Nature was hard to understand. You clip grass and trim bushes and pluck hairs and what do you get? More grass, stray branches and bushy eyebrows. Miss Ball found that she could not cope with nature. Nature was always ahead of her, ahead of everyone she knew.

Miss Ball had been a farm girl. She could remember seeing her father pushing whole barrows of nourishing dung across rotting boards to the fields. She had peeled potatoes, she had awakened in a musty room covered with a damp quilt. That's how it was when you lived close to the ground. It was damp and you were always kicking plants and dirt back into place, sifting stones, building walls, rocking on the porch and watching the crops fail. This was where Miss Ball learned Mother Nature's spiteful ways.

But her operation had cost her a pretty penny and now, with her childhood thoughts of crabgrass and her recent discovery that lungs ballooned and adenoids reappeared, and – most discouraging of all – that Juan had been extremely, shall we say, virile, and now was dead, Miss Ball could not remember if the doctor had given her a warranty.

She had gotten one with her Snooz-Alarm – it was a big green-edged one-year warranty that looked like a savings bond. And she had gotten one with her hair-dryer, her mixer, her vibrator and her juicer. If anything went wrong she didn't have to raise a fuss. She just told the clerk that it was not in working order and she would get a new one, a new dryer or juicer. But she hadn't got a warranty from the doctor.

She had asked herself many times if she needed one and had always decided no. But she had not yet realized her power over men. She had thought she was too old for that sort of thing. She could always reassure herself that Juan was doing it for the money. Was she too old? Harold Potts didn't think so. And that's finally what scared her.

'You look marvellous!' the doctor said with professional enthusiasm as Miss Ball seated herself on the other side of the desk.

'That's the outside you're looking at. It's the inside I'm worried about.'

'There's not much left to worry about,' the doctor said. He was going to say ha-ha, but he changed his mind when he saw the expression on Miss Ball's face. He decided to reassure her. 'What I mean is, you're empty. So why worry?'

'Empty? That doesn't sound too medical to me.'

'I try to simplify things for my patients.'

'I'm not stupid, doctor. You can talk plain to me.'

'I'm talking plain, Miss Ball. Now what's wrong?'

'I want a warranty and I want it now.'

'A what?'

'A warranty. I haven't had a wink of sleep for the past two days. All I could think of was my things, the things you say you removed, only God knows whether you did or not.'

'Miss Ball, I'm a medical doctor. I have taken the Hippocratic Oath. Every doctor takes it – it's part of being a doctor.'

'I'll take your word for it,' Miss Ball snapped.

'About the guarantee . . .'

'Warranty.'

'As far as the warranty goes. Why, I can't imagine why you'd want something like that.'

'I have one for my radio, my juicer and everything else.' Miss Ball laughed helplessly, hollowly, for no reason at all. 'I was foolish to have the operation without getting it warranteed.'

'You want it warranteed, is that it? That's why you came here today – so I could swear out a warranty?'

'You could have been taking me for a ride.'

'A *ride*?' The doctor aimed the top of his head at Miss Ball. 'Do you know what you're saying, Miss Ball? Now you're talking about ethics. Yes you are. You're talking about my ethics!'

'How's a body supposed to know what's going on? You come into the room and stab me with a needle. I fall flat and then you fiddle around for three hours . . .'

'Fiddle around? I take you for a ride to fiddle around, and for this you want a warranty?'

'You know what I mean.'

'I'm a very busy man.'

'I lived on a farm, don't worry.'

'Why should I worry about you living on a farm?'

'Sure,' was all Miss Ball said.

'I want to assure you that I operated on you. I did my level best, as I do with each and every patient. I have not hounded you for the money.'

'You can whistle and wait, for all I care.'

'I have nothing but your health in mind.'

'Don't worry, I've seen things grow back – grass, eyebrows, adenoids. I've seen things go wrong – my toaster, my dryer, my mixer . . .'

'That's a doctor's business – health. We don't try to frighten patients. We are very busy men.'

'Busy my foot. You think you're special, you doctors. That's the trouble with you – you think you're *better* than other people that have to work for a living. You wouldn't know about that, would you? Hard work! Hah! Ever get your hands dirty, real dirty and filthy with hard work?'

'Not that I remember, Miss Ball. I couldn't call myself a doctor if I went around getting . . .'

'And you call yourself a man! Ever wheel a whole barrow of cow manure up a plank? Bet you think it's easy!'

'I never said that wheeling cow manure was easy. It's probably very hard work.'

'Probably,' said Miss Ball in the same tone of voice.

The doctor asked Miss Ball if she thought he was a quack. 'You think I'm a quack, don't you?' he asked.

'Who cares what I think. No one cares.'

'I care, Miss Ball. I care a great deal what you think,' the doctor said softly.

'All right, I think you're a quack,' said Miss Ball.

The doctor bit his lip. He said he had been a doctor a long time. He had healed a lot of wounds, not all of them physical. He had seen a lot of people come and go.

Things grow, Miss Ball thought. Things kept growing and there was little or nothing you could do to stop them. It was Mother Nature's way of getting even with the human race. Everyone suffered. Nature liked ugliness and suffering. Nature wanted fat people and failed crops. Nature wouldn't make you lovely and light. She would keep you fat and fertile. Fertile.

Miss Ball leaned toward the doctor. She almost did not have to act scared. She was scared. But she acted scared just the same, and she shook her head from side to side and up and down, and she said very plainly, 'Doctor, I want you to know I'm a very frightened person. I never get a wink of sleep any more.'

The doctor reflected and was about to speak. But it was Miss Ball that spoke.

'I think they're growing back, and I want a warranty so they don't.'

When all the words reached the doctor he still did not seem to understand what Miss Ball was saying.

'You think *what* are growing back?'

'My things.'

'You mean your fallopian tubes?'

'Yes,' Miss Ball bit her lip, 'those. And the other things you said you took out.'

The doctor started to giggle.

'You think it's funny!'

The doctor could not answer.

'You think human suffering and worry is a big laugh!' Miss Ball began to cry, loudly at first, then worked it down to a whimper. Miss Ball sniffed and dabbed at her cheek with a lace hanky. 'Cruel. You're a cruel, cruel man.'

The doctor apologized. He asked Miss Ball to explain what she meant by the warranty.

After a little hesitation Miss Ball told the whole story. She talked about Mother Nature, about weeds that grew all night and were tall in the morning, about lungs and tonsils, about how she had seen Mother Nature kill her father, about her things –

how they would be back as sure as shooting. The least the doctor could do was give her a warranty so they wouldn't grow back. She finished with, ' . . . I haven't had a good night's sleep for ages.'

The doctor said nothing. He played with his lips for a few moments and stared at the far wall. When Miss Ball thought he was going to laugh once again she started to unfold her hanky. The doctor swiveled his chair back at her and said in a low voice, 'I think I understand.'

'What about it?'

'I'll do anything you say.'

'I want you to warranty the operation.'

'I'll do it,' said the doctor. He took out a piece of paper and wrote on it.

'Make it a five-year warranty, like my juicer. Five years is good enough. I'll be satisfied.'

'No, I won't hear of it, Miss Ball. I'll give you a lifetime warranty for that operation of yours.'

'A *lifetime warranty!* Good God,' said Miss Ball. Her mouth hung open. She could not find the words to express her thanks. Just when he seemed about the biggest quack she had ever seen he reached into his skinny heart and came up with a lifetime warranty. It was almost too much to ask. 'Golly,' she finally said, 'that's the nicest thing anyone ever did for me.'

The doctor handed Miss Ball the piece of paper. He said he had done nothing. Miss Ball protested, and felt like throwing herself at his feet.

On the way out of the office Miss Ball's heart was full of love and life. It pulsed. She felt it thumping there under her brooch and lace like a giant Snooz-Alarm. She was a new woman. Mother Nature could do her worst, could twist nice little tissues into ugly old organs. What did it matter? The wonderful warranty was right there in her handbag.

'When God closes a door he opens a window,' Miss Ball murmured over and over again as she walked home to find out what success Mr Gibbon and Mrs Gneiss had had with their looking around the Mount Holly Trust Company. Personally, Miss Ball felt she could rob a thousand banks single-handed.

## 13

'It's all set,' Mr Gibbon said. He and Mrs Gneiss had found out many valuable things. They knew exactly where the vault was (it was, as a matter of fact, in full view of all the bank customers, as most vaults are) and they had plotted what movements they would make. It would be an elaborate 'quarterback sneak:' the women would be standing by, Mr Gibbon would sneak in with his gun drawn, wearing a disguise. The women would be dressed in very ordinary clothes ('Oh, gee!' Miss Ball said, and slapped the table), and would arrive early at the bank. Everyone agreed that it was a nifty little plan.

The suitcases were next on the agenda. The bodies – or the parts of the bodies – had started making a terrific reek. It was an ungodly odor, Mr Gibbon said, and then he began telling the two ladies about how trenches smelled exactly like that – and you had to sleep, eat, load your gun and shine your brass right in the thick of it. You could cut it with a knife, in case anyone was interested.

Miss Ball said that, for goodness sake, it must have been just like what Herbie was putting up with at that very moment! The thought of the decaying limbs and trunks of the two communists in the suitcases upstairs made them all feel quite close to Herbie.

'It kind of makes you stop and think, doesn't it?' said Mrs Gneiss.

They all stopped, sniffed at the smell that had now penetrated right down into the dining-room, and agreed. It was as if Herbie was in the next room.

But what to do with those suitcases? Miss Ball suggested

burying them. Mr Gibbon suggested that they should put them, for practical reasons, into lockers at the bus terminal. Why? Because after the robbery, as they were carried on the shoulders of a screaming mob of grateful patriots, they would ask to be taken to the bus terminal. In full view of the mob and nation-wide television they would produce the key and throw the locker open, expose its un-American contents to the mayor; they would exchange the locker key for the key to the city of Mount Holly.

Miss Ball called a taxi. The taxi-driver was a bit under the weather.

'Nice to see *some* people get a chance to go away,' he muttered.

'Oh, *we're* not going *any*where!' Miss Ball chirped.

Mrs Gneiss was given the task of depositing the suitcases into the lockers. Mr Gibbon had carefully estimated how much it would cost. He gave Mrs Gneiss two warm dimes when they arrived at the bus terminal, and called a porter to help. 'Give the little woman a hand,' he said. 'I'll be right back.' He winked at Miss Ball.

They should not be seen together in public, it was decided. There was no telling who might be spying on them. Mr Gibbon said that it was a favorite trick of spies to let you go on with your activities and then nab you at the least likely moment, red-handed, with the goods.

'Well, you just leave the goods to me,' Mrs Gneiss said. Mr Gibbon and Miss Ball went their separate ways after whispering that they would meet back at the 'hide-out,' as Miss Ball's white-frame house, ringed by nasturtiums, came to be called.

Mrs Gneiss carried one suitcase, the porter carried the other, heavier one. The porter remarked that it felt as if it were filled with burglar tools.

The moment Mrs Gneiss lifted the suitcase she knew she had Juan. She felt her nice porous skin turn to gooseflesh as she hurried toward the steel lockers.

'They'll fit right fine in this one,' the porter said as he groaned and heaved his big suitcase before a row of big lockers.

Mrs Gneiss looked at the sign and sighed. *Deposit One Quarter Only*, read a sign over a chromium tongue with a quarter-sized circle punched into it. The tongue seemed to be sticking right at Mrs Gneiss. She examined the two dimes in her palm and said to the porter, 'You got anything more reasonable?'

The porter said that at the other end of the terminal there were some cheaper ones, a little cheesier than these.

'Let's have a look,' Mrs Gneiss said.

They hefted the suitcases once again. Half-way across the floor, near the benches for the waiting passengers, Mrs Gneiss heard someone say, 'What's a lady like you lugging a big suitcase like that all by your lonesome?'

The porter ignored the voice and went on ahead.

Mrs Gneiss turned. A sailor stood before her. He was wearing a seaman's uniform: the white inverted sand-pail hat, wide trousers and a tight shirt. He had tattoos on his hairy forearms. He should have been young. It was the sort of uniform young sailors wear. But he wasn't young. He was about fifty, and his pot-belly pressed against his sailor-shirt. He looked jolly. He lifted Mrs Gneiss's meaty hand off the handle and hoisted the suitcase. He asked Mrs Gneiss if she had burglar tools in it.

He alone laughed at his joke. He asked Mrs Gneiss where she was going. He said that he was going to Minneapolis. Mrs Gneiss said that she was going to the lockers at the other end of the terminal. This sent the old salt into gales of laughter.

'I hope you don't mind doing this,' Mrs Gneiss said, trying to get an impish smile on her fat face. 'My Herbie's in the army.'

'Don't say?' the sailor said, interested. 'Is he Stateside?'

'I don't think so. He's in the front lines as far as I know.'

The sailor whistled. 'What's he wanna do a thing like that fer? Get hissel' hurt that way if he doesn' watch it.'

'Not my Herbie,' said Mrs Gneiss. It hadn't dawned on her that Herbie would get hurt. Now, as she said *Not my Herbie*, it occurred to her that Herbie might get his little brain blown off. She blotted out the thought and grinned at the sailor.

The porter had walked all the way to the end of the terminal and now was walking back to where Mrs Gneiss stood with the sailor. He looked peeved. 'I been waiting for you for about an hour,' he said.

'Don't get yer dander up for nothing,' the sailor said.

'Where's my suitcase?' Mrs Gneiss asked.

'Back there. You think I'm gonna cart that around all day you're nuts,' he said.

Mrs Gneiss told the sailor she was in a big rush. She had to get the suitcases into the locker and go right back home (she almost said 'to the hide-out').

When they reached the lockers at the other end the porter held his mouth open in astonishment. ''At's funny,' he finally said. 'I coulda sworn I left the thing right here . . .'

Mrs Gneiss wrinkled up her nose. She did not think it was a great loss. The body that was in the suitcase was not only dismembered – it was dead as well. She was, after all, trying to get rid of it. 'Someone must have filched it,' she said simply.

The sailor suddenly let loose a wild hoot. He seized the shrugging porter by the shirt and began beating him with his free hand. 'Now look what you've gone and done!' he puffed. He shoved the porter up against the lockers with a clang and screamed, 'Look what you're making me do!'

Mrs Gneiss stood quietly and watched. She knew that the sailor would soon get it out of his system. A policeman came by and asked what was going on.

The sailor stopped beating the porter. He was out of breath and could not speak. He shook the porter in the policeman's face.

Mrs Gneiss explained what had happened. She finished by saying, 'I don't see what all the fuss is about. There was nothing very valuable in it.'

'Valuable or not,' the policeman said, 'we don't like this sort of thing happening in Mount Holly. Now you just sit tight and I'll round up that suitcase of yours in a jiffy. The culprit couldn't be far away.' He asked for a description of the suitcase and its contents.

Mrs Gneiss said that it was old, brownish-greenish, and had some personal effects locked in it.

The policeman deputized the sailor and the porter. The three ran out the back door of the bus terminal in search of the suitcase.

Mrs Gneiss quietly placed the small suitcase (Juan) in a dime-locker and went into the bus terminal Koffee Shoppe and swilled down a huge hot-fudge sundae.

Less than ten minutes later the policeman was back with a rat-faced little bum in one hand and the suitcase (Harold Potts, Jr) in the other. The policeman handcuffed the bum to a post and joined Mrs Gneiss in another sundae. Afterwards, he insisted on having his picture taken with Mrs Gneiss: he presenting the lost suitcase to her, she thanking him. It took an hour for the press photographer to arrive, but finally Mrs Gneiss got the second suitcase into the locker. The policeman did the heaving and pushing. He remarked as he was doing it that the suitcase felt as if it were filled with burglar tools.

The sailor and the porter were nowhere to be seen. They were, presumably, still looking for the thief.

'I think I'll just toddle off,' Mrs Gneiss said.

The policeman wouldn't hear of it. He said he'd give her a lift in the squad car. His pal didn't mind. They were both tired of passing out parking tickets. 'The jig's up,' Mr Gibbon said, when he saw the police squad car arrive with Mrs Gneiss in the back seat.

'Gosh, the police!' Miss Ball said. She skipped into the kitchen and slammed the door.

Mr Gibbon pulled out his pistol and flattened himself against the wall behind the front door.

' . . . But just for a sec,' the policeman said as he entered. 'Gotta get back to the station-house.'

Mr Gibbon had carefully unloaded his pistol. Now, as the policeman shuffled in and closed the door, he raised the pistol and brought it down on the top part of the policeman's cap where the bulge of his head showed through. Mr Gibbon had expected a bone-flaking crunch. There was not a sound like that. Instead there was a soft *splok* and the policeman slumped to the floor.

'Charlie!' Mrs Gneiss said.

'Rope!' Mr Gibbon hissed.

Mrs Gneiss looked at the policeman lying spread-eagled on the floor grinning up at her. 'You killed the cop, Charlie, and for no good reason at all, you know that?'

'Get some rope, Mrs Gneiss, and stop sassing me!'

Mrs Gneiss rummaged through her knitting basket looking for rope. She sighed and mumbled, 'I thought it was a bank we were after . . .'

Mr Gibbon peeked out the little window at the top of the door and spied another policeman in the car. He yelled for Miss Ball.

The kitchen door opened a crack. 'Is it okay to come out?'

'Sure, sure,' Mr Gibbon said.

Miss Ball clapped her hand to her mouth when she saw the policeman on the floor. Her eyes popped over the top of her hand. Mr Gibbon leaped in back of her and started to tickle her. On the left side he tickled and held her fast; on the right – where most of the tickling was done – he used his pistol. He slipped the ice-cold gun barrel under her blouse and scrubbed her kidneys with it.

'Stooooop! Paaaalllleeeeeeeeze! Stooooop it! You're awful, Charlie Gibbon! Stoooo . . .'

Her glee found its way through the door and down the walk, past the nasturtiums and into the front seat of the squad car where another policeman sat reading a magazine.

The policeman blew and whistled, fumbled with the magazine, glanced toward the door, shifted in his seat, and then got out of the car, adjusted his tie in the side-window and hurried up the walk.

*

During the night another policeman came and asked Mrs Gneiss if she had seen the two policemen. He described them and gave her the license number of the squad car.

Mrs Gneiss said yes, indeed, she had seen those nice policemen – they had given her a lift home. But they couldn't stay, they said. They drove off in the direction of Holly Junction to give parking tickets.

When the inquiring policeman returned to his car his partner asked him what he had found out.

'Nothing,' was the answer, 'just a nice old lady that doesn't know a thing.'

Mr Gibbon saw the car leave as he sat upstairs in the darkness and looked through a slit in the curtains. He waited a half-hour and tip-toed out of the house to check the squad car that he had driven around back and covered with lilac branches and heavy canvas.

As he sneaked through the nasturtiums he heard, 'Hey, you!' Mr Gibbon froze. He did not move a muscle, did not even brush at a fly that was strafing his wedge-shaped head. He had forgotten his pistol.

A uniformed man came up to him and tapped him on the shoulder.

Mr Gibbon thought of kneeing the uniformed man and making a run for it. But he knew he didn't have a chance. He started to say something when the man spoke.

'Lady by the name of Gneiss live here?'

'Who wants to know?' asked Mr Gibbon, finding his tongue.

'Western Union. Got a telegram for her.'

It might be a trick, thought Mr Gibbon. 'I'll take it. She's inside.'

'Okay, okay. As long as she lives here. Just sign the book.'

Mr Gibbon made every effort to write illegibly in the book. He took the envelope and stayed in the nasturtiums while the Western Union Man walked away, glancing back at intervals until he was out of sight.

The car had not been touched. Mr Gibbon put some more branches on it and then went in the house and gave the telegram to Mrs Gneiss.

Mrs Gneiss opened it and read it. When she was through reading it she reached across the table, took a handful of cream-filled chocolates and put them in her mouth. Her mouth bulged and juice ran from the corners of her mouth.

She chewed and did not stop chewing until the whole box of cream-filled chocolates was empty. And when it was, and she looked worried, she handed the telegram to Mr Gibbon.

REGRET TO INFORM YOU OF YOUR SONS DEATH STOP KILLED GALLANTLY IN ACTION TODAY STOP GAVE HIS LIFE FOR HIS COUNTRY STOP THAT OTHERS MAY LIVE STOP DEEPEST SYMPATHY STOP PERSONAL EFFECTS FORWARDED FIRST CLASS MAIL TO NEW ADDRESS MOUNT HOLLY.

## 14

Dressed in authentic policeman's garb, Mr Gibbon and Miss Ball stood before the full-length mirror in the hall. Miss Ball had insisted on 'being a policeman.' It took nearly the entire night to alter the jacket and trousers, but by morning – and a beautiful morning it was, the sun shining, the nasturtiums about ready to burst and bleed they were so full of color and sun – she was finished, and just in time for the robbery.

'We're *cops*!' Miss Ball said. 'How I wish my kindergarten could see me!' She brushed the sleeve and adjusted the cap and said, 'Isn't it a humdinger?'

Mr Gibbon straightened Miss Ball's tie and said, 'Get them shoes shined and make it snappy, sojer.'

Mr Gibbon had never felt more patriotic. He turned on the

radio hoping for The Anthem. The news was on. ' . . . Tomorrow will be a National holiday in memory of our boys who have given their lives to preserve our way of life at home and abroad, said the President yesterday. The President is now up and around. He brushed his teeth while sitting on the side of his bed this morning and received scores of well-wishing messages from a host of world leaders. He has also been showered with dozens of floral arrangements and directed that some of them be sent to the front lines to remind the soldiers that the country was with them all the way. This morning, with the help of doctors and nurses, he signed his first piece of legislation. Now for the local news. Mount Holly will celebrate tomorrow with a parade through the business districts. Wreaths will be placed and Troop 45 of the Mount Holly Boy Scouts will carry flags. All are welcome to . . .'

'A holiday tomorrow and all on account of Herbie!' Mrs Gneiss said. 'I knew he had it in him! And isn't that thoughtful of the President?'

'We're gonna march, by God!' said Mr Gibbon.

'You're darn tootin' we are,' Miss Ball said.

And then they remembered that it was Friday, a working day. Mr Gibbon called Kant-Brake and said he was in sick bay. Miss Ball called the School Committee and said she was feeling sluggish and headachey. 'A white lie never hurt a soul,' said Miss Ball.

A last check of the two tied-up and gagged (and nearly naked) policemen in the cellar showed one to be still unconscious from the conk on the head the day before. The other was hopping up and down, struggling to get free. He was stooped over because of the high-backed chair Mr Gibbon had tied him to.

'You worried about your pal?' Mr Gibbon said to the hopping man.

The man continued to hop, trying to get loose. Mr Gibbon took this hopping up and down for a 'yes.' 'Don't you worry a bit, he'll be fit as a fiddle in a day or two,' Mr Gibbon said heartily.

Then Mr Gibbon pulled out his pistol. The hopping man's eyes bugged out when they lighted on the pistol. Mr Gibbon tossed his head in a I-know-what's-best manner and said, 'You'll thank me for this someday.' He bopped the man on the head.

When Mr Gibbon came upstairs he said it was zero hour.

'Those two nice policemen are going to catch a death in their undies. It's mighty chilly in that cellar,' said Miss Ball.

Mr Gibbon told Miss Ball to stop worrying her head about little things. There was a country at stake. He went around back, threw off the lilac branches and the canvas from the car, and then proceeded to test each item: the horn, the brakes, the oil, the gas, the siren, the water, and even the windshield wipers. Mrs Gneiss had told him about TV movie robberies that had failed because the get-away car had run out of gas, or the lights had failed, or it wouldn't start. In one of the movies a man had been gunned down as he pressed the starter and got only an *aw-aw-aw* from the engine. Mr Gibbon reflected: what is more humiliating than dashing out of a bank after a successful robbery and getting into an ornery car? It must be damned discouraging.

They had started down the street in high spirits when Mr Gibbon suddenly spun the car around and drove back to the house. He parked around back and said that he'd changed his mind.

'Good,' said Mrs Gneiss. She extracted a handful of jelly beans from her purse and began munching.

'We can't both be policemen,' he said, looking at Miss Ball.

Miss Ball started to pout.

'I don't want to spoil anyone's fun,' Mr Gibbon said, calmly. 'What I said was, we can't both be policemen. That's all I said.'

'But you're the big cheese, Charlie. You can play policeman if you want. Me and Mrs Gneiss are nothing. You're the one who makes the rules!'

Mr Gibbon stretched his lips. He was deep in thought. Finally he said, 'No, you're right. You be the policeman. But remember to follow orders or I'll give you the business.'

'Hot dog!' said Miss Ball. She rolled her eyes and spoofed a face.

'Let's get the show on the road,' Mrs Gneiss said, between mouthfuls of jelly beans.

Mr Gibbon got out of the car and went into the house. He returned dressed in his sneakers ('for quick take-off'), flapping fatigues and wearing a felt hat with the brim turned down all around. He also had a shopping bag with him. He showed the ladies that Old Trusty was inside. He handed both Miss Ball and Mrs Gneiss police pistols.

He had another idea, he said. He had gotten it as they were driving down the street. He would explain it by and by. They were abandoning the 'Quarterback Sneak' plan. They should have scrapped it long ago.

In the meantime he had a few things to do. He made several more trips into the house and came back with some cans of whitewash and a big brush. He looked at the doors. MOUNT HOLLY POLICE was written on the front doors, together with a facsimile of a policeman's badge and the telephone number of the police headquarters. With careful strokes Mr Gibbon painted the front doors white. Then he removed the large chrome searchlight from the right front fender and the long antenna from the back. These he handed to Miss Ball.

'Give you four seconds to put them back,' he said. 'Okay, go!'

Miss Ball scrambled to the rear of the car and stuck the antenna in the hole. When she started for the front of the car she glanced back and saw the antenna start to topple – she ran back just in time to save it. But by then she had used up five seconds and still held the chrome searchlight in her hand.

'Criminy sakes,' said Miss Ball. 'I can't do it for the life of me!' She prepared to pout.

'Now I'm going to show you how to do it proper,' said Mr Gibbon. He whizzed to the back of the car and jammed in the antenna, then huffed to the front fender and, with a little grunt, fixed the searchlight into its socket.

'Think you can do that? Or have I got a real clinker in my platoon?'

After six tries Miss Ball did the same. She managed it in slightly over six seconds. 'How's that for an old bag? Clinker indeed!'

Mr Gibbon stood at some distance from the car and looked at it, closing first one eye and then the other. Finally he took the antenna and searchlight off and put them in the back seat. On the floor of the back he put two buckets of water. A last look at the car, blue and white like a taxi; 'Pretty snazzy,' he said.

They all squeezed into the front seat, and Mr Gibbon explained his new plan in detail. He said they should all be shot for not thinking of this plan before. It was sure-fire. It couldn't miss.

'Oh, botheration!' said Miss Ball. 'How can I drive the get-away car if I can't drive?'

Mr Gibbon told her to pipe down and listen. When he was through talking they synchronized their watches.

It was a little after ten o'clock when Mr Gibbon drove down Holly Boulevard and turned on to Main Street. Apparently many other people had heard about the holiday and had decided to do their weekend shopping. The traffic was heavy; Mr Gibbon leaned on his horn and swore.

They had all digested the plan and were impatient to get down to brass tacks. But now the car was stuck at a red light. Mr Gibbon shut off the engine when he saw no signs of movement in the congestion.

'Tarnation,' Mr Gibbon said. 'We'll be here all day in this traffic. Now you can see perfectly well what a godawful headache it must be to run a country. No wonder the President has to have his gall removed. Why, if he didn't he'd be up tightern'a duck's ass from morning to night. Here we are doing our damnedest to help out the country and we're ham-strung from top to bottom with this traffic.' He smacked his lips and looked around. 'This traffic's thicker'n gumbo.'

There was a dark family in the next car. They smiled at Mr

Gibbon. Mr Gibbon grinned back pleasantly and showed all fifteen of his teeth. He turned to Mrs Gneiss, who was sitting in the middle. 'Don't look now, but there are some You-Know-Whos next door. Hear their radio?' He sighed. 'Those spooks sure need their bongo music.'

The traffic started again. As soon as the cars began moving Mr Gibbon shouted, 'Did you see the nerve of those bastards? Grinning at me like damn fools. Felt like spitting in their eyes!'

Rage had taken possession of Mr Gibbon by the time they approached the Mount Holly Trust Company. He was panting, and wetting his lips. He discovered that he could barely speak. He had made it a cardinal rule that everyone should be cool as cucumbers, but Miss Ball (smiling out the window, hoping to catch the eye of one of her hooky-playing kindergarteners who, skipping by, would see their own teacher in her adorable little cop suit) and Mrs Gneiss (munching dolefully on a Nougat Delite) were the only cool ones in the car.

Mr Gibbon looked over and said in a tone of voice that neither Miss Ball nor Mrs Gneiss recognized as Charlie's, 'Get that fool hat off! You wanna wreck everything?'

Miss Ball took her hat off and smiled. Mr Gibbon at that moment developed a facial tic that stayed with him for the rest of his life.

He drove by the bank and then up a side street to the back. Here he pointed the car in the direction of the front of the bank, a little hill, and said, 'This is it, boys. You know what to do.' He wrenched his hat down over his ears, and got out of the car and told Mrs Gneiss to hurry up. Then he felt in his shopping bag for his pistol and started down the little hill which led to the front door of the Mount Holly Trust Company.

Mrs Gneiss put her Nougat Delite into her purse with her pistol, snapped the purse shut and waddled after Mr Gibbon.

They entered the bank and went immediately to a side table. Mr Gibbon put his head down and muttered, 'You know what to do.'

Mrs Gneiss ambled to the entrance and stood next to the guard. He wore a brand new uniform and looked rather young. Harold Potts' replacement, thought Mrs Gneiss. He smiled at Mrs Gneiss. She smiled back and clutched her purse.

Out back, Miss Ball checked her watch. She stared at it for a full minute, and then took the antenna, the searchlight and the two buckets of water from the back seat. These she put some distance from the car in a little pile together with her policeman's hat. She walked about twenty-five feet away from the pile, which was now between her and the car. She checked her watch again and smiled. Keep cool, she thought.

Mr Gibbon walked towards the teller's cage.

'White folks move aside,' he said.

There were some protests. 'Aw, let the old coot have his own way,' someone grumbled.

Mr Gibbon looked hard at the teller and said, 'Okay, hand over the money.'

The man behind the counter cocked his head and then smiled, 'Have you filled out a withdrawal slip, sir?'

Mr Gibbon put his face up against the bars of the teller's cage so that his nose and chin stuck through. 'Hand over the money, all of it, you hear? This is a stick-up.'

'Beg pardon?'

'A stick-up,' said Mr Gibbon. 'You're being stuck-up. By me. Understand?'

'Perhaps you'd like to have a word with the manager,' the teller said.

Miss Ball checked her watch again. It was almost time. She edged over to the pile of equipment, the hat, the light, the bucket. A man appeared next to her. 'Got a fare?' he asked. Miss Ball smiled, but did not answer. The man got into the back of the car and opened his newspaper.

Mrs Gneiss sneaked a look at Harold Potts' replacement and felt in her purse. As soon as she did so Harold Potts' replacement looked inside, almost involuntarily. Mrs Gneiss quickly took out her Nougat Delite and, grinning, offered him some. 'Much obliged,' he said, 'but no thanks.'

'This is the last time I'm gonna tell you. *This is a stick-up, now hand over the cash!*'

The people who had been in line in back of Mr Gibbon started backing away. They looked at him with the kind of nervous puzzlement that arrives as a smirk. The smirks vanished when Mr Gibbon pulled Old Trusty from his shopping bag and flashed it around. Some people started for the door, but Mrs Gneiss stepped away from the guard and took aim with her Nougat Delite. 'Don't move,' she said.

She heard laughter, and then she heard very plainly, 'Just a couple of old cranks. Might as well humor them – they don't mean any harm. Just two old farts.'

Mrs Gneiss dropped her Nougat Delite into her purse and yanked out the policeman's .38 calibre Colt, looked for the source of the voice, and dropped him in his tracks with one shot.

She waved Harold Potts' replacement away from the door and gestured for the people to back up against the wall.

Oddly, the moment Mrs Gneiss fired her gun everyone in the bank raised his arms over his head; even the girls sitting at typewriters many feet away did so. All talking ceased. Just like on television, thought Mrs Gneiss.

Mr Gibbon pushed his shopping bag over the counter to the teller. The teller stuffed it with big bundles of money wrapped with paper bands and gave the bulging sack back to him.

At this moment a little brown man shuffled around front and, with his hands high above his head, said, 'Don't anyone panic. Just do what the man says. We're insured against theft.'

Perhaps out of fear, perhaps out of the rock-hard heroism that is smack in the belly of every good bank manager, the little brown man smiled and nodded obligingly to Mr Gibbon.

Mr Gibbon sucked in air and snarled, 'I don't want any of your cheap lip!' And he shot the little brown man dead. Like a toy the man gurgled, flapped his dry little hands and went down.

The people in the bank straightened their arms and held them higher.

It was time. Miss Ball picked up a bucket of water and splashed it against the left front door of the car. MOUNT HOLLY POLICE complete with telephone number and badge appeared from under the running whitewash. She did the same with the right front, and on this trip around the car popped the antenna and the searchlight in place. Then she snatched the hat and put it on, pushed up the knot of her tie, got into the car, released the brake, flicked on the siren and started rolling down the little hill to the front of the bank.

The man in the back seat did not look up. He said, 'Oak Street,' and kept on with his paper.

Mr Gibbon was standing next to a huge pile of bills when Miss Ball pushed through the door and said with stage gruffness, 'Okay, don't anyone move. Drop your guns and get your hands up.'

With a clang the guns hit the marble floor of the Mount Holly Trust Company.

'What happened to *him*?' asked Miss Ball, gesturing toward the little brown bank manager curled up in his own blood.

'I didn't *mean* to do it,' said Mr Gibbon.

'Tell that to his widow,' Miss Ball said, in a good imitation of Broderick Crawford. She motioned for Mr Gibbon and Mrs Gneiss to move on. 'Take the money,' she said to Harold Potts' replacement. 'We'll need it for evidence.'

Harold Potts' replacement put the stack of money in the back seat and then got in to guard Mr Gibbon. The man with the newspaper murmured and made room. Mrs Gneiss got in front.

Miss Ball released the emergency brake, flicked on the siren again and, as Mr Gibbon said 'Easy does it,' the car began rolling faster and faster and then coasting at a good rate away from the bank and down the long slope which gave the little burg of Mount Holly its name.

# Epilogue

There is a painting called 'The Spirit of '76' (but better known as 'Yankee Doodle') that hangs in the Town Fathers' meeting-room in Abbot Hall in Marblehead, Massachusetts. It is well known throughout the length and breadth of the United States. The thought of this picture alone is enough to reduce your average American to helpless saluting.

This painting, executed by A. M. Willard, depicts a battlefield strewn with the rubbish of war, a broken wagon-wheel, some pieces of charred skin, a blackened keg. The sky churns with the fresh soot of recently exploded bombs. In the midst of all this rubbish are three figures marching abreast: a sturdy fellow, his head swathed in a bloody bandage, his lips pursed on a flute, marches on the right; a clean little boy in a blue tri-corner hat and beating a drum struts on the left. In the center, wearing a remarkably clean shirt, his head a riot of white hair, a very old man marches. He is prognathic and he is tapping a big drum. At the lower right a wounded soldier raises his trunk out of the quagmire to wave his filthy cap at the musicians and the tattered flag seen fluttering just beyond their heads.

Although nearly three thousand miles from Marblehead, the citizens of Mount Holly know this painting well. And so it was no accident that the day after the robbery of the Mount Holly Trust Company, in what came to be known as 'Herbie's Parade,' Mrs Gneiss, Miss Ball and Mr Gibbon, marching right, left and center respectively (Mrs G. with her head bandaged) and carrying two drums and a flute, and all of them dressed the part, strode through the streets of Mount Holly. It was their wish. Unlike the

92

trio in the famous painting, they did not march in step, for clasped firmly around their ankles were leg-irons. And although it was something they had not bargained on, they had to play their tunes to the clink of their dragging chains.

1969

# The Greenest Island

*I*

They had chosen San Juan because it was cheap that year and it was as far away as they could get from people who knew they were not married. They guessed they would be found out eventually, but to be caught at home, mimicking marriage, playing house – that was dangerous. They were in trouble and ashamed of it, but being young felt the shame as an undeserved insult. They had discovered this island like castaways in a children's story, who stumble ashore and learn to live among the surprises of a tropical place. The footprints of cannibals, bright birds, coconut palms!

But in 1961 Puerto Rico was a poor ruined island. There was no romance – they had brought none. It was green, that was all; and though the green was overstated, there was a kind of yellow delay lurking in the color. They were unprepared and a little frightened. They had nothing but their pretense of audacity and three hundred and twenty dollars. No return tickets: they had no particular plans. The hotel was dirty and expensive – they couldn't live there. By chance, they found a furnished room on the Calle de San Francisco. It was only a room, but here they felt safe enough to write to their families and tell them what they had done.

Paula had hidden her pregnancy from her parents. She had planned to tell them but for four months she had lived with Duval in his college town – another shabby room. She wrote home then; she told them she was in New York working. I need a year off, she said. Her parents understood. There were two other couples in that house – newly married students, with stingy interests, busy with their studies, wanting privacy in their nests of notebooks and term papers. Noisy and hilarious in their rooms, outside they were incurious. Duval saw them on the stairs and couldn't match the night-time laughter to their grave daylit faces. When the spring semester ended, Paula had said, 'I can't go home – they'd kill me,' and Duval had agreed to do something.

He was nineteen, impatient to be older and with a sense that he was incomplete. He read; his imagination blazed; he tried to write. Although he had accomplished little he had the conviction that he was marked for some great windfall, without sacrifice. He believed in his luck, and this belief made him unassailable but solitary and secretive. He could do whatever he chose to; he was confident of his ability to write humorously and well. His spark warmed him like a star and promised that success would come to him with age, in a matter of years. He was certain of it, but that was before Paula had shrunk this future he imagined. Her news had brought the future to his feet, unexpectedly freezing him. He was no longer alone. She was twenty-one, a woman, and she resented the difference in their ages, though she looked younger than he with her sly pretty face and straight blonde-streaked hair and warm skin. He had loved her.

A year before he might have married her. Bur he had stopped loving her, the fever left him, and a month later she had said he'd made her pregnant. It happened so fast there wasn't time to talk about their feelings, and Duval didn't want to hurt her more by saying he didn't love her. Love didn't matter now. The fact was greater: she was going to have his baby. For a confused month when they were apart, in letters, they had argued about the alternatives. The thought of an abortion frightened her. 'Knitting needles,' she said. He calmed her and telephoned a woman in Somerville. The woman said she would do it for sixty dollars and that he should call back. He did a week later. The woman was hysterical; she screamed, she cried. She would be arrested, she said in a terrible voice. But she agreed to do it. 'It's the last time!' Duval never called her again. And it was too late to get married, because now they knew what their marriage would be: a temporary urgency, a trap, the end of their lives. They wanted more than that and they knew they were not in love.

Still, they were afraid; but less afraid when they were together. They would stay together and hope and try to be kind. They had no choice. And yet they wished to believe that some miracle would release them, that they would wake up free one morning. The wish made them restless and it convinced them that if Paula weren't pregnant, if there were no child, they would not be together.

It seemed necessary to flee and hide. Their parents had begun to wonder about them. Duval said he was going to work on a ship; Paula wrote that she was spending the summer in New York. And when their parents were satisfied with these explanations they flew to San Juan. It was like a further possibility of hope: such a great distance to such a strange place; the humid heat, the smells, yellow-brown faces, the sight of palms. The miracle might happen here, on this green island. They waited in their room.

In the morning from their window they could see the high stucco houses of the old city with their clifflike balconies, and the ramparts of the fort and the jutting roofs of the settlement that was pitched between the sea wall and the ocean, the stick and palm leaf slum known locally as *La Perla*, the pearl. There was music, one song played over and over, yakking trumpets, the snap of guitars and sad Spanish tenors. There were cries from the street: the paper seller calling out '– *parcial*,' the chattering of the boy beggars, the ice-cream man with his cart of *piraguas*; and the frantic din of an old woman yelling in Spanish. They heard her for days – she sounded hurt – and then, when they saw her, she was doing nothing more alarming than selling lottery tickets in front of the Colorama Toy Store. She had to scream. Her competitor was a dwarf with tiny legs and an enormous head, who sat in a chair in the Plaza Colon, just around the corner. He looked at first glance like a severed head propped on a chair seat, and most people bought their tickets from him, for charity, for luck.

Duval explored the neighborhood and brought back stories. The people were damaged and crazy, or else very sad. There were homeless boys and old women who slept on the marble benches in the plaza, under the statue of Columbus. The paper seller – his face burned black, his hair burned orange – stood in the sun all day, and at night got drunk and wept hoarsely and shook his penis at passers-by. There was a one-legged man who wore a red scarf on his head and when he paused to beg hooked his stump over the bar of his crutch and glared like a pirate and demanded money. There was a legless man who rode up and down the Calle de San Francisco in a low clattering cart, pulling himself along with his hands. One morning Duval saw a group of excited men being harangued by a soldier. 'They are starting an army,' said an onlooker. 'They will invade Santo Domingo and kill Trujillo.'

It rained each afternoon, sometimes for a few minutes, occasionally for twenty minutes or more It was loud; it crackled like burning sticks and drove people into doorways – the crazy ones, the five-dollar whores from La Gloria, the beggars, schoolgirls, amputees, the recruits for the invading army – and there they waited, watching the rain, nor speaking. After the rain the buildings dripped and there would be a hot hideous smell in the air of wet garbage and yellow sunlit vapor rising from the street. There were few tourists – it wasn't the season. There were sailors from the navy base and merchant seamen who crowded in from the docks and lingered in the plaza where there were whores and shade and cigar stalls.

It looked dangerous – an island of fugitives, temporary people and harmed hopeless souls. Paula and Duval felt they belonged there: such strangeness could make them anonymous. But they were scared, too – worried they'd be robbed, uncertain about the future, so far. Duval went out alone during the day, and at night, when the old city was those harsh voices and songs and the sound of traffic and the roar of the sea near La Perla, he stayed in with Paula. At midnight all the radios in the district played the national anthem: *La tierra di Borinquén, donde me nacido. Isla de flores* – Duval knew the words, but not their meaning.

Their room faced the street. There were two other rooms on that floor, Mr Ruiz's and Antonio's. Mr Ruiz lived in Arecibo. He went home to his family at weekends and on Sunday night returned alone to his room, bringing a bag of mangoes. He said he hated his room. He said, 'It can get very bad here.' He hated the ants, the cockroaches, the darkness. 'I burn the ants,' he said, and then, 'I like to hear the little snaps when they die.'

Antonio disliked Mr Ruiz; Antonio wanted Puerto Rico to be the fifty-first state, Mr Ruiz wanted independence. When he saw Paula and Duval Antonio always called out, 'State fifty-one!' Antonio worked at night – he never said where. In the afternoon he stood in the doorway on Calle de San Francisco muttering each time a woman went past: '*Fea . . . fea,*' ugly, ugly. He said he did it to engage them, and sometimes they stopped and talked and went upstairs with him. He lived in the next room and those times his elbows knocked on the wall and his bed creaked as if it were being sawed in half.

The building was owned by Señora Gonzales, a young plump widow who dressed heavily in black. Her curio shop was on the ground floor, and all afternoon she made souvenirs out of coconut fiber and bamboo, place mats and dolls with witches' faces. She was uncritical without being friendly. She had rented Paula and Duval the room and had asked no questions. She had sized them up swiftly and appeared to know they had run away.

They began going out together, always choosing the same route: down to the plaza, over to the fort, up the hill to the cathedral where Ponce de León was buried, and then meeting their own street at the top end, at Baldorioty de Castro. They spoke to no one; the language was incomprehensible. They bought food by pointing and smiling and showing their money: a child's effort, a child's gestures. Each day they had the same meal: mushroom soup thickened with rice, pineapple, ice cream; Paula drank a quart of milk. They kept a record of their expenses and saw their money trickling away. Dreadful; it was what they expected. This green disfigured place was the world. It was hot during the day and at night it stank. There were cripples everywhere. But they had sought it, and they deserved to be here. It matched their own punished mood. And sometimes they felt lucky to be surviving it. No one here could accuse them of betraying their parents. They were what they seemed, a young couple expecting a baby, anonymous in the tropical crowd.

They seldom quarreled. Although they felt they hadn't the right to be happy, they experienced a tentative enjoyment, a little freedom alone in this restricted place. Their occasional anger they made into silence. Paula decided to study Spanish, Duval to write – soon, to use the time.

Alone; but they were not alone. Both sensed it. There was someone else who crouched darkly between them. They dwelled in the present and moved forward only by time's slow fractions. They did not speak of the future because they would not mention the baby. They avoided all talk of that – the choice it demanded, the rush of time it implied. It was more than a weight: it was a human presence. They spent their evenings talking without consequence of the oddities they saw – the religious processions, the green lizards on the back roof, the amputee in his noisy cart: the sunlight removed the cheating blur of nightmarishness and made each sight a vivid spectacle.

They were aware of their omission. It was as if there were a third person with them, sentient but mute, to whom they could not refer without risking misunderstanding or offense. It was someone they did not know, as mysterious to them as anyone on the island, and contained by Paula – when she came close to whisper she bumped Duval with the stranger. And so their evenings had sudden silences and were usually stilled by the sense of a small helpless listener. They were like people sitting in a room to wait for a signal from that third person, and there was about their gentleness a fearful timidity of waiting that was as solemn as a deathwatch.

Others reminded them of why they were waiting. Mr Ruiz, who gave them mangoes, brought out pictures of his children and named them: Angel, Maria, José, Pablo, Costanza. His wife, he said, was also pregnant: he nudged Duval, trying to share the pride and resignation of fatherhood. Antonio was respectful, and when he saw Duval alone in La Gloria he asked, 'How is she?' as if Paula were ill and Duval needed reassurance. Paula remained healthy, though she complained of the humidity and said walking made her feet swell. So each afternoon she lay down and rested. One day, two weeks after their arrival on the island, she said her ankles felt huge. Duval massaged them and said, 'Does that hurt?' She said no. He pressed harder; she didn't react. He said, 'You're all right,' but several minutes later he looked again at the ankle and saw the deep dent of his thumbprint.

The heat drugged them. They went to bed when they heard the national anthem and did not wake until the traffic and street noise racketed against the shutters. She slept soundly, perspiring, a film of heat on her skin; but just before she dropped off to sleep she thought how cruel it all was. Anyone else would have been happy, expectant, making preparations. She was doubtful and afraid. She wanted something else; she was too young to give in to this. A life she did not want was being forced upon her.

Duval's sleep was shallow, disturbed by the last thing he did before he went to bed. This was his journal. Not a diary – he never mentioned the progress of the pregnancy; he wrote undated paragraphs about what he saw on the island. It was, he knew, the sort of book a castaway might keep, a record of wonders and surprises: the beggars, the difficult heat, the ants, the lizards. He did not write about himself. He wanted to survive, and he still believed in his luck. He went to bed; he remembered; he woke up and dreaded to inquire where he was or why. He felt he was performing a service, obediently, unwillingly, without love – as if he had been assigned this protective task for a certain period.

When it was over he would be free. But he worried. He had already been away too long; he would not be able completely to re-enter that former self. This task, this place, was undoing him, and he feared that having been forced this far he might never go back.

The silence was broken one night by Paula's crying. He tried to comfort her. He said it was hot – he would open a shutter.

'No,' she said. She hadn't moved. She lay on her side, facing away from him. In a small clear voice she said, 'What are we going to do?'

## 2

It was a holiday on the island, Muñoz Rivera's birthday. They had no idea who he was, but the plaza was festive, jammed with buses and taxis and decorated with banners showing Muñoz Rivera's big pink *hidalgo* face. The dark mob, sweating with gaiety, surged beneath the blowing portraits. The shops were closed, there were no newspapers, and even the girls from La Gloria were taking the day off. Duval saw six of them piling into a taxi with towels and baskets of food – off to the beach. Family groups – the scowling fathers walking a little apart – paraded in new clothes up the Calle de San Francisco, on their way to the cathedral.

The activity, the noise, stirred Duval, who was watching it all from the window. He said, 'Let's go to the beach.'

'How much money do we have?' Paula smoothed her blouse over her stomach to emphasize the bulge; she was still small.

'Three dollars.' But it was less. He knew the exact amount. He hated himself for keeping track.

'The banks are closed today. We'll have to bring sand-wiches.'

'We don't need money.'

She said. 'You look like a jack-o'-lantern. I hate your face sometimes.'

He looked away. The music outside jumped to the window, the same song; and now he could make out the words, *el pescador* and *corazón*, a mournful blaring, continuously repeated.

She said, 'I need a shower.'

The shower was in a cement hut on the back roof, where clumsy pigeons sometimes fluttered and nested. Paula took her towel and left, but she returned to the room moments later.

'Cockroaches,' she said, and threw down the towel. It was a command.

Duval went to the shower and at first saw none. The room was hot and damp, the toilet stank. A sign next to the toilet was lettered in simple Spanish, DO NOT THROW YOUR PAPER ON THE FLOOR. There was an old obscene picture scratched on the wall, with a one-word caption, *chupo*. A cockroach scuttled across the floor and vanished through a crack – gone before he could step on it. There was movement in the sink. He turned on the faucet and toppled the hurrying thing into the plug-hole and kept the water running to drown it. Then he pushed the plastic shower curtain aside. Two reddish blobs slid scratchily down and began working their legs. Duval pulled off a sandal and slapped at them with the sole; there was one more from the rub, several appeared from behind the sink, and the last climbed from the plug-hole twitching water droplets in its jaws. When he was done Duval had killed nine of them. They were dark and scablike and some flew in an ugly burring way, falling crookedly through the air.

Paula took her shower. Duval gathered the Pepsi-Cola bottles that had accumulated under the bed and returned them at La Gloria for the deposit money. Antonio was there on a stool, hunched over a tumbler of brown rum. Seeing Duval, he spoke.

'You want a nice beach?' Antonio licked at his mustache. 'Go to Luquillo.'

Duval was mystified; then he remembered the thin wall on

which he heard Antonio's elbows. He said, 'How do I get there?'

'Take a bus to Rio Piedras, then a *público*.' Antonio smiled. 'Puerto Rico – you like?'

'It's okay,' said Duval.

'Too hot. New York's better,' said Antonio. 'I was there. *Mira*, I got a kid too, in New York. But I come back here. You can play with the girls, but your mother's forever.'

Duval said, 'Who is Muñoz Rivera?'

'George Washington,' said Antonio. 'Have a drink. Luis, *venga!*'

'Some other time.' Duval gave the empty bottles to the barman and bought two Pepsis and a greasy *frijole* with the money.

Antonio said, 'Everybody in New York knows me. Ask them.'

Paula was making the sandwiches when he returned to the room. She had hard-boiled three eggs and was chopping them on a plate. The bread was stiff and there were tiny dots of white mold on the crusts. She scraped the bread, then wiped it with watery mayonnaise. She said, 'We need a refrigerator.'

'Those sandwiches will be all right.'

'No,' she said. 'There are ants in the cheese.'

Duval took the small brick of cheese and started picking them off. Paula looked disgustedly at him. He wrapped the cheese and dropped it into the wastebasket.

'I was going to throw it away.'

'You were going to eat it,' she said.

He shook his head. But she was right. The insects no longer bothered him. He believed he had overcome his repugnance. The island was crawling with ants, spiders, cockroaches; during the day there were flies, at night mosquitoes. He brushed them aside; there were too many to kill.

Paula said, 'I don't want to go to the beach.'

'There's nothing else to do.'

They had been to the beach nearby, the one across the road from the Carnegie Library. It lay below a sandy cliff and was rocky and strewn with driftwood and lengths of greasy rope.

They had been watched the whole time by prowling children in rags from the shacks of La Perla. They decided to take Antonio's advice and go to Luquillo Beach: Luquillo was famous – it appeared on the travel posters.

It was a long trip, by bus and public taxi, taking them past marshland slums on spindly stilts, high thick canefields broken by fields of young spiky pineapples, and, in the distance, hills as blue and solid as volcanoes. They arrived at the beach at noon and were surprised to find it beautiful and nearly empty. There were groups of picnickers and there was a yellow school bus parked on an apron of broken cement, but there were few people swimming and there was no one lying in the sun.

The beach was white, a crescent of glare shimmering beside a gentle wash of surf in a green bay. The beach itself was not wide; it was entirely fringed by slender palms, and the long fronds swayed like heavy green feathers, making the dry rustling of many kites tumbling in a crosswind, a sound that rose to a hectic flap when the wind strengthened and finally stifled it to a moan. Among the palms children were playing hide and seek; they were quick stripes of light as they ran from trunk to trunk, and their laughter carried through the trees.

Duval and Paula walked down the beach until the schoolchildren were tiny and inaudible. They spread out their towels and lay under a palm and watched the green sea mirror wrinkle in the breeze and flash spangles at them.

'Jake!' She snatched his arm. He looked over and saw in the sand, three feet from her, a dead rat. At her second cry it appeared to move, but that was the lizards, four of them, dark green, darting away at her voice and giving the shriveled carcass movement.

'It's horrible,' she said. 'Let's go somewhere else.'

The lizards raised and lowered their tiny dragon heads and flicked out their tongues. They crept back and resumed feeding on the rat. Paula and Duval had remained motionless, and now they could smell it and hear the flies.

'Wait,' said Duval. He got up and, putting the lizards to flight, scooped sand over it until there was only a mound where the stinking thing had been. He smiled at Paula. 'Now let's eat.'

The sandwiches tasted dustily of decay, the *frijole* was clammy and almost inedible, but they ate without a word. They listened to the rustle of the palms and watched the surf running and curling against the beach. They kept silent; they were new; it was unlucky to complain so soon. A complaint was an admission of weakness, a tactless challenge to the other's strength. Secretly, they wished for rescue – to be delivered from this mock marriage and the certainty of the child. And they craved protection. They were waiting for everything to change, and yet nothing had changed. The sky was unbroken, the sun bore down on the sand, there was no ship in the sea.

Paula had stopped worrying aloud, and Duval admired that in her, but still his affection was tinged with resentment. She had tricked him. He said nothing about that. He knew she felt the same. They were matched in anger.

But her stubborn calm was disturbed by occasional fears. The closest was that Duval would simply leave her – too soon; that she would come back to the room and find him gone. It checked her temper, this fear of desertion: she must not upset him. And he could go easily – he was so young. He got up and walked along the beach a little way, and she saw him as a stranger. It surprised her again to see how skinny he was, in his wrinkled shorts and flapping shirt, faded already, and kicking at the sand, then looking up and making a face at the palm: just a boy, an unreliable boy, who had fooled her.

Duval continued to look at the palm. He stood at the base of the trunk and high up the fronds formed the spokes of a perfect green wheel, at the hub of which was a cluster of shining coconuts. A tropical beach; the sun on the sea; coconuts. It was what he expected from the island: the castaway's vision of survival in the tropical trees. The breeze stirred the palm. Duval took a stone and threw it hard. He missed and tried again and this time hit a coconut. He saw the large thing nod on the fiber that held it.

Paula watched him with increasing irritation. He was so happy, mindlessly pitching stones at the tree. What was wrong with him? He was determined to play. She would have allowed it in a man, but a man didn't behave that way, and this mood in Duval made her feel insecure. She wanted him beside her, attentive, reassuring, and she called out, as she might have to a child, 'Stop that!'

Duval paused and shrugged and threw another stone.

'Stop!'

He said, 'I want that coconut.' He wanted the little victory, the prize. He would get the husk open somehow and offer her the sweet water to drink. And they could eat the white flesh; it would taste better than her sandwiches.

The coconut wouldn't come down. He had hit it squarely but the stones bounced off without dislodging it. He took a heavy stick and threw it and hit it again. The coconut moved slightly, but did not fall. He tried shaking the tree; it did no good. It was such a simple thing, but he could not do it. He threw another stick. This one crashed through the fronds and landed near Paula.

She scrambled to her feet and said, 'You almost hit me!'

'Sorry.'

'I told you to stop,' she said. 'Now cut it out.'

He left it, and he was annoyed when he returned to her and she looked straight ahead, at the sea. He felt she was mocking him, not because he had tried to knock down the coconut but because he had failed to do it.

She wandered down the beach to the water's edge and holding her skirt against her thighs waded in the shallow surf. Duval looked around; in the distance there were children, and two priests in dark cassocks, brown and yellow stripes between the palm trunks. He slipped off his shorts and put on his bathing suit.

'It's beautiful,' he said, coming behind her.

'I wish we could enjoy it.' She had said that of the explosive sunsets over the cracked Fortaleza; of the cool plaza; of the gaiety at dusk on the Calle de San Francisco. It was her repetition of it that he hated. That was marriage: repetition.

He strode past her and dived into the water, and was buoyed by its brightness and warmth. It took away his irritation. He swam easily down to the sunlit sea floor, yellow, then blue and green flaked, and he faced depths of purple measured by shafts of light, and flimsy weed stalks trailing up from great smooth boulders. In this colored warmth he experienced a brief sensation of freedom: he was leaving everything behind. He saw his future this way, the happiness he had no words for: success, triumph in a casually chosen place. He moved with weightless ease and it was as if he were breathing underwater, his lungs working without effort. Then a ribbon of cold water passed down his body and he turned and circled back to the hot shallows. He threw his head out of the water, and at the shock of air, the dazzle of bright sun, he gasped.

'You soaked me!' Paula was standing at the shoreline, holding out her sprinkled skirt, exaggerating her distress. 'When you dived in you got me all wet. Grow up!'

'It'll dry,' he said, and he went close to her.

'Don't drip on me,' she said.

'Come in – it's fantastic.'

'I don't have a bathing suit.' She had tried to find a maternity bathing suit. There were none in the cheap stores: Puerto Rican women didn't swim when they were pregnant. And at the tourists' swim shop at the Hilton they were too expensive.

'You don't need one,' he said. 'No one's looking.' He went into the water again and pulled off his swimming trunks and threw them on the sand.

'No,' she said, but she looked around uncertainly. It was the hottest part of the day. The beach was empty, there were no people visible among the trees – the children and the priests had gone; so had the school bus. She was alone and felt tiny and misshapen beside the enormous flat sea. She lifted her skirt, walked a few steps into the water and at once wanted to swim.

She went to the beach, and keeping herself low on the dry sand removed her clothes and folded them, making a neat pile. She entered the water. Instantly, all the heat and heaviness she had felt left her. She had swum out of that clumsy body and into her younger one. She was innocent again. The green sea wrapped her and made her feel small and cool.

They swam apart and spent a long time floating – lying back and letting the sun burn their faces, their ears stopped by the water's hum. Duval swam over and embraced her. She hugged him and he was aroused.

'Stop,' she said, feeling him against her. She turned to face the beach. 'Not here.'

He barely heard her. He slid between her legs, and they crouched, up to their shoulders in the water. His face was hot and he could see a dusting of salt on her cheeks and the sparkle of water drops on the ringlets of hair at her ears. She looked tense, and she bit her lip as he moved inside her. Their shoulders splashed, touched, parted, and splashed again in the swelling water, and they watched each other almost in embarrassment, hearing the gurgle their bodies made. Then he moved rapidly and stiffened and his face went cold. She looked bewildered, on the point of speaking. He kissed her. The water was quite still and near his arm a little strand of scum floated like a lifeless creature from the deep.

After that they gathered their clothes and rested in the shade. Paula was sleeping lightly on her side, pillowing her head on her arm. Duval left her and walked through the palms to where they opened into rough low bush and stocky trees with thin yellow leaves. Beyond this, miles inland, he saw the dense rain forest he had seen from the *público*. It was mountainous, shrouded, blue-black, like a tragic precinct of the island's sunlight. The forest was called El Yunque, and it seemed to him then that those great hanging trees and all those rising mists and shadows were what was in store for him if he gave up. His life would be like that.

The forest was blind. He would be lost among the high vines, trapped in their tangle, just another anonymous soul in an immensity of tall trees. The forest warned him as the sea had given him hope, but the forest's threat was worse than any he had known, of a kind of cowering adulthood, promising darkness, the scavenging of naked families. Alone, he could escape it; that forest was the fate of men who were afraid and hid. He was too young to enter it now; it was too early for him to explore such towering shadows, and to be lost now was to be lost forever.

It was after five by the time they left the beach, and they had to wait for a bus in Rio Piedras. When they got back to the old part of the city the lights were on in the plaza and there was about the whole district that atmosphere of exhaustion that follows a festival.

The milk had gone sour. Duval bought a pint from La Gloria and a ham sandwich from a street seller. Paula made a meal of them, then lay on the bed and fell asleep at once, still in her clothes. Duval covered her with a sheet and turned off the lamp. He never felt anything but tenderness for her when he saw her asleep, and he thought if he moved her even slightly she would break.

By the window, in the light from the Colorama Toy Store, he wrote what he had seen that day: the canefields, the green sea, the coconut, the lizards feeding on the rat, and the vast gloomy rain forest. The writing made him hungry; he went downstairs. But in La Gloria he reached for his money and remembered he hadn't gone to the bank. He looked for Antonio – he could have that drink he had promised and borrow some money for a *frijole*. Antonio wasn't there, and seeing all the noisy people in the bar Duval pitied himself.

He considered going for a walk: more hunger, and the sight of the rich eating in the windows of the expensive restaurants further up the Calle de San Francisco. The thought of walking bothered him for another reason: if you had no money you stayed put. He was angry – with himself, with Paula; his anger turned to fear, and the green island became again in those seconds of reproach a dangerous alien place of destitution and ruin, an intolerable trap.

In the room he looked at the pages he had written. He read a sentence: it was foolish, about the beach, an expression of pleasure. He tore out the page and crumpled it and he was about to throw it into the wastebasket when he saw the cheese.

He unwrapped it, glancing furtively at Paula. A few ants still clung to it. It was softened by the heat, and it had sweated, but it did not smell rancid. He knelt on the floor, in the darkness, and nibbled it until it was gone.

## 3

Tame spiders dancing on violin strings; a whiff of ice in the air; rest – wakefulness bleeding from his fingers. The images came to him at the concert; he wrote them down and admired his work. His writing calmed him like music; the concerts helped him think.

They were held every Sunday afternoon at the cultural center, a pretty house surrounded by palms on the Avenida Rivera. The people in the audience were unlikely islanders, pale Spaniards, studious blacks in neat suits, and old frail women in summer dresses. The chamber music was a soothing voiceless encourage-ment to thought, and the room where the concerts were given was clean and air-conditioned. Paula and Duval sat contentedly in the soft chairs breathing Mozart and cool air. It became one of their activities, like the evening walk to the cathedral or the stroll to the fort to watch the sun drop into the ocean. It was free.

In the confidential way they spoke about themselves they began hesitantly to discuss money and to worry. They had spent about a hundred dollars in a month, but even at this frugal rate – there were no more economies they could make – they knew they would have nothing left in two months. The Sunday concert was free; it cost nothing to walk – but there was food to buy, rent to pay. They said nothing about their return tickets. The knowledge of this little money was a slow ache, a dull physical pain like a smudge of guilt, and the passing days only made it keener.

'I'll have to get a job,' said Duval.

'I wish I could help.' Paula was bigger now; she shifted her stomach each time she moved, and she tired easily. But still she spoke of wanting to go to Rio Piedras and study Spanish. She had inquired. The course cost twenty-five dollars. They both knew it was out of the question. Her Spanish, his writing: they had come to seem like broken promises. Whatever he wrote looked incomplete, and though they contained striking islands of green imagery, they were fragments, they were linked to nothing.

Paula said, 'You could go to the Hilton.'

Duval resisted. The Hilton, a mile away, reminded him of what he hated and feared, everything he had left behind; humiliation.

He said he would look for a job, and thereafter, in the mornings, he put on his tie and his limp green suit and set off. Paula wished him luck and seeing her at the head of the stairs he felt sorry for her and pity for himself; he was too young for this – another future was his, not a repetition of this. As soon as he walked into the plaza he lost his will to look. He was hot, he felt tired even before he boarded the city bus. He had no practical skills, he could not speak Spanish. But worse, in the course of those days looking for a job he realized he was spending far more than if he had stayed home: bus fares, lunch, *piraguas*, newspapers. He bought the *Island Times*, the English language weekly, and looked through the classified ads. Secretary, draftsman, chemist, clerk, accountant: there was no job he could do.

But he could write. More and more in this unusual place he felt the knowledge growing in him of an impulse to write, of linking the fragments he had already set down. He could write the sad story he had already begun to live. It was the effect of the green island: surviving here proved his imagination was nimble. To choose solitude again was to become a writer, a heartless choice, rejecting a child to claim freedom.

Without telling Paula he made notes on the concert at the cultural center the next Sunday, and that night he wrote two pages about it. He described the musicians, the palms at the window, the items on the program – he compared it to a menu for a great meal. Rereading it he saw that it was stiffly enthusiastic, full of compliments and meaningless hyperbole, uncritical; yet it was printable. He had worked hard on it. He wondered if he had worked too hard. The light had been bad in the room. He had waited for Paula to sleep before he dared to begin and twice there were sounds from Antonio's room which stopped him.

In the morning, saying that he was going to look for a job, he went to the offices of the *Island Times* and asked to see the editor. The man had his long legs on his desk, his big feet on the blotter. He had a thick black mustache and only nodded when Duval explained what he had written. He passed the pages to the man. Keeping his feet up the man read the article. Duval saw in this posture a lack of interest; he watched for a reaction and he thought he saw the man smile.

Duval said, 'Can you use it?'

The man said – and Duval realized when he spoke that they were the man's first words – 'We'll see.'

Then Duval was embarrassed; he felt defeated and wanted to leave. In the street again he remembered that he had not mentioned money.

That Thursday he bought the *Island Times*. His piece was not in it. The news was of the filming of *Lord of the Flies* on Vieques Island, a few miles offshore. There was no mention of the concert.

He went to the Hilton. But it was not as he had imagined it, American and intimidating. The stucco was discolored by the sea air, touched by pale florets of decay; and the Puerto Rican smells of sickly fruit and *frijoles* had penetrated to the lobby. The desk clerk directed him to the personnel office, where in a waiting-room there were about ten Puerto Ricans, young men and middle-aged women, who looked as if they had been there all morning. A woman at a table was speaking in Spanish to a nervous man with tough Indian features.

Duval took a seat and waited to be called forward.

'Did you see the ad too?' The man next to him was grinning. He wore a baggy linen suit and a string tie. In his southern accent was the lisp of a Spanish speaker. He had a bald wrinkled head and could have been seventy.

Duval said, 'No.'

'I knew you was a gringo,' said the man. His mustache moved when he grinned. 'The ad for their new restaurant – you ain't seen it? They looking for hands.'

'What sort?'

'All kinds – in the kitchen, waiters, pearl divers, people up front to say, "Your table is all ready, señor." All kinds. But not the doorman. That job's as good as filled. By me.'

'So they haven't hired you yet.'

'No. But they sure will when they sets eyes on me.' The old man rapped Duval on the shoulder and cackled. 'I'se a *technician* doorman.'

The woman at the desk gave Duval an application. He filled it out and in doing so invented a new man, one who was twenty-three, who had worked in several restaurants and lived in San Juan for nearly a year; married.

'Help me with this, will you, old chappie?' said the man in a whisper. 'This here writing's too damned small for my eyes.'

The old man – his name was Ramón Kelly – was illiterate. Duval read the application and Kelly told him what to write: born in Louisiana in 1903, a graduate of Shreveport High School; previous jobs on ships, the *Queen Mary*, the *Huey Long*, the *Andrea Doria*; married, three children. Kelly anticipated the questions, but Duval could see that Kelly was lying too, inventing a man on the job application.

'Where do I put my John Henry?'

Duval showed him.

Kelly licked the tip of the ballpoint, then touched the line and made several loops that looked convincingly like a signature. But the name was not Kelly.

The woman at the desk read Duval's application and gave him a slip of paper. She said, 'Go to the restaurant – outside the building and turn left. Report to Mister Boder.'

Duval did as he was told, and when he entered the restaurant, with its empty tables and smells of floor wax and fresh varnish and workmen carrying potted palms, he heard a voice say. 'We got a live one.' Then the man appeared and said loudly, 'I hope to God you speak English!'

Over coffee, Mr Boder said that the restaurant, which was to open in two days, was called the Beachcomber. It was part of a chain of American restaurants specializing in Polynesian food. Mr Boder was general manager of the Los Angeles Beachcomber and had been sent to San Juan to hire waiters and supervise the opening. He was a bluff perspiring man of about fifty with capped teeth which, although perfectly shaped, were yellow from the cigars he chewed. He was friendly, he called Duval 'a fellow sufferer,' stuck like himself on this island of unreliable people.

Duval said, 'It's a dictatorship.'

'I'm glad you told me that.' Mr Boder removed his cigar from his mouth and spat into a wastebasket.

'That's what people say.'

'I don't speak Spanish.' He said that for a few days he had gone to bed with a copy of *L'Imparcial* and a Spanish-English dictionary, but he had abandoned the effort. He hated the island. He was newly married and missed his wife. 'My second wife,' he said. 'She's about your age, and she's starting to whine. You married?'

'Yes.'

'So I don't have to tell you,' said Mr Boder. 'Ever work in a restaurant?'

Duval said he had.

Mr Boder seemed disappointed. He said, 'I hate the food business. The hours, the complaints. The kitchen's always a madhouse. It's ruined my health.' He coughed disgustedly, then said, 'Of all the rackets you can get in, the food business is the worst.'

A Chinese-looking man came out of the kitchen. He was fat-faced and his black suit matched his scowl. He said, 'There's another one in the kitchen. Show them around.'

When he had gone, Duval said, 'Is he Polynesian?'

'Chinese,' said Mr Boder. 'It's all Chinese here. Sure, the decor is Polynesian' – he indicated an outrigger canoe which was suspended from the ceiling of woven grass – 'but the food's Chinese and all the cooks are slants. That was Jimmy Lee. Did he look worried to you?'

'No,' said Duval.

'He's worried. The Beachcomber himself is coming tomorrow. He's always around for the openings.'

A young man came out of the kitchen. He was neatly dressed and looked like the sort of person Duval had seen at the cultural center. He said hello to Mr Boder.

'Speak English?' said Mr Boder.

'Yes.'

'Just asking. You never know with Puerto Ricans.'

'I am Cuban.'

'Okay, Castro,' said Mr Boder. 'That makes two. You're going to be up front with me, boys. Come over here.'

Mr Boder led them through the restaurant to the bar, which was designed to look like a bamboo and wickerwork hut in the South Seas. He said, 'I'm going to tell you one or two things and I want you to remember them, because the Beachcomber's very particular. First, we don't let anyone in here that we wouldn't have in our own homes – company policy. No single broads, no hookers, and no drunks. Never recognize anyone, even if you know his name. Why? Because the woman he's with might not be his wife and maybe he told her his name's Smith. You say, "Evening, Mister Jones," and he's screwed. Better not to use any names at all – that's how you get tips. A little discretion. If the joint's full, steer them over here into the bar, and if you have to buy them a drink to keep them there, buy it, but don't have one yourself. Correction – you can have a Coke.'

The Cuban said, 'Do we have to share our tips with the waiters?'

'That's up to you,' said Mr Boder. 'Now, in front of you are thirty-five, maybe forty, tropical drinks. Shark's Tooth, Jungle Juice, Pago-Pago. Forget the names. If anyone asks you what's in it just say it has rum, fruit juice, and some bitters. Confidentially, they all have the same shit in them, but you don't have to tell the Beachcomber that. You know anything about the food business, Castro?'

'Yes.' he said sternly.

'Ever work up front?'

'I worked at the Hilton in Havana.'

'I'm supposed to keel over,' said Mr Boder to Duval. He stared at the Cuban. 'Know how important the telephone is?'

The Cuban nodded.

Mr Boder said to Duval, 'Pick up that phone and say, "Good evening, the Beachcomber."'

Duval lifted the phone. 'Good evening, the Beachcomber.'

'Say it as if you mean it.'

'Good evening, the Beachcomber.'

'You sound like a mortician,' said Mr Boder. 'Watch me. I'll show you how it's done.' He bared his yellow teeth and spoke genially into the phone.

Later that afternoon Mr Boder said, 'You're on duty tomorrow at four o'clock. Press party, so sharpen up. Don't wear that tie. You're meeting the Beachcomber himself.'

Duval heard a low whistle as he left the restaurant. He turned and saw a man in a military cap with a braided visor, and more braids and buttons on a green frock coat. The trousers had a yellow stripe and white piping on the seam. It was Kelly. He said, 'One cigarette before you go.'

Duval shook out a cigarette and handed it over.

'I told you I'd get the job,' said Kelly. Then he frowned at the cigarette. 'Look at that, old chappie,' he said, pinching the filter tip. 'Should be tobacco there, but there's only cotton. They think they're smart and we get it! I'm going to tell the queen about that.'

Duval lit the cigarette for him and said, 'So you're the doorman.'

Kelly smiled. 'I'se a *technician* doorman. Ain't nothing I don't know about opening doors.'

The Beachcomber was a potbellied man with a bullying voice and a wooden leg. At the press party he banged his cane on the carved figures and chair legs as he limped from room to room. His white hair was cut very short, his forearms stained with tattoos, and when he saw Duval he said, 'Don't stand there like a goddamned Prussian. Look alive!'

He left the island the next day for a tour of the Caribbean, and then the restaurant got its first customers. There were not many; it was not the season. One of the dining-rooms, the Tortuga, remained closed.

At the end of that week Duval brought his pay home. With tips it came to forty-five dollars. Paula enrolled for the Spanish class and they had their first meal in a restaurant, *arroz con pollo* at La Gloria. Duval had wanted to take her to the Beachcomber, but employees were forbidden to eat there; in any case, he doubted whether he could afford it.

The job gave him a routine. He was free for most of the day. If Paula did not have a Spanish class they walked or went to the beach – the narrow, rocky one across from the Carnegie Library. At three, Duval had a shower and then took the bus along the seafront to work. After two weeks of this he felt like a legitimate resident of the island and thought no more of leaving. Now the island which had once seemed to rock in the ocean like a raft looked vast and green. He was aware that he had spent the entire time at its edge, on the shore; the interior he imagined wild, small towns in dusty jungle where people lived ensnared. But he was safe. He had his work.

The work itself was simple. He answered the telephone and took reservations. He met customers at the door and showed them to their tables. He adjusted the volume of the Hawaiian music on the loudspeakers and kept the lights dim. The customers were mainly middle-aged couples on vacation who had come to the island because the summer prices were so low. There were young wary couples who, tanned and uneasy, he took to be honeymooners. There were secretaries, groups of three or four, who lingered over their meals and held conversations with the waiters. Now and then Duval would see a man eating alone, reading a book, and he would want to sit down and talk to the man. But he kept his place. It appalled him to think that he had in such a short time become so old, so obedient.

'The days of the free lunch are over,' said Ramón Kelly, one day. 'They haven't paid me for three weeks. I'm going to have to give up this nice old job.'

'Do you get tips?'

'Chickenfeed,' said Kelly. 'My second wife lives up in Key West. She's rolling in it. I'm going up there pretty soon, open a Melanesian restaurant. Gonna get two tall Cubans for the door – black ones, these big fellas. And serve Melanesian food.' He grinned.

Duval looked at Kelly's feet.

'Them's my Hoover shoes,' said the old man.

Mr Boder told him not to talk to Kelly on duty. Mr Boder had become irritable. 'You're having yourself a holiday,' he said to Duval one evening when he found him reading at the telephone stand. But Mr Boder was servile with customers and Duval noticed that his moments of servility only made him more bad-tempered with the staff, particularly the Cuban, whom he called Castro.

The Cuban resented the name and refused to say what his real name was. 'I don't care,' he said. 'Batista was the one I hated.'

'What was the Havana Hilton like?' asked Duval.

'Very nice.' The Cuban clicked his tongue. '*Muchachas.*'

'Whenever I hear about Havana I think of Hemingway.'

'He used to come in now and then. We kept a certain wine for him – a rosé, nothing special. He always got drunk and shouted. He threw food around the table. "Pass the bread." He throw the bread. "Pass the salt." He throw the salt. Hemingway. People say he is a great writer. But they don't know. I have seen him with these eyes. He is a pig.'

'Have you read his books?'

'I would never read the books of such a pig.'

One meal was included. The employees ate in shifts before opening time, but not in the restaurant. They ate rice and beans in the hotel cafeteria, and Duval's half-hour always coincided with Kelly's. Kelly seemed to grow crazier. He said he was British and threatened to go back to England. 'Back to Piccadilly, old chappie,' he said. He complained that he still had not been paid and he said he wanted to kill Mr Boder with a broken bottle. One evening, in the cafeteria, he asked Duval to write a letter for him. Duval said he would.

Kelly instantly pulled a crumpled sheet of paper from the pocket of his green frock coat. He said, 'Got a pen?'

Duval took out his pen and smoothed the paper. He said, 'Hurry up. I have to go back in a few minutes.'

'I knew you'd help me,' said Kelly. 'Will you write what I say?'

'Of course.'

'Ready?' Kelly folded his arms. 'Dear President Kennedy–'

'Wait a minute,' said Duval.

'Dear President Kennedy,' said Kelly in his lisping drawl. 'I'm an old man and I'm struck on this goddamned island of Puerto

Rico living with a widow lady. The bastards haven't paid me –
you're not writing!'

'I am.'

'Show me.'

Duval pushed the paper to him, but Kelly lost interest in it as
soon as he saw the scribble. Before Duval could begin again,
Kelly said, 'My old woman run out on me and the widow lady
took pity. That was before the Florida business which I aim to
tell you about. Bitch said she was going to Santurce and that's
the last I hear from her. I couldn't find a ship. I been working on
ships since I was so high and I had a right terrible life – goddamned
tax people chasing me, I didn't know which way to turn.
Mister President, sir, you can help me if you read this here
letter–'

Duval had stopped writing. Kelly had begun to cry. In the
cafeteria in his bandsman's uniform, surrounded by chattering
Puerto Ricans, the old man sat shaking his bald head. He
continued to weep. The tears ran into his mustache.

But later that night Duval saw him out front. He was shutting
the door of a limousine and saluting to the man who had just
stepped inside.

'Boder says you're married,' he said when the car drew away.
'Young fella like you. Must be something wrong with you
upstairs.'

After that he avoided Kelly, and the days rolled past without
moving him.

In the cafeteria one evening a girl sat next to him. She had the
cute monkey-faced look of the prettiest Puerto Ricans – dark
eyes and thick hair and a small agile body. She was a room-girl,
she said, and she laughed shyly as she told him how the men
were always trying to flirt with her, saying 'Come in' in the
morning and rushing at her in their pajamas.

Duval told her about himself, scarcely believing what he said.
'I work in the Beachcomber. I live on the Calle de San Francisco.
My wife is going to have a baby.' The room-girl was convinced;

he was not. This man he was describing, this older employee with the wife: it wasn't him.

The feeling came again, that he was living someone else's life. He was using another man's voice, doing that man's work. And he was surprised by how ordinary the man was, how unambitious: a husband, an employee, and soon to be a father. He listened to himself with curiosity. *I live . . . I work . . . My wife.* The life seemed unshakably simple. How easily the green island had abstracted him and made him this new man.

He continued to work. He could not think what else to do. He had tried to write and had failed. He knew why. Could anything be written in such a cramped room, in such poor light? He fitted his life to the job: the afternoon bus, the phone calls, the chance encounters in the cafeteria, the customers whom he hated and envied, the unvarying drone of the Hawaiian music, the sizzle-splash of frying in the kitchen. Without choosing he had become a different man, and he sometimes wondered whose life he was leading, what name he had.

The money was enough to live on, not enough to free him. So the salary trapped him more completely than the fear of poverty had. The job became central, the only important thing; and his ambitions became local: to take a *público* rather than a bus, to eat in a good restaurant rather than La Gloria, to drink rum instead of beer.

Being away from the room for part of every day abstracted him further, and he always returned on the late bus to find Paula asleep, the Spanish textbook beside her, the light on. Nearly two months had passed since they had come to the island and she was now quite large, with new curves, the full cones of her breasts sloping against her rising belly, the veins showing in her tightened skin. She slept on her side; she walked slowly; she never swam.

She studied Spanish; she didn't learn it. At La Gloria one lunchtime she began timidly to speak. She did so with difficulty, and Duval found himself interrupting, saying a sentence he had not prepared, using words he was unaware he knew and only half understood, '*Lo siento. Yo quiero el mismo, por favor.*' The stresses and accents were Puerto Rican, *Joe* for *Yo*, *meemo* for *mismo*.

Whose voice was that?
'Jake!'
He was in bed, being shaken by a damp hand. Paula faced him with tangled hair and her look of worry intensified by the wrinkles of sleep that creased the side of her face.
'Wake up – I'm scared.' There was a low roar at the window: the sea, the fury of a distant bus, the wind – he couldn't say.
'What's wrong?'
'I dreamed I had the baby,' she sobbed. 'It was terrible. You weren't there – oh, God, it hurt. Then they held him up for me to see. Jake, his face was all mangled. It was covered with blood.'
Too soon, he thought. This worry shouldn't be mine. But he tried to accept it. He said, 'All babies look like that – you've seen pictures of them.'
'No – it wasn't the blood,' she said, and she grew very quiet, whispering her fearfulness. 'It was all deformed. The baby's face was twisted and it was crying. "It's yours," they said, "it's yours." It was horrible.'
He didn't know what to say. But he knew her fear. He saw the infant's bloody distorted face, twisted in accusation. He held Paula and then he was asleep.
In the morning he struggled to wake. The summer heat, the dampness in the air lay motionless against him; pressure, keeping him down. He didn't hear the voices from the street, only the song '*El Pescador,*' with its refrain, *corazón, corazón*; its harsh Puerto Rican sadness. He no longer heard the sea. The sea was drowned by the wind; lost. He had ceased to see the island, its greenness. He had withdrawn to his own island, the room, the woman, the job.

## 4

Paula did not tell him how the Spanish classes reminded her of her old life, the pleasure of uninterrupted study in a clean room, the security of a narrow bed. It was the life she had led before she had met Duval: her girlhood. She wanted it back. She had come to hate the changeless green of the island, the late-summer tinge of yellow exhaustion in the color. She did not tell him how, when he was at work, she never left the room; how she would sleep and wake and think it was another day, and sleep and wake again and imagine that in the space of a few hours she had endured days of seclusion. She had said nothing about the doctor she had seen. The office was dusty, the doctor sweating into his shirt, not noticing his smeared instruments. He smiled (the usual reaction: kindly people tried to share her joy) and after examining her said, 'You are – what? – about five months.' She was nearly eight. She took all her questions back to the room unasked.

One hot night she told Duval, 'We can give it away.'

'What do you mean?' But he was stalling; he knew.

She explained that she had written to a friend in Boston, an old roommate, and the girl had supplied the names of three adoption agencies. Heartbreaking names: one was 'The Home for Little Wanderers.'

Duval said, 'They put them in orphanages.'

'No,' she said. 'They give them to people who can't have children themselves. They're very fussy, too – they check up on the people. They sort of inspect them.'

'Then they just hand the kid over.'

'Don't pretend to be shocked! You don't want the baby!' She was shouting. In a moment she would cry.

He said, 'Do you?'

'I don't want to live like this.'

'This is how it would be.'

'It could be different,' she said. 'You could finish college, get your degree–'

'Ir would always be like this – a room, a job.' He could see she was frightened. 'We'd quarrel.'

'I don't want to fight with you.'

He said, 'Married people fight.'

'Single people fight, too.'

'They can walk away.'

She said, 'That's what you want to do with me – you want to walk away and pretend I don't exist. Admit it! You want to leave me.'

'What do you want me to do?'

'I don't know,' she said. She had come to dislike her body; she did not recognize it as her own, it was so swollen and unreliable. And she feared the arrival of the baby – feared it most because she knew she would love it and want to keep it, and her life would be over, like that. 'Help me,' she said. 'I feel so ugly.'

He said, 'You know that doorman, Kelly – the old guy I told you about? I asked him about his job once, and he started to talk about some joint he worked at in Florida. He's got this funny way of talking. He said, "They wanted me inside once. I was young like you. I said, no sir – I like it out here. Fresh air, meet new people. That's why I'm still here," he said, "but I ain't young no more and I don't like it."'

Paula said, 'You're going to leave me.'

'I was talking about Kelly.'

'We have to decide.' She lay on the bed and clasped her stomach as if tenderly enfolding the child. She said, 'The poor thing,' and then, 'No – I don't care what you do, I won't give him away!'

She was insisting he choose, but it seemed to him as if he were past any choice and his life would continue like this, summer after summer, the heat deadening him to the days.

He went to the toilet, which was in darkness. He felt for the light cord and pulled it. For seconds there was stillness, and then the floor moved with cockroaches the heat had enlivened. They ran like large glossy drops and were gone. He had only to wait to see it solved.

The next day was Sunday. Paula awoke, and as if the sleep had been no more than a pause in their conversation she said in an alert accusing voice, 'Make up your mind – what are you going to do?'

'We still have a few months.'

'Six weeks,' she said sharply. 'What is it you want?'

He couldn't say, *I want to be a writer*. It seemed as ridiculous as, *I want to be president*. It was partly superstition: saying it might make it untrue. And yet he saw his books, a shelf of them, as clearly as if he had already written them. The conviction had stuck – not that he was to become a writer, but that he had been one secretly for as long as he could remember. To reveal the ambition was to spoil it. And more, to say it was to commit himself to proving it. He wanted someone to verify it in him, to read his face and say, *You are a writer*.

He said, 'Do you want to marry me?'

'If we got married we'd be divorced in two years.'

He turned away. 'Maybe we've had our marriage.'

'Is it over so soon? Is that all?' She became angry. 'I want more than this.'

'So do I!'

'I hate you for hesitating–'

'Hesitating?'

'For bringing me here,' she said. 'I don't think I could forgive you, even if you did marry me.'

He said, 'I wish I was forty years old and my life was behind me.'

'That shows how young you are,' she said, almost exulting. 'Men of forty aren't old! You don't know anything.'

Later, walking down the Calle de San Francisco to lunch at La Gloria, she said, 'In six weeks there are going to be three of us. Think about that and you won't feel so smart.'

But having said it she grew sad and couldn't eat, and after lunch she said it was too hot for the beach.

Duval went back to the room with her and dressed for work. It was only two o'clock; he was not due at the restaurant until five. He left her on the bed with her Spanish book, in the posture that put her to sleep. A bus in the plaza bore the destination sign LOIZA. He boarded the bus and rode to the end of the line.

Loiza was not as he had imagined, a shady corner at the forest's edge, a frontier. It was simply a leaning signpost where the bus stopped and turned around. The street, wide and useless, continued through a drab suburb of stucco bungalows. There were some palms along the roadside, but they were not green, and dead fronds like the ruined plumage of an enormous bird lay in the broken street. Political slogans with their enclosing exclamation marks were painted on the bungalow walls and on some lampposts were pictures of the president. Muñoz Marin. No sun, only a low cloud as gray as metal radiated humid heat. Duval walked down the sidewalk and saw more of the Sunday emptiness, cracked bungalows, grass growing through blisters in the asphalt, and from behind the dusty hedges the radio's tin rhumba, 'El Pescador' and Corazón.

He walked to a road junction and ahead saw a parking lot filled with cars, and above a sign, CANTO GALLO. He welcomed the noise and hurried toward it.

It was a galleria, a cockpit. He bought a ticket for the middle tier, but as he started through the door he faced confusion – men counting money, men running down the passage, gamblers quarreling – and to avoid them he slipped through a side door and down a short flight of stairs.

The room smelled of straw and chicken droppings and was stacked with wooden cages holding small skinny roosters. They scratched and squawked, but there was in their crowing something still of the farmyard, the shady unfenced Puerto Rican plot with its standpipe and sprinklings of corn. They fussed, yet looked calm, and Duval found it odd to see them in these vertical piles, crammed in such a small space.

He wandered around the room, looking closely at the birds,

noticing their bright eyes, the shine of their feathers, the wrinkled bunch of scrotumlike tissue draped on their heads, their oversized feet and stained claws. He heard Paula speaking, saw her face, and in her face a demand. *Choose, choose*, she was saying.

But each time he framed a reply, a shout went up from behind the wall of this fowlcoop, in the cockpit – triumphant cries of yelling laughter. The cries became more frequent and lost the laughter, and they were accompanied by a stamping of many feet which shook the beams over his head. The howling sounded neither Spanish nor English; it was no language; it was encouragement, anger, jeering, the noise of people watching a small hero, an insignificant victim; a mob's praise.

The crouching roosters on their shelves of cages seemed to hear it. They stuck their heads through the wooden bars and jerked their necks, so their jeweled staring eyes turned in wonderment. Duval paced the room. The cocks pecked hard at their padlocks. *It's up to you*, she was saying.

He was about to go away – to leave the *galleria* entirely – when three men entered the small room. They were excited, jabbering in Spanish, arguing without facing each other. One stayed at the door glowering at Duval. The other two went to the stack of cages and took out two cocks, a black one, a brown one, and quickly trussed them with lengths of cord. The birds fought and flapped while their legs were tied, then lay still, two parcels of feathers, like a pair of brushes. The men were attaching spurs to the birds' legs when the man at the door spoke.

'Go,' he said crossly to Duval and gestured for him to leave.

Duval went upstairs and took a seat in the middle tier. Most of the seats were empty, but near him, in the section that surrounded the circle of the pit, the seats were full, and it was only there, up front, that he saw women, two or three. It was like the interior of a primitive circus. The roof seemed propped on shafts of dusty sunlight; and the rough unpainted wood and the dust rising from the shallow pit and its suffocating smallness lent it an unmistakable air of cruelty.

Brass scales were brought out, the chains and pans jangling, and the trussed cocks were placed in the pans and balanced. The two pairs of bound feet hovered at the same level. The scales were raised for the audience to see. There was chattering throughout the ritual of weighing, but as the scales were removed the gallery became frenzied – men called across the pit, shouting numbers and waving dollar bills. One man vaulted the low fence and hurried across the pit to shake a wad of money in another's frowning face.

The birds were untied, but instead of releasing them the owners faced each other, holding them forward and slowly circling, keeping the beaks a few inches apart, struggling against the flapping wings and angry reaching beaks. The cocks' eyes were blazing as the men solemnly set them down.

Now Duval saw the spurs, inch-long claws clamped to their legs, which gave them a fierce strutting look. The black one began to run around the margin of the pit.

The squawks were drowned by the shouts from the audience, and the birds flew at each other. They did not appear to use the spurs. They fluttered a foot from the ground, seeming to balance on their downthrust wings, and they threw their heads forward and bore down, snatching and pecking with their beaks. The brown one rose higher, pecked harder and pinioned the black one clumsily with clawing feet. He beat him down with his wings and drove his beak into the black one's head. They tumbled in the dust, crazily magnetized, and then chased each other in circles around the pit, with outstretched necks, moving gracefully flat-footed, driving dust and feathers into the air.

*No*, thought Duval, and he was deafened by the cries from the audience. The brown cock flew and settled against the black one, plucking the reddened head.

The black one had started to weaken. One wing was askew, and it scraped the ground with it and tottered on it as it toiled away from the other. The brown one screamed and beat its wings and attacked again. The wing flaps, the flutter of feathers simulating the opening of a Chinese fan, sounded harmless, but it masked the damage. When they were close Duval could see how the cocks' heads were both swollen and their feathers ragged. The audience was excited, beginning to stamp the supporting planks of the gallery and shake the wooden benches.

Like old hindering skirts, the wings of the black cock hung down, and he wobbled in panic around the pit, the brown one behind him, leaping and pecking. The black one fell and crooked his feet against the brown one's attack, and finally, in a helpless effort to fight back, offered his bleeding head to the other's furious beak.

There were cheers; the owners stepped in; the cheering stopped. The audience showed no further interest in the birds. Money was changing hands and men had gathered in groups to argue about the result.

Duval followed the owners back to the fowlcoop. The cocks were placed on a table and examined. The brown one which had been so lively was feebly twitching its legs as its owner ran his fingers through the tufts of feathers to search for wounds. The black one lay as if dead; the scrotal comb was torn and its head was split all over and leaking blood. The owner prodded it gently and murmured in Spanish. Then he lifted its damaged eyelids and said sadly, '*Mira.*' He showed the empty eye sockets of the blinded bird.

*No*, thought Duval again, and back in the street, walking to the bus stop through the suburb that now had a look of pure horror, his reflection came to him whole: *I will never get married.*

# 5

The sun, glimmering and enlarged by cloud, was at the level of the treetops, balanced on the upper thickness of palm fronds, as Duval walked to work. The opposite side of the street was marked by the sunset's pickets of shadow, flung from the palm trunks, and in this broken light women strolled, some singly, some in pairs.

Mr Boder was in front of the restaurant talking to Kelly. What struck Duval at once was that Mr Boder was crowding the old man as he spoke and peering into his face, almost bumping him with his nose. When Duval spoke Mr Boder stepped back.

'Looking at the action,' said Mr Boder, with the kind of disguising heartiness he used on customers. He nodded at the women.

Kelly looked crestfallen. He said nothing.

'Professionals,' said Duval. He winked at Kelly. '*Por la noche.*'

'I'd like to jump all over that one,' said Mr Boder. He licked his lips. 'I'm overdue for a strange piece.'

It was a vicious phrase. Duval saw him taste it. The women wore tight dresses with a slash to show their legs, and they walked with a slow rolling movement and swung large handbags. But it was the shoes that gave them away. The spike heels were worn down from their continual pacing, giving them an unsteadiness that made them lurch tipsily every few steps.

Duval said, 'That one's smiling. I think she likes you.'

Mr Boder's face tightened, as if he had been mocked. He said, 'Come inside. I want to know why you're late.' And without another word he entered the restaurant.

Kelly said, 'Oh, me.'

'What's wrong?'

'I just got me walking papers.'

'He fired you?' Duval was puzzled. 'What for?'

'They owes me money. I axed him for it. He told me I was sassing him.' But Kelly was smiling. 'I'se a doorman without no door.'

'You're joking.'

'Boy,' said Kelly. 'You better go on in there or you're going to be out on your ear, too.'

Duval went inside and put on his Beachcomber blazer. In the

foyer of the restaurant he saw Mr Boder seated at the telephone.

Mr Boder said, 'I've been doing your work for you. Look at these reservations.' He showed Duval the diary with the column of names in his oversize handwriting. 'Now, where the hell have you been?'

'Waiting for a bus.' He would not say he had been to a cockfight. The sight had terrified him and he could not repeat what he had seen: the bright jeweled eye plucked out, the scrap of white tissue in the eye socket, the dripping blinded head of the bird.

'If you're late again I'll dock your salary – your wife won't like that, will she?' Mr Boder stood up. 'What did that crazy old man tell you out front?'

Duval said angrily, 'Did you fire him?'

Mr Boder did not reply immediately. He walked toward the bar and then, as if remembering, turned and said loudly, 'You mind your own business, sonny, if you know what's good for you.'

Duval picked up the diary. It was the Cuban's night off; Sundays were quiet. A dozen customers came and went, and the waiters were impatient, drumming their fingers on their trays, complaining in murmurs, and watching for the front door to open.

Duval went outside. Kelly was gone.

The next night there was a Puerto Rican at the door. It was only when Duval saw the baggy wrinkled uniform on the man that he realized how tall Kelly had been. Duval avoided speaking to Mr Boder that night, and at closing time, he was indignant and sad. He wanted a drink. It was a hotel rule that employees off duty were to leave the premises. The casino, the coffee shop, the pool, the bars were closed to him; and he knew he could be fired for breaking that rule.

Duval went to the hotel's veranda bar, where the drinks were slightly cheaper than inside, and sat and had three shots of rum. He drank them straight, in the Puerto Rican way, finishing with a glass of water. Then he stumbled down the gravel driveway to the bus stop. No one had seen him.

A woman came toward him from behind a palm, her heels clicking on the sidewalk, the revealing wobble in her step. Her hair was drawn back tightly and even in the street lamp's poor light he could see that her dress was soiled. She was short and had a small mouth stamped in her sharp face.

She said, 'Want a date, mister?'

'How much?'

'Ten dollars.'

Duval went through his pockets. He found a dollar and some change. He had spent the rest of his tips at the bar. He said, 'I'm nineteen – don't I get a discount?'

She recognized the word and laughed. 'Even the young ones, they pay me.'

'I don't have any money.'

'*Nada por nada*,' she said. '*Buenos noches, chico.*'

'Wait,' said Duval. 'Where are you from – San Juan?'

'Habana.'

'You like San Juan?'

'I like this.' She touched her thighs and jerked her hips at him. She leered: gold teeth.

That aroused him, and though it was after midnight when he got back to the old part of the city he went to La Gloria. It was closed; a man was stacking chairs on the bar. In the plaza he could see the homeless boys sleeping curled up on the stone benches, small still corpses on the slabs. He walked up the Calle de San Francisco. The street was empty, but he kept walking, looking in doorways. He turned into a narrow cobblestone street and headed down the hill, past darkened shops and small hotels, feeling the rum's warmth still in his throat and a fatigue from work that gave him a nervous inaccurate strength and a quick stride.

He barely heard the woman's greeting. She had been seated on a bench; she rose and said hello as he passed. The sound reached him. She was asking for a cigarette.

He offered her one and lit it, and in the match flare he saw her lined face, the dress a bit too big, the firelit strand of black hair loose at her eyes. She looked cautious, almost afraid.

He said, 'What's your name?'

'Anna,' she said, and glanced down the street. 'You want to go with me?'

'Yes,' he said.

'Five dollars.'

'I don't have five dollars.'

'Four dollars,' she said. 'Let we go.'

He fished in his pockets, knowing what he would bring out. He showed her the dollar, he rattled the change.

She said, 'You don't respect me.'

'Please,' he said.

'No.' She walked away. He followed her down the side-walk, and when she stopped before a storefront he was encouraged.

'Anna,' he said softly.

'You see?' She was tapping the plate glass of the shop window.

He saw a rack of shoes and looked away. They were tiny; children's shoes, small laced things with price tags, mounted on stands.

'Look,' she said, urging him. 'These things cost money.'

It was too late; he had seen the pathetic shoes and the prices and all his desire died.

He entered the room, but did not switch on the light. He undressed in the darkness and slipped beneath the sheet. Paula rolled toward him. She took his head and drew it to her, and he could hear the slow thump of her heart against her breast. He nestled against her, hating the thought that he had betrayed her and was, embracing and kissing her, betraying her still.

Paula awoke in tears, and he felt a helpless sorrow for her as she sobbed. The child, her stomach, shook.

'It's not fair to me,' she said. 'It's not fair to him. The poor baby.'

He knew what to say, but not how to say it. She was so easily frightened.

She said, 'We don't have much time.'

Choose, she was saying. But he had chosen long ago; he had discovered his small green soul on the island, its solitary inward conceit scribbled differently from hers, and now he could read the scribble.

'Poor Kelly,' he said. He saw him, the clown, the limp mustache, the green frock coat and braided cap. The old man moped toward him, chattering, blinded, indicating his flat shoes with a crooked finger: *Them's my Hoover shoes.*

Paula said, 'I'm not staying here much longer – I'm not having my baby on this miserable island. I'm going to catch a plane while they'll still let me. Women can't fly if they're more than eight months pregnant.' She looked at him strangely. 'You didn't even know that.'

'What about the tickets?'

'I've been to the bank. We've got the airfare now – enough for two tickets home.'

'After that?'

'It's up to you.'

'"My baby" – that's what you said.'

She cried again, hearing her own words repeated. 'I don't want him,' she said, her mouth curling sorrowfully. 'I want to go back to school and do well. I want to marry someone who loves me. I want a nice house.'

Duval thought: *I don't want any of those things*; but he wouldn't upset her by saying what he did want.

She said, 'And I don't want to be a failure.'

'You won't fail.'

'What do you know?' she said. 'What do you do after you give a child away?'

'You start again,' he said. 'Alone.'

'You have no more chances. If you fail, then, you have nothing.'

'No,' he said, but he only said it to oppose her, to offer encouragement.

'Nothing at all,' she said bitterly. '*Nada.*'

'It's a gamble,' he said.

'It's a human sacrifice.'

He was deliberately late for work that day, but instead of confronting him Mr Boder ignored him. Duval heard him shouting in the kitchen.

The Cuban was listening, too. He said, 'I hate that pig.'

'Then why do you put up with him?'

'This isn't my country,' he said. 'They could throw me out.' He kicked gloomily at the carpet. 'I got a wife and two *niños.*'

Mr Boder came out of the kitchen. 'What's up – nothing to do? Who's watching that phone?'

The Cuban said, 'I am.'

'Come here, Castro. I've got a job for you.' Mr Boder went close to Duval and peered at him. He said, 'Keep it up. You're asking for it.'

Duval stared at him. He had said that to Kelly.

'Move that chair. Someone's going to trip over it.'

'It's not in the way.'

'Are you deaf?'

Duval moved the chair, and in this tiny act of obedience he saw humiliating surrender. But his timidity was for hire: he was to blame.

'He's worried,' said the Cuban later. 'The vice-chancellor of the university is coming from Rio Piedras with his whole family. He wants to make a good figure.'

It was true. At nine-thirty the man came. He was a thin dapper man with a narrow head and a mustache fringing his upper lip. He held his young son's hand, and his wife followed, shepherding two older girls in white dresses.

But there was a further surprise. At ten the Beachcomber

arrived. It was wholly unexpected and Duval could see the shock on Mr Boder's face when the door swung open and the Beachcomber dragged his wooden leg through and tapped his way forward, rocking on the leg, balancing with the cane. The Puerto Rican waiters barely recognized him, and watched the way he moved with the contempt they offered all cripples.

'Boder!' said the Beachcomber before Mr Boder could speak.

'This is a pleasant surprise,' said Mr Boder, regaining himself, grinning, hesitating in a bow.

'I was in Santo Domingo,' said the Beachcomber. His hair was slightly longer, but he wore the same short-sleeved. Hawaiian shirt that showed his tattoos.

'Fascinating place,' said Mr Boder.

'They shot Trujillo this afternoon,' said the Beachcomber. 'I took the first plane and got the hell out. Why is this place so goddamned empty?'

'Slow night,' said Mr Boder. 'Very unusual. Right this way.'

The Beachcomber paused and shifted his weight from his good leg to the cane. He said, 'Looks like Thursday at the city morgue.'

Mr Boder, smiling, did not appear to hear. He fussed with the reservations diary and then started to speak.

'Get me a drink,' said the Beachcomber and moved off heavily, in the direction of the dining-room.

'Right you are,' said Mr Boder, still grinning, showing his yellow capped teeth at the Beachcomber's back.

The waiters had gathered in a little group by one of the carved Polynesian statues. They were whispering. Duval heard *Trujillo* and *muerte*.

Mr Boder brought a tall glass to where the Beachcomber was sitting. He sat sloppily, his wooden leg propped on a chair, scratching his tattoos, and squinting crossly at the nearly empty dining-room. Duval saw him as a fraud, a tycoon in old clothes, a figure of crass romance. The Beachcomber was staring at the vice-chancellor, who was deep in conversation with a waiter. They were talking about Trujillo. Another waiter came over to confirm it. Duval heard *verdad*. In minutes the whole restaurant knew what the Beachcomber had only muttered.

'Very unusual,' Mr Boder was saying, bowing as he spoke.

Duval was behind him.

Mr Boder turned and hissed, 'Where's Castro?'

'I don't like it,' the Beachcomber was saying. 'You can do better than this, Boder.'

'Eating,' said Duval.

'Get him,' said Mr Boder. 'And make it snappy. While you're at it get another cloth for the table – this one's filthy. Oh, and don't think' – Mr Boder was still hissing, but he was also smiling, half-turned to the Beachcomber – 'don't think I didn't notice you were late for work. I've got something to say to you later. Now move.'

'Boder–' Duval heard the Beachcomber say as he left the dining room.

He went through the kitchen to the hotel cafeteria. The waiters had brought the news here of Trujillo's assassination and there were groups of Puerto Ricans in the corridor talking excitedly. An elderly Negro moved among them slapping his mop on the tiles.

Duval was lost in thought. *Your wife wouldn't like that.* He tried to swallow his anger. Five minutes had passed; ten before he got to the cafeteria. He paused at the door, hating the noise, the plates banging, the voices. They were talking about Trujillo. Already the repetition of this news irritated Duval. He saw the Cuban, eating alone, forking food to his mouth.

Twenty minutes: nothing. But it was too long. In that small delay was his refusal. He winced, thinking of Mr Boder's anger. He could never again return to the restaurant. He was finished here, as lightly as he had begun.

It was – this hesitation – as much of a choice as he needed to make. And he had hung up his blazer and was walking past the floodlit palms of the hotel driveway before he realized the enormity of what he had done. Then Mr Boder, the Beachcomber, the waiters, everyone there seemed suddenly very small, no larger than children; and children had no memory.

It was so simple to go. Now he knew how. You walked away without a sound and kept walking. Beyond the lush hotel garden he saw light, but it was the moon behind the trees that lit them so strangely, darkening the green, like smoke beginning.

He decided to walk the mile home. As he walked on the sea road to the old part of the city the moon rose, seeming to wet the palms with its light. The wind was on the sea, and the waves tumbled like lost cargoes of silver smashing to pieces on the beach.

1980

# Doctor Slaughter

*I*

At first Lauren had liked being new to London and not knowing
a soul. Being a stranger was a thrill, like being in disguise – full
of those possibilities. And she believed that strangers were among
the few people in the world who could be trusted with the truth.
She loved telling them her secrets, and discovering theirs. But the
city, so far, had disappointed her: London wasn't London. She
had not seen anything here that she had expected, and after a
month she had seen too much that she had never expected.

This morning she was standing in her freezing room, wearing
her mink-lined coat, thinking about the General's dinner party
– the incredible thing the guest had said.

'There are five thousand people in the world.' And he had
smiled at those on the left of the table, then – taking his time –
those on the right. Finally, his eyes came to rest on the woman
who had been saying 'absolutely' all evening. She did not say
'absolutely' now.

The people at the table offered one of those silences that was
intended to let the man finish. It had certainly seemed like an
unfinished sentence. But the man just smiled again and lifted his
knife and worked it through the fist of meat bleeding on his plate.

She had found out his name during the first course. Taking
her fork out of her mousseline she had pointed it at the wall just
behind the General.

'That painting looks like a Van Goh,' she said.

'Van Goff,' the General said.

'Fon Hokh,' the man said, and then, 'I should know that, as
a Van Arkady.'

He had done more talking than the host. At these London dinner parties the host often seemed the least important or the quietest person in the room. The host was interesting only because he brought much more interesting people together – so it seemed to Lauren. General Sir George Newhouse, head of the Hemisphere Institute, was famous for his guests and famous for saying very little. He had only opened his mouth once tonight and that was to mispronounce the name of the Dutch painter. But it had hardly been noticed, for Van Arkady was still talking. They were now on the main course.

He said, 'That's it. The population of the world. Five thousand.'

They had been discussing recent catastrophes – the scale of them in human lives: almost a million dead in the Ethiopian famine, half a million refugees in Lebanon, ten thousand throats cut in a massacre in India, and in the most recent Chinese earthquake upwards of two million either dead or homeless.

The Chinese statistic was Lauren's, and when she said it (someone whispered, 'I had no idea there was an earthquake there last year!'), Van Arkady stammered for attention and then delivered his pronouncement about there being five thousand people in the world.

It sank in – he meant just that. It was a very London way of speaking – abrupt and cynical and knowing, like a polite way of starting trouble. Lauren had once asked General Newhouse about a certain Arabic scholar and the General shrugged and said, 'He doesn't exist.' And when you cut someone at a party, she had been told, it was not that you were ignoring the person or that you were turning away – it was that the person was not there: you saw nothing. It was all a London manner she was trying to get used to.

Everyone turned to her when Lauren said, 'China's population has officially reached one billion.'

'That's official,' Van Arkady said. 'I am speaking of reality.'

'Yes, in reality there are a billion people in China.'

'Wrong,' he said. 'There are two people in China.' He was smiling at Lauren. 'I know both of them.'

'I never touch salt,' Lauren said to the man next to her who was offering her a little hopper of salt with a tiny spoon stuck in it. 'But if I did, I certainly wouldn't spoon it out of that thing.' Then her face became radiant and she smiled at Van Arkady. 'Two people in China. I love it.'

'I've been to China,' Van Arkady said.

'Everyone's been to China,' Lauren said, still smiling.

Lady Newhouse said, 'Hugo, did it ever occur to you that you might not be one of those five thousand?'

'The thought never entered my head,' Van Arkady said.

Lauren at that moment seriously wondered: If he's right, am I one of them? It did not come in words. She saw herself fleetingly in half shadow as a small dim rejected figure without a face. She worried for a few uncertain seconds that Van Arkady might be joking. He had talked the whole time, acting as host – pouring wine and pronouncing. Who was he?

The others had become nervous; the conversation had faltered. She hoped it was not a joke. She could not see a joke in it. It was so extraordinary she wanted it to be true.

'And I have a theory,' Van Arkady said – and people relaxed a little, glad that he was managing all the talk; he was ugly and interesting, about her father's age, but dark; and what sort of name was Van Arkady? 'This theory is that if you live long enough you meet them all.'

'It's a metaphor!' Julian Shuttle said – too loud, he was very angry and speaking to the table at large. He was young, about Lauren's age, and had recently been asked by General Newhouse to join the Hemisphere Institute. When Lauren told the General that she had decided not to study China, as she had planned, but to start from scratch on the Persian Gulf, she was put in Julian's office. Julian was an Arabist. Lauren suspected that the General was trying to frighten her into resuming her studies of the Chinese economy. But Julian was not the sort to intimidate her, and when she said that she didn't know anything about the Gulf he said, 'Don't worry about it. That's what fellowships are for.' He was kind and intelligent, and although he was Lauren's age he had an endearing way of behaving like her younger brother.

'A metaphor?' Van Arkady said. 'No, it is not that at all.' His manner was patronizing. He did not insist and it made him seem very sure of himself. 'It is a fact. I can name many of them.'

'Carry on,' Julian said, looking nervous and bold.

Van Arkady said, 'The names would mean nothing to you, young man.'

Lauren admired the man's roosterish arrogance. When she was impressed her face shone, the excitement whipped up her blood and made her prettier. And the man's arrogance somehow went with his ugliness and made him majestic.

'What about the rest of the people in the world?' Julian asked. His voice cracked a little – he was upset, and he seemed beseeching rather than challenging.

Van Arkady ignored Julian. He turned to the other dinner guests. But he answered Julian's question. He said, 'The rest don't really matter. A million dead here, two million there – it is part of a natural cycle. Yes, even massacres. There is murder in nature. Please don't think I'm insensitive. I believe the death of one man can change the course of history, when it is the right man and when we are fully conscious of it. But a million don't matter, because it isn't a number in any actual sense, unless it is applied to money. A million dollars is an easy thing, but a million men is impossible to imagine. My five thousand is reality, but' – and here he smiled at Julian Shuttle – 'a million men is a metaphor.'

Julian seemed to sulk at this, and at the end of the table Mrs Timothy Beach whispered, 'My cleaning lady said, "A blue foulard – that's a kind of duck, isn't it?"'

'We don't feel a million,' Van Arkady was saying. 'You can't honestly say that you miss all those Ethiopians and Chinese. Their deaths don't change anything, and a truthful but callous person might argue that we're all a jolly sight better off without them. We make a pointless virtue out of keeping people alive. It is one of the follies of our century – it is a mere conceit, making us feel powerful. But it is sometimes much kinder to allow people to die in their own way than to keep them alive our way.'

Lauren was thrilled at this – not the details of the argument but the calm cruel way the man stated it, and she wanted him to notice her approval.

Over dessert it became a game. How many of the five thousand were British or German or African? Van Arkady considered each question seriously and answered 'Forty-five' and 'Sixty' and 'None.'

He said, 'And more Arabs than you might think.'

'I do Arabs,' Lauren said.

'The ones I am speaking of are all here in London.'

'In other words, no Bedouin,' Lady Newhouse said.

'What is a Bedouin?' Mrs Beach asked.

Lauren said, 'They're people who like to live in tents.'

The man on Lauren's left – Giles something, from the Foreign Office – said, 'Aren't you going to eat your syllabub?'

'Is that what it's called?' Lauren said, and she laughed out loud. Then she said, 'No, I kind of watch my sugar-intake.'

'And you didn't touch your duckling.'

'I don't eat meat,' she said.

'Did you know Hitler was a vegetarian?' he said, and he scowled and made his eyebrows devilish. Then he relented. 'So was George Bernard Shaw.'

Lauren said, 'I've never read him.'

'You've missed something,' the man said.

'No. I'll never read him. I think it's very unlucky to read Shaw's books. My uncle was reading a book by him when he died.'

Lady Newhouse stood up and said, 'Anyone who would like to–'

'I'm going to miss you,' the man said.

'I'm not going anywhere,' Lauren said.

'You're being summoned,' he said. 'Ladies to the loo, while the men pass the port and cigars around.'

'What a nerve,' Lauren said softly. 'And this is a black-tie dinner.'

'The General is very old-fashioned.'

'To me that always means a complete asshole.'

The man began to stifle a laugh, and then he gave in to it and said, 'But you don't drink!'

'You notice everything,' Lauren said. 'Anyway, it's the principle I object to.'

'Or do you want a cigar?' He had taken two thick cigars out of a leather wallet and he held one under her chin.

'Where I come from,' she said, 'we call that a sour dick.'

She was taken to a narrow parlour-like room with the five other women and they took turns using the adjoining toilet. One by one, they spent far too long behind the door and returned with different faces – like masks made of pastry flour and food colouring: the first time Lauren heard the word 'tarts' she thought of the glazed and frosted faces of these old women.

But one wore no make-up. She was a frog-faced woman who wobbled in her shoes and when she took her turn in the toilet the other women exchanged glances. Lauren suspected it was Van Arkady's wife.

'Five thousand people,' one woman said, mocking the man by making his accent seem foreign.

'He is so full of himself,' Mrs Beach said.

Then Lauren was sure that the frog-faced woman was Mrs Van Arkady.

'Ginnie,' Lady Newhouse cautioned.

But Mrs Beach, who was seated in a chair next to Lauren, was still talking in a low defiant voice.

'He's a fornicator,' she said.

Lauren laughed, and when she saw Van Arkady again in the Newhouses' drawing-room – they were having coffee – she wanted to go home with him. His ugly wife was a burden to him

– she looked unhealthy and bad-tempered. She certainly wasn't one of the five thousand!

'What do you do?' Lauren said to Van Arkady.

The question surprised him, but he looked pleased and said, 'I'm just one of these boring bankers.'

Lauren said, 'I find money incredibly exciting.'

'I sometimes think that money has no existence,' Van Arkady said. 'It is simply something that certain people believe in – and they have given it a kind of temporary reality. It is a bubble – it must be, because in the past it has actually burst. And of course that will happen again.'

He was edging sideways as he spoke, moving Lauren towards the fireplace, where logs were flaming – she could feel the heat against her legs.

'And what is your profession?' Van Arkady said.

She said, 'I do just about everything.'

'Surely not everything,' he said, dropping his voice.

'When I feel like it,' Lauren said lightly.

Just then, Mrs Van Arkady – small, sallow, with shins like knifeblades and wearing big blue shoes – stepped over and claimed her husband, who was still smiling and a little breathless from the way Lauren had seemed to dare him.

But men were so slow, and she felt she always had to do all the work and make it easy for them, and then she had to seem surprised when they at last made a move.

She watched the Van Arkadys go to the foyer, and to be persistent – to show herself again – she went downstairs after them and found her own coat, and waited to be asked whether she needed a lift. But the ugly woman had probably said something to her husband, because he looked a little sheepish and only said, 'What a wonderful coat,' and helped her on with it. She wanted to face him and say that she believed that she was one of the five thousand he had spoken of.

But instead she said, 'Thanks' and let her gaze linger on him. He was a cruel and henpecked man – but just like her father, and like many men, who were savage and brilliant in company, but at home they wore aprons and called their wives 'Queenie' and got furious trying to be helpful.

Lauren saw herself as he must have seen her – standing in her warm coat under the crystal chandelier in the General's foyer in Eaton Row. Her hair was shining and her skin was clear and she was six feet tall in these shoes; she saw herself as pretty and powerful, and she was sure he regarded her as smart and well-off and that he wanted to know her and to get rid of his awful wife. She imagined saying, 'We'll turn heads' and saw herself entering the Ritz with him. Why were men so slow?

Women hate me, Lauren thought, sensing Mrs Van Arkady's poisonous eyes on her. She believed that other women always envied and disliked her and saw her as a threat – it was one of her many satisfactions.

She knew she had left an impression on Van Arkady – she could see it in the General's mirrors – it was the perfect house to be seen in. But she left alone and walked to Victoria Station and took the tube back to her bedsitter. Tube was the perfect name for it at this time of night, and when she got back to her horrible room she discovered her toilet was frozen solid. London!

## 2

The mink-lined coat was her own idea. 'My own design,' she said. But it was a simple design: a good plain Burberry with a fur lining – twenty-seven mink pelts that were hidden when the coat was buttoned up. It was the warmest coat she had ever owned.

Women who wore minks were show-offs, like her mother, who hadn't even needed it in Virginia. This mink lining had once been her mother's whole coat. A second-hand mink was a pardonable thing, but a new one was a crime. A black tailor named Noosie had carefully cut the old thing and fitted it into the new Burberry. Lauren did not pay the tailor, but later the sixty-two-year-old man took her to dinner – she regarded her agreeing to go as a kind of payment – and afterwards in his room she allowed him to take photographs of her neck, from the front. That was Noosie's odd request. 'More neck, darling,' he kept saying.

She unfastened the top buttons of her blouse and sat straighter. She thought: Necko-philia! She wanted to laugh.

But he was very solemn; he was perspiring. His black face was beady-wet like a cold plum. He shot two rolls of film, stepping in a circle around her.

If he wants it I'll go the whole nine yards, Lauren thought. But when he was out of film he made her a cup of cocoa and walked her to the bus stop. She had prepared herself for something else, because she had wanted this useful two-sided coat.

She needed it in this freezing room. She hated the place, and she thought how unfair it was that she should go unrecognized. No one had yet seen how special she was: pretty, healthy, intelligent, well-travelled – and she had style. She had no money – that was a bitch – but money was never hard to find. Yet brains and beauty and health! Did those women last night have any idea how foolish and empty they were, how ugly and neurotic, with a cigarette in one claw and a drink in the other? They coughed like outboard motors!

They hated her because she was young and, somehow, they knew she had been to China and was planning a trip to the Middle East. She could run a fast five miles, she was the first American woman Fellow at the Institute, she had once made love to her art history professor's wife. 'I'm eclectic,' she said. She had represented Culpeper at the Miss Virginia pageant in the State Fair. The professor's wife was an impulse – she had invited Lauren for coffee and touched her hair. Lauren had looked calmly into her eyes and seen a harmless lust, and she said what the woman was too afraid to say: 'I want to scarf you,' and did, there on the sofa, with the woman's dress pushed up around her waist and the woman tipped back and whimpering a little, as if she was giving birth. Lauren counted that afternoon as one of her accomplishments, because she was not sorry and she had not repeated it.

She did not deserve this Brixton bedsitter. It was heated by a small electric fire – two bars on a tin plate fixed to the sealed-up hearth – but it was unsafe and expensive to leave it burning. The day before she had stayed at the Institute and gone straight to the party and in those eighteen hours the toilet in the small cubicle in the hall had frozen. There was still ice in it now and frost on the black windows. London dampness was colder than any ice she had ever seen, and London ice was like dark stone – a kind of dirty swelling marble. Seeing the toilet she had said to herself, as if to a friend, 'And I looked down and saw there was actually ice in the john!'

But she knew she would never tell anyone, which was a shame, because even though it was disgusting it was also very funny. It made a good story, but she knew she would have to be a success before she could tell it, otherwise she would be pitied.

Still in her mink coat she went into the hallway, where there was a pay phone. She found a likely number in the phone book and stood in her warm coat, dialling, and when Lindsay from upstairs passed by her and said, 'All right?' she was pleased with herself, because underneath her coat she had nothing on, and he didn't know it. She enjoyed her terrific secret – standing there naked inside her coat.

'I'd like to speak to the plumber,' she said, when the call went through. Even on the phone she took pleasure in the half truth of being naked inside her coat.

'Yeah, this is the plumber.'

She was oddly encouraged by the stupid selfish tone of the man.

'The most incredible thing happened last night,' she said, and took a breath. 'My toilet turned to ice! I don't know what to do. I mean, what good is a frozen toilet?'

'You American?'

'I sure am,' she said.

'I can't do anything before tomorrow,' he said in a slightly friendlier tone.

'What about this evening,' she said, 'around Happy Hour – or whatever you people call cocktail time?'

He fell silent, but then he asked for her address and she knew he would come that evening.

'Coldharbour Lane,' he said. 'That's Brixton.'

'Brixton is my new home,' she said.

'What do you think of it?'

'Come on over and I'll tell you.'

'Name?'

'Lauren Slaughter.'

Even that – her name – was half true. The gold initials on her briefcase said *L. S.* because it had been her husband's. Leonard Slaughter was English, and very serious. He taught economics at Hull. Hull was horrible! They had met in China and married in Washington and had separated in London. They had China in common, and after they parted she saw his close-set eyes and big serious nose whenever she heard the word China. And anything Chinese stirred memories of her marriage. It was this that influenced her in wanting to change her field of study to the Arab world.

Leonard had not wanted a divorce, but it was pointless to live the way they had been living, making a virtue of merely holding on. Leonard cared about appearances, which made him tenacious. Marriage was not a virtuous thing, only a balancing act, two people pedalling a tandem bike, one behind the other, the man in front. It was absurd and pleasant like that, and just as rare a success as in life – no, it was a short-distance thing and he steered and she pedalled. All marriage had done for her was give her a new name. Her old one was Mopsy Fairlight. She took the name Lauren when she got the name Slaughter. She wondered why people didn't change their names more often. She laughed and then concentrated hard when she saw her old name written on the flyleaf of some of her books – the words, the ink, the signature: where was this girl now?

Last night's dinner party had left her feeling rumpled and dissatisfied, as if she had been stupidly teased. In this mood she went to work. On the Victoria Line to Green Park and the Institute she repeated her sentence 'When I feel like it' and she was pleased by the way it sounded. She liked her reflection in the train window. She was a young woman with a girl's face – the features almost of a child – but she was stronger than most men she knew; she could run faster and farther than they. Jogging at a certain speed, Leonard had always looked as if he was just going to fly apart.

At Stockwell a man got on and sat across the aisle from Lauren. He was a television director, or else an actor, or something in advertising. He was wearing lovely shoes – olive green, probably Italian – and he had nice narrow feet. He also wore a felt hat, innocently gangsterish. A young man who wore that kind of hat wanted to call attention to himself. He was dressed warmly – a Crombie overcoat with soft sleeves, and blue jeans. He was trying to look interesting and self-absorbed and he sat there comfortably with his *Guardian* still folded on his lap unread. Lauren found him sexy and self-assured – but for her they were almost the same thing. Something in his clothes and his manner suggested that he had been to the States. This she found attractive in him. She hated the house-bound English.

She was peering past him, seeming to ignore him. But it was not shyness or lack of interest – she was looking at his reflection in the window and she wanted to give him a chance to look at her.

Then she made her move. She reached into her briefcase and took out *Renmin Ribao* – it was two months old, but how could he tell? She held it up and began reading busily.

'You read–' He smiled and pointed.

She smiled back at him over the top of the paper. 'Chinese.'

He had been quicker than most – seconds – but in that time she had actually found an article she had missed on other readings, and it was related to her new area – something about a Chinese trade delegation to the Persian Gulf. The Chinese were in the oil business, too, and had machinery to sell – this she gathered while the man waited for her to say something more.

He was not handsome but stylish – worldly, unattached, definitely not serious. He looked fun. He was something in television, she was sure.

Lauren folded the Chinese newspaper in half and held it out to him.

'Want to do the crossword?'

He laughed but took the paper and examined it and remarked what an amazing language it was. 'You must be very clever.'

She said, 'On the other hand, I don't speak French and you probably do.'

'You speak American,' he said.

'Don't be cruel,' she said, and tenderly touched his arm.

The train was drawing into Victoria.

'I hate this stop,' she said. 'All the commuters.'

He shrugged and said, 'I'm not going far.'

She wanted to know how far, how long she would have with him, but instead of asking she made an amused face to show that she had not understood what he had just said.

'Oxford Circus,' he said, in explanation.

'I'll join you.'

He said he was a film editor for Olympus Pictures and that he had lived in the States for a year – New York. He then said, 'Do you get back often?'

'Periodically.'

He stared at her and repeated 'periodically' – trying it out.

'You should go to Virginia some time,' she said. 'But there's no point going unless you have me to show you around.'

He did not say anything in reply. He waited until the train

drew into Oxford Circus and then, when the platform was clear, he said, 'I'll keep that in mind. In the meantime, maybe we could discuss it over dinner.'

The serious ones always said dinner. She had not expected this from him. His seriousness slightly oppressed her. They walked up-stairs. She did not tell him that she had missed her stop for him.

'My name's Lauren.'

'Ivan Shepherd.'

At the top of the stairs she took a card out of her wallet. She liked handing over her printed card, with her new name and the two phone numbers and the Institute's embossed hemisphere – the world in gold. It was a ritual that made her feel important and protected.

'The Hemisphere Institute of International Studies,' he said, reading from the card. He had no expression, he was thinking hard; he said, 'You went past your stop.'

'I have shopping to do,' she said, and turned quickly and walked away while he was still gaping at her. And once she was out of sight she ran all the way to the Institute.

There was a seminar that morning on tensions in the Gulf. It was always tensions somewhere – the world was a wreck. This one concerned the war between Iran and Iraq, its effect on the Shatt-al-Arab waterway, but it was being held at London University over in Russell Square. Instead of going, Lauren spent the morning in the Institute library – an irritating morning, as it turned out, because the librarian would not allow her to use the photocopying machine.

'This is for staff use only,' the woman said. 'There's a coin-operated one on the third floor for the use of Institute Fellows.'

Lauren said that Mr Fletcher always let her use this machine.

The librarian said, 'Then Mr Fletcher is breaking the rules.'

Mr Fletcher was a lovely nervous little guy who lived with his mother; but this librarian was an insensitive woman with a chafed face and old brown shoes.

*

Julian returned from the seminar at one. When he was over-worked he looked like an old man – round-shouldered and preoccupied and harmless.

'How about lunch?' Lauren said. 'It's on me.'

In the coffee shop on the south side of Berkeley Square, Julian said that the party had made him furious. He had spent the whole night wakeful, thinking angrily about the man who had said, 'There are five thousand people in the world.'

Lauren thought it was one of the brightest things she had heard in London so far – unless the man had been joking: she was still a little uneasy about that.

Julian said, 'I wish I had said something scathing to him. I hate these people who are full of formulas and magic numbers.'

'He was pretty incredible,' Lauren said.

'He's a monster.'

Lauren did not want to be drawn into a discussion of the man at the dinner – she was uncomfortable talking about things she wanted or people she liked.

'So how was the seminar?' she said.

Julian said that it had been poorly attended, and so they had been able to put a lot of questions to the people who had read papers. He described how the Arabs in the marshes of southern Iraq had been driven away, and their unique settlements which had lasted for thousands of years in this remote place were now destroyed by two trampling armies. The economy of Kuwait had been affected by the war, too. A man at the seminar named Haseeb was organizing a study tour of the Gulf.

'I'd love to go,' Lauren said.

'You should have been at the seminar.'

'I couldn't be bothered to go all the way to Bloomsbury.'

'You're astonishing,' he said, and looked Lauren over admiringly. 'That's a splendid coat.'

'I designed it,' she said. 'I design all my own dresses.'

'My sister does that.'

Lauren was irritated by his saying this. She said, 'But I design everything. I'd design my own underwear, too, if I wore any, except I don't.'

Julian seemed both shocked and grateful.

'I don't buy knickers,' she said, playfully pursing her lips on the word. 'Why do English people like that word so much?'

Julian said, 'Because we're pathetic and repressed.'

Lauren was pinching her empty purse and fussing with it, but before she could say, 'I left all my money at the Institute' Julian said, 'My treat' and insisted that lunch had been his idea, not hers.

'I hope you don't think I'm as coarse as this with everyone,' she said. 'It's just that I feel that I can relax with you.'

'I'm glad. I'd like to see more of you.'

'We can meet,' she said. 'Periodically.'

He smiled at 'periodically' as Ivan Shepherd had done.

'We can bitch about the Institute,' she said.

'General Newhouse thinks your project is super.'

'I'd like to stuff it to him,' Lauren said. 'I certainly never expected the head of the Institute to be a general. It feels like the army.'

Julian said, 'His war memoirs have been compared to *The Seven Pillars of Wisdom*.'

'I've got a theory that it's very unlucky for a woman to read that book.'

Julian smiled in a surrendering way, and she knew she had him.

'I think the General hates the research fellows. I wish they'd get rid of him.'

Julian said, 'Americans come to a new situation and say, "I don't like it. They'll have to change it."'

'What do English people say?'

'"I don't like it. Therefore, I'll have to change."'

Lauren said, 'I always think insecurity or a lack of confidence makes people susceptible to imitation. Weak people haven't got the guts to be themselves. But being yourself is being original! I like myself the way I am.'

She found her face in the coffee shop mirror.

She said, 'Still, he gives good parties.'

'You only get invited to one. It's a sort of welcome.'

'That's awful!' she said. 'That's another reason I hate him.'

She spent the afternoon trying to follow up the reference she had found in the Chinese newspaper about the trade delegation from the People's Republic. She wondered whether Julian was telling the truth about the General — did he really think her project was super? 'Recycling Oil Revenue' was her working title. Arabs were so much more cooperative than the Chinese, and the Gulf was nearer and sunnier and didn't smell of mud and smoke, as China did. She reminded herself that she did not hate the Chinese; but they irritated her — the thought of them, so many of them — and she smirked, remembering Mr Van Arkady saying, 'There are two people in China.' She thought: Or one.

Alone, with no one watching her, she did not want to read. On the tube this morning with that young man across the aisle she had had no trouble concentrating on the *Renmin Ribao* — she'd had great concentration. Now she had none, and the English she was trying to read looked incomprehensible.

At five she saw General Newhouse leave. She put on her coat and followed him to the pavement, where a taxi was waiting.

'Is that your taxi, General?'

'Yes, can I give you a lift?'

They rode in silence towards Victoria. Lauren said, 'Your party was fun. I really liked your friends.'

The General stared at her, and then he said, 'We were glad you were able to come.'

She said, 'We must do it again some time.'

He squinted at this, as if she had just lapsed into another language.

She said, 'By the way, my research is going wonderfully.' She wanted to mock his indifference by lying to him.

'I sometimes think that wealthy Arabs in London are the strangest phenomenon of our century. And someday they won't exist, and no one will understand how this happened in our time.'

Lauren said, 'Isn't there a reception for those Arab information people tonight?'

'I'm on my way there now,' the General said. His face was set in a look of boredom. 'It's by invitation, I'm afraid.'

Lauren smiled, hating the creases in his face and the set of his mouth. She said, 'Unfortunately I can't go – I've got a very important meeting.'

Again, the General seemed to be having trouble translating her words.

They passed a shop in Victoria Street that had a sign that flashed *Sex Show* and *Live Acts*.

The General pretended not to see.

'They're nothing,' Lauren said. 'I saw a sex show in Florida that would take five years off your life.' Then she rapped on the driver's window and said, 'I'm getting out here,' and she did, without another word, leaving the General to pay.

The plumber was late and unapologetic. He looked suspicious and a bit amateur. He had no tools with him. He made Lauren feel like a crank and then she was afraid and sorry she had let him in. But when he saw the toilet he sighed and she was encouraged: now he understood. The ice had thawed to the size of a grapefruit, but it had cracked a pipe.

He said, 'That'll need replacing.'

What was he pointing at?

'Do whatever needs to be done.'

'Who's the landlord here?'

'His name is Reggie. He's in Jamaica at the moment. But I can look after myself.'

The man said something in a low voice. When they were saying something very rude you could never understand them.

He went outside and returned with a bag of tools – a heavy one: it thudded and rattled the windows when he dropped it. He was clumsy – banging, thumping, throwing things down. There was a kind of noise-making that was a clear sign of stupidity in a man.

Lauren sat by the electric fire in the other room, still wearing her coat. The clatter from the hall turned to silence. The last noise was the toilet flushing.

'It's working,' he said, stepping into the room.

'You're marvellous.'

He hesitated. 'Twenty-seven pounds,' he said. 'That includes parts and labour.' He tore a sheet of paper from a pad – the bill. But she did not look at it.

She said, 'Your parts?'

She went to a cupboard and poured a measure of whisky. She gave it to him, she clinked glasses – hers was empty.

'Go on,' she said. 'I don't drink.'

'This won't do you any harm,' he said, and sipped, and his face tightened at the taste of it.

'You're a fast worker,' she said.

'I reckon I am,' he said, and sat down. He had begun to prowl.

'What's your name?'

'Pete.'

'Sneaky Pete,' she said. 'Like another drink?' She took a step towards his chair. 'I want to pay you.' And took another step. 'I mean, I want you to be satisfied.'

He smiled sheepishly, as if he had been discovered naked, and then he grunted, and sipped the drink again. He was waiting for her to do all the work.

Lauren touched the back of his hand, and then moved sinuously around his chair.

'What are you doing?'

'The dirty boogie. That's what we used to call it.' She knelt in front of him and said, 'I think I know what you want.' She unbuckled his belt. He did not object. 'I want to please you.'

He simply stared, and then he looked around and turned the lamp off. He did nothing more for a while. She fumbled with him, then held him tightly and used her tongue and her lips. She felt a sense of power, almost of magic – a kind of conjuring: she held this whole man in her mouth.

The man cried out, and then pushed himself back in the chair, as if slightly wounded – surprised by a burn.

Lauren stood up and switched on the lamp. She wiped a glistening fleck from her cheek, she straightened her dress; she had not removed her coat.

His trousers were down. He was limp, he looked weak and silly and unprotected. Lauren helped him to his feet and reminded him that his bag of tools was next to the chair. He looked at her in a shy amazed way, and then he laughed softly. He was pleased, and he had become grateful and boyish. All his rudeness was gone.

Lauren was holding the bill. She said, 'Now you'll mark that "paid", won't you?'

When he was gone she did her exercises and the room felt warmer. She had a bath. She ate alone: yogurt, an apple, some walnuts, a slice of toasted wholemeal bread and peanut butter, and a cup of herb tea.

Another day – and in many respects it had been typical. For over a month she had been living like this – on nothing – and hating it.

## 3

London was bad air and a sour mood, and on some days its clammy discomfort made her feel physically deformed; on other days she felt the city was poisoning her. But she was fighting it. She jogged down Acre Lane to Clapham and ran around the common listening to the Stranglers sing 'Shah Shah and Go Go' on her Sony Walkman; then she jogged home and had a long bath; and then breakfast of tea and melon, and bran mixed with yogurt. Each thing – the run, the bath, the food – made her purer and stronger. She was reassured, knowing she could keep her health in this senile city.

She wanted to move out of Brixton – this black district made her feel like a failure. She wondered whether she should leave the city altogether. It would mean leaving Britain – it was London or nothing; but the only habitable part of London, as far as she could see, was Mayfair. A man at the party had asked her why she liked it – was it that Giles something from the Foreign Office or had it been Van Arkady? Anyway, she'd said, 'It's really nice – it's just like Georgetown.'

The rest of Britain was dreary, especially Hull, where Lenny – he hated to be called Lenny – still sat, trying to explain China to his students. Once they had gone to Cornwall. The English talked about Cornwall the way Americans spoke of California, but when she got to Padstow Lauren said, 'Are we here?' There was no sun. It was wet and windy, and the sharp ugly rocks made swimming dangerous. She laughed in a hard shouting way when someone mentioned that King Arthur and Sir Lancelot had lived there. 'And Confucius used to live in China!' she said.

Why were English rooms so cold? She had not been in a warm room once – a really warm room, where she could have taken off her clothes and padded around naked. When she grumbled or got sad about that she thought of 'The Cremation of Sam McGee.' She had recited it for the performing part of the Miss Virginia pageant, when she was Miss Culpeper. Miss Goochland played the clarinet but Miss Norfolk won with her roller skates. The Northern Lights had seen queer sights but the queerest they ever did see were those other finalists, and Lauren had looked at them and thought: You're all dogmeat.

She had begun to feel that same disgust in London and she now saw that it had been a mistake to skip yesterday's seminar. But she had had no way of knowing that a study tour to the Middle East was being set up. It would be a good way of leaving London and continuing her project. At the moment she felt shut out and ignored and very cold – the jerks were sitting on her head, and the nice ones were no use at all. She wanted to drop everything and go to the Middle East: she imagined white skyscrapers and clean sand and blinding light. She had no money, but she could find some. The idea was to make a decision and then act. The money would come. She had never felt so left out, and that morning she went to the Institute determined to put things in order.

Julian was already in the office, reading at his desk. There were postgraduate fellows who, when they were studying, looked exactly like timid priests – sort of praying over their books. That was the way Julian folded his hands when he read.

Lauren said, 'I'm going on the tour.'

Julian said he was surprised that she could be so confident of being selected. He pretended to be joking, but he was serious and sort of issuing a warning. He himself did not know whether he would be chosen. They were very fussy, he said.

'Then they're sure to want me,' Lauren said.

The organizer of the study tour, the man called Haseeb, was attached to the Kuwait Embassy. Lauren dialled the number that Julian had given her. She got a crossed line and a wrong number before it even rang, and then no one picked up the phone. She tried again nearer noon and got an engaged signal. Ten minutes later a secretary said that Mr Haseeb was out to lunch. Lauren thought: How can you get out without coming in? At three o'clock he had not returned; at four the number was engaged again; at four-thirty he was in a meeting. And then no answer: the office was closed, and Lauren realized that she had spent the entire day unsuccessfully trying to make one lousy phone call.

The next day was Friday – no work for Muslims; but, being Arabs in London, they had Saturday and Sunday off, too. On Monday the secretary said that Mr Haseeb was out of the office. What was that supposed to mean? Bosses turned their secretaries into liars and guard dogs. People like Haseeb yawned over a magazine and said, 'Say I'm in a meeting.'

Because of these frustrations – not being able to see or speak to the man who could help her – Lauren imagined Haseeb very clearly. He was a brown balding man with a warty face and big teeth, in an English suit, and he weighed two hundred and eighty pounds. He had to wear a special sort of orthopaedic shoe because of his weight, and he had trouble getting out of most cars. He stank of cigarettes. He persecuted his huge wife.

On Tuesday the secretary told Lauren that Mr Haseeb was away for the day.

He had hairy knuckles. His eyes were two different colours. There was scurf on his collar.

'He's on holiday,' the secretary said on Wednesday.

Eating like a pig, and sneaking alcohol. His farts sounded like air brakes.

Then Lauren could not work. In the week since she had made up her mind to go on the Middle East study tour Lauren had put her work aside, because she had been waiting. She could not think or even read a simple article when she was in suspense – it really was like hanging in the air.

'We'll send you an application,' the secretary said on Thursday. Another Thursday and she was on the phone with the same question!

Lauren said, 'I understand they're choosing the candidates next week.'

'Mr Haseeb didn't leave me any instructions.'

'Would it speed things up if I came over and picked up the application in person?'

'Obviously.'

The secretary said this word in that tone of voice because she thought she could get away with it.

'You just missed him,' the secretary said when Lauren entered the foyer. Now she saw the secretary's name: *Miss Humpage*.

Lauren went to the window. The secretary was behind her, gloating – Lauren could feel the heat of it.

The young Arab getting into a black Jaguar wore a dark suit, and a tie like an orchid, and had the physique of a tennis player, and could not have been more than thirty. He looked back at the building and Lauren, who stepped nearer the window, put her hands on her hips and in this way opened her coat. But Haseeb had not seen her – couldn't possibly, or he would not have driven away.

The application called for an academic transcript, and – to satisfy the visa requirements of some of the countries on the tour's itinerary – it asked for a baptismal certificate, as well as a letter from the candidate's bank manager.

Lauren said, 'How am I supposed to get a baptismal certificate?'

'In the usual way, one would think,' Miss Humpage said, coldly. 'By being baptized.'

Did secretaries speak like this because of the awful people they worked for?

Lauren said, 'It's bureaucratic and bigoted.' Miss Humpage did not react. 'It's very demeaning.' Miss Humpage put a sheet of paper into the typewriter. 'And it'll take months. Mine has to come from the States. And what's this about a letter from my bank?'

'Again, that is a visa requirement – we need proof that you have a balance of two hundred pounds in your account.'

'Is that supposed to be a lot of money?'

'I wouldn't know,' Miss Humpage said, lowering her tensed fingers to the keyboard.

'Then I'll tell you,' Lauren said. 'It's not.'

Lauren was grinning, but she did not have this money in her bank account.

'I want to make an appointment with Mr Haseeb.'

Miss Humpage said, 'Fill up this form. Just your name and a number where we can reach you. And your reason for the appointment.'

Lauren did as she was directed, writing fast.

Miss Humpage said, 'Is that a business or a home number?'

'It's the green phone,' Lauren said.

Miss Humpage did not react. She read aloud, '"To investigate the pattern of petrodollar investment—"'

Lauren hated this, the woman reading at her from her own application.

'"—by OPEC agencies in development projects—"'

She spoke in a bored weary way, and at once the project seemed artificial and unnecessary. Miss Humpage looked up from the application.

'"—in Third World Muslim states."'

'And when Mr Haseeb is sober and decides to show up, tell him to take that application and shove it up his ass – unless you'd rather do that for him, too.'

On her way back to the Institute, and feeling frail, she entered a red telephone box that was full of stinks and tried to call Mr Van Arkady's bank. She spoke to his assistant. She heard the words 'in a meeting' and knew it was untrue. What were these people really doing who said they were in a meeting?

The man said, 'What is this in connection with?'

Lauren had called the number without knowing why, but the man's direct question made her realize that she wanted Mr Van Arkady's help and friendship. He was confident and worldly wise; he had contacts; he had money. He would sit down and tell her exactly what to do. Now she hated being alone. Six weeks in London she had not made one friend, but she did not regard this man Van Arkady as a stranger.

'It's a personal matter. We're friends.'

'I'll take your name and we'll get right back to you.'

She said, 'He doesn't know my name.'

'Didn't you say you were friends?'

'Oh, yes. We are.' Then she faltered. 'Only I didn't get a chance to tell him my name.'

After a silence, the man said, 'I see.'
'It's Mopsy Slaughter, but forget it.'
Then she hung up.

'I've got a feeling I'm not going on that study tour,' she said to Julian later, in the smoky, noisy pub. It was almost six o'clock. Julian was drinking a pint of beer. Lauren had a glass of Malvern water. 'I like to buy glasses of water,' she had said and the barman thought she was mocking him.

Julian had a long withered sausage on a chipped plate. He seemed to regard it as a problem. He kept glancing at it but he did not touch it.

He said, 'You don't need to go on the tour. You could probably find everything you need right here. Isn't that why you came to London?'

She said, 'London isn't London.'

'Ah, yes,' Julian said in the self-mocking way that came so easily to him, 'we are not what we were.'

'Don't feel bad. Tokyo isn't Tokyo, and Peking certainly isn't Peking, and Moscow isn't Moscow. Singapore isn't Singapore either. But, Jesus, Calcutta really is Calcutta.'

'I hope Berlin is Berlin,' he said.

'Half of it is.'

'I have to go there fairly soon to look into some archives on Arabia.'

She said, 'All you think about is work.'

'What do you think about?'

'Don't laugh, but I think about my body,' she said. 'The really important things like running, eating, sleeping and washing. I mean, doing them right. Who gives a shit about our research? I'd rather run a marathon.'

In his bewilderment at what she was saying Julian had overcome his nervousness with the sausage and had begun to eat it.

Lauren said, 'How can you put that thing into your mouth?'

'I suppose it *is* pretty disgusting,' he said.

She said, 'Why doesn't the stupid General invite us to another goddamned party? I really hate him.'

Julian watched her with the sausage sticking out of his mouth like a cigar, not biting down on it.

'Eat it and get it over with!' Lauren said. 'You're driving me crazy with that thing.'

When he was done and had wiped his hands she asked him for a loan of five pounds, which he gladly gave her.

The same evening of this long day Lauren was doing her stretching exercises on the floor and heard Lindsay from upstairs shouting that a bloke wanted her on the telephone – English bloke, Cockney-like. Lindsay always gave information in a meddling way. He was from Barbados and always barefoot indoors and had wet glistening eyes. He studied karate.

'It's me – Pete.' The voice was confident and casually familiar.

She said, 'I don't know anyone by that name.'

'The plumber.' Then he cleared his throat. 'Remember?' He cleared his throat again. 'I did that job at your place.'

She said, 'You're the person who fixed my toilet.'

'Yeah,' he said. 'Thought I might come over.'

'I don't need a plumber.'

'Thought you might like a drink.'

She said, 'I don't drink.'

She heard him gumming and ungumming his lips.

'Thought maybe we could get together.'

She said, 'Sorry,' and nothing more.

He became cross. 'Well, what about the last time?'

'That was strictly business.'

This silenced him. He tried again, but hungrily this time. 'I want to see you.'

She said, 'I don't know you. You performed a job for me and I paid you. I don't owe you anything.' And she hung up.

That phone call angered her, but she felt better after a bath, and then she sat in her mink-lined coat with the electric fire on, drying her hair. As the room warmed up old odours were stirred – food, sex, and dirt, all the human smells, the heat revealing the room's former tenants, the sour residue of their lives. London wasn't even pleasant when it was warm.

It was Thursday once more. That was the awful thing about failure: it humiliated you again and again by repeating the same empty days. She thought: I should have done Sino-Soviet relations – Chinese grants were easy these days – already people were sick of going to China. Then, remembering China, she saw Leonard's nose. Or the EEC, she thought: Paris was still Paris. She saw herself lecturing at a podium in Paris or Brussels, wearing her blue high-necked dress and white shoes. Then she thought: I would like to run a big hotel catering to the business traveller – he has special needs.

Julian entered the office from the library. He walked stiffly – he had been reading in his prayerful posture. Lauren knew that a mistake would be made and that he would be chosen by that little queer Haseeb to go on the study tour. She pitied Julian – he was wrong, incredibly naive, painfully truthful and timid, and always apologizing.

'Want a drink?' he said, in his embarrassed way, as if expecting her to say no.

She said, 'When you offer me a drink you actually mean something to drink.'

'Yes,' he said.

'But with other people, yes to a drink means yes to everything. And why is it always a drink?'

Julian had begun to look hopeful.

He was rummaging in his briefcase. 'This came for you this morning,' he said, and handed her a rectangular parcel in a padded bag. 'I signed for it. It came by messenger.'

'Just a book.'

'Okay then?' he said. 'The Duke of York?'

She said no in a resigned way and went home in the dark,

leaving all her library books and her file of photocopies on her desk.

It was not a book. It was a book-shaped video recording. It had no label, and the parcel had no return address. She had a small black and white television set, but no video machine. Lindsay had one. He was a member of a Brixton video club; he rented pornographic videos, and ones about karate, and Nazi prison camps. His favourite was one called *I Spit on Your Grave*: rape and murder.

'Hello, stranger,' Lindsay said. He was dressed like the kung-fu hero on the poster near his bed.

She said, 'I want to borrow your video machine. All that means is I want to borrow your video machine. Don't offer me a so-called drink.'

'You're a really funny kid. I rate you.'

Lindsay stood up. What was there about karate that attracted undersized people? Lauren took a step back.

'Just the machine,' she said.

## 4

She watched the videotape in her room as she did her stretching exercises – naked, on a long straw mat, the blinds down, and the electric fire blazing and filling the room with dusty heat. Her exercises were like a dancer's warm-up – flexing her arms, and tugging one heel and then the other against her stomach, and finally salaaming slowly towards the television screen.

*–This young woman earns two hundred pounds an hour.*

The narrator spoke in a flat insulted voice and the film showed a woman hurrying through strolling groups of people in Park Lane. It was not a cheaply made film. It was a television document-ary, well-edited and with good sound – perhaps a BBC program that had been taped. The woman was seen from a number of angles, and Lauren noticed that she was very ordinary and overdressed, with podgy shoulders and a chubby chin and a big bum. Dogmeat.

*—Her takings for a single week might be several thousand pounds —*

'And she weighs three hundred pounds,' Lauren said, stretching.

Now the woman was introducing herself to a swarthy moustached man who actually looked impressed and grateful — his libido on the boil and his tail wagging. The poor man was half the woman's size and he stood in his tiny Italian suit on stiff skinny legs.

*—She is one of a growing number of young women who work in London's newest industry — the escort service —*

His tone was interesting. It attempted stifled horror and distaste, but Lauren didn't believe it — she was sure the narrator was as fascinated as she was. With hidden cameras and bugged phones, the film progressed in a patchwork way, explaining the various girls-for-hire agencies that operated in Central London.

The girls looked unattractive and stupid — and they were certainly overpaid. Large sums were mentioned, but Lauren was still new enough to England to think of plain shapeless lumps whenever she heard the word pounds.

*—It's much more than they're worth,* said a cherubic hooker in dark glasses. *That's why it's not prostitution!*

*—I agree.* This was a soft-voiced black woman with a vast shiny handbag. *Prostitution is lowering yourself like, but this is just the opposite.*

The customers seemed to Lauren unexpectedly young and well-off. The ones who were interviewed were excited at the prospect of meeting a girl. Most of the men were foreign, many were from the Middle East, a few were Americans. And an Englishman — but then Lauren remembered that this was England.

*—I like the simplicity of it,* one of the American men said. *I hate hassles.*

The man looked like Archie McComb from Culpeper – just as big and pleasant, the same beer belly, the same spiky hair. But this one had money.

*—Usually it's just a bite of something,* the man explained. *You get lonely. It's company. Sure, a bite of something and then you take a hike.*

It was apparently a discreet business – practically all the arrangements were made by telephone. The makers of the film stage-managed an appointment. The narrator's tone of voice prepared the viewer in a sarcastic way for a kind of viciousness; but Lauren found the operation reassuring and practical, if a little comic.

*—Jasmine Agency. May I help you?* The voice at the end of the line seemed trapped in a small bottle.

*—I'm ringing from the Hilton,* the man in the foreground said. Hyde Park was visible out the window. *I'd like an escort for the evening. For dinner and, um –*

*—Give us your name and room number and we'll ring you right back.*

*—Why is that necessary!*

*—It's just a precaution, sir.*

Of course, Lauren thought. The man gave the information and then put the phone down. When it rang again he resumed.

*—I'd like to know how much it costs.*

*—One hundred pounds, plus twenty-five agency fee.*

*—What happens then?*

*—The rest is by arrangement with the lady. Shall I book an escort for you?*

The screen went black, the sound became echoey, and now it was as if the cameraman was squashed behind a door and squinting out. A doorbell rang loudly; there was gabbling, and the indistinct motion of several humans, and the friendly scrape of a Scottish voice.

*–We don't take personal cheques.*

When this woman crossed in front of the camera Lauren could see that she was expensively dressed, with an unnecessary and rather flashy scarf. But physically she was very plain. She had freckles and fat knees and she was definitely uneducated.

*–Mind if I smoke?* she said, lighting one.

Lauren laughed at the stupidity of it – the silly woman stinking up the small hotel room with her cigarette, and then coughing into her stubby fingers as she counted the man's money.

*–What did you say your name was?*

*–Samantha. Samantha Buckingham.*

Lauren jeered at her. 'Samantha Buckingham! I love it!'

*–Pleased to meet you. I'm Frank Harris. I want to take you to a party.*

*–I like a good party,* the woman said, and Lauren smiled at the accent – how ignorant and ridiculous it was.

*–Then maybe later we can pop back here for a nightcap. You don't mind that, do you?*

*–Might cost you extra, depending on the time. Do you always talk this much? There's nothing to be nervy about, darling.*

The next shot was of a party in the ballroom of a London hotel, a throng of shouting people – women in bright gowns and men in dark suits.

*–Most of the women in this room are social escorts being paid anywhere from fifty to five hundred pounds to stand and smile. In some cases, rather more is required.*

Their faces were crusted with make-up; they had gooey lips and lacquered piles of hair. Lauren saw mingled greed and gratitude in their eyes. And she thought they were pathetic – not for their lack of style or their silly sequined dresses, but for their heavy flesh and dull skin. They were hideously unhealthy.

The camera moved to a bright-eyed Arab at the party trying to speak to one of the girls and mumbling shyly.

*–Here, what do you call that, then?* the girl said, jerking the lower edge of his headdress.

'A ghotra,' Lauren said.

–*Ghotra*, the man said. *It is for the sun and sand and windstorm.*

–*Very useful in London that!* The girl screamed with laughter.

Slob, Lauren thought; but the man was gently laughing with the girl.

–*The Jasmine Agency has been operating for three years from their offices in Shepherd Market. Every evening of the year girls are dispatched to customers in London's hotels.*

The narrator described the innocent-seeming premises of the Jasmine Agency, and their mysterious directors, as a small figure hurried out of the office door and approached a Daimler that had just drawn up to the kerb.

–*This is Captain Twilley. He has been a farmer in Rhodesia and a sultan's bodyguard in the Persian Gulf. He has twice been arrested for firearms offences – carrying an unlicensed revolver and being in possession of a stolen weapon. There is no record of his having earned the title 'captain'.*

A young and rather haggard woman emerged from the Daimler. Captain Twilley took her by the arm and escorted her to the door.

*Madame Cybele. Her last known employer was the Hotel Bristol, Beirut, Lebanon, though her duties were somewhat obscure.*

A reporter suddenly appeared in the foreground of this shot, startling the woman.

–*I have a few questions for you.*

The woman recovered and gave him a corrosive stare.

–*I cannot help you.*

Her voice was faintly foreign, and her slight accent and the over-correct English made her seem all the more rude.

Captain Twilley loomed.

–*On your bike!* he shouted at the reporter.

The Captain had bushy eyebrows and a tweed tie and wore a thick baggy suit which had a bristly nap and a weave like sacking.

*–Certain aspects of your business seem rather strange to us.*

*–Stranger things happen at sea*, Captain Twilley said.

Madame Cybele's pale weary face was framed by a black fur collar. She had large eyes and large lips, and Lauren was interested to see that someone so young and attractive could also look so used up.

*–You will excuse us, please?* Madame Cybele said.

Captain Twilley shielded her and swept her into the offices of the Jasmine Agency.

This was not the end of the videotape. There were sequences of women at dances and dinner parties, and shopping in the West End – smiling at tiny watches on trays; they were shown at embassy functions, in restaurants, and at national day receptions under multi-coloured flags and banners. They were all paid for this.

Lauren was struck by how plain they were, how little conversation they had; their accents were uneducated and their health was mediocre; they had bad skin and wore too much make-up. They had heavy legs. They smoked. They were dogmeat.

She had stopped doing her exercises. She sat cross-legged, naked on the mat, still watching. And for the duration of the film London seemed a habitable city – it was human and workable. What had been incomprehensible to her before was now clear. She saw order: a pattern was revealed – motives and results, too, and for the first time something potentially friendly. The city no longer seemed foreign and half dead to her. She was thinking how much prettier and better she was than those women, and how powerful she could be. When the tape ended she felt invigorated with a peculiar strength. In this foreign place she saw something familiar and alive. And the most important thing of all: in this huge city of strangers someone knew her very well. It was the person who had sent the tape, and Lauren felt that this person – he or she – was still whispering encouragement to her.

*

Lauren tried on her Thai-silk dress, pale yellow with bright stripes, and her Italian shoes – two narrow straps and a three-inch heel that was so sharp it jammed in escalators. Her shoulders were bare, her hair upswept, and her thickest gold chain round her neck – Noosie, the Brixton neck-freak, had drawn it tight and photographed the welt it had left. Now Lauren posed in front of her full-length mirror and smiled: Party time! She had worn this dress to a cocktail party at the Hemisphere Institute and to General Newhouse's dinner party. She knew that as a political economist she was disconcerting in it, and she loved the tactical advantage in being disconcerting.

This dress would not do – it wasn't right. When she took it off, the rustle of silk and the sight of her own nakedness aroused her. She felt queenly. Then she parted her legs and teased herself with one fingertip and she shuddered with pleasure at the white length of her body.

She put on a dark tartan kilt, and a white pleated shirt that she buttoned to her neck. She drew on her oatmeal tweed jacket.

She said, 'I think this recession can be explained by a credulous over-dependency on supply-side theory.'

She fastened her grandmother's brooch onto her lapel and turned back to the mirror.

'On the other hand, in China until very recently all external debts were settled immediately in cash, taking no notice at all of the float possibilities.'

She tugged her hair back and wound it and fixed it with an old tortoiseshell clasp – her 'librarian clasp'; and she glanced again at the mirror.

'Petrodollars are definitely bottoming out. If they hit the tape at one-twenty your oil producers may begin to sell gold.'

She pulled on her boots and stood up and stamped in them.

'As seen from Mayfair, the downside risk is lethal but worth taking.'

And lastly she put on a pair of gold-rimmed glasses.

'I'm now a virgin,' she said. 'You break it – you pay for it.'

It was ten o'clock in the morning. At one, a Fellows' meeting was scheduled in the Situation Room of the Institute – cheap wine and cheese sandwiches and a pep talk from the General. There was time, there was time.

The videotape had suggested sumptuous offices by showing a plaster façade painted in the dead white of a Nash terrace and with ornate grillework, and the sort of pompous brass name-plate that the Institute itself had mounted over its porcelain bell-push. This one said *Jasmine Agency.*

Lauren rang and entered – as a smaller notice demanded – but instead of stepping into comfortable space and warm light she found herself at the bottom of a steep flight of stairs. And it was chilly, too – like being at the bottom of a well.

On the landing high above her were two men in robes, snatching at their heads in frustration. It was an Arab gesture that looked like a frenzied benediction. They were speaking to a receptionist, who was seated at a small desk with her morning paper and her cup of tea. Lauren had expected to see Madame Cybele at the top of the stairs and she was disappointed by the girl at the desk – another bulgy bitch, like the ones in the program.

Each of the men – she now clearly saw that they were Arabs – wore an English suit jacket over his white robe. They were jabbering in a hurt, puzzled way. The language barrier so often made foreigners look stubborn or childish – it was what Lauren hated most about having to speak other languages: she felt infantile saying 'Please' and 'Thank you' and 'Very good' and all that talk in the present tense, like a silly novel trying to look brisk and important.

Lauren shut the front door and the men stopped talking as the door-slam reached them. Now they looked down the steep stairwell at Lauren rising.

'Hi!' she said. She was smiling and even after that long climb she was not winded.

The men backed away as if to receive her, and one blinked in satisfaction and said, 'We want this one.'

*

It was the first time she had ever been early for a Fellows' Meeting. She sat primly, waiting for the others. They entered self-consciously, heaving briefcases and not speaking – Julian, Fairman from the Asia Section, Stringer, Willymot, and Bridgid Doyle, an affected girl ('ashoom' she said instead of 'assume') with broken teeth who rode an old bike and never took off her greasy raincoat. Apart from Julian, they all hated Lauren: Fairman because she had been to Chengdu, Willymot because she had stuck him with a restaurant bill their first week, Stringer because she had borrowed his cheap fountain pen and lost it; and Doyle – obvious.

Julian whispered, 'Any luck with your application?'

'What application?'

'Haseeb,' he said. 'That Kuwaiti chap. The Study Tour.'

This delighted her. She had completely forgotten all that. She said, 'Fuck it!'

Julian pinched his face. He did not understand.

She said, 'Don't care!'

The General entered and addressed them in a tone that was both bullying and patronizing, speaking of their research projects (fat Bridgid was doing famine relief!). What Lauren hated most about his tone was that it showed no trust in them, no interest, only a sort of vague irritation that these research fellows existed; and, all the while he spoke, he wore the expression of a man who hears a mosquito buzzing but can't see the creature he is impatient to swat.

'Finally,' he said in the little homily he always saved for last, 'the Arab world. A word. I don't have to tell you that it's on our own doorstep. I know some of you' – he looked at Lauren – 'have met with a certain resistance. Don't be discouraged and above all don't be foolishly suspicious or wrong-headed. Your efforts will be considerable but so will your rewards. The Institute's relationship with the Arab world has grown out of an unprejudiced enthusiasm for the land and its peoples, and should any of you decide to pursue your researches further it would give the Institute a tremendous strategic advantage in applying for gifts from Arab agencies trading in the U K –'

The two men had taken her to the coffee shop of the Hilton and bought her a cup of espresso and a large piece of Black Forest gâteau. They took her protests for friendly excitement, and she said no so vigorously they ordered her a second piece of cake. She broke the first cake apart in a ceremonial way, to show she was grateful; but she did not taste it, nor did she drink the coffee. When she ate even a tiny morsel of something she didn't like she could taste it for two days.

Each of the men ate a slice of baklava, and then one wiped his mouth on his handkerchief and said, 'We go?' to Lauren.

They left the other man at the table grinning at his wristwatch. He had shown Lauren the watch. Its face was a solid gold ingot weighing fifteen grams. He had also, that same morning, bought a large stuffed bear and an air pistol. The teddy bear was for his wife, he said tenderly, and he was going to shoot birds with the air pistol. There were many birds in his country – many, many birds to shoot at. He was still yapping about bird shooting when his heavier friend swallowed and said, 'We go?'

'What's in the bag?' she asked.

He whisked it open as if at a customs' check.

'A book!' she said. 'What's the title?'

An Arab with a book: it half scared her.

'No, no,' he was saying, and pulled it out. He lifted one of the hard covers and plinking music began, the first few bars of 'The Floral Dance' but even a few bars was enough to get this man wagging his head happily.

'Ah, that's better – a music box,' Lauren said. 'A book is a pain in the ass, isn't it?'

The man was still wagging his head to *pinka-pink, pinka-pink*.

She could never tell the ages of foreigners. This man might have been thirty or forty, or more – she believed that middle-age was a certain musty soapy odour, and he had it on him. He gave her a hundred pounds in twenties from a canvas money belt that looked as if it held slugs of ammo. Then he went to the bathroom and washed noisily, and he stood by while Lauren washed, supervising her in a fussy way that had nothing to do with sex. When she lay naked on the bed, he knelt between her legs and lifted his robe. He had not taken it off even to wash. His penis was thick and dark and looked like an old pickle. He entered her, pushing hard, and only minutes later he ground his teeth, and cried, 'Khallas!' and was done.

She was washing, using the bidet, when the second man slipped into the room. She had left the bathroom door open in order to keep an eye on her handbag, and then she saw this second man come towards her to watch. And the hotel room door slammed: that was the first man leaving. They had it all worked out!

Without speaking, this man took a sock-like purse from his pocket and a plug of bills from the purse. When she had finished washing herself, he handed it over. Lauren took five long strides to the bed and tumbled in. The man peeled off his skullcap and massaged his shaven head as he contemplated her. Something was wrong – he seemed distracted, at once modest and impatient. She reached for him but he drew back, keeping his hands from her, as if fearing contamination. Then he shuffled towards her and gave her a little slap on her hip – an animal pat. It was an order. She understood and turned on her stomach.

'Take it easy,' she said, facing the headboard and seeing his dim reflection in the varnished wood.

But he had started with his finger and already it hurt. He was lost in a gabbling monologue with himself, and using her hip bones as handles he shoved himself into her abruptly, surprising her.

The swiftness and the slight pain made Lauren sob, which seemed to please the man. He pushed in deeply and rode her and then lay the length of her with his teeth clamped on her neck and squealing softly like a sudden rabbit.

'Any questions,' she heard the General saying.

183

She frowned, remembering, then said, 'No, sir.'

She had agreed to meet Captain Twilley at the Jasmine Agency that evening. The videotape was still so fresh in her mind that she felt as if she was part of the same film – but a vast improvement over those tacky English girls and that fat Scot who had coughed as she had counted her money.

Captain Twilley was much smaller in the flesh and very gruff.

He said, 'Escorts don't normally come to the agency, so don't make a habit of it. Use the telephone instead. We'll keep track of your appointments and send you a weekly invoice. That's all I need from you – your name and your telephone number. Your real name. We guarantee absolute discretion. If you want to use another name for work, that's fine. We don't ask awkward questions. This is like the Foreign Legion.'

'I want to use my real name.'

'That's very unusual.'

She said, 'I'm not ashamed of what I'm doing.'

Until that moment he had been scribbling on a pad and only glancing at her. But now he looked up and kept his eyes on her as he leaned back in his chair.

'You're a bright spark,' he said. 'But I'm less than ecstatic about your outfit.' He spun one finger in a winding motion that he intended as criticism. 'Have you got anything a little more colourful that would emphasize your figure?'

'If you think a social escort is just tits and a tight dress you have a very old-fashioned idea of what this job requires,' Lauren said.

'What have you got that it requires?' he asked.

She said, 'I'm user-friendly.'

'Good,' Captain Twilley said. 'We get all kinds of punters.'

The next night she was summoned to the Savoy by a tall French boy, eighteen at most, who greeted her in his room wearing a red baseball hat with limp cloth horns – like cow horns – sewn to its crown. Their meal was sent up. He ate in his underwear, the hat on his head. She peeled an orange and ate three segments. They watched television. He kept his money in a paper bag. 'Tarzans,' he said, stirring the ten pound notes. 'Tarzans.' He paid her and then went to sleep with his head in her lap. He woke and wept when she said she had to go home, and then he screamed and frightened her, and slammed the door as she walked quickly down the corridor.

She felt wonderful afterwards, as if she had walked a tightrope and won the grand prize. Her only regret was that she had to go all the way to Brixton to be home. She wanted something nearer – a flat in Mayfair – perhaps a short distance from the Institute; she wanted two lives separated by a few streets.

That same week she was sent an invitation to a reception at the Dorchester. It was to welcome a delegation from the Bahrain Ministry of Information. The minister himself was there, and so was the ambassador. The invitation had been delivered by a messenger to the Institute, and it was only when Lauren saw Captain Twilley waiting in the lobby that she was sure that she was representing the Jasmine Agency and not the Hemisphere Institute.

Captain Twilley took her upstairs and into the ballroom by a side door, bypassing the receiving line and a beefy-faced Englishman with side-whiskers and a red frock coat who was shouting the names of the arriving guests.

'Look for Puddles,' Captain Twilley said, and hurried downstairs for another of his girls.

Lauren saw Madame Cybele approaching.

'Puddles?'

The woman's frown meant yes. But Lauren thought: if someone's called Puddles you don't ask why. Lauren liked Madame Cybele's dark eyes and cruel fleshy mouth, but something else disturbed her. The high collar of her dress did not quite hide a grey bruise on her neck – the top of the splotch just showed. This bruise, there, seemed to Lauren very decadent – what was it about necks that made men crazy?

'Follow me,' Madame Cybele said, and she snaked through the room. It was mostly men, and nearly all of them Arabs – in *besht* and *thobe* and red-flecked *ghotra*, like a desert gathering; and others in suits, and in various military uniforms. They were unusual clothes and made the party seem festive, like a fancy dress ball: these men dressed as Arab sheiks and those as potentates and those as stage-generals. Most of the men looked wealthy, and they had bad posture, as if they did nothing but sit or ride or be carried.

Madame Cybele stopped at a group of three men. Now she raised her voice and became charming. 'Gentlemen, I'd like you to meet a young friend of mine.'

Each man smiled and spoke his name quickly, like a sentence in Arabic.

'They're very generous, but ever so naughty,' Madame Cybele said, in an affected way that did not go with her intelligent eyes or her bruise. 'Be very careful, Lauren, they're from Kuwait.'

'I wonder whether you can tell me,' Lauren said to the men, 'what effect an Iran-Iraq war has had on the tribal people living in those immense marshes north of Basra and the Shatt-al-Arab waterway. I mean, the Madan and the Faraigat.'

The men stared at her, and then one spoke.

'Very trouble,' he said and put on a sorrowful expression.

Another said, 'Yes, too much trouble for them. But I am living in Bahrain today.'

'He keeps inviting me there,' Madame Cybele said. 'One of these days I'm going to surprise you and say yes.'

But Lauren was still closely attentive. She said to this man, 'I have great admiration for your pipeline.'

'Well, well,' Madame Cybele said.

'Awali to Dharan,' Lauren said.

'You'll excuse me,' Madame Cybele said, a trifle coldly, and slipped away.

'And Sitrah. And Jebel ad Dukhan,' the man said. 'You know

Zahran.' He showed Lauren his foot. 'I buy this shoes in Zahran. This is the most expensive shoes in the world.'

'I hope you've got two of them,' Lauren said. 'Then you can show me around the Gulf and not get sore feet.'

'Please visit Kuwait,' the third man said. He had been watching with bright squirrel-like eyes, and smiling each time Lauren spoke. He was intelligent looking and had a good accent – none of this 'Very trouble' or 'zis shiss'. He was chafing a small string of worry beads in his fingers.

'Nice beads,' she said.

'Mogaddimeh.' And he pressed them into her hand.

They were heavy and cool – perhaps jade, perhaps something even more precious. The clasp was gold. She smiled, feeling powerful again, because without any effort she was a success; and what could they possibly deny her when she was trying hard to please them – she knew that she had an unusual capacity to please men. It had everything to do with forgetting her own pleasure and being a willing slave.

'I wanted to go to Kuwait,' she said, handling the beads in her long fingers. 'But Haseeb at your embassy flatly refused to see me.'

'I have no embassy,' the man said.

'But you know Haseeb!' one of the other men said. 'Haseeb is just a small boy. And a lazy boy. I will arrange your visit. No Murphy's Law, no very trouble.'

'What do you think?' Lauren said to the man who had given her his worry beads.

'I think you should come with me,' he said, 'so that we can discuss this' – and he smiled – 'at the highest possible level.'

He pinched the tip of her elbow and steered her towards the door. Then he released her and hurried forward to embrace someone – another man. They kissed and greeted each other with great formality – murmuring; but whether it was English or Arabic she could not tell.

'Meet my friend.'

Who was being introduced – she or the man? Then it didn't matter. The man was Hugo Van Arkady.

At the General's he had seemed swarthy and heavy; in this gathering he looked thinner and rather pale and intense. But it was merely the difference in the setting, she was sure. He registered no surprise at seeing her.

'We've met,' Van Arkady said. 'And I was sure that we would meet again. You're keeping good company, Dr Slaughter. Don't let this man's enthusiasm discourage you.'

She said, 'You remembered my name!' She was pleased, for why would he bother to remember her name if he did not think she was one of his special number? It was magic more than memory: she was suddenly part of the city, and now everything in London seemed possible. That was an important moment for her – his easy assumption of friendship and her delight. And he didn't judge her, nor did he seem to care whether she was an escort or a research fellow. It was as if he had known her for a long time – that, rather than the other way around, because she also found him a little scary looking, and if she had not felt like a success she suspected that she might be afraid of him, as she had been – slightly – at the General's.

'We must make arrangements,' the man said.

Van Arkady said, 'You both look very happy. It is wonderful to see you – wonderful.'

In the nightclub the man said his name was Karim and that he hoped they would meet again soon. He said, 'I know what you want.'

She said, 'I want you.'

'That is a great deal,' he said. 'But if it makes you happy' – and he made a face at her at the dark and candlelit table.

'That man Van Arkady is an old friend of mine,' she said.

'Oh, yes,' he said. 'I could see.'

'But there's nothing to be jealous of,' she said.

Karim nodded gravely at this and then ordered a feast of

lamb and chicken kebabs, with a great bowl of rice and lemon soup.

Lauren did not eat anything. Karim picked at one kebab, but when he murmured that Lauren really ought to eat something – it was good, a traditional feast, it made you strong and lovely – when he said this, Lauren grasped a skewer.

'There's something sexy about these,' she said. 'The way it's raw where the skewer pierces the meat. I love these skewers. I even like the word skewers.'

These skewers were swords. Karim presented her with one, wiping it on his napkin and telling her to take it home.

'But why?' she said.

'Because you are my chicken.'

## 5

In the daytime there was the Institute, and at night the Agency, but she found the work similar in many respects; and when people (day or night) asked her what she did the rest of the time she said, 'Research,' and she thought: I've gone the whole nine yards.

She saw Karim often. It was always business. He said she should get a flat in London – he innocently believed that Brixton was not in London.

'I'd love a place in Mayfair. Half-way–'

She was going to say 'Half-way between the Institute and Park Lane,' but she forced herself to be silent. She wanted to keep her two lives separate – she was superstitious in a routine way, and she was also practical. And she had succeeded in dividing her life: at the Institute she let everyone know that her real name was Mopsy, and they called her Mopsy; at the Jasmine Agency, and to most of the men she was sent to, she was Dr Slaughter – it was Van Arkady's greeting that had given her the idea. 'Cheerio,

Mopsy!' Julian said at the Duke of York, and an hour later she would be speaking into a house phone at a hotel: 'This is Dr Slaughter. I'm in the lobby—'

'Half-way,' Karim was saying, urging her to finish her sentence.

'Half-way through Mayfair.'

'Yes, yes, yes.'

He was glad in the way that wealthy men became glad: she had never seen this in anyone else. These men had everything they wanted – they had so much that they could not imagine what someone else might want. They could grant any wish, and yet they lived in a rather saturated world in which people seldom expressed a wish. It was maddening for them, and that was why Lauren's saying 'I'd love a place in Mayfair' made Karim grateful.

A few days later he took her to a small flat in Half Moon Street, at the Piccadilly end, number three. Here he photographed her as she sat naked in clear plastic chairs or as she pedalled a Finnish exercise cycle. He took his pleasure that way, talking to her the whole time.

'Is this yours?'

The question embarrassed him: he was still taking pictures.

'The flat,' she said.

'You like it, don't you?'

She said, 'You know what I want.'

'Yes, Doctor.'

'You're an awful pimp,' she said.

She was just teasing, but he didn't laugh.

She thought a moment, still pedalling as Karim knelt with his camera, and she said, 'There are a lot of things I don't have. But I'm not greedy. I don't want a car. I'd rather have my own room and the freedom to do anything I want in it. I don't want to be bossed around. If there's one question I hate it's "Where have you been, young lady?" I don't care much about jewellery. I don't care about the things I'm being denied now. I want the things I was denied when I was twelve years old.'

There was as yet not much furniture in the flat on Half Moon

Street, but even so she became attached to it, and she disliked having to leave it and take the tube to Brixton. These days Karim always used the flat, photographing her and talking. Was this sex? If so, it was the oddest slowest kind. Sometimes he took an hour or two. That was the trouble with the kinky ones – they needed time. The others were different. She prided herself on being able to blow an average guy and be at the door in fifteen minutes, shaking hands – that was always how they wanted it – and leaving. She was never kissed. Karim did not even touch her.

He shared her with his friends; they were bad and boring, but no worse than husbands – and they paid. She agreed to it because there was no jealousy, because it was business, and because with Karim's friends she was allowed to use the flat on Half Moon Street.

Often with these men there was no sex, but instead long noisy nights – too much food, and too much talk; and back in Brixton she fasted and exercised. The men were a useless combination of wealth and laziness, but they were so kind. They were always exposed, always waiting, always self-conscious and they always gave her too much money. She always felt she had the advantage. She still called it dating.

Some others were American – businessmen: they would answer the phone while she licked at them. 'I'm a little tied up at the moment – I'll get right back to you.' So many of them were vain about their hair, and one put on a rubber bathing cap before he got into bed with her. Another one told her in explicit detail how she was to take him into her mouth, and then he added sharply, 'But don't touch my hair.' They wore gold chains and expensive pendants around their necks. When they were violent or very stupid Lauren said, 'I've got to get up real early tomorrow!' and left quickly. If they protested at this, she said angrily, 'Don't you treat me like a hooker!' London was full of vulgar brainless bitches who would do anything for a weekend in Spain or a new pair of boots, but how many of these bitches had a masters in economics and a doctorate in international relations?

'I've just flown in from Hong Kong.'

'I've been there,' she said.

'I closed a pretty big deal.' They were both cautious and boastful.

She said, 'When I was in Hong Kong I was using the archives at the university. They've got some fantastic stuff on the People's Republic.'

But the men could be pathetic.

'My name's Lauren – what's yours?'

'Anthony J. Pistorino,' one man said.

He swallowed and blinked, because it was a lie – an hour later he forgot the name; but whenever she remembered it she laughed.

Another thing about the men was that they were seldom young. And when it was late and they were tired they looked older; their fatigue gave them a grief-stricken expression. Lord Bulbeck was like that – sorrowful eyes at midnight. He was well-known for his charity work and in his flat he kept photographs of himself receiving awards for his efforts. One night as Lauren was leaving Lord Bulbeck's flat in Queen's Gate, she paused and peered at a photograph. The foot of some aeroplane steps: Lord B. hugging a white-haired man.

'He was a very important man.'

She said, 'Really?'

'A very great statesman,' he said, as if to a tame little whore.

Lauren said, 'Ben Gurion, yes. That whole issue makes me feel very leftwing. But, before you say he was greatly misunderstood, I will tiptoe away.'

Lord Bulbeck looked up, amazed that she knew the face.

She decided that he was a lonely man. He said he had no friends now and often did not feel safe. That was why he had gone to the Jasmine Agency, and that was also why – after the first few times – he would not accept anyone but Lauren. One evening he took her to dinner at Claridge's. He was celebrating, he said. 'I'm seventy years old today.'

She said, 'I'm flattered that you included me.'

'There is no one else.'

Then she wanted to justify herself and gave him a little encouragement, too. She said, 'I've got a PhD, you know. In international relations. You didn't invite a dummy to your birthday party.'

He said, 'I know all about you. A man with my views has to take great precautions.'

'What sort of views?'

'The sort that are not changed by discussion,' he said, and that was that.

When he paid the bill he said, 'As a boy I used to walk past and see that man out front dressed in his fine uniform – his top hat and gold braid. I wanted so badly for him to tip his hat to me, and open the door. "Good evening, my lord."'

'But that's exactly what he did to you tonight.'

'Yes,' Lord Bulbeck said.

She said, 'I know just what you mean.'

He shook his head. He smiled at her, because it was too much trouble for him to explain. He began, saying, 'My father sold scrap iron in Limehouse. I was always a Labour man,' and then he gave up, though she knew that he was only trying to tell her that he had been made a Life Peer in one of the Honours Lists – did he really think an American wouldn't understand a simple thing like that?

She went home with him. She said, 'One of these days I'm going to take you to my place on Half Moon Street.'

'In the meantime, let us make do with a tango at Queen's Gate.'

Was it 'tango' or 'tangle'? Anyway, that was what he called it. She liked the way he talked. He said, 'Another bottoo of wine?' He said, 'Peepoo can be horriboo.'

These old men still had life left in them! They were slow to get started but could go on for ages. Lord Bulbeck always said, 'I've been planning this for days.' But another old man paid her double the rate to give her enemas.

He too had come through the agency. It made her wonder

about security. But then she discovered an answer of sorts. She asked another girl at the party. 'Arabella' – they all had assumed names like that – just laughed.

'Security? Don't be silly – whatever for?'

They were so stupid! Lauren wanted to say, 'Don't you know that you're an incredible security risk?'

But they didn't know – so they weren't. Their stupidity was a form of security. And only Lauren knew that she needed a baptismal certificate and a bank statement and her grandmother's maiden name on an application to go to some of these countries – but she could take all her clothes off and sit on the ambassador's face on the recommendation of Captain Twilley or 'Puddles'.

She knew that Captain Twilley found her cold.

He said, 'Karim likes you' or 'Lord Bulbeck wants you back' in a disbelieving way, and sometimes – not obscenely but with genuine curiosity – 'What have you *got*?'

'An education,' Lauren said. She did not like the man. He talked too much about the army.

He said, 'It doesn't take an education to get fucked.'

'No one fucks me,' she said, staring back at him. 'I do all the fucking. It used to annoy me, but now it suits me fine.'

She guessed that Captain Twilley must have told this to Madame Cybele – Lauren still could not bear to say the word 'Puddles'. The young pale woman invited her out for a drink and mentioned it: Lauren liked her big soft lips and idly imagined kissing and biting them. This was at the Ritz, both women drinking Perrier (four pounds for two glasses of water, but it was a lovely place), and Madame Cybele repeated Lauren's remark. It had been polished by the retelling and had the sound of a 'saying'.

Lauren said, 'I was thinking of Karim and his cameras. And that flat of his on Half Moon Street. Have you ever seen it?'

'He doesn't live in Half Moon Street,' Madame Cybele said.

'His studio, let's say,' Lauren said. 'I'd give anything to live there.'

'Don't ever say, "I'd give anything." It can be dangerous.' Madame Cybele looked at her from across the table. 'I know. I got here the hard way.'

Lauren said, 'That sounds awful.'

Madame Cybele seemed to read the questions in Lauren's eyes. She said disgustedly, 'The things they say to you!'

Lauren said, 'I hate the ones who don't wash.'

Madame Cybele shrugged. Why was it that her bruises never quite vanished, but lingered as faded inky stains on her very white skin?

Lauren liked her for saying then, 'They never think about a woman's pleasure.'

'All they ever want to do is bum me,' Lauren said. 'I always come home feeling like I've been riding a bike – they're killing my ass.'

Madame Cybele smiled – it was the first time Lauren had ever seen her do so, and Lauren was encouraged to ask her the question that had remained unanswered for weeks.

'Did you ever send me a videotape?'

'No.' But Madame Cybele became watchful.

'That's why I looked you up that first day. It was a program about escort agencies. Yours was in it.'

'I know. It was a stupid program.'

'So who could have sent it to me?'

Madame Cybele stood up and kissed her and said, 'Be very careful.' Lauren returned the kiss tenderly and felt the young woman's frail body beneath her winter coat, like a bird's bones under its feathers.

Usually, she was glad that she seldom saw Madame Cybele, and she avoided Captain Twilley. And the girls she saw at parties were too busy hustling to talk. She was alone. She preferred it this way. She regarded herself as a success, both at the agency and at the Institute.

'I've got so much work to do,' she said. But she only went through the motions; she never intended to finish. What was the point? Being an escort had calmed her and made her undemanding at the Institute; and her wide reading had made her a sought-after companion. Now Captain Twilley was polite when he called to give her an appointment, and General Newhouse spoke of extending her Fellowship.

She wrote a paper on the possibilities of a banking crisis precipitated by the overproduction of oil and consequent pricecutting. Her emphasis in the paper was on the economics of Third World countries and their defaulting on debts. The arguments were hers, but Julian had helped her substantiate them by turning over to her all his notes. Afterwards, the General said, 'One word, Miss Slaughter.' It was never 'Mopsy' or 'Doctor.' 'I think that theme is well worth pursuing for publication, but you desperately need documentation.' She remembered this, because within the next half hour a man she had never seen before was kneeling against her and saying, 'Lauren, put this in your mouth.'

The time came for the Study Group to leave for their tour of the Gulf. Julian said, 'We'll miss you.'

'Send me a postcard.'

He misunderstood. He said, 'If it was any other year, I'm sure you'd be going instead of me.'

That was the sort of gentle, dumb remark he made.

Lauren had over three thousand pounds, cash, stuffed in the coffee pot she never used. She had standing invitations in Kuwait, Bahrain and Qatar. Lord Bulbeck had a regular date with her on Wednesdays and once he had said, 'I don't know what to do about my will. There's my flat, my books, and all my furniture – I shall do whatever you tell me.' She had had a long discussion with the editor of *Arabia Today* ('Pretty much the same as yesterday,' she had said when he told her his paper's name; but she had proven her seriousness by asking about the Sunni-Shia split). 'Anthony J. Pistorino' had wanted to take her to Geneva for a week. Karim was always saying, 'Use my driver.' She believed that she could have anything she wanted.

She said sweetly to Julian, 'One of these days I might get lucky and go. Tell me all about it. But be careful in Kuwait. You'll go in a tight end and come out a wide receiver.'

He inclined his head at her.

'It's a football expression.'

He said, 'Not English football.'

The day Julian and the others left Lauren met a man named Shafique at Half Moon Street – one of Karim's friends, though when she mentioned Karim the man denied that he knew him, and he mysteriously said, 'Who do you work for?'

'Myself,' she said.

One day Ivan Shepherd called the Institute and asked Lauren to dinner. It seemed odd being called 'Lauren' here, but she looked at her appointment book and said yes – tomorrow – and what was the name of his hotel?

He said, 'Ivan Shepherd – don't you remember me?'

'Yes,' she said, 'a long time ago on the subway!'

'Six weeks ago on the tube,' he said. 'How about it?'

'I'm really much too busy these days,' she said; but she wanted to say, *You've got to be joking!*

'Busy doing what?'

Instead of replying she said, 'Hey, did you ever send me anything in the mail?'

'No,' he said, and repeated, 'Busy doing what?'

'Having dinner, actually,' and hung up before he heard her laugh at his presumption, for even if he meant dinner – and he probably didn't – he would be getting free what a grateful man would pay two hundred pounds for.

That was the usual price and they *were* grateful, too, because when she said, 'I want to give you pleasure,' she meant it.

The paradox that particular day, when Ivan Shepherd invited her for dinner – why did men always mention food when they meant fucking? – that same day, Roger, the Assistant Librarian, saw her in the Reference Section and squeezed her breast as if he was honking a horn and she said, 'That *hurt*!' He said, 'If you tell anyone, I'll kill you,' and looked crazily at her.

Also, that same day – this was why she gave up her diary, because there was too much – Karim sent her to visit one of his Kuwaiti friends and the man spent the whole evening drinking tea and earnestly describing desalinization schemes.

It was not sex so much as safety these men looked for. Most of them were wealthy men whom this big foreign city turned into bewildered boys. They knew very little about life in London. They had never heard of Brixton, they thought that a hundred pounds for two in a restaurant was about right, and they were afraid of the dark. They knew nothing.

Lauren said, 'A girlfriend of mine's toilet froze over a few months ago.'

'No.' The man was German. This was at the Inn-on-the-Park. They were in his room watching a pornographic video in which a toilet figured.

He said, 'Your friend was lying to you. It is not cold enough. In Hamburg, yes. In London, no.'

'That's what she said. She never lies.'

'Impossible.'

It made her feel like a heroine; it made her hate her room. She smiled, determined to move out.

'You like it, *ja*?' The German was pleased. He thought she was smiling at the man and the woman and the toilet.

The following Wednesday she told Lord Bulbeck that she was looking for a place to rent in Mayfair. 'Or Queen's Gate?' he said, suggesting that she might want to move in with him; but she was not ready for that. He said he would look around. Some days passed and then, impatiently, she asked the agency to get in touch with him – that was the procedure: a girl could not telephone a client directly. Lord Bulbeck phoned her and said he would gladly find her a flat – and he would pay the rent. 'You don't understand,' she said, but then he rang off saying a motion was being proposed. She tried him twice through the agency, and twice he returned her call: he had one or two leads, he said.

The second time Lauren signalled that she wanted to get in touch with Lord Bulbeck, Madame Cybele said, 'I shouldn't say this to you, but you are being very stupid.'

Lauren said, 'You're right. You shouldn't say that to me.'

And then she had her wish. Karim took her to the flat on Half Moon Street – to photograph her, she thought. But, no: he toured the three rooms with her. There were cushions and carpets where there had been bare floors, and the room with the clear plastic chairs and the Finnish exercise bike now had plants and bright curtains.

Karim said, 'It's yours. I know the landlord. He needs someone reliable like you. An academic person.'

Of course – because it was people like Roger who treated her like a hooker. *The only person who ever assaulted me and threatened me with murder was an assistant librarian.*

Karim brought her the papers; she signed, she paid, she got the keys and a one-year lease. And she moved into the top floor flat on Half Moon Street, number three.

The street itself was nothing – a narrow connection to Piccadilly, the backs of buildings, a small hotel, some black railings, the pale smooth pillars of the Naval and Military Club. But the flat was special, and it made her so happy that when she thought of herself in it, or saw herself in a mirror there (she had always liked the suddenness and the teasing glamor of mirrors: there were five big ones here), she felt important and beautiful and very proud. The first thing she wanted to do at Half Moon Street was call Hugo Van Arkady and say, 'Come over for drinks some evening.' That meant everything. She also wanted to call Lord Bulbeck and treat the good old boy to a free night – it would mean a lot to him. But she couldn't call either man: agency rules. She didn't complain – this isolation as an escort left her free to go to the Institute. And in any case one day soon Lord Bulbeck,

and probably Van Arkady, would call her and come to the
flat and say, 'Ah, you've arrived!'

Half Moon Street was at the very centre of things. She had
found the middle of London. And the most remarkable thing
about the flat was that though Lauren was often alone in it she
was never lonely. That was the test of all property and that was the
measure of her happiness on Half Moon Street. It was everything
she wanted, and she found her solitude delicious.

She had left Brixton without telling anyone. She had wanted
to vanish without a trace – those very words occurred to her.
What did Brixton know of Mayfair? This was the London she
had always imagined herself in, and as with many people whose
fondest wish is granted she felt very healthy, and stronger than
ever. She slept soundly. She became very conscientious about her
food. Long ago she had banned salt, white sugar, milk, cream or
anything with preservatives. Now she banned what she called
animal products – no meat at all, not even chicken bouillon
cubes. She ate fresh fruit and steamed vegetables, brown rice,
lentils, roasted nuts, mushrooms and yogurt. She tried to include
half a cup of bran a day. She made stock from potato peel, she
drank herbal tea and bottled water, and after a run she had
honey on wholemeal toast. Her weakness was for peanut butter.
'I do one of these a week,' she told Rahman – one of Karim's
friends – holding up a jar of Harrods' Peanut Butter. Occasionally, she ate fish – poached or broiled, but never fried. 'Like the
Hindus say, fish are a kind of sea-vegetable.'

She ran without stopping entirely around the edge of Hyde Park
every morning, clockwise from Hyde Park Corner to Kensington,
then north to Bayswater Road and along it to Marble Arch, and
down the broad walk parallel to Park Lane. It was seven miles.
After a shower – she had four showers a day but only shampooed
her hair once – she went to the Institute: library in the mornings,
an apple and a piece of Cheddar for lunch, and conferences or a
seminar in the afternoon. The place was unusually quiet – nearly
all the Fellows had gone on the Study Tour to the Gulf, even

Bridgid, who was supposed to be doing starvation somewhere else, and Fairman the Asia man. Willymot was upstairs counting nuclear warheads, but she never saw him. In the evening after her stretching and a spell on the exercise bike she took agency calls.

It was surprising how many of her dates – she hated Captain Twilley's calling them 'punters' – were interested in eating right. Not Arabs, of course – they stuck to traditional food and were (as well as being generous) the most inflexible and narrow-minded people she had ever known. But Americans, Germans, and all the Scandinavian people liked talking about what Lauren called the dynamics of diet. The sex was predictable – with Karim's friends it was always perfunctory and nearly always bumming; and everyone else wanted to be sucked off. So much for the varieties of sexual experience in Western Civilization! Yet it made life simple and she was glad of that.

But afterwards at the late supper she never ate she often talked about food.

'These tomatoes are very bad for you,' she said. 'They're full of acid. Potato skins are good roughage and loaded with vitamins, and there's a lot of goodness in these snowpeas – unless they boiled them. People are always boiling the goodness out of things. But stay away from these dumplings and that gravy. I always think sausages are just plain destructive. I'm a salad person–'

She could tell how civilized a man was by his willingness to listen to reason about his diet. Savages were the real junk-food freaks, and drinkers and smokers too. She hated smokers so much she refused to kiss them – it was the only line she drew – but kissing in the traditional way was the rarest act she performed. They hugged her and squashed their hands on her; they pushed her head down. But she didn't object. Her power was in making them feel powerful, and sex often made her feel like a ravishing witch, for after they had come they were small and weak, and they would need her again to make them strong: the crude magic worked. She said, 'Fuck my face,' and helped them struggle, and when they were done she swallowed and said, 'It's good, you know – it's all protein.'

She considered writing a paper on diet and health, using Lévi-Strauss's studies of Indian culture and food as a model for Arabia. She wanted to look at high blood pressure and heart disease among the super rich in the oil-producing countries. And what about gastric ulcers and respiratory ailments – all that drinking and smoking by simple desert people? But General Newhouse said no. It was not that sort of institute.

'Unless you plan to publish your findings in *The Lancet* I suggest you carry on with your study of the recycling of oil revenues. What a pity you weren't chosen for that Study Tour.'

She told Karim that she wanted to talk to Van Arkady. She wanted the victory of his visiting her in Half Moon Street.

Karim said, 'He is very busy. He can't speak to you.'

'Is his bank connected with your embassy in any way?'

'In a way, yes,' he said, challenging her with a smile, 'because I have no embassy.'

'You're being mysterious again.'

'Because you are asking improper questions,' he said. 'Now take your clothes off, my darling. Do you mind?'

'Why should I mind?' And she laughed as she flung them off. Karim was so generous. He had found her this flat, he had given her most of the furniture and that Finnish exercise cycle and a leather chair from Barkers and a Lalique panther made of lead crystal from Harrods. 'But I hate your friend Latif. He's a bully.'

'What does he do?'

Karim was using a large gun-like camera – making a videotape of her pedalling the bike.

She said, 'He spits in my mouth.'

'Lift your knees a bit higher, darling.'

She was not posing but really pedalling for the sake of the film. She said, 'This is great exercise!'

'Stop smiling,' he said. 'What about Rahman?'

'I always confuse him with Raheem.'

'But Raheem is the hungry one.'

'How do you know that?' and turned around to face him.

Karim said, 'Keep pedalling.'

'Yeah,' she said. 'He bites me. Sometimes he leaves marks, and I have to wear my tracksuit to hide them. Some of your friends are real animals.'

'Perhaps only with you,' he said.

She said, 'That's very true. Only I know what they're really like.'

Karim said, 'Go on.'

'Forget it,' she said. 'Rahman gave me some perfume. Tina Farina. In a limited-edition bottle.'

Karim said, 'I don't leave marks,' over the whirr of his camera.

But Lauren was thinking of that terrible German and his toilet movies, and the man who made her put on rubber underwear ('I don't even wear the normal kind!' she complained), and the Spaniard who commanded, 'You must give me a black kiss. Do you know what is a black kiss?'

That was what they were really like: they had small hot secrets.

She said, 'There's no sex any more.'

Karim had stopped listening. His camera was whirring. He said, 'Pedal harder!'

This sex: a virgin could do it and remain a virgin. It was virginal sex, or rather, not sex at all. It was service: she did not feel violated. She was asked to cooperate or perform; to see or be seen. The men groped across her body, some did not touch her at all but merely watched her use her fingers on herself. Often, nothing but her attendance was required – at a banquet or a party. She was once in the same room as the Duke of Edinburgh. The rest was physical, and some of it high school stuff, but it was not sex – not fucking anyhow – and though it frequently confused her it left her feeling pure. Now she understood Madame Cybele's distraction, and those bruises on the young woman's white skin.

## 6

When a man asked for more time all he wanted was time. At dinner he might say, 'I want you for breakfast, too,' but he would then spend the rest of the night snoring beside her in his king-sized bed, or else showing her off to his friends – towing her in and out of rooms for them to admire. So greedy, so eager, so puny! Most of them had nothing but money, which seemed to Lauren like the cruellest form of destitution. They overreached themselves, these men, in sex as in their business lives. Their loneliness made them unreasonable. But usually they just submerged themselves in sleep.

All that was required of her was tact – don't mention the uneaten meal, the sudden sleep, the unused and useless portion of the jeroboam of champagne; not a word about the hopeless fumble and apology, that bump in the night: 'Sorry, I don't think – oh, never mind–' She wanted to say, 'You don't have to apologize, darling.' They were demanding by nature, but in the circumstances in which she saw them they were children. She wanted to say: *Your eyes are bigger than your – et cetera!* They made her feel like third helpings. And there she lay until they woke up blinking at her pretty face and honey-blonde hair.

Often they wanted no more than her companionship. One man, a superstitious Portuguese – banking – spent hours showing her his good-luck charms, and they included a shrunken head – a hard hairy prune with sewn-up lips. A man from Needles, California, who was working on an oil rig in the North Sea, had a gold belt buckle engraved *If You Ain't Oilfield You Ain't Shit*. With such men it wasn't sex. It was that they did not want to be left alone and lonesome in this wet winter-dark city. Sometimes it was just like a sink.

This particular man asked for a weekend. He said his name was Guy, and Lauren knew he wasn't lying – Guy was not the kind of name you made up.

'What did you have in mind?'

Once a man had said: *What kind of knickers–*?

'Nothing special,' Guy said.

For a weekend! But really it was just the sort of vagueness she expected for this length of time. He was like the rest of them, except that he was being honest.

She said, 'A weekend's a long time.'

'In the country it passes quite quickly,' he said. He sounded cute and nervous. 'We'll be staying with friends. It's all arranged.'

He picked her up late Friday afternoon at the Institute in his Triumph. He was young, about twenty-eight – but some of these English people could look much older than they were, wearing incredibly ugly clothes and with terrible posture, and there were thirty-year-olds in London who had grey hair. Guy was surprisingly good-looking and probably played tennis – he certainly didn't smoke. He walked on the balls of his feet in a tennis-player's way. Now Lauren was glad it was going to be a weekend.

The agency fee for this was three hundred pounds. Lauren considered asking only another three hundred, she liked him so much, but she didn't want him to think she was a hooker, so she decided on an even thousand. She kept the price to herself for the moment.

He said, 'I love finishing work on a Friday and leaving London. It's like breaking out of jail.'

He drove too fast – over seventy: the English were so childish about speed, and the other Europeans were worse, French and Italians especially. But at least he kept both hands on the wheel.

They were on the Great West Road and had now passed the suburbs of semi-detached houses, the vegetable fields farther on, the airport. Now it was dark, and just the occasional scatter of lighted windows far off the road indicated a town or a village. Now and then a sign saying *Wales* or *Oxford* flew at them from the darkness ahead.

His dog woke up and began barking. Lauren had taken the thing for a hairy blanket in the jump seat. She felt his damp nose

at the back of her ear and something else against her hair –
perhaps his jowls or his flapping tongue. He stopped barking,
he slurped at the side of her head; and she smiled, remembering
much worse men.

Guy said, 'Get down, you stupid dog!' and the animal
retreated.

'He doesn't bother me,' Lauren said.

'He thinks he's a person, that's his problem. He's really neurotic. He prevents me from having anything like a worthwhile
relationship with anyone else. He gets jealous.'

Lauren was enjoying the solitary pleasure of smiling in the
dark. She had not been this happy for months. Yes, she thought.
They never had animals, and they were never so young, and never
so relaxed. Guy was an unusual fellow. He wasn't shifty or
apologetic. I could even stand the dog, she thought. She saw
herself walking the beast in Hyde Park on Sunday mornings and
buying newspapers at the corner and bringing them back to Guy.
He wasn't like any of the others. This weekend was going to be
fun.

'What's his name?'

'Him? Shmuel.'

'What's it mean?'

'It means he's a special sort of mutt, like me.'

Lauren said, 'I think you are pretty special.' When he laughed
at this she added, 'I think I am, too,' and he stopped laughing.

Answering one of her direct questions, Guy said that he worked
at a merchant bank. He startled Lauren by saying, 'I have a
rather lowly position at the moment, but if I get a transfer I'll
move up a few grades. I've put in for Hong Kong.'

Lauren said, 'There's much more money in the Gulf. Dubai,
for example, would be perfect. I've been to Hong Kong – so I
know. The Gulf is my field now.'

Guy said, 'The Gulf might be awkward for me.'

'Not if you want to do business,' she said. 'You should see the
profiles of some of these Gulf banks. Mega-bucks!' There was

not much light on Guy's face, but he seemed to be smiling and nodding in agreement. She said, 'I bet we've got a lot in common.'

Why didn't he say something?

She said, 'We could meet there. It might be fun travelling together.'

He smiled again, but was staring straight ahead at the empty road. Finally he said softly, 'I'm sure you know much more than I do about the Gulf.'

'Want to know a secret?' Lauren said, but she had already started to laugh. 'I don't know shit about the Gulf! I chose it because it's the opposite of China that was my husband's big thing. But the Gulf – God, I don't know the difference between emirates and interest rates, and I'm supposed to be able to talk Gulf economics! Hey, I'm just sucking my thumb.'

Guy's expression did not change. He was still smiling in a studious way at the tunnel his headlights made on the road ahead. Lauren wondered whether she was boring him.

She said, 'I don't know why I told you that,' and frowned. 'Maybe it's because I've never told anyone else.'

He said, 'You've got a husband.'

'*Had* a husband.' He had missed the point – seized on the most unimportant detail.

'And China!' he said.

He really had missed the point by a mile. She said, 'You've never been there or else you wouldn't be so wild about Hong Kong. China's just boring and depressing, but Hong Kong is worse in a different way – if it was human you'd say it was tasteless, spoiled, overweight and had high blood pressure. When the lease expires in 1997 the PRC is going to take over and kick the shit out of it. People are already leaving – and you want to go there!'

He said, 'You know these places intimately, of course.'

'Sure. My Chinese work got me the Hemisphere fellowship.'

'What about your escort work?'

'It's not work.'

He said nothing. It was an English habit not to hit the ball back. You sometimes had to serve again and again.

'I'm flexible,' she said.

He kept driving.

'I can fit anything in,' she said.

Maybe he hated himself for being with her.

'I live alone, so most of my evenings are free.'

He said, 'So you're not seeing anyone at the moment.'

She laughed. 'I'm seeing a lot of people! But not steadily. Do you know what I mean by a sex-partner?'

'Approximately. Have you got one?'

'Not at the moment.'

'And yet,' Guy said, 'something tells me you've got your hands full.'

She said, 'You'd be surprised how much I can handle.'

He chose not to reply – well, what could he say? And he was concentrating on his driving. They drove off the motorway onto a dark twisting road, walled by thick hedges which showed in the headlights.

Lauren meanwhile had been reflecting in a hopeful way, and now her mind was made up. She said, 'I'm sure it would work out.'

'Sorry?'

'You and me,' she said. 'In the Gulf. Dubai, for example. A kind of working vacation at first. I'm sure we've both got a lot of contacts there. We could just play it by ear and share expenses – see how we get along. It might be fun.'

He said, 'I put in for Hong Kong, but even if I tried to get a transfer to the Gulf it might not go through for another year.' He sniggered in a self-deprecating way and added, 'I don't fancy my chances.'

'You'd get it easily!'

'You don't know a thing about me,' he said, almost sternly.

Then Lauren realized that she had gone too far, planned too much – she was always skipping ahead. But she had been dealing with rich successful men; she wasn't used to young struggling executives who called themselves 'middle management' and were anxious for a one-rung promotion.

'It's not far,' Guy said. 'Just a few more miles.'

Lauren said, 'You don't have to apologize, darling.'

He had been there before – she could tell by the way he raced up the driveway, taking the two curves fast and scattering pebbles as he braked before the stone canopy at the front door. Lauren was saying, 'Hi!' to the old man approaching the car, but Guy said nothing, only gave the man the key to his boot, and then Lauren realized she was warmly greeting the butler – the servant anyhow – babbling at him. She was embarrassed but decided to make a democratic virtue of the gaffe and kept talking to the old man as he heaved the bags at the door.

She sensed something like hostility in the man – fear and anger – he was trying to drive her off and save himself, because how could he explain to his employer – the woman who was walking slowly towards Lauren – that this American girl had insisted on chatting with him?

'Guy!' the woman cried and lifted her hands to his face. She was tall and bony and sure of herself. She wore a shapeless grey suit and had white streaks in her hair. But Lauren saw that she was not more than thirty-five or so – she had young skin and lovely hands.

'And this is your young lady,' the woman said, turning to Lauren. 'You must be the lovely Julia.'

'I'm not,' Lauren said. 'Does this mean I have to go back home?'

Guy said, 'Maura, this is–'

'Dr Slaughter,' Lauren said, putting her hand out. 'But you can call me Lauren.'

The woman did not take her hand, and so Lauren stood there feeling like someone who had just dropped something.

Maura said, 'I'd much rather call you Dr Slaughter.'

Lauren said, 'If it'll make you feel better.'

Maura was still speaking. 'Like someone in Trollope.'

They had been walking quickly as they spoke and were now past the hall and approaching a long room where two men and another woman were sitting before a fireplace. The men got to their feet as Maura entered with Guy and Lauren.

'I always like a little Trollope in bed before I go to sleep,' one of the men said and smiled at Lauren.

'So does Sam,' the other man said.

'Wasn't it Harold Macmillan who said that?'

'Surely it was Lennox Berkeley?'

Lauren saw that each person in the room was sneaking glances at her and, as they knew Guy, probably sizing her up. Was she good for him? Were they serious? Did she have anything to offer? Did she have a nice figure? You silly fucks, she thought.

The other woman, introduced to her as Sidney, asked – apropos of what? – 'Are you interested in music, Dr Slaughter?'

She said, 'I like playing the mouth organ.'

'Do you know English music?'

'I think it's tremendously underrated – particularly in America,' Lauren said.

'There!' Maura said.

'The Stranglers are way ahead of their time,' Lauren said. 'They're practically geniuses.'

'You're a very brave girl.' Was that man smiling?

Sidney said, 'I'm not familiar with the Stranglers, I'm afraid.'

'"Shah-Shah a Go-Go"? "Baroque Bordello"? "Walking on the beaches, looking at the peaches"? "Rattus Norvegicus"?'

Lauren stared at them as she spoke.

'Slaughter,' the woman named Sidney said in a thoughtful way. 'Don't I know your father from Nairobi?'

Maura said, 'I'll show you upstairs.'

They had separate rooms, she and Guy, and not even adjoining ones.

Lauren said, 'Is this going to work out?'

'Perfectly.'

'You'll need a map!'

But she wanted to say, *I hope these people aren't good friends of yours, because I sort of hate them.* Instead she said nothing; she liked Guy too much to embarrass him. She saw that he was a few years younger than she and she wanted him more: *My young husband* . . .

She knew they were trying to mock her, but she did not know whether they were succeeding – and that was maddening. They were certainly telling private jokes, which was a way of ignoring her; but were they ridiculing her?

'Americans put such extraordinary things on their feet,' Maura said, after Lauren and Guy returned to the long room.

They kept saying things like that. But this time Lauren decided not to let it pass.

She said, 'Every time I see an Englishman I think, "What's that stuff on his head?"'

She felt their gaze on her.

She said, 'And it's usually hair.'

Alan – Maura's husband – said, 'You're new in London, I take it.'

'Sort of. I could have had Peking, but I'd been there before. I figured I'd try London and if it didn't work out I'd look at my options.'

'I understand,' Maura said. 'She said to herself, "I'll suck it and see." That's very American.'

Did they know something?

Alan said, 'I can't think what's keeping Sam.'

Guy said, 'He's probably speaking. You know Sam.'

'Yes,' the woman named Sidney said. 'He's a very passionate man in actual fact, isn't he?'

'On certain subjects,' Guy said.

More private jokes, Lauren thought: mock the guest by keeping her in the dark. She had an urge to say: *There was a girl named Roberta Wiljanen at my school who had six toes* –

'Your young lady must be ravenous.'

No, just bored stiff – and she hated to be spoken about in the third person: the big English thing. She said, 'I'm not hungry at all. I had an apple, some walnuts and plain yogurt just before I left London.'

Maura, suspecting, looked annoyed.

'Vegetarian,' Lauren said, and beamed.

She had kicked off her shoes. They looked at her feet.

Maura said, 'There's roast beef for dinner.'

'I'll just have a little salad.'

'Perhaps we can organize an omelette for you.'

Lauren let disgust flicker across her face. 'In some ways eggs are worse than meat.'

'Now I never knew that!' the second man said. His name was George – 'Geo,' the others called him. He had seemed fascinated by what Lauren had said, but it was all show. He turned abruptly to Maura and said, 'Next week at this time you'll be in Les Houches.'

'Aren't you going this year?'

'Been,' he said. 'But we're fed up with Chamonix.' He smacked his lips and said, 'Val d'Isère. Fabulous. Powder. Three thousand metres. Scared Sidney rigid.'

Guy said, 'I was at Mégève over Christmas.'

'Was it fabulous?' Maura asked. 'I've heard Mégève's heaven.'

Guy said, 'I think I marginally prefer Klosters. Greta Garbo lives there, but so what?'

They were off, they kept talking, and they had turned their backs on Lauren. No one addressed a word to her, and it took her some minutes of listening to work out that they were talking about skiing. From this conversation she was totally excluded – she wondered whether it had something to do with her having blurted out that she was a vegetarian. God, she had enjoyed telling them that. It always wrong-footed a hostess when you saved that for the last minute.

She hated this skiing business – people they knew, places they'd

been, heaven, fabulous, exquisite food. It was all incredibly boring, just a recitation of names, because how could you discuss skiing except to say that one place was good and another was lousy? It was stupid and the proof was would anyone talk this way about swimming? And it was the same kind of thing.

But the worst of it was that Lauren had never been skiing.

'I'm told that Les Arcs is really superb. We didn't book in time. You fly to Geneva and take a coach. The pistes run right up to the hotel apparently.'

Should she say that she had skiied but had given it up after a serious leg injury; or still skiied every year in Aspen – yes, we have lots of skiing right in Colorado; or should she mock the whole idea of it and say that it was like talking about swimming? But no one asked her. The conversation did not come her way. She didn't count. And when Guy became solicitous and asked her in a whisper whether he could get her another glass of Malvern water she began to dislike him and to wish that she had never come.

They're really and truly awful, she thought, and she grew a little sentimental thinking about the busy breathless man she would be with tonight; she thought of Karim, and of Lord Bulbeck, and their loneliness. She had liked Guy on his own, and she hoped it would be like that again upstairs.

'I much prefer the food at the French resorts.'

They were still talking about skiing!

'Bumpy gave me a new pair of boots for Christmas,' Alan said.

'I got a really chic anorak,' Sidney said. 'And matching salopettes.'

Anorak? Salopettes? Lauren wanted to laugh at them.

Perhaps they noticed her smiling, because Maura said, 'Do you ski?'

'Periodically.'

Then an alert listening look brightened Maura's face. Lauren had seen that look before on other people – it was a house-owner hearing the sound of someone in the driveway. It was inaudible to everyone else; you had to own the house to hear it.

'That must be Sam.'

Maura went into the hallway and after a suspended silence she shouted at her guest and there was a commotion – stamping feet, the banging of a suitcase, a loud kiss, a slammed door.

'He's here–'

And now the men were calling across the long room, and bantering, 'We'd just about given you up, Sam,' because the guest was so late, and in this chatter Guy said, 'Hello, uncle.'

Lauren was thinking: Another one. And since they all pretended to be old-fashioned here she decided to keep her back turned and go on toasting her toes until they got around to introducing her. She sat with the cat on her lap, thinking about skiing, how she had never gone. But you couldn't do everything.

Now the guest was in the room, treading the carpet.

Guy smiled with a kind of insistence at Lauren – he wanted her to get up and greet his uncle. His uncle! England was all relatives!

'And this is Dr Slaughter,' Maura was saying. 'She is rather preoccupied at the moment with our cat, Rudy. Perhaps she is a vet? Dr Slaughter, I'd like you to meet Lord Bulbeck.'

She turned quickly and saw that he was smiling. He shook her hand and said, 'Pleased to meet you, my dear.'

She could not see either affection or anger in his smile, and feeling off balance she looked for Guy. He was talking with Sidney, the younger of the two women, who was so self-assured with her big knockers, pretending she didn't see them swinging. Guy looked interested and responsive, that flirtatious energy, that nervous thirst, and Sidney was enjoying his discomfort and turning her headlights on him. Guy was different now from the circumspect young man who had driven her up from London. If Lord Bulbeck had not been there she would have taken Guy aside and whispered, 'I'm going to sneak into your room upstairs and eat you.'

But Lord Bulbeck was still smiling vaguely at her, with a kind of forced politeness. And, when Maura told him she was off to Les Houches, he said, 'I know it's not an originoo thought, but the French have no principoos.'

'That was a very flattering profile of you in *The Times* last week,' Geo said.

'I don't find it flattering when journalists refer to my nose as bowbus.'

'I meant your part in those Middle East peace talks.'

'I'm just an errand boy,' Lord Bulbeck said.

He had the floor. When he spoke everyone listened.

He said, 'It's a horriboo errand.'

Lauren loved the way he talked, his little bubble-blower's mouth puckered under his fat nose: *originoo . . . principoo . . . bowbus . . . horriboo.* And she was sorry that he was probably mad at her for finding her here with someone else. But that was tough luck for him: everyone paid, which was why she was free.

The hostess seated Lord Bulbeck next to herself and separated Lauren from Guy, so that Lauren was stuck with Geo, the middle-aged man who said, 'I came to skiing rather late,' and then began boasting, in his English way, about what frightful risks he took and how bad he was.

For Lauren, all dinners were very long: it was her being a vegetarian that made this so – she knew; and as a non-drinker she found most parties interminable. Her only diversion was in seeing how carnivores and boozers underwent a personality change as they crammed the junk into their mouths. Meat-eaters grew tired in an animalistic way – did they know how long it took flesh to be digested? – and drinkers just got crazier. Now, after the meal, everyone was clumsier and louder, sort of stumbling like squinting zoo monkeys after their feed. Lauren almost ran from the dining room when it was over – she hadn't exercised all day: that was the trouble – but Lord Bulbeck headed her off, and before the others overtook them he said, 'You're looking well.'

'I hope you're not mad,' she said. 'I never met these people before. I came with Guy.'

'Of course—'

'You probably want to kill me. But I didn't know he was your nephew.'

'If he wasn't you wouldn't be here,' Lord Bulbeck said. 'And neither would I.'

'I don't get it.'

'I'll explain everything later,' he said. 'Upstairs.'

She said, 'I'm a Fellow at the Hemisphere Institute,' because the others had entered the room.

He said, 'You're a lovely fellow!'

But upstairs, after midnight, Lord Bulbeck did not explain anything. He came to her room and in his big soft funny-uncle way he held her and told her how beautiful she was.

She said, 'So it was a trap.'

'I know all about traps,' he said. 'People try to trap me often enough.'

'But it's a pretty roundabout way of getting me into bed,' she said.

'Very roundabout, very safe.'

She said, 'Think how safe it would be in France.'

'Frants,' he said. So he found her pronunciation funny, too!

She said, 'I want to go skiing, Sam.'

'Anything you want, ducky, but please don't call me Sam at breakfast.'

It was a perfect weekend. She was two people, and it worked so well she had at times glimpses of a third – the person she believed in and trusted. On Sunday evening she drove back to London with Guy, and neither said a single word.

7

They had traveled in the same plane to Geneva; but in different sections – Lord Bulbeck flew under the name Green in First Class and Lauren was Mopsy Fairlight (it was an old passport) in Tourist. They went through Customs at the same time; but Lord Bulbeck was waved along by an official and he was picked up by a Mercedes flying a United Nations flag, while Lauren took a taxi. They were both staying at the Holiday Inn, but in separate rooms. And yet at midnight they were together – in his room – and again he marvelled at her beauty.

'You Americans are so big and healthy.' He spoke with gratitude and even humility. He said, 'I'm so lucky to know you. I feel puny and old.'

'That's why you don't want us to be seen together.'

'That's not the principoo reason.'

She laughed hard, and she laughed again when he said the word, 'genitoos.'

'You'll be real healthy after the skiing,' she said.

'We shall see.'

That was their first night in Geneva, which seemed to her an uglier and duller place than shoreline Chicago, which it somewhat resembled – Chicago with mountains. Lord Bulbeck told her that his committee would keep him there for a few days and that he would follow her to the resort.

'You're going tomorrow,' he said. 'Get an early start. The car's coming for you at eight. It's a four-hour drive to Bourg St Maurice, and I'm told the hotel is on an impossiboo road at 1,800 metres.'

'You have to promise on the Bible to be there.'

'The Byboo is not my book,' he said. 'But I promise.'

Lauren left him in the dark early morning and went to her room to pack. The driver was young and very silent, but she saw his eyes in the rear-view mirror; and she was reminded of a taxi driver in London, who took her back to Brixton and demanded nine pounds because it was after midnight, and she had said, 'Come upstairs – wouldn't you rather be paid there?' and she had done him in a few minutes and sent him down exhausted. That was fun, but that was before. She thought: I'll only do it for fun again, and if I want it.

They crossed drearily into France on wet gritty streets which continued for miles, and then to Annecy where the snow was coated with a black lacework of soot. The lake was an improvement, and soon the light was better and they were in sight of high mountains, and an hour later they were climbing them. They made their way along the sides of valleys, the road like a gutter hacked across the steepness. There was snow everywhere and vast knobbed icicles hung from cliffs and from the glacial sluices in the crevasses between the valleys.

Beneath the rising road was a loud, almost demented-sounding river battering greeny boulders and crashing along the deep stone trough, uselessly shoving at the walls. The mountains had no peaks: they penetrated a ceiling of cloud that was like sky-stuffing and that in places had slipped sideways to reveal in torn holes sky the color of tropical water – aquamarine that seemed as pure and soft as a harmless gas. She thought that oxygen must look like that. The snow by the roadside was pushed into precipitous heaps, and nearer Bourg St Maurice what people she saw were either skiers or peasants – wearing absurdly bright colors and ridiculous hats, or else dark heavy coats and black boots.

The last ten miles to the high slopes of Les Arcs were a twisting ascent in which Lauren began to imagine herself upraised on a skyhook that made everything around her vanish – the cliffs, the ice, the pines, even the road – everything but the car in which she sat. The car seemed to tremble on an air current. Her ears crackled like static. She was in empty space and only she was real; but no – it was the whiteness of the snow.

The next day was sunny and bright, and she was amazed that at this altitude, among all this snow, she was comfortable and not even cold. She left her ski suit unzipped. She was in a beginners' class, on rented skis, very short ones; the resort was famous for this method.

'Are you alone?' It was an American woman sitting beside her in the chairlift. Lauren had taken her for a German – she had German eyes: ice-blue, humorless, lovely.

Lauren said, 'At the moment.'

'I was just wondering if you had a partner – a husband or a friend.'

'I have both,' Lauren said. 'Periodically.'

'I like you!' the woman said. 'My husband's a great skier, but he's so competitive! He's at the Aiguille Rouge today. What's that – ten thousand feet? He wants to get dropped out of a helicopter somewhere around Mon Blong. I got sick of staying in Vence, that's where we live, he's with GE. But I hate being a beginner. I was watching you stumble up to this lift and I thought: She's just as bad as me. I'm Ellen.'

She had said too much; she had spoiled it, so all Lauren said was, 'How big is the class?'

'Just the five of us from last week, and you, and that new guy.' Ellen was pointing her ski poles at the man in the swinging chair in front of them – his head made smooth and compact by a snugly-fitting ski hat.

'Here we are,' Lauren said, seeing the man glide away from his chair at the top of the lift.

'Don't knock me over,' Ellen said, and just as they arrived she panicked, shoved Lauren sideways and then tripped her.

Lauren was emptying the snow from the inside of her gloves when Ellen hobbled over to her. But, instead of apologizing she said, 'Those chairlifts are hell!'

Lauren said, 'I know how to fall.'

But Ellen was looking at the new student. 'I'm probably prejudiced but I have to laugh when I see blacks on skis. He's probably a Hindu or something. Doesn't he look a little out of place?'

Lauren said, 'I've seen them in all sorts of places,' and there was an edge in her voice that did not invite reply from the woman.

Stumbling and slipping, falling in ways that looked comic but that were painful and embarrassing, the class – growing more frightened and less determined as it fell – zigzagged to the foot of the long slope. The instructor, a woman with red peeling cheeks and a faded blue ski jacket, stamped her skis and muttered in French. 'Non, non, non,' she said contemptuously as one by one each person in the class fell, negotiating a little half-hidden hump of snow.

Later in the morning, Lauren found herself next to the newcomer in the chairlift. She had wanted that, but had he helped? He was very calm, hardly looking at her.

'I'm studying the Arab world,' she said. 'Where are you from?'

He said, 'The Arab world,' and smiled. 'But my business takes me all over. My parent company is based in London.'

Why was it that only Arabs and Indians used expressions like 'parent company'?

She said, 'We must have an awful lot in common.'

'Then we should have lunch.'

'I'm just going to have an apple in my room.'

He said nothing. They were arriving at the top of the lift. They struggled off without falling and shuffled to where the class was waiting.

'Do you have two apples?' he said.

At noon, he knocked on her door carrying a large basket of fruit wrapped in cellophane and ribbon. He had a yard of French bread and a small wheel of Camembert and two bottles of wine. Typical Arab overkill: he could have brought one apple. But she was getting to like the needless gesture and found it a comfort.

She said, 'I don't drink, but I sure do like bananas,' and removed one from the basket and peeled it in a slow unzipping way, with her teeth.

They sat by the window and stared at the luminous blue snow

and the white sky and the spindly black pines. Now it looked very cold outside.

Lauren said, 'I should tell you, I'm alone at the moment, but I'm waiting for someone.'

The man nodded; had he seen something outside?

'My father,' she said.

'We'd better hurry,' he said, and touched her, though he was still peering outside.

'We've got plenty of time.' She began wriggling out of her ski suit. 'I hate wearing all these clothes.'

They missed the afternoon class, and when they awoke from the short deep sleep – was it the sex or the altitude? – it was snowing. The flakes were large and loose, as big as fur balls, and swaying past the yellow lamps that lined the buried path beside the hotel.

His name was Sonny, but probably not, and he might have been from Syria – he was very vague and he also mumbled when he seemed unwilling to reply. She did not want to know more: there was always a commitment in asking questions and expecting replies, and she knew she often became unreasonably eager when she heard things like 'I'm looking for someone to run my Qatar operation.'

He was handsome – watchful, appreciative, very strong. He made love to her in an old-fashioned impaling way – it had been months since a man had done that, and he surprised her by chafing her into orgasm. Then it was like levitation, a mid-air feeling, and all her nerves singing – energy in her fingers and toes – until the orgasm shook and scorched her and she fell back to earth and began to cry. She tasted her tears; she was proud of them; she gave herself to them and faked them a little more until Sonny was pleased and frightened.

'This has never happened to me before,' she said.

'Some women never have one.'

'I mean, the crying,' and she let the tears dry on her cheeks.

After that they skipped most of the classes. She used the sauna and the exercise cycle in the hotel's health club, and Sonny fed francs into the electronic games in the resort's game room. Lauren liked watching him play the idiotic video games, seeing him amaze the young French boys with the rattle of his enormous scores. 'They call this "Frogger" in England, but here it is called "Jumper."' He played that croaking one reluctantly. He preferred the high-speed rocket chases and machine-gun games that were full of asteroids and explosives.

It seemed a just revenge on the skiers, who were either experts or incompetents. People came for one week to learn how to ski! Then they came next year for another week! It was exhausting, dangerous, expensive and – Lauren thought – pure show-off. Did anyone ever ski alone? The idea was to have someone watching you do it better than they could. Something in the whole ski thing reminded Lauren of details she had heard about health spas a hundred years ago – immersion cures and colonic irrigation and 'taking the waters' and generally going to a lot of trouble in order to justify eating well and meeting people and getting laid at a high altitude.

The first two days she forgot about everything except meeting Sonny and making love. This was the kind of sex she had been denied in London. She needed him for it; she loved it, she ached. It was certainly better for you than skiing. It was always in her room, and he always gave her time to herself. He had a lot of sense for an Arab: he cared about her pleasure.

'What about your father?' he said on the morning of the third day.

'My father—' She looked pained: agony. Her father was dead.

Then she remembered.

'I'd better call him.'

It took her the whole morning to get a line, and when she reached the Holiday Inn in Geneva the line was bad. 'Speak louder,' the operator said, but Lauren was already shouting. She screamed her name, she spelled Lord Bulbeck's, and then hung

up, hoping the operator was deafened by the crash of the receiver
– but they never heard more than a click, did they?

The phone call worked. That evening there was a telegram:
REGRET UNABLE TO MEET YOU. WILL RING
YOU ON RETURN TO LONDON. No signature – what
a cautious man! – but she knew who it was from.

Sonny was playing 'Moon Landing' in the game room,
working a jolting vehicle and firing with it at looming monsters.
A crowd of French children had gathered around him and looked
very impressed.

'He's not coming.' She didn't say 'my father' – it gave her the
creeps to say the word now.

Sonny said, 'I've earned five credits. That's a free game.'

'You know where I'll be, darling.' She went to the hotel to
exercise and change. She liked this life here: she wanted more of
it – not the skiing, but everything else.

She waited until ten o'clock. Her certainty and her anticipated
pleasure made her patient. But just after ten she craved an orange
and called Sonny's room to remind him to bring some. The
phone was dead. She dressed and went looking for him. His
room was locked. He was not in the game room. On a whim she
asked at the front desk.

'He checked out two hours ago. He is gone.'

Why did the French seem to take such pleasure in giving a
person bad news?

She went back to London and at last, after an unexplained two
weeks without seeing her, Lord Bulbeck phoned her at Half
Moon Street and said he wanted to take her to a play. It was a
West End revival of *A Streetcar Named Desire*, but she insisted
on leaving at the intermission.

She said, 'Tennessee Williams would hate my guts. But it's a
phony play, so that doesn't matter. Only a fairy could have
written that play and gotten everything wrong.'

Lord Bulbeck said, 'I can't imagine anyone hating you.'

'I'm the sort of healthy open-minded girl that people used to call a nymphomaniac,' she said.

They went to the Savoy Restaurant. Lord Bulbeck asked to be seated in a corner, away from the view of the Thames. Lauren had two appetizers and nothing else. Lord Bulbeck had smoked buckling, and then steak and grouse pie, and finally sherry trifle.

'You're killing yourself,' Lauren said.

Lord Bulbeck wiped his mouth and ordered a schooner of port. He said, 'I missed your dire warnings. And I missed other things.'

'I thought you'd forgotten about me. You never came skiing. It was fun.'

'I had to return suddenly to London.'

'You still haven't visited me here!'

Lord Bulbeck said, 'But you moved to a new place.'

'That's just it. I wanted you to see it.'

He said, 'I wonder if it's safe.'

'Everyone worries about me!' Lauren said. 'I can take care of myself!'

'I meant me,' Lord Bulbeck said. 'I have to be very careful you see.'

He was eating the sherry trifle still. His conversation was always full of maddening pauses when he was eating.

'It's my views.' He chewed and swallowed. 'I'm on a certain council – I'm chairman. Improbable as it may seem,' and he chewed and swallowed again, 'some people have threatened me with trouble.'

As always she was fascinated and distracted by his pronunciation. He said 'sherry tryfoo' and 'cownsoo' and 'improbaboo' and 'peepoo' and 'truboo'. But what was he talking about? She wondered whether it was an upper-class accent, and she suspected that it wasn't. But it was lovely in its way. Why was the poor man looking so serious?

'–getting used to peroo,' he was saying.

Could that be *peril*?

Now he changed the subject, perhaps because she had been so interested in his accent that she had not said a word. He said, 'I suppose you've been seeing other men?'

'Seeing them, yes.'

'I imagine they just want to get you into bed.'

'*Bed?*' she said. 'Bed? I haven't been in bed with anyone for weeks. You're the only man I go to bed with.'

Lord Bulbeck said, 'You're joking, of course.'

'I'm serious,' she said. 'On a table, on a chair, on an exercise bike, in the bathroom – yes. But not in a bed.'

'How is it to make love on an exercise bike?'

Lauren said, 'He was taking pictures of my thing.'

'And a bathroom,' Lord Bulbeck said, making a face. He was hardly listening. Sex was so often a completely private set of fantasies.

'We weren't making love,' Lauren said. 'He was shaving me.'

Lord Bulbeck said, 'But not shagging you.'

'No. But last week I came close. I've got this other guy who takes me out. He's an American engineer, working on weather satellite technology. He's got this girlfriend, Debbie. She's from Scotland and she's got this really neat accent. Usually we go to his place and he puts on a video. It's always something dykey. Then we watch it and he gets Debbie and me to start kissing. I mean, we really make out. Is that what shagging is?'

Lord Bulbeck had become very intent. He swallowed, concentrating hard, and said, 'Then what happens?'

'Then he fucks Debbie while I watch and then we all go out to dinner,' Lauren said. 'But I never eat anything except salad. I'm a salad person.'

'Go on about the other thing,' Lord Bulbeck said.

What *other thing*? she thought. She said, 'Well, you mentioned bed, but there isn't much of that. Men don't want a woman. They want an object. I mean literally. "Stand very still," they say. They want me to be a pillow or a chair or a table or a pet rabbit. They want me to be a *thing*. It's ridiculous!'

Lord Bulbeck said, 'I'd like to go to your flat with you right now and take you to bed.'

'Yes, yes,' she said. 'That'll be a change.'

'I'm quite in the mood,' he said. He paid the bill and they left the restaurant.

She said, 'It's good for you to leave the rest of that dessert. And coffee is just horrible.'

They went to Half Moon Street. Lord Bulbeck went into each room, sniffing, touching, looking out of the windows. 'There's the famous exercise bike,' he said. He reminded her of a detective searching for clues, and when he was satisfied that there were none he undressed with his usual care, one cuff button then the other, and shaking each leg out of his trousers, and piling everything onto a chair. It was the clear plastic chair. She had not told him about that – how she pressed herself against it for Karim.

She wanted to say, 'Sex isn't sex – at least, that isn't.' It was rarified and distant and private, the small corners of private fantasies. Now she and Lord Bulbeck were in her bed at Half Moon Street for the first time, and he was stroking her slowly: like a lover, she thought. That was it – the men were not lovers. Most of them did not even touch her. She found it impossible to enter the feelings of these men. She tried: she wanted to share that thrill and to know that satisfaction. But there was only the ritual, the solitary orgasm, and no satisfaction. They probably didn't have any feelings at all. Sonny the great lover had just ditched her!

'Did I hurt you?' she said.

'A littoo,' Lord Bulbeck said. 'Why?'

'You moved!'

But she was joking, because he lay beside her, exhausted, looking mugged.

Later, she said, 'I'm really glad you finally came here. This flat is special.' She felt his hand on her: he had tried hard to please her. She said, 'And you're special.' But she could not use the word lover for someone with so many secrets.

226

## 8

When Karim said, 'There is someone I want you to meet,' she was prepared for anything. It was a silent man with a suitcase. The suitcase made her reflective. The ones who used props always seemed a little unsteady emotionally – even Karim and his camera, the way he poked the thing at her. And as with some of the others Karim insisted that she take this man to Half Moon Street.

That day, Lauren had agreed to read a paper at the Thursday seminar which covered topics of current interest – General New-house called the papers 'backgrounders.' Lauren did not have a paper, nor had she submitted any work to the Fellowship Committee. She gathered newspaper clippings and wire service reports, and she filed and cross-referenced them with the financial analyses – anything to do with oil revenue investments. But all revenue was oil revenue! She wished she had never begun the project – China would have been easier, food would have been more fun; but she would still have had to face those scraps of paper and those fat files. She could gather material but she could not write.

Writing was so hard. It was not just setting down your thoughts or putting those clippings into a narrative, but more like learning how to think and then teaching yourself to write. It was not just hard – it was impossible for her. Her hand stiffened on her keyboard after the first *bop-bop-bop*.

She thought: I should get one of these word-processors.

The Institute had a computer, with a telescreen and a printer. She sat at it with a stack of notes. *Chk-chk*. And then, *chk-chk-chk*. But it didn't think. It was a glorified typewriter. There was a game they played every Fourth of July on the courthouse lawn in Turkey Hollow – the peanut race. You pushed a peanut with your nose, six feet to the Civil War Memorial. That's what writing was; and she looked at her notes: this is my peanut.

And the task was much larger and sometimes when she was trying to write it was as if she were trying to invent the written word – like originating language itself. Impossible. And what about spending every night with those men? She was strong but she did not have time enough to write and also live her other life.

She did not write a seminar paper, but instead spoke from her notes. Suspecting that the others would think she was frivolous if she wore a dress – it was almost April but very sunny, and warm enough for her Laura Ashley pinafore – she decided on her tweed jacket and severe blouse and grey flat-heeled shoes. It was her usual escort outfit, her librarian look. 'I'm naked underneath,' she said, if a man questioned the style.

The title of her talk was 'Work in Progress' – she wanted something loose and ambiguous. She had organized her notes around various headings – investments in energy schemes; buying foreign currency; recycling petro-dollars; and spending on leisure. Because she was talking to historians and political scientists she decided to include some basic accounting terms and she began by describing the implied differences between expenses and expenditure, and other misunderstood financial terms. Then she turned to her headings and illustrated each one with a particular person – 'I think the most effective methodology is the case study' – and she made her points by describing various men she had met through the Jasmine Agency: where their money came from, and where it went. She did not mention the agency. How shocked those men would have been! She said, 'In an interview, the subject disclosed–'

'Salim is fifty years old, from Qatar, and has a number of business interests, mainly in oil-related industries. On a recent trip to London he met with an American manufacturer of solar panels and placed orders totalling a half-a-million dollars. These were trans-shipped not to Qatar but to Pakistan, where Salim is developing an agriculture scheme. When interviewed, the subject disclosed–'

When interviewed the subject had been just behind her, furiously bumming her against a mirror. And similar impressions came to her when she discussed 'Mamoun,' her foreign currency case-study; and 'Hamid' the film importer; and 'Ahmed' and 'Jabari' and 'Fazal' – the last three were all friends of Karim whom she entertained at Half Moon Street, and whom she suspected of being arms dealers. But she used them to illustrate property and leisure.

General Newhouse, as chairman, summed up her talk by saying, 'This can hardly be called rigorous analysis, but a study of this kind has great charm and subtlety as well as insights. There is considerable merit in this. Questions, please.'

Lauren loved answering questions, and she easily turned them to her advantage: 'And this reminds me of something else I meant to emphasize–' Her talk was not well-documented – it was not documented at all. But she knew that it was appreciated for being fully human. She had made events and abstractions understandable by describing the men behind them. The men had paid her for her companionship or her sexual performance – but so what? It really was scholarship, of a kind, and later when she was praised she thought: I've earned that.

It was on the afternoon of her successful talk that she received what had become a daily call from Madame Cybele. Somehow, she expected her to say, 'Bulbeck.' She said, 'Karim.' And Karim said, 'There is someone I want you to meet.'

He did not at first show her his suitcase. He met Lauren at a pre-arranged spot – the gazebo in the centre of Berkeley Square: she watched the daffodils tremble as she waited – and it was as they were walking together back to Half Moon Street that he produced the metal valise. One minute there was nothing, and the next minute this heavy thing was bumping his leg – certainly heavy, because his arm was straight and tugging his shoulder at a slant. He said his name was Zayid – volunteered it, and so she knew he was lying. People seldom lied to her: what was the point of lying to a stranger? A stranger was one of few people in the world who could be trusted with the truth.

Lauren's successful talk that morning had made her confident and bossy. She took charge and became inquisitive – Where was he from? What did he do? How long was he staying in London? He said nothing, which unsettled her – silence always did – and then when she persisted, for her own peace of mind, he said, 'I am engaged in various sorts of business,' and no more.

His English was good: he could have explained. But he stayed strangely silent – so different from the boasting men she was used to.

Zayid grinned at the room, at the street, at the pavement below, at the rooftops. It was a grin of wonder – his smiling lips and bared teeth expressing incomprehension. Lauren had seen this grin on the faces of nervous men in hotel rooms when they faced her. But Zayid was facing the windows.

'Will you have a drink?'

'That will not be necessary at the moment.'

He had the foreigner's pointlessly good English – too many words. In this way he reminded her of Madame Cybele.

He did not 'require' any food, he did not 'use' cigarettes, he had a 'very sweet tooth' and where was the 'parlor'? Talking this way he seemed to be turning aside – Lauren always found formal English suspiciously evasive. And she could not understand anyone until the person acted. Because this man was not saying or doing anything she did not know him. She had weeks ago stopped looking for motives in men's faces. She could handle men. After she made them come they were silly and embarrassed. It was one-sided sex – she got nothing – but she sometimes maliciously thought of it as castration. Men were so empty afterwards!

When Zayid took out his camera Lauren relaxed – the voyeurs were always the silent, reticent ones, just spying on a body, hiding near it and possessing it at a distance, like certain travelers. The voyeurs were harmless. Taking pictures was not sex – that act was a private moment, later, when the pictures were developed: hot hands and bulging eyes.

But Zayid's back was turned. He was pointing his camera out of the window.

Lauren said, 'The Naval and Military Club. They don't let women in. Isn't it awful?'

He did not face her. Had he heard?

She said, 'But then, you probably approve of that.'

Nothing.

She wanted to call Karim and say, 'Hey, where did you dig this guy?'

He was a small cold man. His grin which looked like under-standing was incomprehension; his frown, which appeared to be concern, was complete indifference. I can understand sex, and I can understand the fetishism that turns things into sex, she thought; but I can't figure indifference.

She said, 'I've got to make a phone call.'

'No phone calls.'

'Don't say "No phone calls" like that! You're not my father. I want to call Karim.'

'Karim is no longer present in this country,' Zayid said.

'What's that supposed to mean?'

Zayid frowned: he didn't care. 'Ring him if you like.'

She tried – anxiously aware that she was breaking agency rules – but there was no answer.

'He's probably out.'

'He is definitely out.'

It worried her that he seemed to know so much and that he did nothing. He had put his camera away and had stopped pacing the room. He sat down in a chair by the window and went to sleep: was he going to spend the night there?

Lauren did not want to go to bed while he was in the chair. She started doing her stretching exercises, then became self-conscious and stopped. She lay opposite Zayid on the sofa with a pillow under her head, but her interrupted routine – the presence of this man – kept her awake. She did not mind missing dinner, but missing exercise made her restless.

'Where are you going?' Zayid said, without moving in the chair.

'Out. I can't sleep. I'm going to run.'

'Stay where you are,' he said. 'You forget I have paid you.'

Six hundred pounds in a brown envelope – such a thick packet she had had trouble crushing it into one of her shoes in her closet. But she had forgotten the money, because she hadn't done anything to earn it.

She said, 'What do you want me to do?'

'Exactly what I say.'

That worried her and her worry increased when he remained silent for the next three and a half hours, his lids not completely down and his nighthawk eyes shining through crescent slits.

Just before dawn, he said, 'We go.'

She was ready: she had not taken off her track suit.

They walked to Berkeley Square down wet yellow-black Curzon Street, passing a policeman and then two gamblers – who else would be just here at this hour? And she was reminded that Zayid had a gambler's wordlessness. At the top end of the square Zayid stopped next to a BMW and he told her to get in.

'I'm always trying to get into the wrong side of the car,' she said, crossing to the passenger side. 'In the States the steering wheel's on the left.'

He said nothing, but his driving put her on her guard: he drove one-handed, too fast, always speeding when the light changed, and turning sharply, trusting to luck that there would be no one crossing the road.

She said, 'I hate these butch cars,' hoping that talk might slow him down.

He sped south, past the Palace and across Westminster Bridge. She watched the signs and looked for something familiar.

'I know someone who lives here,' she said, seeing a sign to Brixton. She was speaking of herself, in that room, in that house, hating London. She could not connect that girl with this woman, the past with the present.

'She's amazing,' Lauren said. 'She makes popcorn and feeds it to the birds. She's real strict about her diet. Like she eats carob? And bean curd? And about a ton of bran a day? She used to be married but she left the guy, because they were always arguing about curtains and whose turn to cook. She started off writing this book about Kissinger, and that got her interested in China. But she's been everywhere. She's always saying that the Chinese have beautiful skin, and Hindus never wear wigs, and Africans have perfect ears and – get this – Arabs never wear second-hand clothes. Jesus, do you have to drive this fast?'

He neither responded nor slowed down.

She said, 'This isn't your car.'

He glanced at her.

She said, 'You weren't driving a car last night when you met me.'

'How do you know that?' he said, surprising her with a full sentence.

'Because if you had come in a car I would have seen it and remembered the license number. I always do that, just to be on the safe side.'

'What is the number of this car?'

She told him the three letters and the three numbers that she had seen when she had crossed behind the car to the passenger side.

'I knew last night that you were very clever,' he said, and drove faster.

'Clever doesn't mean smart in the States,' she said. 'It means something else.'

He said, 'I mean something else.'

'Where the hell are we going?' she suddenly demanded.

His fast driving was like a reply. They made their way through Surrey, and dawn struck at them – long fragments of light from the end of a long brown set of meadows. She stared at the rising sun until it became a bonfire on those meadows, and it gave the packed clouds in the high sky the texture of smoke. This was old orderly England, looking senile but safe; she preferred this to the trampled edges of London.

'Where are we going?' she asked. She was sorry her voice had a slight tremor of suspicion and fear in it. Perhaps that was the reason he did not bother to reply.

There was no conversation, so she read road signs.

'Godstone,' she said. 'Piltdown.'

But saying these names into the silence made her uneasy.

'Listen, where are we going?'

He frowned and it meant everything.

Did he know where he was going? Perhaps he was just following any old road in order to speed. She had felt so differently yesterday. *There's someone I want you to meet.* And she had gladly agreed, because her seminar talk was out of the way – little accomplishments like that relaxed her and made her lazy again.

She felt she should deliberately try to make herself feel hopeful.

'I think it's so important to know when to relax. Some people don't know how.'

There were wide hills in the distance with long smooth summits and shadowy hollows, and nothing behind them but great tumbling fume-like clouds.

She said, 'Do you know where you are?'

He snatched at the gear shift and said nothing.

She said, 'I want to go back.'

He ignored her. He looked up each side road that they passed – fifty feet off the main road they narrowed to country lanes.

She said, 'I have to go back. I've got things to do today–'

She had taped her seminar talk. If she got someone to transcribe it and she did a little work on it, she might be able to publish it. She wanted to get that going today, have a good night's sleep to make up for last night.

Zayid turned his face to her, but his eyes were not on her. He was looking past her at a narrow side road, and then he swerved suddenly and aimed the car into it, skidding as he went. Now they were racing down a country lane that was wet black from a recent shower.

She said, 'Unsafe things always look lovely to me, like certain bridges and certain roads, and ice on a lake in the winter.'

She was terrified and could hardly breathe.

'Would you mind slowing down?' Talking helped her get air. She only asked questions when she was afraid.

'Jevington,' she said, as they passed a low black and white village sign. 'Please stop.'

But he swerved again on a yet narrower lane, hardly more than a path, that carried them steeply up a hill into some trees; the curves surprised him, but he did not let up.

She was sure that he had no idea where he was going. He was turning on impulse, looking for the narrowest road, the most hidden place, because – why had she gone when he grunted, 'We go'? – he wanted to harm her. She felt freezing waves of a kind of murderousness coming at her from his body like a strong smell. She thought: He wants to kill me.

He was looking for a place, hurrying towards the end of this empty lane.

She said with useless anger, 'What do you want?'

He stopped the car so quickly she felt a sense of forward movement for a few seconds after he stopped – it was a stomach-sickening weightlessness that was also fear.

He faced her and fumbled in his pocket – for a weapon, she was sure – but she already had the door open and was heaving herself out.

'Stay where you are!'

He said that last night when I wanted to run, she thought; and now she would run. She shouldered the door shut, wishing that she could tip the car over.

'Good morning,' a gentle voice said. It was an old man, dressed for bad weather. He had a puffy friendly face and was carrying an umbrella and wearing a flapping raincoat. He stumped towards her in big muddy boots. Then he saw Zayid getting out of the other side of the car and grinning. The man blinked and said, 'You're not local.'

'No,' Lauren said. He wouldn't touch her while this old man was near.

'I hope I haven't kept you waiting.' The man took out a large black door key and said, 'After you.'

There, through an iron gate, and planted in the narrowness at the end of the path-like lane, was a small country church with a low thick steeple – more of a plump tower than a steeple. The church was made of flint which, in the morning sun, looked like pieces of broken bone set into the sandstone walls.

Zayid was still grinning at the man. It was his wondering grin of concentration, all teeth and no pleasure. Then he grinned at the bone-white church. And then at Lauren. Whatever happens, you'll be sorry, his grin said.

The old man swung the heavy door open and said, 'We don't usually get people this early. You must be keen.'

'Tourism,' Zayid said, as if replying to an immigration officer's question. He began talking, saying how pretty the church was. Lauren noticed that his English was much poorer when he was speaking to this old man than when he spoke to her. Everything about him worried her.

'Down from London?'

'No. We were in Brighton. Vacationing and seeing the sights.' He stared at her, daring her to challenge the lie.

'Eastbourne's much quieter,' the old man said, and the church walls cushioned his words. 'I often go down on a Sunday afternoon if the weather's fine. Planning to be in England long?'

Zayid said, 'That is entirely up to my wife.'

There was something about this obnoxious lie that made her certain that he intended to kill her. The word 'wife' was like a rope around her neck.

'This church goes back to the tenth century,' the old man was saying. He pointed with his umbrella. 'That sculpture in the wall is even older – it was found in a stone chest under the floor of the belfry. It's Christ killing a demon.'

A biscuit-coloured chunk of stone sealed into the wall like a huge tile showed in relief a smooth almost featureless Christ driving a spear into a beast's open mouth.

'That's Saxon. Fifth-century, you could say.'

Zayid grinned at this: his grin was fury and frustration. He walked down the centre aisle, his footsteps ringing on the hard floor. The church smelled of cold paint and waxed wood and damp stone and dangerous roof beams. Hammer beams, the old man was calling them. The bare altar was set in a small enclosure, with an arched entrance.

'Chancel arch,' the man said, hurrying after Zayid, who was grinning at the stained-glass windows. Lauren was backing away. 'See those squints?'

He drew Zayid aside to the narrow openings.

'You'll never guess what they were for.'

Zayid showed his teeth. It was his way of struggling.

'Lepers,' the old man said. 'But they were cut on the slant so that the lepers could see the altar from outside the church. You know what lepers are?'

Zayid's gaze lingered on the old man's tongue, as if the words were still there, and he turned his back on Lauren for the first time while he examined the squints in the arch, saying, 'Leprosy?'

By then Lauren was pushing open the door to the porch and before the door swung shut again she was away, running hard down the lane and through a wet meadow, which was a long hillside at the edge of the Downs. From the top she saw the open sea and at the shoreline in a flat valley the town of Eastbourne – though she did not discover its name until she was well inside it and running towards the station.

The train arrived in London just before noon. In the taxi she resolved to pack and go, to leave London at once. Her fear had left her and now she felt a trembly euphoria that she was still alive – lucky!

Out of caution she alighted from the taxi at Stratton Street and walked slowly to Half Moon Street, making sure that no one was watching her. Then she hurried upstairs to her flat. She opened the door and stepping into the room she fought for breath – she steadied herself against the door-jamb so as not to fall.

The flat was empty. It was not robbery – robbery was a sort of piecemeal plunder, the smash and clutter of things opened and broken. This was something else: it was clean and complete. Everything that had been there was gone – every stick of furniture, every carpet, every picture, every fragment of decoration. Her shoes, her money, her precious coat, all her books. It had been totally emptied, and she was frightened by the nakedness of the place. There was one object – the metal suitcase that Zayid had brought. It was pushed against the wall and in its small solitary way it looked dangerous. The other thing about empty rooms was their obvious stains – the faint trace marks where everything had been.

The bare flat – everything gone – gave the place an absurd nightmare look and convinced her that someone had intended her to be part of this scheme, taken away like all the things she owned: someone wanted to kill her. She felt weak and terrified as if what she was seeing in these hideous empty rooms were symptoms of a fatal illness.

## 9

Now the flat seemed very dangerous – like a deep unmarked hole – and the cracked bricks on the buildings of Half Moon Street squinted at her in a threatening way as she passed them, hurrying towards Shepherd Market. She had nothing, she was naked under her tracksuit, she was cold without her mink-lined coat. She did not have her briefcase to take to the Institute – not even a pen! But what was the point of going to the Institute? She was finished here, she had been plundered: they had removed everything but her body. It was a fright that convinced her that she was helplessly close to death.

The Jasmine Agency was shut, though she went there anyway to make sure, not knowing whether to barge in and take a chance or to lurk outside. She lurked long enough to find out that it was closed. But it was usually closed in the daytime: the sleazy greedy places and the ugly girls were for the afternoon in this part of Mayfair.

It would have been a relief to her to find Madame Cybele. There was no one else Lauren knew who would offer help. She could not call up anyone and say, 'Help me – I'm in trouble' – no one in that whole city knew her well enough: no one knew her at all or understood both of her lives. To those who knew her as a Fellow at the Institute she would have to explain how she came to be in this situation; so the Institute was out. And all those other men had paid her: there had never been any question of friendship. She had wanted it that way. Friendship was dangerous and cheap.

Karim had put her in this position. She hated him for sending Zayid to her. She wanted to call him and scream, 'You failed – I'm still alive!'

But where was he? Zayid said he was not in the country. And what of Lord Bulbeck? The old secretive man now seemed as suspect and cruel as any other man she had known, and in her fear she began to hate him for everything he had hidden from her.

Men stared at her as she moved through Mayfair wondering what to do next. But only one move was possible: she had to leave. She had a little more than thirteen pounds in the shallow pocket of her tracksuit – the change from a purple twenty after buying her train ticket from Eastbourne.

Shepherd Market was full of travel agencies and ticket offices.

She chose the agency with the most posters and asked the man at the desk the fare to the United States.

'Which city?'

'Washington,' Lauren said. 'No. New York.'

'Is this first class or economy?'

Lauren pouted and said, 'First class.'

'When would you be travelling?'

'Immediately – today or tomorrow.'

'That would be full fare, I'm afraid. Six hundred pounds, single. Just under, actually. Shall I book it for you?'

Thirteen pounds. Lauren said, 'I'll be back.'

Then she stepped into the street and a harsh voice behind her said, 'I've been looking all over for you!' And at the same time a strong hand grabbed her roughly by the wrist.

Now she was naked on the floor of a darkened room and the man was standing above her and saying, 'You don't sound as if you mean it.'

'I *do* mean it,' she said, in a pleading voice.

'No,' he said. 'You're lying. I don't believe you.'

'Really,' she said, and her voice broke. 'It's true.'

She pushed herself sideways to see his face. He was smiling. He wanted her to beg.

The man was short and had popping eyes and was bald under the nest of hair woven on his head. His penis was a blunt little thing, like a pathetic vegetable tucked under the hairy basket of his belly.

She said, 'I'm dying to take you into my mouth.'

'You're not going to get anything, my girl,' he said, shielding the silly thing with his cupped hand. Then he was encouraged and he caressed it with his stubby fingers.

'Let me do that,' Lauren said. 'I'd love to do that. I want to touch you.'

He said softly, 'You can watch me.'

'Yes,' she said, and now she understood. They were always so

240

evasive! 'Let me watch you' – and moved nearer. 'I love to watch you do that.'

'Do you?' he said, and he repeated it. He was stalling. And he was stiffening – the vegetable had changed colour and now filled his hand.

'That's nice,' she said. But seeing him struggle she wanted to laugh. What a misshapen and ridiculous thing the penis was! Half of them didn't even work properly and all of them looked pathetic and detachable, like some wrinkled sea creature – like something you'd find goggling at you and swaying in an aquarium.

She had not touched this man. He had told her roughly to take her clothes off and to lie down on the floor ('Not on my bed!') and then he pulled the little demanding thing out of his pants and throttled it in his hand. Now he was whimpering as he dripped it on her and all its life was gone.

She said, 'I love that,' and propped herself up so that he could see her face. She was daring him to deny that she was telling the truth. 'More,' she said, and it was like mockery: he was done.

'Don't go,' he said. 'Please.'

'If I stay it'll cost you another hundred' – she was already pulling on her tracksuit.

'Then go,' he said. 'You're a slut.' He was at the door, fumbling with the locks. 'You've got diseases. I wouldn't touch you for anything.'

Lauren knew she had to leave quickly: men could be terrible just afterwards in their humiliation. She had never seen their famous sadness, but only guilt or anger or resentment, or a sullen silence, as they realized they were temporarily castrated – and how did they know at that moment that it was not temporary? No man had ever completely satisfied her, or had touched her as tenderly and deeply as she had touched herself. But she always knew when a man's little frenzy was finished: they came with a pathetic finality – one squirt and the rest dribbled and that was all. This dope was still muttering as he shut the door on her.

Following the signs to the Fire Exit she turned a corner and saw a man entering a room.

She paused and stared and so surprised him he held the door open. She said, 'I bet your room has a terrific view.'

'Dynamite,' the man said, after a stutter of trying to find the word. 'Want to come in?'

'It'll cost you,' she said, and stepped nearer and whispered. 'I'll do anything you want. I just want to please you.' She implored him and stooped slightly and said in a slavish way, 'Any-thing.'

The man showed a flicker of hunger and she knew she had him.

By five-thirty she had turned nine tricks – the term seemed hugely appropriate. Tricks were what most men wanted. She had never solicited this way before; it excited her and took the edge off her fears. The men were eager – she guessed that they were able to smell other men on her. And most of them, at last, were glad to see her go – something to do with the daylight and the street noise and their shame. It was so different from the night, when they procrastinated and behaved like husbands, and whined when she said she had to go. This afternoon showed her the laughable weakness of men – how they hurried, how impatient they were, how easily baited, how willing to pay. She stared, they faltered and fell. They were looking for her! She had almost twelve hundred pounds.

The good boutiques and chic stores were closed, but Selfridges was open until eight tonight. She bought shoes, tights, a handbag, a Burberry and a lovely umbrella, and a silk dress. She left her tracksuit in the changing room. Returning to Park Lane she stopped an Arab dressed handsomely in a *thobe* and *besht* as he was entering Grosvenor House Hotel.

'Yes, please, madam,' he said.

But she had only smiled.

'Can you come with me?' he said.

He brought her to a third-floor suite and a man in a *dish-dasha* opened the door and let Lauren in. He waved the other man away.

An Arab wrapped loosely in a towel lay sprawled on a bed, and the man in the *dish-dasha* returned to him and in a loving way massaged him.

Lauren said, 'I can do that.'

The masseur glared at her, but the man being massaged said, 'Come here.'

She did so, towering over him. He took one of her buttocks in his hand and squeezed it and said, 'I want this one.'

'If you bum me,' she said, 'it's four hundred.'

He said no, but in his eagerness to send the masseur away he miscounted and she got six hundred.

'Stay,' he said afterwards, but she said she was busy – she did not have time for the drink, the dinner, the belly-dancer and the groggy argument at midnight over where she would sleep. She felt enterprising and alive again: she had very little time left. Her goal had been a thousand pounds, but now – even after having bought those things – she had over twelve hundred again and she decided on two thousand pounds even, like a gambler aiming for higher stakes in the middle of a winning streak. She would work all night – she had never stayed up all night before; she would leave in the morning with her money and her first-class ticket. Her tremendous panic was gone. She thought: I've got a hot hand.

She felt powerful – excited and greedy; she felt more willing now to take a risk, having survived what she was now sure had been an attempt on her life. She had nothing to lose; there was no one left to impress. She was indestructible. All she had to do was stay away from Half Moon Street.

She stopped men on Piccadilly. They wanted to be stopped by a pretty girl. She said, 'I'll do anything you want. It'll cost you, but it'll be worth it.' The mention of money made the men eager, for the only thing they had was money.

She sat at the bar of the Hilton and touched the man next to her and said, 'Do you want me?'

He murmured.

She said, 'Lead the way. I'm your wife.'

After midnight the men were louder and rougher. She met them in doorways and they hurried her to their rooms. They had been drinking. The whiners of the afternoon were now asleep; these others were wilder and alcoholic and barely intelligible, but full of insistent and elaborate instructions. One man made her suck him off in the bathroom in front of the full-length mirror; another gave her a vibrator and explicit directions and he photographed her using it on herself; a third had her kneel over a chamberpot and piss while he drunkenly swayed before her and ejaculated against her cheek.

By the time the casinos were closed – three-thirty or four – she had been photographed again – but with her face turned away. She was bruised and had scratches on her arms, and she was saddle-sore from the bummings and the pokings. And yet no man had lain between her legs and simply fucked her as Lord Bulbeck had done last week: they were too frightened, too shy, and they were indifferent to her pleasure. Did they know how identical they were in their fears?

She had lost track of the men, of the foolish routines, of the numerous showers that still had not removed that hot oystery smell from her. But in the Ladies' Cloakroom in the Dorchester she counted her money. She had two thousand three hundred and forty-three pounds in cash. She thought: I'm free.

There were lights burning upstairs at the Jasmine Agency. She had seen them first in the early hours of the morning as she had passed under the window with another nameless man, and she had thought fondly of Madame Cybele. Lauren's bruises inspired a sort of affection and pity for the woman.

But this ache made her feel slightly diseased, too, and there was something like an illness in the male smell that she could not wash away. The past hours had given her an understanding of Madame Cybele, and she wanted to see her to say goodbye.

She had to say goodbye, because she knew she would never go

back; and what she had once regarded as enjoyable, the calculated frolic of a double life that had granted her a kind of power, she now saw as a sickening weakness, a feeble plotting to serve a bad habit.

She hated men now – hated them for being bullies and not caring about her pleasure. She hated their gross bodies. She hated their smoking and drinking – their decay. Most of all she hated them for not having any secrets. Their real malice lay in being both stupid and strong. They could have anything. They wanted the worst things. She thought fondly of Debbie, and how they had kissed and licked like two cats in front of the video while that man watched them.

The street was empty. She was walking in the direction of the agency. She felt sisterly towards the woman. She wanted to tell her that she understood and she was free. And she had a desire to warn her – to tell her to get away and escape while there was time, as she planned to do herself on this new day. Lauren was out of danger, but this realization made her want to save one other person. It was only fair.

The steep stairs reminded her of her first visit the day after she had seen the videotape – the stranger who knew her well and sent it had never admitted the fact; and then the two Arabs had said, 'We want this one,' and she had been flattered, and she had so easily stepped into this other life.

She took the stairs softly, one at a time, and heard low voices – one was Madame Cybele's, the other was a man's, perhaps Captain Twilley's. She knocked and there was a silence – the darkness of dead air. She listened at the door and knocked again.

She heard a drawer shoved into a desk.

'Come in.'

Madame Cybele was alone, at the secretary's desk, looking up, trying to speak.

Lauren said, 'Why do you look so surprised?'

Madame Cybele struggled to speak and then, unable to make

any noise, she got up and rushed forward and hugged Lauren so
tightly she was on the verge of tipping the tall girl over.

'Hey, what's up–'

'Who is it?' came a complaining voice from the other room –
not Twilley.

Madame Cybele said, 'Run!' and Lauren realized that the
woman was trying to push her out of the door. But Lauren was
having trouble standing. Madame Cybele did not say anything
more – did not have time – for in the next instant the speaker
from the other room came to see for himself who the visitor
was.

'Let go!' he shouted.

Lauren looked up, but she choked when she tried to speak –
she was suffocated with fear. She stared at Hugo Van Arkady,
who hissed at her in furious surprise.


## 10


He had taken charge, but he had not said much. He had paused
only to gather his raincoat and his wide-brimmed hat and then
he had hurried her to Park Lane and hailed a taxi. The streets
gleamed – it always seemed to rain in London at this dark hour
of the morning. He was giving the driver directions and she was
helpless to resist. She was tired and shocked – they had made a
fool of her. What affected her most was not the surprise that she
had seen Van Arkady in that place, but the humiliation that he
had seen her.

Now they were at Victoria in a first-class compartment, with
the shades drawn, drinking coffee out of plastic cups. The train
was at the platform being loaded with mailbags and bundles of
newspapers – every few moments there was a thump or a clang.
Lauren faced the gaunt man. Ever since the taxi she had been
asking him questions in a trapped and wounded way, but he had

hardly spoken and he had not replied to her. Then, unexpectedly, he answered.

'You are catching the ferry to Calais.'

'And you?'

'I'm making sure you catch it.'

'I could have flown,' she said. 'I've got plenty of money.'

'Money!' he said in a pitying way, as if this was the most meaningless thing on earth. He recovered from this word and said, 'They'll be watching the airports. And you don't have much time.'

'Why?'

He shook his head. 'You'll be a great deal safer if you don't know.'

'Where's my stuff?'

'Disposed of.'

'Just like that,' she said.

'Every bit of it is replaceable,' he said with the same pity he had used to mock her with the word money. 'Your worry about it proves how young you are. It was such innocent junk.'

She said angrily, 'And you were going to dispose of me, too!'

'Zayid was supposed to take you away. His plane was leaving from Gatwick yesterday afternoon. That's why you ended up in that part of Sussex–'

So Van Arkady had been listening to her questions and pleadings in the taxi: her story of the car journey and the little flint church near Eastbourne.

'–He might not have killed you. It wasn't in his orders. But these people sometimes use their own initiative. It is cheaper to kill someone – and less trouble, and it's final. Don't say "murder." Simplicity can often seem very savage. This coffee is disgusting.'

'He was a savage.'

Van Arkady considered this. 'Because he didn't make love to you?'

'How do you know that?' But she had the answer as soon as

she spoke. 'You bugged my flat, you knew everything, you set me up.'

He said, 'You were our bug,' and seeing Lauren wince, he added, 'You were a live wire.'

'You and Karim knew all those men.'

'Not very well. We were listening to them, not you. We've never had a bug like you. Education is a wonderful thing.'

'That's why you needed me,' she said.

'Not really. You asked them good questions, but it was more a matter of security. You were one of the few people I trusted – you were completely reliable in your innocence. When I saw you at the General's party I realized you needed us.'

She said, 'You're the person who sent me that tape.'

'I thought it might interest you. You seemed ambitious.' Now he looked at her almost in admiration. 'God, you were busy! You must be very healthy to keep up that pace. But you were also very lucky, you know.'

'I used to think so.'

'Yes. You might have been killed.'

'By one of your slobs.'

'By anyone. Listen, it's dangerous to sleep with everyone.'

'You're a pimp and you say that to me.'

Van Arkady said, 'I hate that word.'

There was a whistle, and the banging of doors, one after another, and shouts. Then there was silence and the train started, without any more sounds. The posters slid by, then a brick embankment, a bridge, a power station, rooftops and back yards looking derelict in the drizzly light.

Van Arkady smiled at the gloom. At lamp-posts a soft brown murk surrounded each saucer shape of light. He said, 'London is an excellent place for murder.'

She followed his gaze and then looked back at him. He was still smiling.

'It's quiet and peaceful, the police are unarmed, and if you're caught you get a fair trial. There is no torture, no hanging, no firing squad. The sentences are remarkably short and the prisons are clean. Do you know that the best-fed people in Britain are prisoners? Any murderer can study for a degree in sociology. Our people are used to a different sort of justice.'

She said, 'You do mean murder, don't you?'

'Never mind.'

'It was something to do with the flat on Half Moon Street and my name on the lease. What is it, a hiding place?'

He said, 'I hate intelligent people. You can't shut them off. Ignorant people can be nags but they're much more useful.'

She said, 'I know it's Half Moon Street.'

'Your personal effects are gone. You should be glad they are, instead of sitting there pleading for them back. Zayid was just a courier, and you don't know anything.'

'Why did you mention murder just then?' she said, and when he didn't reply she said, 'You're an incredible phoney. If those people at the party really knew you, they'd despise you. You're a pimp, you're a sneak, you run an escort agency in order to spy on the poor fuckers you don't trust.'

He said, 'I find you extremely ugly.'

'And you're planning to kill someone.'

He said, 'You worked for us, darling.'

'I could talk,' she said.

'You won't. No one would believe you. And you'll never come to London again.' He gestured out of the window at the last straggling suburbs, the semi-detached houses, the allotments, the black canals. 'If you come back, you'll probably be arrested.'

'I don't have to go back to London to talk.'

He did not hesitate. He said evenly, 'You can still be killed.'

She looked out of the window and saw a woman raising her arms to hang out a blue shirt on a clothesline, and in the foreground a brick-yard and *Builders' Merchants* behind a rusty fence; she knew at that instant that this was printed on her memory and that she would always see the woman and the brick-yard and the sign and the fence when she remembered *You can still be killed.* Even in themselves they were horribly shabby, but they also signified his threat. These alone were reason enough for her never to come back and be reminded of what this man had said at the very margin of London.

In a small surrendering voice she said, 'How long were you using me?'

'From the first,' he said, and seemed triumphant. 'Didn't you ever suspect?'

'Yes,' she said. 'Periodically.'

He smiled broadly at her and she felt fooled in her lie.

'What if I hadn't moved to Half Moon Street?'

'We would have found someone else. London is full of people like you. The world is. That's why it is so easy for us.'

'What do you mean "us"? Who are you?'

He said, 'The five thousand.'

He did not speak again until they were near Dover. He fixed his eyes on her and his steady gaze seemed to emphasize the distance between them. She had no more questions.

'Don't look so sad,' he said. 'You're safe.'

She thought: But I wanted to save someone else. She looked away from him, and now they were in a tunnel and her side window had become a mirror. Perhaps the other person I am saving is also me.

She did not relax when he was gone, nor when she was on the ferry, for she knew that though she could not see him he was still watching her in his own way. The surface of the Channel moved like a length of cloth in the turning wind. Lauren sat inside with a sad severe look on her face. At Calais the Paris train was enormously waiting at an empty platform. In Paris she bought a green leather suitcase and a cup of yogurt and stayed that night in an American-style hotel. She was exhausted but slept badly, because she was frightened, even here. And what was happening in London?

On the train to Roissy the next day she tried to put the past two days together. She puzzled with them but there was a large piece missing. And yet the rest was vast. There was too much. She thought: It hasn't happened to me yet. She was still trying to make sense of the first terrible day.

At the airport, all the papers on the news-stand, French and English – and every other language – had the same simple picture on the front page. It made a black pattern that ran through the display like a rack of wallpaper or linoleum. She bought *The Times*, the *Sun*, and the London Arabic paper, *Al-Arab* – in this one the picture was repeated larger than in any other paper, which was why she bought it. Here the fallen man not only had a face but an expression – surprise, anguish, and his eyes were whitened with fear. His hand was folded crookedly beneath him and great stains soaked his coat.

'Excuse me, miss.'

One shoe was twisted away from his foot, and his narrow elderly ankle was showing. His frailty was obvious in his thin legs and in his brittle posture – he looked as though he had been thrown on those stairs, and broken.

'Are you–?'

But it was this corpse's strange contorted posture that revealed his identity to her. His head and legs set so carelessly gave him an attitude that resembled ecstasy. She had seen him awkward and reckless like that a dozen times, and the last time exactly a week ago all twisted and looking murdered by his passion for her – and right there, too, on Half Moon Street. Horriboo, he would have said. She giggled a little and then began to sob.

'Are you actually reading that paper?'

She shook her head: No – and startled the stranger with her wet eyes and the way she pressed her lips into her mouth in grief. She made an animal motion with her hands – fear – and the man turned sharply away. Was he trying to pretend he hadn't said anything? But even as she watched him go she was still afraid and felt ugly.

1984

# Dr DeMarr

# I

Out of nowhere, and after years of silence, George showed up one July day and put his face against the screen door and said, 'Remember me?'

He was clowning in the way that desperate people sometimes do. He said, 'Deedee?'

Gerald did not want to open the door. How could he have forgotten the man who had destroyed his life? He wanted to say: *I thought you were dead*. He had often hoped so, but his pessimism told him that it could not be true. George was his brother, his twin, or else he would not have let him in.

The spring yanked the screen door shut with a smack, like the lid of a trap, and the brothers were both inside, jostling.

George was nervous, fussing with his hands and breathing hard, trying to be helpful. He followed Gerald into the kitchen and tripped him – almost knocked him over – he was so eager to please. Wherever Gerald turned he came up against his hovering brother. How different they were, and yet it had always been like this! Years ago, walking side by side, they had bumped shoulders, tramped on each other's toes, hit elbows – 'You go first,' 'No, you.' They got in the way, one kicking the other's feet, usually George kicking Gerald's, which was why Gerald resented the memory of being slowed and pushed by that little oaf. That was another thing: they were physically small – just over five feet in high school, and they did not grow any more. Gerald blamed his size on George, too. If it had not been for George he would have been a whole man.

Their father, who had no other children, used to introduce

them at parties, saying, 'I believe in having two of everything!' and he insisted they sing 'Daisy, Daisy' while he sat there beaming. In those earlier years they wore the same outfit, had the same haircut and shirt. They wore shorts, knee socks and big-toed, Buster Brown shoes. Because of their size and their comic clothes they were always taken to be much younger than they were. Their father's intention was to make them look the same, but Gerald believed the matching clothes only tended to exaggerate their differences. Yet people did not regard them as two boys, rather as one irregular being, a four-legged freak.

Gerald and George DeMarr were identical twins.

The hateful shriek was, 'It's impossible to tell you apart!' That statement set them apart – it made them enemies. But, being twins, they could not be separated. They were a matched pair. From the first, Gerald and George were not allowed any existence away from this mirror image: each one was a reflection, or an instance of human repetition, or a small biological stutter. They were seen as a double image. Gerald thought: *I am a shadow*, and it was an early mournful memory of his that as a twin he had been buried alive.

They seemed unusual, as physical echoes, and so they were goaded to perform.

'Do something together – sing, dance, recite a poem, pledge allegiance to the flag.'

This was 1951. Their clothes were always costumes – just right for skits and party pieces. They sang songs, they tap-danced until their bow ties shook loose, they did alternate stanzas of 'Flanders Field' and 'The Concord Hymn' (*By the rude bridge that arched the flood . . .*). It was all the hackneyed upbringing of twins – the freakishness of it, the puppet show. People called them the Deedees, or the Dancing DeMarrs. It prevented them from maturing, it destroyed their will-power, and coupled with their small size this meant they would always be treated as grotesques or as children.

'Are you sure *you* feel all right?' a person would say to one when the other was ill, as if it was impossible for them to escape each other's illnesses. They were not two individuals: they were aspects of one.

Their names, too, were given interchangeably, as if it hardly mattered. 'You must be George,' people said to Gerald, and delighted in their mistake, because it was caused by the twins' supposed sameness – and in consequence their flaw was that one was superfluous.

They grew up in Winter Hill, a place that was both a town and a neighbourhood of Boston – from the high ground in the center of it, looking east, they saw the Custom House tower, and to the west were wooded hills. The area itself was a barely respectable ruin of three-decker houses – dry, rust-colored shingles and sagging porches – on the steep streets at the very edge of a small city.

Mr DeMarr was a salesman in a men's clothing store that still called itself a haberdashery. It was a badly-paid and boring job, and unworthy of him, but his work had become an easy habit. He was given discounts on his clothes. He dressed like a trial lawyer – pin stripes, a Homburg, a cashmere topcoat. As a young man he had worn spats. He was slightly taller than his boys and very proud of his tiny feet. He told jokes: his wisecracks somehow fitted his natty clothes. The jokes revealed his sadness and his sentimentality. He was tearfully fond of his wife and always spoke to her in a shy grateful way – no wisecracks – because she never judged him and said what he feared, that he was a timid show-off, nearly a coward, who had pinned all his own failed hopes on his twin sons.

'Give them hell,' he always said, when he goaded the boys to dance.

They were Catholics, and there was something about their version of Catholicism that took away their ambition and made them morally lazy: they had heaven and the confessional and the consolations of secret rituals. There was a theatrical element in the Holy Mass, too: it formed the twins and gave them a sense of timing and decorum. You had to perform to be a Catholic! They were altar boys, and then Boy Scouts, and later they tap-danced in the church hall: 'for the Glory of God.' They were discouraged from joining any teams, since competitive sports would inevitably have emphasized their differences. A brief spell on the Saint Joe's softball team proved that – they couldn't both be pitchers, and George was the stronger hitter.

They were routinely given identical haircuts and identical clothes. For birthdays and at Christmas they were presented with identical gifts. Aunts and uncles were warned. If there were not two available of a particular thing, they went without – one was unthinkable unless, and this became common, a joint gift was given: they were told to share it equally. That happened, as the years passed, with the rocking horse, the Meccano set, the pup tent, and the radio; each gift – *To Gerald and George, best wishes* – provoked a bitter and damaging quarrel.

For their first fifteen years or so they seemed to share a life as undifferentiated sides of the same person, one standing for the other, or else the shadow, or sometimes the ghost of the other – a sort of maddening mimicry that was vivid because their father had deliberately made them overlap. They lived a strange unseparated life, full of the hot secret dreams that are the sweats of frustration. They were in each other's company the whole time; they went to school together, they slept in the same room, they were never alone. It was symmetry of a kind, but it was ornamental, it went no deeper – all that effort purely for the design.

They had hated each other from an early age; but they knew they had no one else. They were like the last two survivors of a race of people, with their own language and habits and customs, constituting an entire culture, the smallest society on earth, a nation of two.

Yet each believed himself to be totally different from the other. The very fact that they were twins made them obsessive about comparisons, and they never looked at each other without narrowing their eyes in scrutiny or, indeed, without discovering yet another crucial distinction. They glanced at each other in the way that people glanced at mirrors, but they never saw reflections, only differences.

Gerald looked at George and saw a shrimp, with tiny moles on his forearms that were more numerous in the summer; George looked at Gerald and saw a small pudgy coward. 'You're pigeon-toed,' George said. 'You're worse – dink-toed.' Gerald had a cowlick, George had a chipped front tooth. 'You're got big lips,' George said. 'Not as big as yours.' They recognized a vague similarity, but this made them monstrous-looking to each other. Each one seemed dark to the other and thought: I have a light complexion.

They knew that most people lived with the satisfaction that they were single and unique; but it was the fate of twins to be always weighed and compared. For the whole of their early life they were unhappily chained together, and it was torture to them, for the few likenesses they saw seemed like nothing more than ugly parody.

Their parents had connived at making them seem the same, but it hadn't worked; it never worked; the differences of twins were always greater than the similarities, yet only twins knew that. Gerald and George believed this. If they had been in the habit of confiding in each other they might have discovered that in this respect – in this one belief – they were identical.

When their mother died – they had just turned sixteen – their father held them tighter, consoling himself with them, treating them as toys, and goading them more fiercely. He demanded that they succeed, so that he would not be seen as a failure, although he did not know what he meant by success.

They were still at school. 'George did ten laps,' a gym teacher said once, challenging Gerald, who had been ready to give up after eight. He forced himself to do two more, and the next day he ached terribly from the effort.

'What do you mean you don't know how to do quadratic

equations?' the maths teacher said to George. 'Gerald is a whiz at them!'

They supposed that George was being stubborn. He had to put in hours of extra study, and still he never got the hang of them.

This dreary competition inspired one day an unexpected response.

The scoutmaster, Mr Seagrave said, very loudly, 'You don't know how to semaphore?' He always shouted when he meant to be sarcastic, believing that sarcasm was not a choice of words but rather a certain degree of loudness. 'But Gerald knows how!'

They were senior scouts and wore identical green uniforms with white leggings.

George put down the flags. In a flat insolent voice he said, 'I'm Gerald.'

Gerald looked up from his wood carving, and then smiled at his knife. How easily Mr Seagrave had been fooled! It was a crucial victory, because it seemed to disprove what they had instinctively felt, about their differences being so obvious. They really weren't taken seriously at all, they weren't known, they didn't matter – no one looked closely enough to see them properly. It was the world's fault, either indifference or contempt. They thought: We are Chinese.

It proved that no one cared about them. There was no subtlety, no nuance. They were a pair – that was all, like bookends or a pair of shoes. Their own father had not bothered to distinguish between them: 'I believe in having two of everything.'

It made them cynical. When they saw how easily they could be mistaken for one another they played upon the confusion. George took Gerald's driving test, and Gerald took George's French final. George appeared in court as Gerald on a charge of reckless driving – it seemed less serious that way. And Gerald worked as George at the Star Market. This last ploy worked so well they decided to share the job, putting in three evenings a week each, bagging groceries and stacking shelves. This was in 1959, the year they graduated from high school.

All this had unexpected results. Their taking turns made their differences even greater. Gerald, who had never really learned to drive well, seldom used the car. George was incapable of simple algebra, Gerald was ignorant of history, George of French, and Gerald would have failed art except for George's effort. Gerald had flat feet: the imprints on his foot examination were George's; but it was Gerald's good teeth that saved George from the dentist's drill.

Cynical people, who regarded them as freaks, had made them cynical and freakish: the two boys passed themselves off as one nearly perfect specimen while remaining – they knew – deficient themselves in many ways.

George was the more composed of the two – a talker, an easy conversationalist, full of schemes and deceits. He attended all the college interviews and he made a good impression, both as himself and as Gerald. Gerald had become a silent and somewhat fearful person, and the more George acted on his behalf the more his confidence ebbed.

But the college interviews marked the end of the odd team effort, and soon the pretense was dropped and they were returned to themselves. Their father died – that dapper man who hid himself in his expensive clothes; that puppeteer, that sadist. Gerald and George were relieved and hopeful, and they began to recover, as from a long illness. This death had released them. The important witness was gone. They realized now that their parents while living had intimidated them, made them guilty, and robbed them of glory. Now the twins could quietly succeed or fail, and now that they were free, each saw enormous changes in the other.

Once, they had needed each other in distinct ways. Arriving home late in the day, Gerald had greeted his mother or father with, 'Where's George?' or 'Has George called?' – and George had usually done the same. Each had to know where the other was – what he was doing, and with whom and why. And each was uneasy and vaguely anxious until he had the answer. If anyone had asked them they would have said that they felt closer to one another than they did to their parents.

But the twins were alone now and whatever it was that had bound them together – a fear of death was what Gerald felt – anyway, it was gone. Alone now they often felt hateful, and each received hostile vibrations from the other. This hatred hummed like a bad smell. They were free and they were alone, but what good was it if they were still a pair? Gerald understood what was in George's mind, because it was in his own, yet his was more muted and kinder.

He wanted George to leave him; but George wanted him to die – and not just die, but for the earth to crack open beneath him and for him to be swallowed by the murk and vapor in the abyss. George's poisonous emanations, that smell, said *die*. Gerald felt that hideous wish in George's looks – his eyes darkened at him; in the casual violence of his touch – he had a way of nudging Gerald with his horny little knuckles; in his harsh arrogant voice. And Gerald sensed it sometimes at a great distance, the odor that wished him ill.

Using the insurance money they went to college – different ones; Gerald chose Boston University and George chose Harvard. George flunked out in his second year, was immediately drafted into the army and was sent to Vietnam. He was not killed – Gerald would have been informed of that as next-of-kin. It was one of the sorrows of his life that he did not know what had become of George; he brooded on his brother and felt sad and thwarted when he realized that he too wanted his brother dead.

Otherwise how could he live? He earned his degree, a BA in economics, and he worked in the Boston Navy Yard as a statistician. Sometimes he described himself as a Vietnam veteran and spoke about his adventures.

He could even impress many of the older men – some of them veterans of the Second World War – with the stories. The one about the snake he had found in his bed – not on getting into bed, but rather the morning after, when it had wrapped itself in five coils around his ankle. The tale of the lunatic with whom he had shared a pup tent on bivouac – only when the man had talked in his sleep had Gerald realized the grave danger he was in from this mumbling murderer. The tropical fungus he had contracted, on a shirt imported from the Philippines, that had given him six months of misery and the mottled skin of a giraffe. The nightmare journey under fire from the jungle outpost to the garrison at Danang, dragging his wounded buddy. And this was strange, because he had never been to Vietnam and he avoided war movies, and any mention of the war by a genuine veteran frightened and upset him.

In the stories he told that weren't about the war he was a highly-placed comptroller doing budget projections for Northrop Aircraft Corporation in Long Beach, whose crucial work had produced in him a massive nervous breakdown; or he was a graduate of Harvard Law School, a frequent visitor to London, England, where he went to the opera and watched the Trooping of the Colour, and he had once lived there in a flat near the famous Hyde Park – it was Bayswater, actually, for any listener who was familiar with the city – and in that year of sheer luxury he had spent the vast sum he had won in a card game on the cargo plane that had taken him from Saigon to Frankfurt, a C-130, as a matter of fact. There was a '68 Chevy in the belly of the plane and the GIs, Gerald included, had sat in this air-borne car, playing gin rummy at ten bucks a point.

None of it was true (although Gerald often thought, *But it must have happened to someone at some time . . .*). He was not ashamed of his lies. On the contrary he was secretly pleased and strengthened, and he despised his co-workers in the Navy Yard office so heartily for believing his lies that he became incapable of telling the truth. That habit isolated him and kept him apart and alone.

He lived in the house his father had bequeathed him – George had received a sum of money. Surely he was dead? Twice, Gerald had almost got married – the women were plain and seemed a little desperate and eager to please; but it was they who left him.

Gerald went on living in the three-storey house where he had been born and raised. He lived in a slow spare way, almost monkishly. When he thought about George he felt like a shadow and he blamed George for this. Not that George had done anything in particular that displeased him, but George was alive. Whispers in Gerald's mind told him maliciously that they were still being compared, and this convinced him that he was living in a dumb and buried way and that in certain respects he had already started to decompose. Terrible thoughts – but he lived alone and told lies and there was no one he knew who could dispute his morbid thoughts.

Living alone, he frequently felt invisible, or only partly visible – patchy and far off. It was a feeling of being half there. Sometimes it was misery, and just as often it gave him relief; it added satisfaction to the only real pleasure of his life, which was peering into people's windows.

This spying thrilled him especially in the colder months, in the early darkness of winter afternoons, before curtains were drawn or shades pulled. He could look into lighted rooms and see people eating or standing at sinks. They stared, they fingered their buttons, they touched their faces. It made him short of breath to see these private acts taking place; and the sight of a woman in loose houseclothes, alone, combing her hair before a mirror, always held him and slowly throttled him. It gave him a taste for night-time walks, and for trains; for back yards and certain streets. Until they pulled it down, the elevated train from Sullivan Square had allowed him wonderful window views. How he missed the curve where the train screeched and slowed between Thompson Square and North Station: several nearby windows in a gray house were his particular favourites, and he knew the furniture in most of them and most of the people. All rooms fascinated him from the outside. Just the interiors, those secrets, had an obscure eroticism and always an excitement. But he knew it was pathetic.

This looking through windows stimulated Gerald and gave him imagery for the letters he wrote and the phone calls he made. He imagined that the women he sought were in rooms like these, sitting on those brown sofas with their legs crossed, between the kitchen and the bedroom, wearing a slip or a house-coat, and with the bathroom door ajar.

He wrote often and at length to a number of people, women mostly, ones he had known from long ago, and others who answered the personal ads he sometimes ran (varying his description) in the *Boston Globe*. His letters were moody, allusive, extravagant and full of innuendo – he teased, he gave advice, he depicted himself as eagerly interested in pleasing them but just a bit too busy at the moment to oblige. His sincerity was in his humour and his certainty: a man this sexy and humorous was worth waiting for. He strung them along until they became impatient – irritably demanding that he do something – and when he vacillated they stopped writing.

There was always someone else. He was a good letter-writer. He had the time, he had the solitude, he was lonely enough. He could be chatty on paper, talking easily about himself (the snake, the lunatic, the war stories, law school, all the rest of it), asking questions, being a friend; and in this way he elicited confidences. He was trusted. In his letters he was usually a businessman, a vice-president ('We make an unbelievably boring product called money . . .'). The letters never revealed what his company actually did, though Gerald always hinted broadly that his best customer was Uncle Sam, as he put it. 'Defense contracts,' he sometimes said. He had a strong sense that it was involved in the weapons industry – not conventional arms, but high-tech armaments, fiber optics, laser guns, heat-seeking missiles. 'Military hardware,' he sometimes let drop. 'Components for the Stealth bomber.' He knew these women were impressed.

His letters were long and fluent and goading, and they frequently alluded to sex – nothing personal but always specific, such as a detailed description of a scene from a movie – *Body Heat* was a favorite source, and so were *The Postman Always Rings Twice* and *Don't Look Now*, and movies with alarming or unusual sex-scenes. Gerald saw most movies, he went twice a week or more, depending on when the programs changed at the cinema complex – ten screens – at the foot of Winter Hill. But often, after a particularly vivid letter, the woman did not write back, and he knew he had gone too far. He hated that. He did not want to outrage them: he wanted them to write back in the same vein.

His phone calls were similar to his letters. He teased, he chatted, he made oblique references to sex. He mentioned his company, his foreign travel, his experiences in Vietnam. He could talk for hours. Most of the women he had never seen. He liked it when they complained of illnesses they had, or aches and pains, for then he would give them detailed advice on how to get well. He recommended home remedies, food cures, exercises, sleep, fresh air – and he imagined them undressing or changing and doing as he had advised. Medical matters gave him a thrill of power and authority. He enjoyed discussing specific areas of a woman's body – the shooting pain in her arm, the lump in her breast, the tightness in her throat. Then he could ask: How tall are you? How much do you weigh? Do you smoke? What sort of work do you do? Do you sleep well? Any recurrent nightmares? What do you like to eat?

The women were the strangers he saw in those rooms – from the train, from the street. He knew he was lonely and pathetic, and he saw this as an addiction. He was addicted to these whisperings and scribblings, and so were they.

And it gave him a hatred for the young. He did not know why. He had feared and despised youngsters his whole life, but now his hatred was corrosive. He saw them shambling around Quincy Market. He enjoyed their ruin. They were most conspicuous in the summer months, squandering their health and shortening their lives on drugs. He overheard things. 'She's living with this incredible guy!' or 'He's absolutely devoted to his kids!' Such remarks enraged him. But there was justice in all things: they would get the early death they deserved; and he who had never really been able to choose – what twin ever did? – would go on living his shadow life, for he had been shoveled under from birth. And where was George?

Now Gerald was forty-six. People said that twins had two lives, but he knew he had hardly one. Sometimes he remembered the skits and songs – they were mingled with religion, too: God was the unblinking audience for whom every Catholic had to perform his heart out. It was much worse than an embarrassment. Gerald saw that its solemn foolery, its clumsiness and its grotesque pathos made it actually tragic. Tragedy was putting on the wrong clothes and clowning and failing to be funny.

## 2

So the visit that July day, two weeks before Gerald's summer vacation, amazed and frightened him. The face against the screen. 'Remember me?' The big kicking feet. And one other thing.

'Deedee?' the man said. He smiled at the secret name.

Except for that childish word, Gerald would not have recognized him, and even so there seemed something diabolical about the man in the doorway. The strong summer light behind him had darkened his face and caused the man's shadow to fall like a shroud over Gerald. The man seemed calm in his darkness, but what unnerved Gerald was the man's size: he was precisely Gerald's height. Their eyes were level.

Hateful kids, some of them no more than twelve or thirteen – girls of eleven! – were his height. They roused his fury, yet he did not feel threatened by them. But now he had the experience of looking a middle-aged man squarely in the eye, and it terrified him to think that the man was his brother George.

'Where's your wife?'

Gerald hesitated, then took a breath to explain that he had never married.

But the man said. 'My marriage was a failure, too.'

'I'm not a failure!' Gerald said loudly, but the way he said it revealed how frightened he was – it was a hollow protest.

'Don't be afraid,' the man said – more calmly now. 'I need a place to stay, for a while.'

Gerald said, 'Why did you come back?'

'I never left.'

Still, Gerald wondered: Is it George? George was the past, like an old coat and crippling clothes that Gerald had been forced to wear. He had nearly suffocated from the nearness of his hovering brother.

'Please go,' Gerald said.

He opened the screen door but he stood his ground at the threshold, blocking the man's entrance.

'Are you alone?'

The man peered behind Gerald, and Gerald saw a stripe of light on the face – sunken features, dry lips, bright eyes. It was a glimpse of illness.

'Help me.'

The man moved again, gave his face to the light. It was a small pale mask of hunger, and there was despair in the bony shape.

'Please,' he said.

Gerald stared back, wishing he would shut up and go.

They watched each other, broken-backed, in the same pleading way.

'Deedee?'

That name again: Gerald gave in. He stepped away and that was when George began bumping into him and tramping on his feet.

George did a feeble dance step, tripping twice and looking around.

'Dad's chair,' he said.

It was red leather and its arms were darkened with age and it had itself the look of a seated man – a big red man reading. Some buttons were missing, there were nicks in its black legs. The matching footstool was pushed against the wall.

'He used to sit in it, looking so pleased with himself. He must have been. He certainly wasn't pleased with us.'

George sat on it and hitched himself back, and, dwarfed by the chair, he seemed like a small boy being obedient.

'I don't mind that my feet don't touch the ground when I sit down,' George said.

He bum-hopped forward and got to the floor and went to the mantelpiece. He picked up a souvenir plate from Niagara Falls.

'Except when I'm on the hopper,' George said, finishing his thought. 'It's so embarrassing. I've never told anyone.'

Neither had Gerald, and Gerald had a fleeting glimpse of the little secrets that had once bound them, hating, together.

'It's a good thing you can lock the door of a john,' George said, and frowned at the plate. 'They went to Niagara on their honeymoon. What an obscene cliché. "The honeymooner's second disappointment." They always talked about their ride on "The Maid of the Mist." Memories, Deedee!'

Gerald hated George's contemptuous reminiscences. He wanted him to go; but George kept prowling, his eyes darting from object to object.

'That rocker, the so-called Salem rocker,' George said. 'He was off it, wasn't he?' – and hardly paused. 'This cigar box. Typical of him to smoke cheap White Owls, real El Ropos, and have an expensive monogrammed humidor. What is it with people who love monograms? What aristocratic fantasy do they have in their heads?'

Gerald said nothing, because he was proud of his mono-grammed cuff-links, dress shirts, pyjamas, ties, his gold-filled belt buckle. He told George again to go. George smiled, hearing nothing.

'Their clock. Their carpet – it still smells of Mum's cooking and Dad's White Owls. We used to fight over the knife.'

'It's a letter opener. It's from China.'

'Oh, sure,' George said. He had never believed it. 'That lamp. "You're going to ruin your eyes."' The mimicry of the old man was perfect. 'You did all the reading, Deedee. I was the man of action.'

*Then go* – but before Gerald could put this thought into words, George was talking again. 'Doilies. You don't see those any more. More monograms' – a dinner plate. 'He used to say, "Pass the mouseturd." He called raisins "dead flies."' George put the plate down and picked up a silver cup, monogrammed GDM. 'We used to have two of these. We used to have two of everything. Where are the others?'

'Lost.'

Destroyed – burned, broken, chucked away, junked, sold. Gerald wanted to say so, but he knew it would make this little man linger.

George lifted the flap of the piano and – still standing: he was the perfect height, he could stand and play without bending, the way a child bangs on the keys – he began to play. He clawed chords on to the keys. He sang *Peg of My Heart*.

And his face brightened. It had been waxen, but now it thickened with colour. The tempo changed. He sang *Bye Bye Blackbird*.

They used to dance to that, and found the song melancholy and spooky.

'You don't seem to realize that I am very busy,' Gerald said.

But he wasn't busy at all, and George must have known that. How was it possible to keep a secret from your twin?

'The Victrola,' George was saying. He lifted the lid of the phonograph, turned the crank and put on a record – one from the top of the black stack.

*Mexicali Rose*, sung by Gene Autry. Before it was over, he plucked it off and played Bing Crosby singing *Sweet Leilani*, and interrupted that too, plopping down Handel's *Largo*, played by Fritz Kreisler, which he left on until the end – he was transfixed by it, and so was Gerald.

Then the needle scraped and repeated in the dead-sounding groove, and Gerald said, 'You have to go.'

George simply stared and put on another record.

'Not many people know that's the *Poet and Peasant Overture* by Franz von Suppé,' George said, whistling through the gap in his teeth.

But the gap in my teeth is much smaller, Gerald thought.

'What do you want me to do?'

'Nothing,' George said. 'You don't have to do a thing. All I want is a quiet place to stay. I'm just paying a visit.'

His tone was almost resentful, as if he wanted Gerald to thank him for asking such a small favor. That was typical. Because George wasn't asking more, Gerald was supposed to be grateful. It was brother logic, and also the tyranny of twins. George's attitude had always been: *Be glad that's all I'm asking – my small request is a favor to you!*

'I don't want you in my life,' Gerald said.

'We only have one life.'

'That means two things,' Gerald said. 'And I mean one. This house is my life – I don't want you in it.'

Gerald was afraid and spoke in a stilted speechy way, occasionally stammering. The *Poet and Peasant Overture* had ended. The needle was scraping again in the groove.

'Look at me, Deedee.' It was one of George's comic voices but it only increased Gerald's fear. George stared at him and did a dance step.

Gerald stammered on, weakening under his brother's gaze. 'But I won't refuse to help you. I know you're desperate.'

'I'm not desperate!' George said and lost his balance.

His genuine panic had a calming effect on Gerald.

271

'If you're not desperate,' Gerald said – slowly, as if teaching him English, so that he would remember the pain – 'then why did you come home?'

As soon as he said it, he was sorry, because there was no possible reply. George just stood there and sagged a little in silence. He knew that *home* was failure. They both knew that.

Gerald said, 'The top floor's unoccupied. I'll give you a week. But I don't want to be here with you. I'm going away–'

'Did you keep Dad's cottage at the Cape?'

'–and when I come back,' Gerald went on, afraid of George's sudden interest in the property (he had an equal claim), 'I don't want to see you here. Promise me that.'

'I promise,' George said, and when Gerald handed over the key, George caught hold of his brother's hand lightly – just a squeeze, the same temperature, the same pads of flesh on the snagging fingers, and such a close fit that Gerald hurriedly shook his hand loose.

'Where's your car?'

'Took a bus,' George said.

'One week,' Gerald said, 'starting tomorrow.'

So it was final. George's back was to the window, and shadows had gathered on his face again – the small dark mask that had first frightened Gerald.

George said, 'You look terribly worried.'

'Never mind. That shouldn't concern you.'

'It doesn't. I'm glad! When I see other people suffer I actually feel a whole lot better – sort of relieved that it isn't me! It sounds awful, doesn't it? But most people think that. Most people have devilish thoughts that they would never admit to. They don't even know that you have to be half full of evil in order to go on living. Do you still go to church?'

Gerald only watched, and what looked like worry on his face was anger – the hatred brimming in him at the way his brother mirrored his own empty life.

'I don't want to see you again.'

'You won't,' George said. 'I know better than to ask a favor of you.' It was his *Be grateful* tone. 'I know when I'm not wanted.'

But the key was in his hand, so he had it both ways, as usual. He had the favor and he also had the malicious satisfaction that Gerald had begrudged it. And just before he turned to go upstairs he did another soft-shoe shuffle and a little lisping flap of his feet. That was George: when he wasn't stepping on Gerald's toes he was dancing lightly in front of him – but each was a form of gloating.

George had got what he had come for. Gerald thought: But what about the sickness in your face?

Gerald took his vacation then, two weeks early, and left the next day for the Cape.

He went slowly in his Datsun down Winter Hill and struggled through Boston traffic to the South-east Expressway, the speeding, contending cars bumping over the broken highway. How come it was never fixed, it only got worse, the traffic more aggressive, the road more dangerous. At the *Globe* he saw the time and temperature blinking alternately *July 13* and *81°*, and then the familiar landmarks, the wooden clubhouse of the Dorchester Yacht Club, on stilts like an Asiatic dance hall from one of his jungle lies, the gas tanks childishly multicolored in stripes that mimicked spilled paint (and one was said to be the profile of Ho Chi Minh), the junction ten minutes farther on, where the right road said *Providence – New York* and the left said *Cape Cod.*

Merging left, he studied the landmarks, a familiar sequence: Grossman's lumberyard, the low buildings in the pines, the photographical lab, Exit 13 with its fast food signs, the Howard Johnsons and *All you can eat, Rocky Nook* at Exit 7 (seeing it, George had always murmured 'Nooky Rock'), the totem pole at Exit 5, *Plimouth Plantation* at Exit 4, and *Heavy Weekend Traffic – Expect Delays*, and the first sight over the tree-tops of the hump of the Sagamore bridge span, like a hill in steel. There was a freighter swilling the water of the canal as he crossed it. He sped on to the Mid-Cape Highway and took Exit 2. There, papers were blowing in the road and were flattened against the chain-link fence: the dump. Then the Wing School, the motels, the gift shops, the real estate agencies, the tracks, Colonial Market. How long had they been loaning videos? The cottage was at the marshy end of Plowed Neck Road. The lawn needed cutting, the front door stuck, the inside smelled of damp upholstery – salt, sand, mildewed sheets, and the foody smell of decayed wood.

He looked around at the lamp, the light, the mirror, the sandpails, the ship's wheel, the broken oar, the stencilled crate, the smooth bits of seaglass – treasures from the tidewrack – and he imagined George saying *I remember this* and *We used to have two of these* in his proprietorial and mocking way.

Gerald bought a frozen pizza at Colonial Market, and baked it, and ate it at the window, looking at the blue-leaved trees and gray sky this gloomy day. He sat down and clamped his teeth together when he imagined that someone was staring in at him – an old woman with a crippled and misshapen mutt on a leash. The craziest ones had dogs like that.

Then he locked the door and fretted, mumbling to himself, on the verge of crying. He knew he was hiding. Buried again.

It was his first visit of the year. He had begun to neglect the cottage as he had neglected his life. The place was full of junk, and it was junk that George would covet – the way someone drowning clings to flotsam, saving himself and staying afloat by hugging a hunk of greasy styrofoam cushion. There was just such a cushion at the cottage. He made a sudden pile of it all – the stack of newspapers, the *National Geographics*, the wine bottles, the paint cans, the jelly jars he had washed and saved, and all his odd frugalities – the drawers full of string and screws and rubber bands and reusable envelopes; and the toys, two of each, everything that linked him to George, the snorkels, the flippers, the goggles, the kites, the skates; he junked it all. He crammed it into plastic bags, and whatever would not fit whole he broke and tore, dismembering it.

A black sea-drizzle crackled like hot fat in a frying pan and the roof became slick with leaks. Someone drove a car too fast for these slippery roads, heading towards Plowed Neck. Once, long ago, George had tumbled out of a dune buggy and run shrieking up the driveway, across the lawn.

*I've just got arrested –*

But he was laughing.

*–for driving illegally on Spring Hill Beach*, he said. *In the prohibited area! Near the nesting terns! We were racing!*

Why was he laughing? Gerald was using paint stripper on a chair, and repeating to himself the sour and precise word *glue*, and wearing yellow rubber gloves – feeling that he looked like a housewife doing dishes.

*And you'll have to pay a fine!*

*No – you will*, George said. *I showed him your license.*

It was the same face to anyone but them.

*I'm you, Deedee! You did it!*

He went to the Town Hall to pick up his dump sticker. But when he asked for it, the clerk – a girl not more than sixteen or seventeen – did not look up. She was talking to an older woman who was leafing through a travel magazine.

'England's real pretty at this time of year. Plus all that atmosphere. Flowers and that. Grass. Bricks and stuff.' That was the older woman, her head bent over the magazine.

The girl said, 'England,' She took a deep breath, thinking hard. 'I'd kill to get there.'

And then she turned. Such violent words from so sweet a mouth – no make-up on the face, no lipstick on the lips. Gerald watched her. He would not have trusted her an inch.

'Dump sticker, please,' Gerald said when she turned to him.

'One landfill permit,' she said, correcting him. She did not even notice that on this rainy day he was wearing a genuine

Burberry. Never mind that he bought it in Boston. What did she really know about England?

He studied the calendar that lay on the counter. He had left Winter Hill on the thirteenth. George would have to be out by the twentieth, when he returned.

'I'll have to see some identification,' she demanded. How he hated her. 'Your car registration.'

He produced it, and she seemed not so much to read it as to smell it.

She clumsily copied his name into her log book, and he was reminded of how poorly coordinated unintelligent youngsters could be; how she started to write and then looked around and lost her place; how she started again. She had no concentration, her fingers hardly seemed to work. He imagined that someone so young and blundering could have no sexual sense at all – no violence, no tenderness.

She handed over the sticker, she lectured him on which window of his car he should display it, and he left.

He took miserable pleasure in using it, throwing away the bags he had filled – the toys, the goggles, the flippers, the skates; all George's – and he sat at the dump in his car, among the screeching seagulls, watching the bulldozer push the crates and bags into the pits of the quarry-like place. And the man in charge, with his rake. He liked the dump this week. He enjoyed seeing the filthy refuse covered, and there was something about this great noisy burial of things worn out and used up or pointlessly thrown away that he found consoling.

It was the perfect solution to error and waste and embarrass-ment, to the toys that had belonged to George. They were lifted by the jaws of the bulldozer and crunched and planted deeper. He imagined that George was in the jaws, lying still – the odd small man – and then lifted and swung around by the bulldozer's shovel-mouth and buried under the burst cushions and the rusted Weber grill.

Then Gerald panicked and had to leave the dump, because

only then – with the destruction of Gerald's possessions – had he seen that for nearly the whole of his life he had wanted to kill George, and never more so than now. The thought that he wanted his brother dead, that his genuine happiness had come from the suspicion that his brother was in fact dead, probably killed in Vietnam – this morbidity drove him from the dump that day. He did not want to think of himself as someone with such bitterness in his heart.

But he went back there. The dump was a process of life, and it excited his mind. He chucked away bottles and papers and trash bags with more of George's things; he felt he had junked his brother's childhood and taken possession of the house.

And he sat and watched the gulls squawking over the torn-open garbage bags. He saw apple peels, grapefruit rinds, crumpled letters. He had once written hundreds of letters to a woman who accused him of being a wimp and a dreamer. *They're just words*, she said. But words were wonderful. He told her that: *Words are magic.*

The pronouncement enraged her, and she sent his letters back, nearly all of them – there were so many – in the old manila folder in which she had saved them. She said she was glad to be rid of them. 'I care nothing for them,' she said. Before Gerald destroyed them, in a low negligent mood, he put them on his lap and began to read them. He went on reading, with mounting fascination. They were funny! They were interesting! They contained daily happenings, some of which were true. They were full of life, and they were loving too – always asking after her, cheering her up. Her own letters were flat and complaining and monotonous. Her ingratitude proved that she was selfish and demanding. His letters showed him that he was a good man.

It rained most of the week, so it was either the dump or the movies. And the movies hadn't worked. The movie was one of those summer ones, for kids: a family on a farm, 'If we all pitch in we can make it work,' a sadistic neighbour, some dead kittens, the famous 'drowning scene.' When the struggling bag sank Gerald burst into tears and sobbed into his hands.

His hatred for George was making him ill. It did George no harm at all, he knew, but it was poisoning him. This hatred for his brother was like swallowing his own venom.

He gave it an extra day, to be perfectly sure, and then he drove home – embarrassed as he passed the gates of the town dump, where he had wasted those hours.

There was no sign of George at the house. But he had not come in a car the first time – perhaps he didn't have one?

*I will take no notice of his absence. I will pretend it never happened.* Yet he wanted to be sure, and so he was alert to every sound. As he unpacked his suitcase Gerald heard a mutter in the wall.

He ran to the back stairs. A radio was playing! So George hadn't kept his promise. Gerald noticed a tap dripping as he crossed the kitchen. *Now you've got to leave.* Gerald braced himself for an argument and trembled thinking, *You gave me your word!*

George was in an armchair. Obstinate: he did not look up. Gerald spoke his name. Very pale and plump – George was dozing. 'Listen!' But George was obviously very sick. Gerald raised his hand to touch him, but the dry grey skin repelled him. His flesh was the colour of microwaved meat. So he whispered 'Deedee?' in a kindly way. But George did not respond, and then he knew that George must be dead.

Turning aside to whimper – it was a strange sound, like his soul leaving his mouth – he saw the hypodermic needle, the bottle, the ashtray, the addict's junk, and was that spilled soup in his lap?

## 3

Gerald had never known such a shock. Even the death of his parents and his guilty clinging grief had been nothing compared to this. This was physical in a paralyzing way, but it was slow and unstoppable, more like a rising tide: wave upon wave of emotion heaving within him and numbing him – sadness, surprise, relief, guilt, doubt, anger, joy. One caused another, washed up and broke, spilling useless surf and rattling his soul loose. Afterwards, he felt purer and slightly weak, as after a sickness.

For Gerald, George's death was more like an amputation – one that had been successfully carried out on his own body. It was as if a diseased and disfiguring part of himself had been cut away, like a blackened frost-bitten finger. It was a horror, and yet he could not think about it without feeling a little sentimental. It had been a necessary thing and, as with the death of his father, it had granted him another measure of freedom. There was justice in its cruelty and, like all natural deaths in a family, it had a savage element of sacrifice.

George had brought it upon himself! The sick gloating man who had said how the sight of people suffering secretly pleased him – he had suffered and died. He had come home and killed himself, either accidentally or on purpose – pushed a needle into his arm and puked his guts out. His face still wore the urgent expression of the moments before death: defiance – he had fought back – and the only signs on his face that he had lost were his blue lips and cold eyes. His small cheeks were full, he was canted forward, plump and surprised.

And then Gerald wondered: Who is this man and why did he come here?

He feared that it might be merely a macabre joke being played on him; and what if he were not George, but just a small stiff corpse, propped on the chair to terrify him – not his brother at all? George was capable of a deception like that; it was the sort of thing George would enjoy. *You're next*, the staring eyes seemed to say. It was so easy to scare someone by surprising him, even if it was only to shout *Boo*!

The belongings in the man's pockets were too few to convince Gerald that it was George. It would have been so easy for George to have planted them. The dead man's face was bloodless and unrecognizable: pale unfamiliar flesh. Gerald caught himself pitying this stranger. Or perhaps it was the sort of convulsed and choking drug death George had endured that had changed his face and removed the resemblance.

What if – Gerald was pacing the room downstairs, glancing at Boston through the front windows – what if it really had been George the other day, but that George had put this corpse here and dressed it in his clothes, given it his wallet and handkerchief: killed this man and thereby faked his own death? It was possible. And if that was the case he was depending on Gerald to report him dead, while he counted his money in Mexico or started a new life in California or wherever, and continued to cast his shadow over Gerald.

In the wallet there was some money – just over forty dollars – and standard wallet items, credit cards, social security card, all George's. No driver's license. There was a razor and shampoo in the bathroom, and last week's *Globes*, a sequence of three – Wednesday to Friday. Today was Monday. Did that mean that the man had been dead for two days, or had things been arranged for it to look that way?

None of this matters, Gerald thought. But one thing does matter: secrecy. Gerald was certain he would not go to the police. If it was George, why should he dignify his druggy brother's memory with a decent burial? If it was not George then certainly George had planted it, and he would not do George the favour of reporting the death and aiding him in his pretense.

They were the family reasons. There was a practical reason, too. The third floor was empty because it was for rent – so was the second floor, for that matter. There would be no possibility of a tenant if news of the death got into the papers.

Once, when they were children, the DeMarrs had been visited by their uncle Frank, who drove up in a green Cadillac. Frank was a simple soul and very proud of his car – practically new!

'Let's go for a spin,' he suggested.

'You can drop us off at church,' Mr DeMarr said. He felt Frank was a dangerous driver, especially when Frank was trying to hold a conversation. But it was raining hard, and it wasn't far to Saint Joe's.

On the way, Frank said. 'You won't believe this, but I only paid two hundred dollars for this beauty.'

Mr DeMarr sniffed and became thoughtful.

'Stop the car!' he said at last.

It was so loud, Frank pressed the brake and spilled Gerald and George off the back seat and on to the floor. The four DeMarrs got out and walked the rest of the way to church in the rain, and it was not until they were inside that Mr DeMarr spoke. He did so in a frightening way, hissing the sentence into his children's faces.

'Someone died in that car!'

And someone had died in Amato's duplex – years ago, and the place was still empty. 'You'd hardly know someone died in there,' Amato said. The *hardly* still bothered Gerald.

These recollections came to Gerald as he labored with the body, slipping it into the plastic bag and sealing it, and then dragging it into the garage and cramming it into a barrel. Upside down, and with the knees tucked up, it was just the right size. That brought back a memory: the pair of barrels they'd had in their act, and how they had been rolled onstage to the well-known song, and the twins had tumbled out and danced.

*Roll out the barrel*
*We'll have a barrel of fun!*

That memory continued, offering Gerald another glimpse of himself and George – George standing on his shoulders and wearing a long coat that reached to the floor, so that one on top of the other they made a whole man. It had been a life as little men, dedicated to dressing up and performing, and remembering it roused all the old hatred for George.

The next morning he awoke with a determination to get rid of the barrel. If it was George it was just what he deserved; and if it wasn't, why should Gerald worry? And there, lying in bed, still bitter about his hidden life, he hit on the perfect burial.

He was soon driving down the South-east Expressway, keeping well under the speed limit. After Braintree the traffic thinned out.

The road was straighter, flatter, bordered by scrub oak and dwarf pine. It was a road with few landmarks, the sort that made you reach for the radio knob. The lumberyard, the restaurant, the swamp, the river, the marsh, the totem pole, the distant view of the prison farm – but mainly it was the exit numbers and the place names on signs that indicated your progress on the route – Rocky Nook, Norwell, Kingston, Pembroke, Plymouth, Marshfield, Whitehorse Beach; and for anyone who knew the road well, the smells. Gerald was penetrated with the vibrations of the wheels and he lapsed into a driver's reverie.

In a world of straight flat roads and low trees and cloudy skies he had needed fantasy. He knew that this plain familiar landscape made him yearn for foreign places, for mountains and deserts and oceans, settings in which he saw himself as an adventurer. He felt it was better to dream, to expect no more than dreams; he had been a success that way. If he had seen real mountains and moors he might never have known such triumphant fantasies.

It was only as he bumped over the steel seams on the Sagamore Bridge that he remembered the load in the trunk; he began watching for the exit. And wondering how George had lived his life.

The dump lay behind a chain-link fence, and today the man in charge was examining dump stickers – making a business of it, halting each car and then, as it came to a stop, hurrying it, motioning with his hands in a peevish way and frowning, as if he found it all intellectually exhausting. Gerald was delighted to find the man there and not guarding the ditch with his rake. Gerald was examined and waved on. He drove down the slope and parked near the narrow trench – it was just the width of the bulldozer that was filling it with the rubbish people heaved out of their cars in sacks and boxes. Among the dust and groans of the bulldozer were the seagulls – large nagging birds that mobbed the edges of the trench, occasionally tumbling in to tear at a burst bag.

Gerald waited for the other dumpers to drive away, and then he slid his barrel out and tipped it against the lip of the trench with the crates of grass clippings, and the smeared cans and broken beach chairs. He rolled it forward and it came to rest just beneath the bulldozer scoop, which covered it with half a ton of sand.

This must happen all the time, he thought. And he imagined the dump to be full of dead men and nameless fetuses and discarded mistakes, and all of it covered with yellow sand and household junk.

He remained – pretending to sweep out his car – until the trench was nearly full and the barrel completely buried. He trusted the incurious dump workers, but he had no such faith in the hungry seagulls. He drove away satisfied with what he had done.

'I'm still on vacation,' he said to the empty road ahead. He had the solitary person's habit of holding conversations with himself and always meeting opposition in these dialogues. 'Call this a vacation!'

It seemed incredible that in such a short time he had managed to discover and hide a human corpse. He was a moderate, fastidious and decent man – he felt this strongly. Perhaps this accounted for his efficiency. He had always talked of his adventurous past, and talking had been enough. But now he had acted, he had taken a turning – for the first time in his life – and he had to keep going, to finish what he had started. The burial had made it complete.

He was alone, and so he was solitary in his deceit. It made him feel lonely, but not weak. In fact, he imagined that this secret gave him Power, or at least an authority over his life that he had never known before.

He raced forwards under hot gray clouds that had the shapes of sundaes and luffing sails. The horizon was a row of grinning faces, with monkey cheeks.

As soon as he had crossed the Cape Cod Canal he knew he had succeeded. The canal was like a break in time. He had left the past behind on the far bank: he was safe. There was nothing at all here off-Cape to connect him with the corpse. It was perfect, a buried secret. And anyway, who was there to tell?

He followed Route 3 towards Boston until, at Marshfield – feeling very tired – he pulled into the rest area and parked. The sight of the North River winding through the tall grass below the highway into Norwell heartened him, because it was lovely and unspoiled, and his certainty that it was beautiful gave him hope: If I know that, then I'm still worth something.

He saw that he could leave the whole matter now and go home. No one would ever know. But another mystery, that of George's life, would be his to ponder for the rest of his days.

He sorted the credit cards and rummaged in the wallet as he turned the matter over in his mind, wondering whether to pursue it. That was when he found the laundry ticket – or it might have been for dry cleaning. It gave him a task and a decision. He had a free day and the laundry ticket tempted him. He would follow that lead, and if that did not reveal the life of the dead man he would forget the business and go home.

Printed on the ticket was the name of the laundry and a serial number – no more. There was something important in the little ticket: it had been folded and tucked away. It mattered because it had been forgotten and seemed unintentional. And everything else had appeared so calculated.

He had been so preoccupied with getting rid of the body that he had not considered what his next move should be. But this suggestion could hardly have been easier. It was the Wong Hee Laundry on Stuart Street, the Chinatown exit. If nothing materialized he could just beat it down the expressway to Winter Hill. That was his new guiding thought: See what happens.

It wasn't ghoulish, it was a favor – picking up the dead man's laundry. And Gerald was again reassured by the simplicity of it. It was so easy it could not be wrong.

If he challenges me or asks, Gerald thought, I'll say I'm Charles Leggate – with an 'e' – and my car is double-parked in front of Jacob Wirth's, and I'll have to move it before I can explain how this laundry ticket came into my possession.

And then I'll go underground and never return.

But the elderly Chinese man showed no curiosity and did not even pretend a polite interest in him. He held the ticket close to his face and matched its number to a large parcel in a tall stack. He handed it over and told Gerald the cost: fourteen dollars. That seemed rather expensive for shirts, which was what he guessed was in the parcel. He went to his car and tore off the wrapper and saw that he was in possession of four linen smocks, folded in tissue paper. They were the sort of white smocks worn by so many people these days, not only dentists, doctors and pharmacists, but also art teachers and certain mechanics who carried out car repairs in the more expensive garages.

If it had been shirts he would have headed straight home. But *smocks*?

He could not imagine George the art teacher or George the mechanic. But he clearly imagined a plausible George DeMarr DDM, gouging a root canal, drilling for all he was worth, bearing down hard on a bleeding gum as the patient gagged, his mouth yanked sideways with the hissing drain of a mouth-hook.

Behind his white mask George was smirking with satisfaction over the pain he was inflicting.

With this vision of George the dentist, Gerald saw him standing on a stool in order to work at the correct height. But would his vain brother have done that? It was true that dentists were the greediest, the most complaining, the most demanding members of the medical profession, with the highest suicide rate. They simply grubbed for money in people's mouths. That was George's general profile, but George was the wrong height.

He walked back to the laundry and showed the man his ticket.

'I think there was something else in here,' he said. 'Some shirts.'

'No shirts,' the man said.

'Can I see the receipt?'

The man nodded and pulled out a shoebox filled with receipts. After a moment of foraging in the box he clawed out the correct piece of paper.

'Four smock,' he read. 'No starch.' He pushed it sourly at Gerald.

Gerald smiled at the success of his ruse. This was what he wanted to see. D. MARR it said in wobbly capital letters, and there was a telephone number.

D. MARR: was that George's alias or just a Chinese mistake in transcription? The smocks he could see had been hand-tailored. They were not standard issue, but rather custom-made. They were as beautiful as surplices – they could have been priestly garments. Could it be that George had become a priest?

Gerald was the only DeMarr in the Boston telephone directory, and no one named Marr was listed. On a hunch – because of the smocks and because the place was so near – Gerald enquired at Tufts Medical School, just across the street. Doctor Marr? Doctor DeMarr? But no such person existed.

He called the telephone number he had memorized from the receipt. It rang repeatedly – hopeless, he thought: he was calling a dead man's number.

'Doctor DeMarr's office.' It was a woman's voice, and yet not as crisp as it might have been. Perhaps an answering service?

When it sank in – the Chinese laundry clerk had simply written what he had heard – Gerald said, 'Yes, I'd like to speak to the doctor, please.'

'I'm afraid that's impossible,' the woman said. 'He's not available.'

'When do you expect him?'

'I'm not sure. Who's speaking, may I ask? Is this Mr Scarfo?'

Without hesitating, Gerald said, 'No. I'm a consultant immunologist and I'm just up from Plainfield, New Jersey, for the convention here on immunology and,' he took a breath, surprised by his fluency, 'I thought I'd look up my old friend–'

'So it's not an appointment,' the woman said.

'I did want to make an appointment for my wife,' Gerald said. 'It's rather urgent.'

'I was just going to say, we're not taking any new appointments until further notice. Perhaps I can get back to you?'

'It might be easier if I called you some other time. I'm not sure when I'll be back in Boston. Perhaps I'll write a note. Would you mind giving me your address?'

The woman dictated the address: it was a suite on the fifteenth floor of Riverview Towers, Kenmore Square.

The woman repeated, 'Doctor DeMarr is not taking any new appointments–'

'I'll see that all the details are in my note to him. Perhaps you'd be good enough to see that the doctor gets it.'

'It will be on his desk with the rest of his mail.'

Why was this woman being so obstinate and unhelpful?

After he hung up, Gerald parked at the Common Garage and went to Kenmore Square in a taxi. Riverview Towers was not a new building, but it was a stately one, of brick and granite, with ornamented stone around its windows and at its edges, and a heavy stone canopy over its front door that somewhat resembled a movie marquee. Gerald counted the floors to fifteen, and he marveled at how he had spent his whole life in Winter Hill and had never seen this building or realized that George might still be around. But, thinking about it, he ceased to be surprised; after all, he had always imagined that he had lived a buried life. And now who lay buried?

Still carrying the parcel of smocks – it was like a key to the whole puzzling business – he entered the building and examined the lobby board for names. Among the doctors and dentists, George was listed twice. Gerald gathered that his office was on one floor and his apartment on another. Gerald saw the security guard and thought: I am George's twin – I have a right to be here.

But the security guard did not ask for identification.

'How ya doing, boss?' The guard was black, he looked big and uncomfortable in his chair, the book in his hand was a Bible.

'Warm out there,' Gerald said, with a patronizing smile.

'And it going to get a lot hotter, bo.'

*Bo* was what the man said. So that was short for *boss*?

Gerald smiled to think that George's security could be so lax – and he was probably paying a fortune for this sloppy protection! The guard smiled back at Gerald, and that emboldened him to take the elevator to the fifteenth floor, and he stepped out and saw the brass plate bearing his brother's name. He resisted ringing the bell. Somehow, he knew it was a waiting room, with a five-foot palm tree, and armchairs, and last month's magazines, and a vast meaningless painting on the wall.

The painting was yellowy-red, the gluey, rubious, ketchuppy paint spread heavily on the canvas like an entire Mexican meal smeared sideways – and Gerald mentally named it *Melting Combination Plate*. It was terrible but it was bright. George had chosen it for its brightness, its colour, probably its size too. Gerald at first hated it and then saw the point of it – and it was better than that waiting-room standby: Norman Rockwell's poster of a freckly big-eared youngster being examined by a kindly old quack with a stethoscope.

He walked up a floor, just to sniff around and see the apartment door, and then he descended to the basement and the parking garage. He prowled on the cool dimly lit floor of cars and saw that the numbered spaces corresponded to the apartment numbers, and that at 1602 there was a Mercedes – lovely, even under its coat of dust. It was a two-seater, light cream with red upholstery, and as with the building and the fresh smell of the corridors and the 'Doctor,' Gerald thought: yes – it all pleased him. And what was oddest was his lack of interest in cars. He drove badly and often said, 'I'm car-blind – car-bored, really' – he couldn't tell one from another. But he knew this one, the 190SL, he wanted it, he was happy here and he was gnawed by temptation.

Everything fitted except the man with the puffy and slightly ruined face who had appeared at the house a week ago and said, 'Deedee.'

Gerald wanted to go home. It was lunchtime. He could sit and fret quietly. I don't know enough, he thought. That worried him. That meant he knew too much.

In the elevator, he told himself that he had punched the wrong button. He got out at fifteen and told himself that he would get the next elevator down. He sniffed and rang the office bell and told himself that he would not go in, even if someone answered. No one answered. He sniffed again.

That was settled then. He called the elevator and waited, wondering what he would do with this parcel of laundry. He had no use for smocks: he would mail them to this address.

The elevator light went on, the warning bell rang, the doors shot apart and a young woman stepped out.

Her stare froze him: she seemed to recognize him, and yet she said nothing. She looked almost fearful, as if she might be wrong. It was an expression he had often seen on a woman's face, though not lately.

This woman had the compact and self-possessed face of a cat, but her skin was sallow and she seemed weary. Gerald saw her eyes flick – she was holding her breath, touching her hair, and in one motion moving her fingertips from her loose blue blouse to her light skirt.

'George.' She made it a sharp word, almost a question, and there was a small sob in the way she spoke it.

She had caught him off-guard, and the words he had been rehearsing seemed feeble and unconvincing: *Just trying to get some information . . . Looking for my brother . . . Consultant immunologist . . . Found these smocks delivered to my office . . . I called the other day about an appointment . . . Just visiting . . . Has anyone disappeared?*

It crossed his mind, just then, that he had killed George and buried him secretly and run off. He was a murderer and his instinct was to conceal what he could and deny everything. The young woman's hesitation, her faltering voice, gave him courage and, fingering the parcel, he began to smile.

'Yes,' he said. 'Are you surprised to see me?'

'No–'

He had made her nervous! But he was annoyed to see that she didn't know the difference. It was that childhood feeling of discouragement when people ignored him by mistaking him for George.

The woman had turned to the door and was fumbling with the lock, trying to be cheery and apologizing for being late back from lunch.

'Don't worry about it,' Gerald said, and stepped inside and thought: He owes me this.

## 4

He kept on, still sniffing, still sleepwalking, without looking back. He justified himself: I'll get to the bottom of this; then mocked himself with an overtaking thought: It will be over in five minutes.

But he found a reason to feel triumphant. He had not been mistaken for George – no, he had displaced his dead brother. George was dead, and Gerald was no longer a shadow.

The young woman behind him – MISS T. JORDAN had been lettered on her desktop nameplate beneath the five-foot tree, he had been right about that and the bad painting, too – was speaking in a halting way, trying to begin, 'I was getting worried . . .'

'Glad to be back,' Gerald said briskly, and didn't turn. She *had* looked worried. 'I've had nothing but trouble for the past week,' he went on. 'I was seriously wondering whether I'd make it.'

He knew from a droning ache in his skull that the woman was staring at his head.

'At least I've got these,' he said, and slapped his parcel of freshly starched smocks. 'So I guess I've done the right thing.'

There were other doors at the side of the office – his portion of it. One door led to the examining room, with a high platform-like bed, and a set of scales, and clothes hooks; the room next to it was densely shelved and held bandages and medical supplies – bottles and coils of tubing. Gerald moved swiftly around the office, searching and committing to memory everything he saw – photographs, books, trays of files, unanswered letters, a diary, an appointment book, and the framed degree displayed on the wall.

He took out a smock and put it over his shirt and trousers. Now he was more comfortable, more convinced of his right to be there: these were the right clothes.

The wording of the degree was in Latin, but any fool could make out that he was a Doctor of Medicine. So George had graduated from Columbia? There were other certificates on display: he was a member of the American Medical Association, he had been voted Man of the Year – two years ago – and here was a framed badge and scroll testifying that George DeMarr had been an Eagle Scout.

Eagle Scout! Gerald knew this was false. Neither boy had earned the necessary merit badges to achieve that rank. Gerald did not mock, but instead was reminded of a shameful occasion at work when someone had mentioned the Scouts, and he had lied, 'I was an Eagle Scout . . .'

The phone rang. Gerald wondered whether he ought to answer it. Surely the secretary would pick it up? It continued to ring.

'Yes?'

'It's Tallis.'

*Tallis?*

'You must think I'm crazy,' she said. 'It's just that you took me by surprise out there . . .'

So Tallis was T. Jordan, the secretary.

Gerald said, 'Come in for a moment, will you?'

She was more relaxed this time – she had composed herself – happy to see him safe, he guessed, and also glad that this stranger was in fact the doctor. He knew she felt apologetic for almost not recognizing him, and he was uneasy, knowing himself to be responsible for her awkwardness.

'I cancelled the morning appointments. There were only three. I hadn't heard from you, I had no idea where you were.'

'You did the right thing.'

'There was another of those urgent calls this morning.'

*Another?*

'He's going to write you a note,' she said. 'And that Mr Scarfo was here all morning. He wouldn't go away. Mrs Florian is scheduled for this afternoon, and so is Mrs Naishpee – the one with the hyperactive child–'

Gerald was nodding, as though he knew this already; but he was anxious. Who were these incomprehensible patients? And how was he to help them?

'I warned them you might not be in,' Tallis said. 'I could move their appointments. I could cancel. I could do some juggling–'

Gerald was tempted to cancel the whole day – or to agree to it all. He had no idea of the consequences of no, or the conditions of yes. He thought: George was a *doctor*.

Tallis broke off, looking troubled, as she had when she had first seen him outside the elevator. She said, 'I hope you don't mind my asking this, but is there anything wrong?'

Gerald found it easier to face the woman when he saw that she was disturbed. He could not stand a cold stare or a direct question. If she had been blunt he would have felt very small under his smock. But she was tentative, and so instead of feeling like an impostor he could reassure her. He had merely forgotten part of his past. He did not know what sort of doctor he was, or what his mood should be. He had no driver's license, no keys, no clear image of George the doctor. He knew he seemed vague, but he did not want to stumble so soon. He could not question her. All he knew about this woman was her name. He smiled at her.

He said, 'I'm going to tell you something and I want you to swear to me that you will never divulge it to anyone.'

'You know you can trust me,' she said. 'You have plenty of proof.'

That meant something.

He said, 'And you know you can trust me.'

'I think I do now,' she said. She smiled, and her smile cost her so much effort it seemed to prove the opposite of what she had said – that she had been wounded. 'I mean, now that you've come back.'

He felt that if he was kind he could rely on her.

'A terrible thing happened to me over the weekend,' he said.

Tallis raised her hand involuntarily, as if to protect herself from what he was about to say.

'I had a massive shock,' he went on, gaining confidence.

Tallis had become conscious of her raised hand, and now she covered her mouth with it as she listened.

'Don't be frightened,' Gerald said – Tallis seemed as if she were about to scream. 'I won't tell you what it was. But it's had the most amazing consequences. I feel different, and I have a slight case of amnesia. Certain details, certain objects.'

'I see,' she said blankly. And then, 'Did you say amnesia?'

'Yes, please help me. I don't want anyone to know I've had this unfortunate – this shock. They'll think it's a weakness and try to take advantage of me.'

She smiled again, but without effort now, and without pleasure: it was a memory surfacing in her eyes and mouth. She said, 'You haven't changed.'

What had he done to make her say that?

'Amnesia would be hilarious if it weren't so inconvenient,' Gerald said. 'For example, I can't remember what I did with my keys. I couldn't get into my apartment this morning. Maybe I've lost them.'

'They arrived last Friday,' she said, 'with your driver's license and your medical I D. They were found somewhere in Boston and an honest person brought them in. I didn't know where you were, or I would have notified you.'

She retrieved a bag of objects from her desk, and the keys clanked as she set the bag down on his side table.

She said, 'Don't you believe me?'

He wasn't listening.

She said, 'There are still some honest people left in the world.'

He was thinking: And if I am a doctor, what is my specialty? What do I eat, what do I drink? Am I your lover? But buried in this ignorance was his thrill at not knowing, the risks he was running in being there. That thrill made him incurious and reckless.

He took a step nearer and said, 'Tallis.'

Her features softened and now he believed what she had told him earlier, about being worried when he hadn't come back. She looked so pale. He meant only to touch her hand, but she took his and clasped it.

'I was feeling desperate,' he said.

He had only meant to gain her as an ally, but it seemed to him that she misunderstood. She drew close to him, and then her body rose against his and he could feel her shudder.

Tallis said, 'I know what desperation is.'

So she had misunderstood; but it was a mistake in his favor. He took it as encouragement, he moved his hand to her arm and helped her closer to him. Beneath her sleeves her arms were so thin! Her pallor and her look of starvation gave her a hungry beauty that Gerald found impossible to separate from illness. He felt mingled pity and desire – he wanted both to feed her and devour her.

She said, 'I'm glad you haven't forgotten everything.'

'How could I?' he said.

It worked: she gave him a sorrowful grin and said, 'I was desperate, too – I felt crazy! Forgive me–'

She suddenly broke free of him and stepped away. She had heard something.

Gerald was about to caress her – of course, he forgave her! – when she said, 'It's the two o'clock appointment.' She was walking towards the outer office.

'Are you still making appointments?'

'Naturally,' she said. She did not turn. 'I knew you'd be back.'

'I need a little time.' He said he was hungry. Would Tallis go out and buy him a sandwich and coffee? He said he'd talk to Mr Scarfo on the office line.

'Listen' – the voice clouted his ear – 'you're going to help me this time, ain't you?'

Am I – was George an abortionist? Gerald wondered. This

man's voice sounded both urgent and threatening. 'I'll do my best.'

'Just do what I want.'

He told Mr Scarfo to come back the next day, but he knew that everything depended on his next phone call. The bogus Eagle Scout scroll and medal had been the first clue; and he suspected the Man of the Year award to be merely window dressing. He decided then to verify the most important document.

'Registrar's Office,' the voice said.

'I'm inquiring about a certain George DeMarr, who apparently graduated from Columbia Medical School in 1972,' Gerald said. He spelled the name and waited until the graduate records were examined. He was transferred to another line; he heard the clack of computer keys and the mutters of another secretary.

'We have no listing under that name.'

He tried the Boston branch of the American Medical Association, and was put on hold. He looked at George's driver's license and snorted at the mug shot. How could Tallis have been taken in? There was no resemblance at all! But he felt there was justice in this, and it was the fact that he was certain to be exposed as an impostor that made him bold. He would fail, of course – he would wake up from this – and it would be a glorious failure, a wonderful awakening.

But in the meantime he deserved a period of successful stealth. He had spent his whole life meagerly as the dim half of a double image, and it was only today that he had felt any excitement in living. It was like coming back from a sort of underground prison. He did not care about living George's life. I wanted to live my own, he thought – the one I've been denied.

'I'm sorry to keep you. We have no one of that name in this AMA branch. Perhaps it's a new entry–'

This was excellent news, and it excited a responsive feeling in Gerald: with each succeeding falsehood connected with George, the more confidence he had in his own truth. Tallis, in those moments beside him, had helped, too. By returning his affection – he really had wanted to put his mouth on hers.

And he liked the risk – liked it best because it did not matter whether he failed. Even if it all ended now with this patient saying 'What have you done with Doctor DeMarr?' it would be worth it, because he had discovered something that delighted him. George was no doctor – his degree was a forgery. George himself was an impostor!

Gerald ate his sandwich by the window, and then drank his coffee, and carefully brushed his teeth. George was a quack! He dialed Tallis and said, 'Send in the next patient, please.'

She was Mrs Florian, a square-faced woman with beautiful eyes. In her dark dress she seemed heavy, and she moved slowly, staying stiffly upright and using her shoulders in a way that attempted sensuality without quite achieving the effect. It was only when she was seated that her sadness was evident, and then she looked lumpish and stubborn. She brought a strong aroma of syrupy perfume into the room, and there was a pattern on her dress, glittering on the dark silk, of dead birds.

Her file lay before him – the typed particulars and nearly illegible notes.

Mrs Florian said, 'I thought your watchdog wasn't going to let me see you,' and she moved her eyes meaningfully without moving her body.

Gerald smiled in the direction of the outer office, where Tallis sat.

'She said you were busy. That always means something, because busy doesn't mean anything.'

Gerald said, 'I've had a heavy week.'

'I thought she meant you were sick. And then I started wondering who your doctor is. I thought, "Why should I go to him? I should go to *his* doctor!"'

Gerald said, 'I look after myself.'

But Mrs Florian seemed bored as soon as he began to speak. She folded her arms and Gerald guessed that she was referring to her ailment when she said, 'I did what you told me.'

'You did? That's excellent.' He set his face at her benignly to hide the fact that he was totally mystified.

'And it didn't work.'

'What a shame.'

'So you were wrong.'

She was playing a role – using pauses and coyness. That made it especially difficult for him, because he was concentrating hard, hoping for a clue.

Her eyes were deep-set and though they were large they had an oriental cast to them – it was their loveliness – that gave nothing away. Gerald could see pleasure in the pout of her jowls: she was enjoying this.

'And you were so sure of yourself!' she said.

It was a self-satisfied tone – not quite triumphant – and the gloating in it was friendly rather than belittling. It was a sort of bullying intimacy, and it confused Gerald. He wished he had been able to decipher the scribbles in her file.

Mrs Florian said, 'I think it might have made my condition worse.'

Made what condition worse?

'That's extremely . . .' he began in a ponderous way, and paused, inviting the woman to interrupt.

'I understand how cutting down on smoking might help,' she said, filling the silence he had created for her. 'As you suggested.'

This was a start. Gerald said, 'It was only a suggestion.'

'But don't you see how the anxiety of going without cigarettes might have irritated it more?'

Irritated what more?

Gerald shrugged, and she said, 'Isn't there anything I can take for it?'

'There are many things you can take, but will they do you any good? I'm not sure what the best answer is.'

Because I don't know the question.

Mrs Florian said, 'I've been getting these sharp pains again in the upper abdominal region, and I know it's not peritonitis –

we've been through that, haven't we? Sometimes it's agony. Can't you X-ray it?'

'It doesn't always show up on an X-ray.'

'Even with barium?'

He was grateful to her for this. He said, 'Barium's a funny thing. It doesn't always behave itself.'

'Drink lots of milk. That's what my mother would say,' Mrs Florian said. 'But what did she know about ulcers?'

Ah. Gerald said, 'Some of these folk remedies can be very effective. Milk's not a bad idea. With ulcers you have to be careful in your diet. And alcohol – particularly on an empty stomach–'

Hearing this, Mrs Florian looked hurt. She said, 'I'm obsessive about what I put into my body. I don't eat junk. I don't drink crap. If you want to know, I'm kind of a fanatic.'

She was a big solid woman who, seated, seemed like part of the chair. She was apparently alone and unhappy, and she had the powerful appetite that substituted for a friend in some solitary people. Her loneliness had made her a stuffer. And she was so wounded by Gerald's remark about drinking that he was almost sure she was lying.

He said. 'Obviously, you take care of yourself. That's very important.'

'Worrying about ulcers can give you ulcers!'

'Now this is very true,' Gerald said. He did not know how to go on from this. He smiled at her. She was calmer now. He said, 'Was there anything else?'

She looked amused and resentful, as if he were trying to hurry her.

'Aren't you going to examine me?'

'Ulcers are very hard to examine.'

'There's a sort of swelling,' she said.

'Let's have a look,' Gerald said.

She rose and went to the examining room: she had done this many times; she knew the moves. Gerald heard her sigh as she removed her clothes, and there was something coquettish in the way she sweetened her voice and said, 'Ready.'

She was naked under a short paper smock that she had found somewhere in the room, and she lay on the examining table like a badly wrapped parcel – a body in a small paper sack. Her arms were behind her head and her knees drawn up. Where she was not blackly tanned she was puffy and mutton-colored, and this unnerved Gerald more than the dead flesh of the corpse he had found in his house and tipped into the dump at Cape Cod.

He fumbled with his stethoscope – listened; fumbled with his watch – felt her wrist; then grunted and touched Mrs Florian under her breasts, his fingers spread as if playing a chord on her ribs.

'A bit lower.'

He moved his fingertips as she suggested.

'Do you feel anything?'

She said, 'Don't *you*?'

He said gently, 'I see what you mean,' and stepped back, so that she could see him in a reflective mood, pondering her symptoms.

'You can put your clothes on,' he said.

'Aren't you going to palpate me?'

'Of course,' he said, and approached her frowning in order to look serious: he did not want to betray his bafflement. *Palpate?*

She opened her legs and they made a smacking sound as if she was unsticking her thighs. Her face turned aside: he hoped she wasn't smiling. He touched her tentatively, then tried again. He knew now that he could not pretend – he was nervous, and she knew.

'What's the hurry, Doctor?'

He wanted to say: *Don't you see? I'm not the Doctor!*

She said, 'You're always in a hurry.'

Always!

He said, 'I'm sorry.'

'You always say that.'

And then he knew he had succeeded.

The next patient was a woman with a damaged face, Muriel Dietrich. He hoped that she had not come to him about her face. She had not. She wanted him to sign an application that would allow her a license plate saying that she was handicapped. She said that she could never find a parking place and was sick of walking two miles every time she came into Boston.

'They ask me to describe your handicap,' Gerald said, examining the form.

'Old age – that's the worst handicap of all, God help me,' she said. 'You know what to write.'

He invented a disease and created a Latin name for it, and he defined it in parentheses: 'Progressive wasting.' He was pleased to be able to conspire with this woman against the young traffic cops.

Mr Lombardi – another patient – said he had emphysema. It was an illness Gerald had heard about. He wondered whether Mr Lombardi was telling the truth when he described how he could not breathe and how he slept badly.

He coughed terribly, he said. He used the word 'sputum.' 'I throw up every morning,' he said. He reeked of cigar smoke.

His file showed that George had been treating him for three years for various ailments.

'I'm still taking the medication,' Mr Lombardi said.

He too demanded to be examined.

Gerald took his time and afterwards said, 'Come back and see me after another three thousand miles.' This delighted Mr Lombardi.

'It's my skin tabs,' Mrs Brewster said.

She had come with her husband, an overweight and bosomy man, sixty or so, who had his wife's way of clasping his hands between his knees. He said nothing. When his wife spoke he became nervous and his eyes twitched in flutter-fits of blinking.

Mrs Brewster was asking to be treated with the latest methods. She demanded laser beams.

As she was being examined, she said. 'There's something different about you.'

This made Gerald wary.

'You look happy,' she said.

Ms Frezza made the same comment. She was thirty, she was 'spotting.' It was the Pill, she said.

They were experts on what ailed them. They described their symptoms, they guessed at causes, they suggested remedies. Their physical condition did not match their complaints: they all seemed fairly healthy. Gerald decided that they were reporting progress – they felt a little worse, a little better. Gerald listened carefully and tried to be sympathetic. The rest was ritual – the stethoscope, the tapped lungs, the deep breathing, the pulse-taking, the simple rubber bulb device for checking blood pressure.

Gerald saw that they were not looking for advice. They were suspiciously full of information. They were looking for agreement. Most of all they were in the mood for more medication, and three of them demanded prescriptions.

Between Lombardi and Brewster there had been a phone call.

'You were recommended,' the voice said. It was a tentative request, but when Gerald encouraged him he stated it. 'Thought you might be able to write me a prescription. I'll pay the going rate – I know you're not cheap. The thing is, I've got to have it right away–'

They were not really sick, Gerald thought, sitting with Mrs Naishpee and her ten-year-old son, diagnosed as hyperactive. She was a heavy woman with a drugged and drawling voice that Gerald found maddening.

'How are you?'

'I'm good.'

Her child was practically a monkey, but it was not hard to

explain how he had gotten that way. Mrs Naishpee, too, wanted more medication.

Prescriptions were the one item he could not provide – later, perhaps, as he told the man on the phone (who angrily swore at him and hung up). He could not write them, he had no knowledge of drugs, he could not even find George's prescription pad.

But that was his only problem, and it was a small one. He had begun in the confidence that George had been a phoney. Seeing patients was slow work – they were so talkative! But Gerald's nervousness had kept him going and made him attentive. He watched the patients closely, alert to everything they said. They were uninterested in him. They had the selfish concentration of people who believe themselves to be unwell. They were ordinary people whose imagined illnesses had made them super-stitious and turned them into egotists. By the end of the day's appointments Gerald was sure that everyone was a hypochon-driac. It seemed hugely appropriate that each one had come here to see Doctor DeMarr, for who was better at treating a hypochondriac than a quack?

'I've developed a polyp,' Mr Henry Byron Haggin told Gerald, the old man tapping himself on the lower buttons of his shirtfront.

The President of the United States had a polyp. It was on the television news. Gerald had seen it – seen the polyp, too – on the Cape, at the cottage.

'Do you have any substantial reason for thinking this, Mr Haggin?'

'A swelling and a pronounced tenderness,' Mr Haggin said, seeming to quote, 'in my abdominal area.'

'You're quite a diagnostician.'

Gerald found it easy to smile at the patient from across his businesslike desk.

'Yes. This polyp as I say is in my lower intestine.'

So was the President's polyp.

'Would you mind taking your shirt off, Mr Haggin?'

The large feeble man sighed and obeyed and then sat hunched

forward, his big pale belly upright and swollen, like an unwrapped joint of meat he held in his lap – loin of pork, something damp and disgusting until it was cooked.

Gerald asked him to sit up straight, and then he felt for the polyp with his fingertips as Mr Haggin winced.

'We'll have to have you in for tests,' Gerald said.

Mr Haggin smiled; that was how the President's polyp had been dealt with.

When there were no more patients, Gerald could think clearly – and it was then that he realized that he had not consciously tried to imitate George. He had not been aware of impersonating his brother. He had been himself, without any pretense. It was his own triumph – George had had no part in it. Gerald's skill was his common sense. It was not necessary to think about George. But when he reflected on his success he decided that it had not arisen out of imitation but was instead a result of his having improved upon George. He was, simply, better than his brother: 'There's something different . . . You're happy.'

The day had started with a burial; but that burial had set him free.

He could not show his delight. He didn't dare. And yet his feeling of satisfaction relaxed him and made him solemnly garrulous – he wanted to take that woman Tallis into his confidence.

'I think I should tell you the reason for my shock,' he said. She had come into his office with the same suffering look that had touched his heart when he had first seen her. He realized that she was the first young person he had ever wanted to help.

She said, 'It's not necessary–'

'Please, stay.'

She turned to him, looking apprehensive. 'If it'll make you feel better.'

'It was my brother. He died over the weekend.'

He was then very sorry he had said it. Tallis looked stunned, and Gerald imagined for a moment that she had stopped breathing. He saw how thin she was – so frail in her summer clothes – and he saw, too, a stiffness, a teetering resignation. Tallis looked like someone who had just drowned.

'Are you all right?' he said. He found himself reassuring her.

She said in a slow, underwater voice, 'I didn't even know you had a brother.'

# 5

He had taken possession of the office; now he unlocked the door of George's apartment on the next floor and sized it up. It was empty and cool on this summer evening, and its stillness said that it had been abandoned. It was hard to be in a dead man's home and not think that you were in a tomb: it brought back his old buried-alive feeling.

The place was very orderly, and moving from room to room Gerald saw that George had lived here alone. It was obvious in the undisturbed order of the rooms, the walled-in shadows, the position of the one large chair, the single taste in the décor – orangey walls, an unlikely terracotta color that was, Gerald thought, perfect really. The bathroom – everything in it – told him that only one person used it, a vain and rather foolish man who pampered himself in a superficial and self-deceiving way and lingered here in that silk bathrobe, among these mirrors and these expensive bottles, looking at his own awful face.

George was dead. Gerald searched the rooms for drugs. Perhaps there were none here; perhaps they were well hidden. In any case, it was a mistake he had no intention of making – it had killed George, so it would save him: George's death gave him life.

Apart from the drugs, George's life had been fairly tidy. Gerald saw that he could make it perfect.

He found the liquor cabinet and poured himself a glass of vodka. He threw open the windows for the evening breeze. He was high enough so that the street noise was muffled, even somewhat comforting – a low clatter and drone, adding to the raffish atmosphere of this downtown apartment. The bedroom had a textile smell – curtains and bedspread, and what were those ridiculous candles doing on the dresser? But when Gerald lit them he saw the room in a new way, the flames jumping on the wall, the mirrors on the headboard of the bed glittering, and he savoured the sweet tang of warm wax. He filled his glass again and tried to resist gulping it. But his thirst was powerful – all those years of dullness and denial, his shadow life as a twin. He drank and soon he possessed the apartment too.

Before he was fully drunk he took a shower, believing it would sober him. He changed into one of George's lightweight suits. What pleasure it gave him to pull on those socks and slip on the jacket – a perfect fit. The low chair was just the right height.

He thought: It had to be George, because he was small enough to fit into the barrel.

He instantly forgot that thought.

What am I trying to remember?

Something – a crystal – began to form from broken splinters in his mind. He took another drink to help it along, and then he sensed it dissolve. He was glad it was gone. He suspected that it had been a fear.

The phone rang. He was laughing softly as he answered.

It was Tallis. Already this life seemed wholly circumscribed!

'I hope you don't think I was being insensitive. I am very sorry about your brother. If I had known he existed I think I might have been able to say something sensible. But it was such a surprise – that you had a brother, that he was dead.'

Gerald said, 'Why not come over?'

His triumphant feeling, which was a feeling of wonderful lungs, had returned to him with her call.

'Would it help?' She was presumably thinking of the death.

In a guarded way she said, 'I'm still a little afraid of you. And it's late.'

He was glad she said that, because he was a little afraid of her. But she had spoken first: he felt protected by her fear.

He said, 'The way you touched me today–'

There was a sound of air in the phone – had she sighed?

He said, 'I felt like someone completely different. I was alive, in a kind of time warp. Nothing else mattered. I wanted you so much. You'll never know how that reassured me. Energy passed through your hand and strengthened me, and–'

He faltered, becoming self-conscious at her prolonged silence and wondering how long he had been talking – was it minutes or hours? He felt enlarged and noisy and stupid with vodka. He was afraid in a helpless way that he had gone too far with her and had been talking through his hat.

Still she said nothing.

'Are you there?'

He forgot her name.

'Yes,' she said. 'It's strange hearing you say that.' Had he blundered?

'That was one of the first things you ever said to me.'

What had he said?

'You're so sweet, George,' she said sorrowfully.

This was perfection. What was it the woman patient had said? *You always say that.* Perfection.

Tallis said, 'You have changed, haven't you?'

'Yes, yes,' he said. 'What is it?'

She was crying now, and in trying to stifle the sobs she was making them more distinct.

'You know what I need,' she said at last.

But her sobs had frightened him. He said, 'Maybe you're right. It is pretty late.'

'You've got a terrible day tomorrow,' she said.

Another mystery. He said, 'Excuse me?' pretending he hadn't heard it, so that she would rephrase it – perhaps explain it.

'Those scary-looking guys are coming tomorrow,' she said.
That didn't help.

'But I'm pretty desperate, too. What about tomorrow night?
If you really mean it.'

'I mean it!'

In saying so he convinced himself that he had known her for
years and understood her. And as if to prove it, in that same
moment he remembered her name.

'I mean it, Tallis.'

'We'll do it the old way and take our time, like we used to.'

'Yes,' he said, 'like we used to,' and saw it all – candles,
mirrors, her long pale body in his bed, and her shadow making
a witch on the wall.

He was asleep soon after that, and all night the roaring in his
ears from the traffic in Kenmore Square had a sound like a
slipstream and gave him dreams.

Just before he woke he dreamed of a woman whom he was
passing on Boylston Street. 'What are you doing here?' she
mouthed. She was small and old, she had a child's face. She drew
a gun from out of her oversize coat and shot Gerald in the chest.
He sank slowly, sinking to his knees with each step. It was a toy
pistol – he had known that before it went off – and yet the
woman's face had terrified him. The woman was his mother.

While he was dressing the dream came to him – the pistol first,
then the rest of it. But what fascinated him was the realization
that he had had that same dream ten thousand times or more.
He just now grasped that he had been dreaming it most nights
of his life.

A patient was waiting in the reception area. This was the reason
Tallis greeted Gerald in a formal way.

'Good morning, Doctor.'

Gerald smiled, thinking: Doctor of what?

But he was pleased. There was something about Tallis's
formality that suggested there was passion beneath it – exactly

like the fine grey suit she had on: it was for him. She was being efficient, giving nothing away; it distracted and aroused him.

She has made love to me before, he thought. Soon, I'll make love to her.

'Any messages?' he said. When she handed over the sheaf of pink slips he muttered, 'Prescriptions, prescriptions.'

She said, 'Are you surprised?'

'I couldn't find my prescription pad yesterday,' he said.

'On your desk.'

'No' – he had looked for it, he was absolutely sure.

Today the pad lay at the corner of the blotter. Gerald thought: I must be careful.

The patient was Murray U. Stone. Gerald saw from his file that he was eighty-six years old. He was full of complaints – back pains, indigestion, sleeplessness, wind. How strange that this man on the verge of death should care about his stomach and his sleep – he was snatching at another month of life. The old man thought it might be his prostate – that was the sort of thing he had to expect at his time of life, wasn't it?

Gerald quizzed him on his diet and told him to cut down on ice-cream.

Mr Stone wanted to go on living. Two days earlier, Gerald would have found this pointless and selfish, and in an old man a kind of insanity. Now he saw the point of it. He sympathized with the trembling man. It wasn't such a crazy wish, and Gerald was all the more attentive when he remembered the humiliation and boredom of his own other life.

'Aren't you going to have a poke at my prostate?' the old man said.

In time, Gerald thought, I will understand this business. But it was not a job – it was a whole life. Already he had begun to accept its demands. He was glad of that: he wanted to live this life. But there were certain tasks he could not perform. He could not carry out a convincing examination, he was too disgusted by the sight of their underwear to be able to concentrate; he couldn't write prescriptions, he knew nothing of drugs.

He was made speechless, or at least short of breath, by their nakedness. Poor pale flesh – it did not fit them. So he stalled. He played charades with the stethoscope, he muttered. He sent Mr Stone away with a tube of ointment he had found in a box of samples.

Mr Libby, the next patient, entered the office bent double, as if he was straining to touch his toes. He stayed in this stooped position, speaking sideways about wanting to see a chiropractor.

Gerald was genuinely annoyed that Mr Libby wanted to be recommended to a specialist. He said. 'Don't you trust me to treat you?' and fished out a bottle of Valium from among the samples.

'Valium's for depression,' Mr Libby said.

'It has many uses,' Gerald said in a peevish way. It was the one drug he understood and this stupid man was contradicting him! 'It relaxes muscles – all muscles. That's why it's good for tension, that's why it's good for bad backs. Don't you want to get better?'

There were phone calls after that – demands for prescriptions. They made him feel inadequate. He considered taking a vacation – maybe to Florida, where he could bribe a pharmacist to show him how to write prescriptions for the important drugs. With a professional letterhead on his pad and a medical degree on the wall, he could make it all look legitimate. It was not dishonest, he felt – it was just complicated and hard to explain. But it was idealism all the same. He saw it clearly, and then it struck him that it was exactly what George had done.

I'll find another way, he thought.

That was the morning. He was wondering whether to go out for lunch when Tallis buzzed him and said in a whisper, 'Mr Scarfo's just got out of the elevator.'

He heard the thump of the reception room door and, almost in the same moment, his own door was shoved open and the man was upon him, with Tallis close behind, handing Gerald the man's file.

Mr Scarfo was young and haggard. He had a gray complexion and yellowish eyes, and he limped – but he seemed careless rather than crippled. He was thin and round-shouldered, like an awkward boy. His hair was tangled, he needed a shave. He wore a wrinkled shirt, and it was from the pocket of this that he took a folded-over swatch of twenty-dollar bills. He placed the money on the desk.

'I'm not going to argue with you this time,' Mr Scarfo said. 'Just give me the prescription and I'll go.'

'You'll have to be a bit more specific,' Gerald said.

'You know what I'm talking about.'

The gaps between his teeth seemed to indicate that he was unintelligent. Yet the man was persistent and oddly energetic – dry-mouthed in a nervous sort of way, but defiant, like all the other hypochondriacs he had seen in this office. But which others had tried to palm money to him?

'I've been having a hard time,' Mr Scarfo said.

Gerald had concealed the file, but even so there was nothing on it when he quietly sneaked a look – the name and address, nothing else; no record of illness, no prescriptions.

Mr Scarfo was still talking: 'And these doctors you recommended – they wouldn't give me anything.'

'I'm sorry about that,' Gerald said, trying to calm the man with a show of sympathy.

'And you went away,' Mr Scarfo said. 'I was sick. I didn't know what to do.'

'Let's have a look at you,' Gerald said, and reached for his stethoscope.

This made Mr Scarfo angry. 'You're always doing that. You're stalling. You're wasting my time. Are you going to give me a prescription or not?'

Gerald said in a kindly way, 'I can't give you anything at the moment.'

'I told you the last time, I'm running out of stuff. I won't have any in a few days – and then what?' But he did not wait for a reply. He said, 'It's not fair!'

Gerald said, 'I want to help–'

'You *have* to help,' Mr Scarfo said. 'You gave prescriptions to three people I know, four hundred bucks apiece. This is five hundred, Doctor–'

'I don't want your money.'

'Rizzo – you gave him one. I seen it!' Mr Scarfo stood up, and even though Gerald himself was standing the man towered over him. 'I could pinch your head off so easy.'

For the first time, Gerald became frightened. He did not know anything about narcotics. He could humor a patient, but this was something different: he was helpless.

'And a guy named Ferrara. You gave him one!'

Who were these people and what had he given them?

Gerald moved away from Mr Scarfo, to place a safe distance between them. He did not want to argue. He wanted the money, he wanted this life, and he already hated this man enough to give him exactly what he wanted, and the more lethal the better. But he resisted. This was precisely where George had gone wrong.

'You'll have to go,' Gerald said.

'I'm not moving.'

'I'll call the police.'

'Beautiful,' Mr Scarfo said. 'Then I'll tell the police about all the shit you got for these other guys.'

'If you do,' Gerald said crisply, inspired by his anger, 'I'll never get anything for you. Are you willing to risk that?'

Mr Scarfo stood up. He said, 'I'll be back.'

It was a snarl, a threat – he spoke it darkly; and it rattled Gerald terribly. It was now after two o'clock, with another patient on the way. There was no time for lunch.

The next patient had a similar request to Mr Scarfo's. This was Toby – another blank file: he was underweight, twenty or so, with a skeletal smile: clearly ill and addicted. He said, 'How about it?'

'I can't help you,' Gerald said.

'That's what you said the last time.'

Good, Gerald thought. He said, 'I want you to understand that.'

'I don't understand nothing. You cost me a lot of money. I paid for this office. That desk. That crappy lamp. That's my money.'

Gerald resented the young man's tone, and the mention of the lamp – he particularly liked the stainless steel desk lamp. There was much in the office that he realized he had wanted his whole life.

'I can't give you a prescription,' he said.

'I think you like saying that. It gives you a sense of power. You're paranoid.'

Gerald hated ignorant people who used technical or pompous words to intimidate him. The young man was stupid, and yet Gerald was hurt by his insolence. He suspected that it did not arise from the young man's own weakness but rather from his seeing that Gerald was helpless.

'Your time is up,' Gerald said, feeling trapped.

'I'm leaving, but I'm not going anywhere. Get it?' He stood up. 'I'll be around.'

There was another phone call: 'You were recommended.' There was a man named Hume who said the pimple on the back of his neck was a boil that needed lancing. And there was Archdale.

Archdale was a Harvard student; he looked pathetic with his thick grubby textbooks, and Gerald knew before the boy spoke that he wanted a prescription. Archdale pleaded. He had money with him, he said. He looked worried and began to cry, saying that he might be able to get more.

'Please,' Gerald said. He wondered whether he should offer to examine him. He was afraid to touch him.

He said, 'You've been here before, haven't you?'

'Yes–'

And then Gerald saw that it was in this that George had gone wrong. He thought: I will not become George.

Archdale had not heard him. He was still talking, saying, 'I realized what it was. You didn't want money any more. You said no–'

Had George said no?

'It's very smart, really. It's a kind of strength, saying you don't want money any more.'

Gerald did not know what to say.

'I can't buy you, because you've already got money,' Archdale said. 'But ask yourself – how did you make all that money?'

Now the young man was going, but he paused at the door.

'Ask yourself.'

When the young man was gone, Gerald was so shaken he told Tallis that he could not see any more patients. He had begun to understand how messy George's life had been: he did not want to make the same mistakes. He needed time, in order to succeed.

He said. 'I'm going up to my apartment.'

'What time do you want us to meet?'

He had forgotten that – anxiety had taken away his desire. He wanted to be alone, but he did not have the heart to tell her. What would George have done?

He said, as candidly as he could, 'I'm not sure about tonight.'

'What do you mean by that?'

He was vague because he was tired and fearful, but she seemed to think it was lack of interest.

Before he could reply, Tallis said coldly, 'I never know whether to trust you.'

'You can trust me,' he said, trying hard to reassure her.

She smiled. She said, 'You let me down once.' Her smile broke and she began to cry. The weeping had a ruinous effect on her.

She looked like one of the most unhealthy people he had ever seen, and a great deal sicker than any of his patients.

He felt pity for her. No other person so young had ever moved him in that way.

## 6

Pitying her, Gerald felt powerful and kindly. Her weakness roused him. He was happy and hopeful, because he knew that he could help her. Unlike George, he could be good to her. Certainly George had borne some responsibility for her. *You let me down once* – that was a judgement on George.

Gerald drew courage from his knowledge that he only resembled his brother in a physical way. Inwardly he was another man entirely. His private image was of two identical bottles, the same shape and size and colour; but one contained poison and the other its antidote. And that was also why only one person in the world could heal this woman; only one woman deserved his love.

He said, 'Tallis' and touched her, and she looked at him with such passion that he wanted to hold her and kiss her. And as always, when he looked hard at her, she seemed desperately afraid and forlorn.

The Maison Rouge on Newbury Street was a restaurant that Gerald often fantasized about being in, with a woman, drinking wine by candlelight.

'You and your French restaurants,' Tallis said, but warily as though she was afraid of going too far. Had she been there before with George? Would the waiter remember? Would the waiter remember George's credit card and see that Gerald's was not the same? Of course not.

She was wearing a long-sleeved dress, silky black, with a

pattern shimmering on the fabric. The pallor of her skin that had made her seem so ill now gave her a haunting beauty. Her face was thin and intense, and she did not take her eyes from his.

She said, 'I can hardly believe this.'

Gerald, enjoying himself and happier than he could remember, took her fragile hand and held it gently.

'You look lovely,' he said and, inhaling her perfume, he could not stop himself from saying, 'Lavender. It's so familiar–'

'Your mother used to wear this perfume,' Tallis said.

It was true – she knew everything except who he was. But what mattered was that she and George had a long past, a history that included secrets and intimacies and perhaps passion – almost certainly passion. Gerald was shocked by how much she knew, but he was emboldened by the one crucial fact she did not know. Her ignorance gave him power. But he did not want power – he wanted love, friendship, the sort of happiness he felt at this moment.

He said, 'Why shouldn't we always be as happy as this?'

'You know why,' Tallis said. She was suddenly resentful. 'You've made it so hard for me. You've put me through hell.'

He stared at her. He had to be mute. He was the ignorant one now.

'I almost didn't come tonight,' Tallis said and lowered her eyes.

'Look at me,' he said, at once inspired, and when she refused to obey he said it again, urging her, 'Tallis – look at me.'

She was ashamed, he guessed that, and she was angry. She was slight but her will-power gave her an aura of largeness, as though she were bulkily built. And there was a suggestion of violence and danger in her silence.

So was it to be one of those dinners, where the woman agreed to join him for a meal only to use the occasion to scream at him or weep and tell him how he had failed her? One of those testing dinners, like a set of hurdles, where the woman made him submit to her abuse before she rewarded him much later – always too late – with sex, and not enough of that. Please no, he thought.

She was crying again. He had forgotten that he still held her hand in his. He released it – his own hand was no larger. Her small size would certainly have made her attractive to George. There was so much that Gerald could have asked her about him.

Tallis said something tear-sodden and inaudible. Gerald asked her softly to repeat it.

'I feel terrible,' she said.

It was an unhelpful and ambiguous statement, yet he was overcome by his feeling for her, and he began to babble.

He said, 'Please don't worry, my darling. Let me pour you a drink. This is how I want it to be from now on. Let me feed you, let me love you–'

He poured the wine. He caught sight of the label. He said, 'This Schramsberg *blanc de blanc* is as good as any French champagne you can name. Thirty-eight dollars is nothing. The Krug is over a hundred. California wine is vastly underrated by wine snobs. They pay no attention to the vintage Mondavis. Your Sonomas. Your Niebaum-Coppolas.'

Now she smiled and her mood lifted.

'Oh, George,' she said, and sighed. 'Why do you always pretend to know about wine? You know it's all booze to you, just another anesthetic.'

'You like it, at any rate.'

She looked piercingly at him.

'You know what I like,' she said.

Gerald could not go on looking into those eyes. He glanced down, but her voice found him and pierced him further. 'You know what I want,' she said.

What was it? Her hand reached his leg, her fingers gripped him.

'You know what I need.'

Only when the waiter approached them again did she let go. And then she said she wasn't hungry. She said she would have some pheasant consommé and a small salad. Gerald ordered the lobster bisque to start, and he told the waiter he was torn between the *goujons* of monkfish and the tuna *niçoise*. The waiter pursed his lips as though in warning that he had a thick French accent, and he said that it was yellowfin tuna, from Hawaii, and it was fresh – and something in the way he lisped, making a fishmouth on the word fresh, made Gerald choose the *goujons*.

Tallis' expression still said *You know what I need.*

He felt he did know. He loved being in the presence of this woman, and as though for the first time ever he saw the point of eating a meal with someone you desire – being near to her, so close to her face as she ate gracefully, putting food into her mouth and smiling and returning his gaze, watching him. This sort of tempting meal was a way of controlling and exciting desire. He wanted it to continue, he wanted to go on looking at her, stroking her with his eyes.

In the past such meals had been painful for him. He had sat like a man being judged. The woman across from him forked food into her turned-down mouth and wore a sour expression, as though she were about to choke. Yet she would go on chewing and frowning, looking disgusted, as though the whole experience happened to be physically painful. *Take the prisoner away.*

He was sorry that this woman Tallis had shared a past with George – sorry for her, for what she had had to endure. But that same awkward past helped him too. The preliminaries were over, and that was always the embarrassing part: Gerald had always been too slow or too fast. Only his letters had ever really worked, but they were letters to strangers. George had begun with Tallis, but Gerald could carry on from there – loving her, pleasing her, impressing her. He had a strong assurance, as he sat there eating in the Maison Rouge, that he was already her lover. That suspicion made him very calm, and it steadied him in his chair.

'I haven't told you anything about my week off,' Gerald said. 'Don't you want to hear the details?'

Tallis looked alarmed – the same look of anxious surprise

which had been on her face when he'd stepped out of the elevator that first time.

She said, 'Why do you always smile like that when you're angry?'

'I'm not angry.'

'When you're accusing me of something,' she said.

'I'm not accusing you.'

'I don't want to hear the details of your week off,' she said.

He reached for her hand once more, and he said, 'I don't think I've ever told you about the time I was in Vietnam.'

'That's practically all you ever talk about,' she said. 'But I don't want to hear about how you almost became an addict. I don't want to hear drug stories. Talking about dope makes me want a fix.'

Her talking reassured him. So George fantasized too – or had George really served there?

He told his snake story. He said, 'We were out on patrol one day and got pinned down by the Cong. Under fire for about six-seven hours – and I was lying there, firing back, lobbing grenades, waiting for air-cover. Suddenly the firing stopped and we decided to move on. As I walked along I started to limp. I looked down and saw that a huge snake was coiled around my ankle.'

Gerald smiled at her; she smiled back. She didn't look the least bit impressed.

'God, you've got a terrible memory,' she said.

'What do you mean?' He hated saying it.

'*Then* what happened? You always tell me about the snake, but you never tell me how you got it off your ankle!'

Gerald leaned forward, as though to kiss her. 'That's the point,' he said. 'Let's go, I want to tell you later.'

In the car he remembered that it was his father's story – a Cape story: his father sitting on a grassy bank and the copperhead coiling itself on his ankle. The old man had never revealed how he had rid himself of the thing. Perhaps he too had been lying.

Tallis said, 'Where are you taking me?'

'Guess.'

She was eager, and in the elevator, when they kissed – his first with her, but that kiss had a turbulent history, he knew – she hugged him tightly, seeming to cling fearfully, until she opened her eyes and looked at him.

He wanted nothing to change. He held her and hoped. And in the apartment – George's apartment, but already Gerald felt at home and confident enough to walk through it in the dark – he did not switch on the light. He sat with Tallis on the sofa, loving the delay, savoring his fantasies.

'You know what I want.'

'I want you too.'

Wasn't that what she meant? She seemed to be frowning in the dark. He kissed her and found that her face was wet with tears. Had she always wept this way with George?

'I thought you never wanted to see me again,' she said.

'No,' he said, in a moan of protest.

'I thought you hated me.'

Gerald held her tightly, though he was aware of her fragile bones, the basket of them beneath her silky dress.

'I thought I hated you,' she said, and she shuddered. 'It was a nightmare.'

Gerald was fumbling with the dress, pushing at it. Tallis lay back on the cushions, and he felt her body with his fingers as he murmured over her, swallowing, breathing hard, blinded by his own eagerness.

He was abruptly shoved back, as she stiffened and protected herself with her thin arms, to keep him away. She cried out but it was not a human noise – it was a cat's hiss.

'What's wrong?' Gerald said, in a fearful voice.

'Who are you?' Tallis said, and edged away from him and switched on the light.

Gerald stood up and dragged at his trousers as he staggered. It was a clumsy gesture of surrender. He was on the point of telling her everything.

'Oh, George, I'm so sorry.'

And she knelt before him and held him.

'You seemed like a stranger in the dark,' she said.

After that, they made love. The darkness that made her timid turned him into a little brute and at one moment he thought he might have hurt her badly. But he realized when she shrugged it off that he was small and harmless and that she was, even in her weakness, much stronger than he would ever be.

She woke him once in the night, moaning, 'Help me, George,' and he pretended not to hear. Later when the early sunshine of summer knifed the blinds she said, 'You will help me, won't you?'

He said he would, he wanted to more than anything else.

He kissed her. If he had seemed to her like a stranger in the darkness, she seemed in this embrace like the most desperate creature he had ever touched, and he promised again to help her.

'It would make everything right,' she said.

That was exactly how he felt.

Help – that was all she wanted. He was glad that she had asked. Was there any better way for him to prove his love to her? He felt that he owed her his life, for she had already helped him, by rousing his desire. He was forty-six years old. Two years before, a woman had left him. He had not regretted her departure. She was the one who had sent his letters back – those wonderful witty letters. He had thought: How could I ever have pleased her? His sexual charge was diminished, flickering out – soon, he had felt, he would not need a woman, and then he would be truly alone.

But Tallis had changed that. From the moment he had seen her he had desired her, and he had been thrilled by a renewed hope in the future. He became optimistic, he felt younger, he wanted this woman.

Because his desire for her was new to him and revealed new aspects of himself – that was why. It gave him hope. Love was another word for life – real life, real vitality. Loving Tallis he could live longer and be happier. He wanted to go on being that loving man, and for that to happen he needed this woman as his lover.

She left early to go home and change, but she was back in the office before nine, her sallow complexion and her thin face still giving her an odd vulnerable beauty, that of a frail child.

There was a patient at nine-fifteen: Tallis showed the girl in. She was very formal now – 'Here is Miss Franda's file, Doctor.' 'Thank you, Miss Jordan.' The charade thrilled Gerald, because under all the formality desire lay like an ache, and he clearly saw their struggling sexuality of just a few hours ago. That secret was an excitement. And it was surely something that the brusque George had never known.

When the patient, Gail Franda – she was just eighteen – seated herself in the examining room, Gerald went to the lobby and smiled at Tallis. He went near to her and touched her face. He said, 'I love you.'

She looked pleadingly at him. Her eyes were gray flecked with green.

Miss Franda's file listed a two-year history of bulimia, a condition Gerald was familiar with – Dot Vincenzo at the Navy Yard office (first at the cash desk, then in Receipts) had a daughter (Lauren? Lorraine? Lorretta?), a model, who binged and purged. Why was it that the word model always seemed like a synonym for prostitute? And yet models apparently worked very hard. Bulimia was not sexual, not at all, Dot had explained – not like anorexia, which was very suspect. Bulimia had to do with self-image, a girl's shape – her figure, how she thought she ought to look, usually too thin. And yet she would gorge and wolf everything in sight before sticking her finger down her throat.

Surprisingly, Miss Franda was plump.

She said, 'I've started again. Last weekend, at my cousin's wedding. I ate like a horse. I was up the whole night.'

'The main thing to remember is that bulimia is not sexual in origin,' Gerald said.

'That's what you always say, Doctor–'

George had told her *that*?

Miss Franda was still talking ' – but eating is sort of sexual, isn't it?'

'Of course it depends on what you eat,' Gerald said, wondering whether he was stalling or making a valid point.

But the problem – the reason for Miss Franda's visit today – was that she didn't know whether to tell her mother. She wasn't asking for medication. She simply wanted to know if she should tell the woman that it had begun again and that she was determined to work on it.

Gerald urged her to confide in her mother and then to return when she had her mother's reaction.

'We can work on it together,' Gerald said, and thought: I would have made a good psychiatrist.

Mrs Caputo's son just had a sore throat, but typically she claimed it was tonsillitis. That was the hypochondriac's characteristic response to an ailment: making it much worse, turning every lump into a tumor, preferably malignant.

Gerald told the silent feverish boy to open up, and using a wooden tongue depresser he looked into the quivering mouth.

'It's a sore throat,' Gerald said. 'I'd advise plenty of rest and liquids.'

'He's in agony, he can't swallow,' Mrs Caputo said. 'Why don't you put him on a course of antibiotics.'

They imagined their ailments! They imagined their cures!

Gerald smiled tolerantly and made sure Mrs Caputo registered the smile. He said, 'Do you want a violent case of diarrhea on your hands? Do you want a child in full spate? Because that's what penicillin usually means to an eight-year-old.'

'What about tetracyclin?' Mrs Caputo said, looking obstinate.

Gerald chuckled at the woman. 'I'll do the prescribing around here, Mrs Caputo, if that's okay.'

He did not say, though the knowledge stung him, that he was unable to write a prescription for an antibiotic or any other drug. But so what? People were better off without them. He was not going to encourage them in their hypochondria, as George obviously had.

Yet they weren't all hypochondriacs. He had more phone calls – two sounding distinctly threatening, demanding prescriptions, saying they would stop by. Another man was almost in tears – desperate, he said. And the last was from Scarfo.

Scarfo said, 'I'm coming over. You better have something for me.'

That thuggish voice. Wasn't there any way he could be stopped? And yet Gerald wished he knew what Scarfo knew, because Scarfo knew George.

The only afternoon patient was a man with a loose thumbnail and an infection at its base. It was a deranged and ugly thing his file called a paronychia. Gerald looked it up in George's well-thumbed medical dictionary (it shared a shelf with an equally well-thumbed *Physicians' Desk Reference*). Then he looked again at the swollen thumb and curling nail.

'It seems to be healing nicely,' Gerald said. And he scissored off the rest of the bandage and dressed it again, using a method he had learned in Boy Scouts, First Aid merit badge.

Scarfo appeared as the man with the paronychia was leaving. He ignored Tallis. He loomed at Gerald's door and without hesitating entered, slamming the door shut. He was big and unshaven.

'I can't help you.'

'I want a fix right now,' Scarfo said. 'Then I need a prescription for more. You're going to give it to me.'

Gerald said, 'If you don't leave my office this minute, I'm going to call the police.' He picked up the phone. He stabbed at the numbers. 'You think I'm kidding?'

It worked, and Gerald was amazed at how quickly it did.

Scarfo backed away, but before he left he said, 'There's lots of other suppliers, I'll get some. But you've been jerking me around – lying to me. I know you're a dealer. I'll be back. Think about it. You're going to pay for those lies.'

And Gerald thought: George was hiding from Scarfo – obviously. But why, if George was an addict and a dealer – the classic conundrum, the sick doctor – had he stopped supplying drugs to these people?

Tallis was also asking for drugs. That was the help she wanted. She entered as soon as Scarfo had left. She said, 'I've locked the office.'

Gerald's desire was roused by her simple statement and an awareness of their isolation here.

Tallis was pulling the blinds shut as Gerald held her and kissed her.

'First I need a fix,' she said.

'After,' he said, and drew her closer to him.

With that promise and hope brightening her eyes, Tallis responded to him, and then slipped her dress off and lay on the sofa.

'Take the rest of my clothes off,' she said.

Gerald approached her with trembling hands.

'Now, George, now,' Tallis said, and woke him – he had fallen into a doze from the effort of making love to her. He got to his feet and dressed and kissed her tenderly.

'I'll be right back.'

But he was desperate. He knew he couldn't write a prescription. He wondered what drugs he could find in the city.

He took a taxi to the lower end of Tremont, where it began to decay, and he walked, lurking, seeking a likely person. He saw a black man and held his gaze. The man offered marijuana. Gerald said he needed heroin.

'I don't deal that shit,' the man said, and seemed offended. 'That stuff's death. It fuck you up.'

Then it was dark, and he was too frightened to walk farther.

He went back to the office and found Tallis crouched on a chair, breathing hard, shivering, clearly suffering.

Gerald took her cold fingers and said, 'I will help you. But it may take a while.'

Tallis said with sudden bitterness, 'I thought you'd changed.'

'I have changed,' Gerald said, trusting the truth of it. He was a different man! 'I'll prove it. I love you.'

'I hate you for saying that.'

'Give me until tomorrow.'

'I can't wait until tomorrow,' Tallis said. 'You're incredible. This is exactly what happened the last time. You bastard.' She watched him hurry to the door. She said, 'You're going again.'

'It's very important.'

She didn't blink. She said coldly, 'That's what you said the last time.'

## 7

Scarfo's home was in East Boston – according to the file – a sharp right turn after the tunnel, all tenements and hanging laundry, and big badly-made houses intersected by narrow streets. He had left the taxi at the first set of traffic lights, and now he was walking. He walked down London Street, past Lombardo's Lounge, into the maze of three-decker houses. From the airport came the roar and boom of planes, but here the night-time noises were clear voices, dishes being clanked in a sink, television laughter in little bursts of pressure, and the whispers of people in the darkness of their porches and front steps and wooden fire escapes. The sounds were unselfconscious and strangely intimate. The neighborhood was poor Italian; it smelled of laundry and cooking – scorched tomatoes especially. Roy's Cold Cuts, Gino's Autobody, Christie's Pizza, Homemade Slush, a café or a meatmarket on every corner. The dark cluttered air gave Gerald the sense that he was walking under water.

He turned into Bennington Street and saw the house. The newness of it surprised him: it was in bright repair. In a row of tall square-sided tenements, wood-framed, with dingy scratched shingles on their fronts, this house had white-trimmed windows and fringed awnings, a screened-in piazza and brick steps. It was a proud little bungalow. Gerald was bewildered and somewhat encouraged by it.

He had been frightened. He had gone there wondering what decision to take. If the house had been a decaying tenement he might have been too fearful to knock, he would have gone away. But his curiosity overcame his timidity: the house did not tally with the man. He had not decided what to say, but now at least he could discuss matters. He wanted to help; he did not want to make George's mistakes. Scarfo's threat had truly terrified him.

Walking past, he saw movement inside – people behind curtains, a woman in a kitchen window, and in another room a flickering blue phosphorescence on the ceiling from a television screen.

He could make a deal – just a simple deal. He would offer to sell him some prescription blanks – or give them to him, providing he used them in another city, providing he would say he had stolen them if he were arrested, providing there were no more threats. It was a compromise, but it made sense and Gerald felt it might rid him of the man.

Gerald was relieved that he could not push drugs on to the young man, because he disliked him enough to do it; he was tempted. Yet he did not have to worry about the morality of it, nor the fact that it was crooked. He simply did not have the skill to write prescriptions.

He rang the bell. He heard, 'I'll get it!'

A small boy came to the door. His T-shirt said RED SOX.

'I want to speak to Mr Scarfo,' Gerald said through the mesh in the screen door.

'Mom!' the boy yelled, turning his back on Gerald.

Standing on the front steps in the darkness, Gerald could see into the house, past the entryway to the foyer and a long corridor. The man did not appear. The child ran to the far end of the corridor, and yelled again.

Gerald saw a young woman in a print dress take off an apron and walk towards him. She seemed happy and unconcerned, and that fascinated him. There was something very private and self-contained in her posture. This was Scarfo's wife? She smiled at Gerald. She said, 'My husband's at work.'

'Sorry to bother you this late,' Gerald said. 'It's just that I was hoping for his signature on our petition' – he took out his chequebook and waved it, certain that the woman could not see it in the dark. 'Do you know about the proposal to raise the tunnel toll to a dollar? It's going to affect all of us – everyone in East Boston.'

'What did you say your name was?'

'Charles Leggate. With an "e". I live over on London Street, across from Lombardo's.'

'About the toll, huh?'

'Yes,' Gerald said. 'I don't know about you but I'm furious.'

'The thing is, I don't think Sal wants to be disturbed at the station.'

*Station?*

Gerald said, 'Right. I won't bother him. I didn't realize he was working nights. The North End's a madhouse. That's where he is, isn't it?'

The woman smiled and said, 'Storrow Drive. That's worse. It's all traffic duty and drug busts.'

'I'll catch him tomorrow. Take care.'

But no sooner had he turned into Visconti than he saw a cab, and hailed it, and told the man to take him to the station house on Storrow Drive. Gerald knew the place – it was just behind the Mass General.

Gerald had to see the man in his uniform, and he wanted the

man to see him. That would be enough. He would not be intimidated by this policeman, as George obviously had.

In this new life, in which he had taken over the appearance of George, he wanted everyone to know that he was different. Let them believe that George had changed, he thought. Then I can be myself.

'I'd like to see Officer Scarfo,' Gerald said, to the policeman at the desk.

'Salvie,' the policeman called, turning aside.

Behind him sat Scarfo, just inside a small room, and he was obviously preparing for the evening. He was shining one shoe – the shoe in one hand, the black brush in the other.

He was not the starved wolf of the afternoon, but rather a relaxed policeman – a husband and father – who had been interrupted as he prepared for night duty. He was clean shaven, his hair was combed – he had the rosy just-peeled look of someone who was still damp and pink from his shower. He stood up, slightly unbalanced by the sock on one foot, the uniform shoe on the other. It was Scarfo – transformed.

Seeing him, Gerald stepped back – down the stairs and on to the sidewalk. He decided to run, but just a fraction too late: Scarfo got a glimpse of his face a moment before Gerald dashed off.

'What are you doing here?'

Gerald ran, in a panicky way, frightened by the slap of his feet on the sidewalk. Later, after he was safe in a taxi and speeding through the tunnel, he remembered that the barefoot man could never have caught him. He had another recollection – that it had all happened before: he had experienced that whole episode – discovery and chase – from an old dream.

He went to George's apartment on Kenmore Square, but only to get rid of his brother's unlucky clothes and to find a telephone number. Tallis's. She would be back in her own place by now.

'It's me,' he said. He did not want to say George. That was over.

Tallis said, 'What's wrong? Where have you been? Why do you sound so–'

'I've just found Scarfo,' he said. Tallis said nothing. He said, 'Did you hear me?'

'I heard you.' Her voice had gone cold.

'Tallis – he's a phoney. He's completely different. He's a cop!'

He was struggling against her silence.

'Are you listening?'

Tallis said, 'Where have you really been?'

'I'm trying to tell you. Scarfo's house. I saw him at home!'

'You got to be lying.'

'He was trying to set me up!' Gerald said. 'He's no junkie. He wanted to get me arrested.'

She said, 'Do we have to go through all this again?'

'It's serious.'

'Yes, but it's not news. You knew what Scarfo was up to. You're making excuses.'

'I'm scared, Tallis.'

She said, 'Exactly what you said before, when you ran out on me.'

He could not speak.

She said, 'You haven't changed at all. You really have lost your nerve.'

'I have changed,' he said. 'I'm going straight – no more phoney prescriptions, no more lies. I'm going to live right.'

She said, 'I've got to see you. Please don't go away again. You did say we could meet – we're lucky to have another chance, George–'

George is dead, he thought, I am alive. Being George had given him a taste for life. Before, the thought of dying had not worried him. But now he wanted to live; so he bolted. There was only one place he could go.

He found his old car in the Common Garage. The sense of desperation was still vivid in his mind. George must have felt this way – no, George had felt worse: George was George, and Gerald was himself. George had been fleeing from his only life. Gerald felt some sympathy for his brother now, and when he reached home and locked the door and washed, he looked into the mirror over the sink and saw a resemblance. It must have been something like the face that George had seen in his own mirror. But in Gerald's sympathy there was smugness and relief: he was home, he was safe. He thought: I'm not dead.

And yet he did not sleep well. He had slept much more soundly last night in George's bed. He thrashed, trying to dive and submerge himself in sleep, but each time he ended up on his back, awake, his face to the ceiling, watching car headlights move from one side to the other.

An hour passed; another hour. One set of headlights moved more slowly than the others, then stopped before they reached the far wall. They slid a bar of light across the ceiling, and there it stayed, a slanted stripe over Gerald's bed. He sat up and listened.

The car had entered his driveway. Gerald looked out and saw only shadows inside, though just after turning away from the window he thought he heard the click of a car door being shut very carefully.

Gerald did not bother to dress. He hurried to the back stairs and climbed to the empty apartment on the upper floor where George had been. There he waited, hiding himself, wondering whether to sit down in that dreadful chair. Let them take what they want, he thought, and then he sat down.

He covered his face: My poor brother. He was thinking about himself most of all. He was both of them. And he always felt especially small in the early morning.

Dawn had reached the windows – a yellow-green early morning sky behind the telephone poles, that forest of black crucifixes. There was no sun yet, but instead pale seeping colors that brimmed like liquid around the old house.

The door opened quickly and a large startled man said, 'You're still here.'

Then Gerald was dazzled by the man's flashlight, and the weak sunrise was not strong enough to outshine it. The man was hidden behind it and, perhaps realizing what he had just said, he repeated it in amazement: 'You're still here!'

The light shook as it moved towards Gerald, paralyzing and blinding him. He was at the mercy of the man, but the man was breathless – still exclaiming, and almost laughing as he spoke.

'I'm alive,' Gerald said.

'Course you are.'

'Turn off the light – please.'

The man did so. Gerald saw that this large dark man had a short neck – no neck at all really; his head was crammed between his shoulders, and when he turned his head he turned his whole body. But he had the sleepy harmless look of someone who has just woken up. He was still on the verge of laughter, with eager eyes, as if he was listening to a good story and wanting more.

'You know me.' he said. 'Right?'

'No,' Gerald said, and felt safe.

'You don't know me!'

Now the man did laugh, and watching him, Gerald laughed, too. It was a good joke – after all he had been through, he was relieved by the apparition of the laughing man.

Gerald pondered the situation: I think I do know this man. I think I have been here before.

The intimation had been frequent over the past two days: his dreams had prepared him and had made this strangeness familiar. He was sure he had dreamed this: the empty room, the visiting man's unexpected laughter. He had seen it all, more than once.

'Why ain't you asleep?'

That sounded familiar, too!

And when Gerald said, 'I couldn't sleep,' it sounded to him like another echo.

The man's face was bright – he was smiling, perhaps thinking:

He should be in bed! There were footsteps on the back stairs. The man wasn't alarmed. He walked easily over to the door and opened it to the visitor, a young woman.

'Tallis,' Gerald said.

Her face was sallow and bony, her clothes were shapeless on her body – they hung in vertical folds. Her thin ankles showed at her trouser cuffs and her little toes were twisted in her sandals.

'He's still here. He says he doesn't know me,' the man said.

Tallis smiled at this – the smile tightened her face and made it even thinner. She approached Gerald with her hands in her pockets.

'It's the same guy!' The large dark man said. 'He woke up!'

Gerald said, 'You're going to laugh when I tell you – you're laughing already – but I really don't . . .'

Only seconds had passed since Tallis had entered the room. But Gerald was fascinated by her. She was all he wanted of George's life. She was lovely in a pitiful way and she looked hungrily at him – still smiling slightly. She had lovely lips and large eyes: they were part of her hunger.

Tallis drew her hand out of her pocket and Gerald saw something between her fingers. She lifted her arm and her sleeve slipped back; and he saw scars and blue punctures where her sleeve had been. She held the pointed thing like a dart. It was so narrow and she was so nimble with it, it seemed like a part of her hand. She found the plunger with her thumb and let the needle glitter at him.

'Now I'll show you how it's done,' Tallis said.

'Are you talking to me?' Gerald said.

'Both of you,' she said.

He thought for a moment that she meant George and him – the idea of George still clung to him, and he had been dragging his brother around like a flat shadow. But no – she meant the man, who was now behind him.

'But this time you don't wake up,' Tallis said.

Gerald turned and saw that the man, still smiling, had raised his hands and spread his thick fingers to take hold of him.

'You killed George!' Gerald said, but the man only laughed.

Tallis said, 'He could have saved me a lot of trouble if he had done this right the first time.'

Gerald said, 'Wait–'

And then the fingers were over his mouth.

Still Tallis manipulated the needle. Her eyes went small and cold, and losing their light they became black with hatred and fixed on one unswerving purpose – now Gerald saw – to kill him.

Before Gerald could jerk himself out of his chair, the stranger's thick fingers tightened and clamped him down. He was helpless, his body was being squeezed and pinched, he pitied himself for being so small.

'This is for coming back from the dead,' Tallis said. 'This is for lying to me twice.'

She slipped the needle into his arm and pushed the plunger, and a freight of ecstasy like hot syrup surged into the pinprick and enlarged his arm, and his whole body, making him blissful and buoyant. For an hilarious instant he understood everything, and then he was dead.

1990

# Bottom Feeders

Hoyt Maybry was calling aliens 'fruit pickers' again, though I could not imagine a better name than aliens. He was describing them with breathless, unsmiling praise in a tone that was a little too reasonable not to be sarcastic. Talkative people tend to be awful drivers. He was impulsive and distracted behind the wheel, gunning the engine and braking hard and muttering at other cars.

We were stuck in traffic in front of the old Harborfront Tower near the Maidan where our former offices were being gutted.

In the back seat, Kinglet Chee said, 'What's that wood panelling in there – teak?'

'Mahogany,' Hoyt said.

'Good for salvage,' Kinglet said.

'Insure it and burn it,' Hoyt said.

'How would you deal with the claim?'

'Mug them with a rusty razor,' Hoyt said. 'Give them paper in return for bureaucrap.'

Kinglet said, 'So what do you think, Mr Grillo?'

'Seems a little rash,' I said. 'But then, we're bottom feeders.'

'This isn't the Peace Corps, Grillo,' Hoyt said. 'Be a lawyer.'

Bow tie, blue shirt, tight suit, cowboy boots – he was overdressed for Singapore, but that was his image, corporate, with Santa Fe accessories: his watch on a silver bracelet, a turquoise stone on a silver ring, a silver bear-claw belt buckle, tooled boots, a racy monogram on the shirt. It was Hoyt's intention that when you saw him you did not think lawyer. He wore aviator glasses. He chewed gum. Hoyt's gum seemed more obnoxious than the cigarettes it replaced. He had a motorcycle too. When we skied, as we did each January in Telluride, Hoyt wore a black leather biker's jacket with a skull and crossbones airbrushed on the back. You did not notice all these things at once, but over time they became obvious and important. Another thing: today his thumb was bandaged.

'Just incredible,' Hoyt said, changing the subject back to the United States. 'You want to know the reason for this miracle of social engineering. Is it money?'

Hoyt had just returned to Singapore from San Diego, the run we called the shuttle. Kinglet was on his way there – same deal, the Southern Tech joint venture, the funding for the offshore assembly of their third-generation memory chip, a very big deal; 'our blue chip,' Hoyt called it. From this chip and Kinglet Chee's confidence he expected to make almost eight hundred thousand dollars. But there was first the matter of Kinglet's American visa to attend to at the embassy.

'My parents were wealthy,' Hoyt said. 'What does that make me? Just a lucky sperm. I was a lucky sperm, weren't you?'

Kinglet Chee's silence was the Chinese answer to a leading question. He lowered his window to see the condemned building better, and into the car rushed a Singapore gust of fried noodles, the eggy stink of sweated chicken meat, the coal-tar tang of soy sauce and the grit of street dust, with yakking voices and hot steamy air. Singapore looked tidy but it stank of its wealth – car fumes, the reek of its busy harbor. Its gases were like complaints and errors. You could bottle them and give them to someone to snort and he would straightaway know the city intimately and see it as a failure.

Hoyt inhaled and made a face and said, 'The thing you have to remember about a tiny city state like Singapore is that it is something between a summer camp and a small town. In other words, a penal colony with superior facilities. Name another country where you actually get spanked for doing something wrong.'

He slammed on his brakes and cursed and hit his knee against the steering column. This impulsiveness and over-reaction made him accident-prone. He fumbled things and dropped them. I had never known a lawyer who had sustained so many hard-to-explain stitches. That bandage on his thumb was typical. It was wrong to ask.

'Your fruit picker is always so small, so dark, so silent – so necessary,' Hoyt said.

Kinglet winced. 'I could send one of my men in to remove the panelling,' he said tentatively.

Ignoring him, Hoyt said, 'On my way to, um, Tom Bradley Airport in Los Angeles, I remembered how back in ninety-two I saw smoke rising from South Central – the LA riot. Oh, sorry, did I call it a riot? I meant to say a disturbance. At the time I got sad and thought, "What is this place coming to that they're incinerating inner-city commercial space and tying up freeway traffic?" But if I witnessed something like that again I would feel that it was a legitimate expression of social discontent. It's a kind of eloquence. Gunfire from a high-calibre automatic is a statement with an American accent.'

'Or even remove it myself,' Kinglet said. 'I like to keep busy on the weekends. And that old detail is great. What do you call it? Urban archeology?'

There is single-mindedness bordering on obsession in people who are able to ignore someone's interruptive questions as they are talking. Hoyt was like that. He could not be sidetracked. Yet he filed the question away. When he was finished with what he had to say he would reply to the question he had been asked ten minutes ago, with a verbal efficiency that bordered on rudeness.

Chewing for emphasis, as he used to puff smoke for emphasis, Hoyt was unstoppably monologuing about what he had seen in America: the teenagers with rings in their noses, the youths with their caps on backwards, the welfare mothers with their many children, the panhandlers, and more – the President, the politicians, the liberals, the guns, the traffic, the aliens.

'We have to do more for these unfortunate people,' Hoyt said.

He sounded forceful and indignant and a bit strident. His tone might have confused Kinglet, though it was impossible to tell what his silence meant.

I turned to Hoyt and asked, 'What's it like to be back?'

'I can't express it in words,' Hoyt said.

Hoyt could be pleasant but was not a naturally humorous man and so when he laughed, his laugh seemed whinnying and insincere, more like a loud gloating that matched his aggressive and unsmiling sarcasm.

Kinglet replied by suggesting he go to Harborfront Tower on Sunday. Just detach the panels from the walls and stack them for removal.

On this recent trip, Hoyt said, he had run into Indians – 'dot Indians, not feather Indians' – in airports. You had to understand their patriotism, he said, in order to know why they cut in front of him and pushed and shoved. Their children had grown huge and clumsy on American food. They were happy in America.

'Hey, now and then you hear of a wealthy old widow who takes in a tramp, thinking that he will be grateful to her and that her kindness will do him some good. She takes pity on the unfortunate down-and-out. I think the word is "outreach." And the tramp rapes and kills her and goes on living in her house.'

The traffic had begun to move. Hoyt drove on, snapping his gum.

Kinglet stared at him, the smooth mask of his face a challenge to say more.

'If paying for ambitious social programmes is the price of progress, isn't the answer, "Pay"?' He was driving with a fixed grin and staring eyes. 'Surely "lots of money" is the meaning of the word "proactive."'

At last, stirred by this, Kinglet said, 'But it's your money.'

'I was wondering whether you were listening. Of course it's my money.'

'Maybe it's a waste,' Kinglet said, his tentative voice trailing off.

Hoyt found his client's face in the rear-view mirror and said, 'It's an investment in the future. Isn't it, Grillo?'

'Whatever you say.' I hated Hoyt in this mood.

'Oh, it shouldn't take more than a few hours to strip it off,' Kinglet said. I looked back and saw that he was smiling. 'I could go over with a crowbar and a claw hammer.'

At the American embassy, Hoyt swerved into Visitors' Parking and, cursing an oncoming car, scraped a post. Hurrying to get out, his confusion rising, he opened his door too hard and dinged the next car. He was in a terrible mood when inside he asked for the consular officer, Victor Scavola.

'He will be out just now,' the Chinese receptionist said.

'He will be out shortly,' Hoyt said, correcting her by biting his words with white precise teeth. His hands were two fists which he held by his side like pistols.

There were other people waiting for visas or interviews – Indonesians, Chinese, Malays, Filipinos, Indians, Thais, Vietnamese. Hoyt said nothing. He sized them up. He winked at the portrait of the smiling American President.

He turned to Kinglet and said, 'Are you insured?'

Kinglet Chee smiled a bit carelessly, as though the question was ridiculous. Before Hoyt could say anything else, Victor Scavola appeared, pink-faced, in a tight white shirt and blue tie and plastic picture-ID badge pinned to his breast pocket. In his chubby hand he held Kinglet's file and ignored us while he looked through it.

'Before I issue this visa I want to remind you that as the holder of a Tongan passport you have one month, and when your time is up you must exit the United States. This is non-renewable. Do you understand, Mr Chee?'

Hoyt said, 'Given the present situation in the States it's easy to understand why he would want to stay a lot longer. Maybe get proactive.'

'No problem,' Kinglet said in a submissive, peace-making tone.

Scavola sighed and stamped the passport and scribbled on it. I sneaked a look at it. I had not realized Kinglet carried a Tongan passport. Tonga was – what? A little coconut kingdom somewhere in the vast Pacific?

'A lot of people do overstay,' Scavola said.

Hoyt laughed in his whinnying, gloating way.

On the way back to the office Hoyt said, 'There's a certain fragrance in the air. The sea. The sky. The flowers. There's a kind of energy. No, it is not hysteria.' He raised his eyes at Kinglet in the rear-view mirror. 'This is my home. Get some insurance, Mr Chee.'

Kinglet smiled the Chinese smile of bewilderment and uneasiness and incomprehension.

'Because if you get injured you might sue us.'

'I would never do that.'

Hoyt laughed; it was the instinctive reflex of a lawyer hearing the word 'never.'

'You might have to sue us,' he said.

'Help him with that,' I said, seeing Kinglet fidget, as though he had been insulted.

'It's a no-brainer.'

'Take him through it, Hoyt.'

'You trip, you fall, you sustain severe trauma to the base of the skull, you're paralysed from the neck down, you've got the reflexes of a beanbag, and there's a loophole in your policy big enough to drive a truck through. Plus, you're on a respirator. Round-the-clock nursing. Your medical bills hit seven figures. You're desperate. You don't want to sue me, but you have no choice. You take legal advice. You have no money. There is only one course of action. Sue.'

The logic of this was irrefutable.

'So put a rider on your policy and you're welcome to salvage anything you like from the old office.'

*

Kinglet returned from San Diego just before Christmas, when Singapore was thick with Santa Clauses – sleighs, fake snow, reindeer on the walls and roofs of hotels and office buildings; lights were strung along Orchard Road and reflected in the Singapore River; carols were played as elevator music.

Hoyt said, 'I like Christmas this way,' and I could not tell whether it was more of his gloating sarcasm. He gave his annual party, and it was grander than usual. Alison, his eldest child, had returned from her college in Oregon. She said, 'Daddy bought me a new Jeep Cherokee!' When Hoyt and I talked about having had a good year and began to tot up our earnings, profit-sharing and bonuses, Hoyt said, 'There's more to come. We just need a few signatures.'

He meant Kinglet Chee's joint-venture contract, the memory-chip project. Just after New Year, Kinglet closed the deal. We held a partner's meeting and were told of our bonuses. Hoyt's share was a million-eight.

'You think that's a lot of money,' Hoyt said. We were in his office, the two of us. He scowled at me. 'That is not a lot of money. Not in my tax bracket.'

Was he being sarcastic again? A million-eight was much more than he had been expecting.

'But this is something else,' he said.

He eased the door shut. His scowl softened and became a smile.

'This is tax-free,' he said.

It seemed to me a fool's smile, and yet he was confident and happy – I had never seen him happier.

'I'm not American any more,' he said. He was very nearly tearful with gladness. 'I handed my passport back. I'm a free man.'

## 2

'Some lawyers flatly deny who they are,' Hoyt said to me once, 'like those Germans in Florida who claim to be Swedish when they meet Jews on the golf course.'

When I joined the firm, Hoyt told me, 'You know how much a person matters in your life when you realize you're constantly quoting him.' I was struck by the truth of that, and the fact that I have just quoted him shows how much Hoyt mattered to me.

'You might have to sue,' was a Hoyt line that seemed like a precept. I once confessed to Hoyt that I had originally wanted to become a writer.

'What are writers?' Hoyt said to me. 'Know what? Words for sale! That's a writer!'

Hoyt was my partner, my client, my friend. I was with him when two of the other partners, Elfman and Warfield, mentioned renunciation of citizenship as a possible solution for him, and it was I who explained in detail the risk factors and the total downside.

Everyone says lawyers are the lowest form of life. We are green bubbly scum. Something happens to people's eyes when they utter the word 'lawyer,' and they usually swallow hard afterwards. It is more self-consciously subtle than just blinking and gulping; it is the sort of cold glaze you see in the eyes of a cornered animal, gagging with fear. 'Attorney' sounds somehow worse, and even I have hesitated at times, muttered 'corporate counsel' or 'jurisprudence' or 'litigation,' but never within earshot of Hoyt Maybry, the enemy of equivocation.

This widespread public perception is not entirely without foundation, and yet what the public does not seem to understand is that the true haters of lawyers are other lawyers. Warfield? Personal injury? After he won the settlement of seventy million for the blind smoker who lit the wrong end of his filter-tip cigarette and suffered severe trauma he became a pariah among other lawyers in Chicago and joined us in Singapore.

Ours was a busy firm. The day after our embassy run with Kinglet Chee, Elfman spent the morning in conference with a pharmaceutical firm that wanted to sell asthma inhalers in China. I had a sandwich at my desk while taking a deposition from a woman who had experienced sensory loss in the fingers of one hand after removing a jam-filled Wacky Cracker from a toaster. 'Overheated jam acts like napalm,' I wrote. In the waiting room a woman renegotiating her pre-nuptial agreement was telling Hoyt, 'A divorce after ten years means I am no longer viable on the marriage market. Either that's reflected in the settlement with fifty per cent, or I'm not signing.' Our local partner, Loong, had found a case in the *Chinese Gazette* which stated that the unique fold of the fortune cookie had been invented by a particular individual in China and proposed patenting them. It was Loong – not Hoyt – who said, 'A patent on the fortune cookie could have worldwide implications,' and wanted to beat the bushes to find this Chinese man and sign him up as a client.

Some lawyers ask for trouble. Yet Hoyt did not drive a white Rolls like Burton Elfman, whose vanity license plate was lettered SUE EM. Why all the jokes? Like Hoyt, I cannot stand them: the imagery of death and rape, disgusting acts, horrible creatures, sharks, wolves, snakes, the sort of jokes that are told about despised minorities. 'What do you call twenty lawyers in a cesspool?' sent one of his twins, Mallory, home from school in tears. Hoyt said, 'Mal, get used to it, they're just ignorant,' and she sniffed and said, 'I told them you're a dentist, please back me up, Dad.'

Hoyt told me: 'God Almighty, for that alone I would have slapped a personal injury suit on the school, howled, "You're toast!" and gone to war – lien on the property, declaration and seizure of assets, whatever – except they would have said, "See? They're all like that!" and completely lost sight of my daughter's damage and emotional distress. I am not a dentist.'

\*

345

When Hoyt described what happened at his renunciation appointment at the embassy, I could see it all clearly because we had been there together such a short time before.

Those Vietnamese and Indians and Malays and other hopeful people were still waiting in the vestibule of the consular section when Hoyt arrived. He did not pay much attention to them. The irony that they were eagerly awaiting the very same passport that Hoyt was on the verge of renouncing did not impress him. When I mentioned it, he said, 'Which of those fruit pickers was taking a tax hit on a million-eight?'

'So you didn't think anything when you saw them?'

'For the first time in my working life I didn't resent them,' he said. 'I knew I didn't have to pay their medical bills any more, or educate their kids, or listen to them bitch about affirmative action.'

I saw him fidgeting, knocking over a stack of leaflets as he snatched a magazine from a table. I saw him scowling at the seated people – no chair for him. I saw him winking at the President's picture.

Scavola appeared with witnesses. The witnesses goggled and seemed nervous, as though they were unwilling accomplices to an illegal act. It was an undramatic ceremony – paper shuffling, oaths, signatures, rubber stamps. The only detail that made it memorable, Hoyt said, was that a plump, dark secretary in a sari was eating some food she had hidden in her handbag. While Hoyt was signing the renunciation papers and swearing his oath, and witnesses were conferring, this Indian woman was reaching into her propped-open handbag and eating – prawn crackers, he thought, from the sound of them.

'Don't we have some rule about that?' Hoyt asked.

Scavola smiled, welcoming the comment and wanting more.
'Rule about what?'

'Eating on duty. She's a federal employee. She works for Uncle Sam.'

'You're not an American, Mr Maybry. It's no concern of yours.'

As he spoke he brought his hand down – a bit harder than was necessary, Hoyt thought – and stamped VOID on Hoyt's passport.

'One last document,' Scavola said. 'Raise your right hand. Repeat after me. "I hereby renounce my citizenship of the United States of America, and all rights, obligations and privileges."'

Hoyt repeated the formula, sealing his renunciation.

Far from being the solemn ceremony he had expected, it was the sort of business that Hoyt always referred to as 'bureaucrap.' The fans were croaking, the paper fluttering, the stacks of files were sweat-stained, the Indian woman was still covertly munching prawn crackers out of the crackling cellophane wrapper in her bag, as Scavola said, 'I trust you are aware of the implications of this.' Hoyt hated him all the more for that 'I trust,' a kind of wordy and meaningless pomposity that made Scavola seem even more stupid.

The paperwork was mostly signatures and initials. It was a legal act in which blanks had to be filled in on the standard forms. Horrible music was playing – someone's radio. They allowed this? It reminded Hoyt of his first divorce. His only annoyance was that he had found himself tapping his toe to the music.

'Afterwards I was the same person,' he said. 'Except happier. I knew I was free.'

Lighter, freer, stronger – but these were hard-to-define feelings. He felt in control. He felt liberated. He felt wealthier. In the days before income tax and welfare and parasitic fruit pickers and criminal rappers, he said, men must have felt just this way when they closed a deal and made a profit. The whole amount was theirs – a big chunk of cash. They had then been able to act more boldly – start a railroad or a steel mill, dig a canal, found a city.

'Grillo, that is a very American feeling.'

'But you're not an American, Hoyt.'

'I'm American,' he said, and then as though to a child he said slowly, 'But I'm not *an* American.'

I must have looked sceptical, because he then repeated it and said, 'You understand the difference between essence and status?'

'What did you do after you renounced it?' I asked.

But he had already streaked past my question.

'It's like the difference between the flag and a flag. You can't burn the flag. It is a large and noble symbol. But you can burn a flag. That's just a piece of cloth.'

'What flag are you talking about?'

'Ours. Stars and stripes. The American flag.'

'But it's not your flag. You're not an American.'

'Not an American.' He raised his shoulders and smiled. 'I'm American.' He dropped his shoulders. 'You call yourself a lawyer?'

He peered at me, pitying me for my stupidity, and then he answered the question I had asked a few minutes ago.

'I went back to work,' he said sharply.

He was impatient. I had missed the subtlety of his philosophical distinction.

'You have some idea that by giving up my US citizenship I dropped out of the world – just tuned out. Bye, everybody! No, I'm working harder than ever. I have never worked like this in my life. I feel pure, I feel strong. I am free.'

He said he had stayed late, and his saying it made me recall passing his office when I left and seeing him inside, tapping away at his computer, smiling at the screen.

'When I was done, about two a.m., I clicked on my calculator,' he said. 'I figured out my savings in tax for that day alone. I did the billable hours, the expenses, the profit projections. And I realized that every penny was mine.'

The following evening, he and Vickie and their twins, Mallory and Dana, went out for a meal. They chose the Singapore Hilton, because of the restaurant there, called Main Street, which served all-American food. The twins were not told what their father had done – it was a business matter – but they were well aware that the meal was a celebration. They called Alison at Willard and told her they loved her and that they were eating her favourite food.

'The fish is good there.'

'The only fish I'd eat is a cow that had drowned,' Hoyt said. 'I had prime rib. The kids had burgers and fries. I had two Buds. They had shakes. We had hot fudge sundaes for dessert. I haven't had a sundae for years.' He shook his head. 'OK?'

'It sounds like fun.' Odd though: one of the few virtues of Singapore was its peculiar cuisine and its noodle stalls.

'What did Vickie think about you renouncing your citizenship?'

'She has this superstitious idea – a lot of people do – that renouncing American citizenship is the equivalent of damnation,' Hoyt said.

Deep down it was the way I felt. When Elfman brought the subject up he had sounded like the devil. I did not say so, because the deed was done, and nothing could undo it. And Hoyt was saying this, I was sure, as a prelude to telling me that it was not so.

'Give it up, and you'll go to hell – that's what she thinks. That you're a kind of outcast, the man without a country, wandering the earth,' he said. 'She's a Catholic. She believes in Original Sin.'

It sounded convincing, but I did not contradict him; he was still talking.

'She does not yet understand that it's the opposite – an elemental and purifying act,' Hoyt said. 'I'm like the guy in the soap commercial. For the first time in my life I feel really clean.'

'I guess she'll understand it eventually.'

'She surely will,' Hoyt said. 'All my American assets are in her name now. Vickie's going to realize that I've made her a very rich woman. Hey, she's high maintenance.'

Victoria Maybry was the sort of woman I wanted to marry. She was attractive, she was bright, she was a great cook and had a cheerful disposition. She had a warm way of saying, 'Hi, gorgeous' – even to me, and later, smilingly, 'M'bye-bye.' Yes, it must have been an act, but it was a good act. She was secure and tolerant. And so her pretense of being submissive and of letting Hoyt hold forth was a sign of her strength. She was in all ways the perfect wife and mother, for that was what Hoyt needed most. She did not complain about Hoyt's long hours or his travel, nor the many clients he brought home to entertain.

She did not have an easy life, and sometimes it showed – she had begun to go a bit gray – and more than ever she had begun to look and act as though she was his mother. Hoyt's talking had turned Vickie into a listener, and she was so silent at times it was as though he had talked her personality away and simplified the poor woman, the way rushing water smoothes a boulder.

She was a trained nurse who had never worked as a nurse – Hoyt had married her just after her graduation from nursing school. But given Hoyt's proneness to accidents, her medical knowledge was helpful, and she was often called upon to give him first aid. More than that, she understood his ailments and ministered to him. Like Hoyt she was from California, was a competent scuba diver, spoke Spanish, read the new novels and, even if she did not agree with all of Hoyt's political opinions, at least she did not contradict him in public. She became prim, pressing her lips together, when Hoyt said 'fruit pickers.'

'Caning is good – it teaches a lesson,' she said once. It was the eternal Singapore topic.

'Hanging's even better,' Hoyt said. 'There's plenty of that here, too.'

'I'm for gas,' Vickie said. 'Or lethal injection.'

'Too humane,' Hoyt said. 'My father had a collie dog. Lovely creature. The dog began killing our chickens. My father hung the dead birds around the dog's neck. Broke my mother's heart, but it taught the dog a lesson. "Whip 'em with barbed wire," my dad used to say.'

Hearing these stories I often tried to imagine old Mr Maybry, Hoyt's father.

350

Hoyt said, 'I frankly don't understand why they don't have public executions. There's your deterrent.'

When Vickie was asked to think for herself she deferred to Hoyt or else went silent, her gaze faltering, and clasped her nervous fingers. In this fear she became stubborn and sure once again and, with an irrational certainty, spoke in her husband's voice. Lorelei – Lori – Elfman was a spender with a coarse sense of humor. She called oral sex 'making jewelry.' Warfield's wife was a golfer. Loong's was a partner in another Singapore law firm.

Although Vickie called herself a homemaker, her servants had usurped her role in Singapore. Each summer she arranged a rental in Martha's Vineyard, yet instead of spending those three school-vacation months there she dutifully followed Hoyt back to Singapore with Alison and the twins after two weeks. Each winter she supervised the condo rental in Telluride, for skiing. She flew ahead of Hoyt and put the place in order in anticipation of his brief and frantic visits.

Hoyt loved her, but that was beside the point. It was an unequal marriage of an old-fashioned and unfair sort, full of understandings and trade-offs. It seemed indestructible because she accepted her submissive role as handmaiden, and because her submissiveness was an illusion. Once, returning from a snorkeling trip to one of the outer islands of Singapore harbour, I saw Hoyt sit next to Vickie; then he slipped down and hugged her like a little boy. He was tired from the sun and the swimming, and blotchy with sunburn. When Vickie held his head against her breasts and looked down at him with a slit-eyed Madonna smile, I understood her power.

Vickie kept her American passport. Hoyt was alone in his renunciation, he said. Only then did the obvious question occur to me.

'If you're not an American, what are you?'

'Ever heard of Guinea-Bissau?'

## 3

Squinting at the small print in my *World Almanac*, I read that Guinea-Bissau (capital Bissau) was a tiny West African country, formerly a semi-destitute Portuguese colony, now a destitute independent republic, containing almost a million people, four per cent of whom were classified as 'white.' One of those white Guinea-Bissauans was now Hoyt Maybry, who used to describe the inhabitants of such places as 'cannibals and communists.' More than half the native Guinea-Bissauans were illiterate, most of the roads were unpaved, the life expectancy for men was thirty-eight years. There were no daily newspapers. The average per capita income was two hundred bucks a year in pesos, the local currency. I imagined many people being shocked, but the more I read, the greater my belief that Guinea-Bissau was Hoyt's kind of place. They exported cashew nuts. Hoyt liked munching cashews!

Hoyt's passport was dark green, its text was Portuguese, he had bought it for forty thousand dollars from the Guinea-Bissau Consul-General on Orchard Road, behind Tang's. Hoyt secured investor status in Guinea-Bissau, a country whose resources (apart from cashew nuts) were salt, sugar cane, bananas, coconuts, pozzolana ('a siliceous volcanic ash used to produce hydraulic cement') and peanuts. But the briskest business these days was the trade in passports. Kinglet Chee's Tongan passport was a hedge against Hong Kong's handover to the Chinese, and it had clearly influenced Hoyt's decision.

Hoyt said that he had been bold and that he felt free. But almost from the first this Guinea-Bissau passport seemed a nuisance.

Most Saturdays we went to Johor Bahru, just across the causeway in Malaysia, to play golf at the Royal Johor. Returning, we normally flashed our US passports and sailed through the immigration check. Not today. Hoyt's green one interested the immigration officers. They stopped us. They asked to see this odd-colored document. They passed it around and muttered over it. It was no reassurance to hear one of the men laugh out loud. They ordered Hoyt out of the car and asked him where Guinea-Bissau was and why he had no Singapore entry stamp in his passport.

'Fill up this form, Mister,' one officer said.

Hoyt did so, standing in the heat, scribbling on the clipboard, looking absurd on the causeway in his golfing gear: yellow pants, two-tone shoes, pink shirt, cowboy hat.

'Your address is – what is this place called?'

'Bissau.'

'You live in this place?'

It was a cruel question.

'Obviously.'

'Not obvious to me, lah,' the officer said, his goofy grin masking his shrewdness. 'Why you put down your residence care of this business?'

'It's a bank.'

'You live in a bank?'

'That's my mailing address.'

'Not postal address, we want your home address.'

'I don't have a home address.'

'So where you live, lah?'

'I don't live there.'

'You say you live in Bissau' – the man pronounced it 'Bissoo.'

'That's a figure of speech. I am a citizen of Guinea-Bissau.'

All this time, Indians and Malays and Singapore Chinese were driving past the checkpoint in cars, staring out the window at the large hot man in the golfing duds being interrogated by – so his badge said – Officer Tan.

'You're a Guinea-Bissau person?'

'No. I am a citizen.'

'That means you are a Guinea-Bissau person.'

Hoyt's pink face seemed to swell as he compressed his lips. A grunt came out of his face.

'Right.'

But this dispute had only made Officer Tan more suspicious.

'I never see one before.'

Hoyt was told to wait. I parked the car and joined him. He apologized for the delay, and we watched what appeared to be a little family being shouted at by another Singapore policeman. They were Indians, probably Tamils, the sort of people we saw all the time doing menial work. This being Singapore, the quarrel was in English.

'I am not in possession of documents because I am leaving pouch of documents at my residence.' The dark man had close-set bloodshot eyes and he gestured with bony fingers that had claw-like nails. 'For sake of safety.'

'How do I know that? Just because you say it doesn't mean it's true. You can say anything. People say anything.'

'I am speaking the truth!'

The Indian woman, his wife, shrieked; the children cried and clung to her sari.

'You are making my lady wife upset!'

'Go back to your country.'

'My home is there,' the man said, pointing past the far end of the causeway, his voice rising and becoming hysterical as he stepped forward to plead.

The Chinese policeman pushed the man's chest, making him stumble. The wife wailed again, the children joining in a miserable chorus.

Hoyt said, 'What in the hell is going on here?' and looked combative.

But I tugged his arm. I said, 'Stay out of it.'

'This is ridiculous. It's simple for them to run a check on his Singapore ID.'

I said, 'Do you really want to call attention to yourself? You could be next.'

Hoyt took a breath, as though to speak, but he said nothing. I had never seen him identify with a victim like this before. Such people were usually the targets of his bitter sarcasm. Only if you were billable were you a true victim. Yet this encounter interested me, as a display of Hoyt's sudden outrage, and for the way it vanished, as though this tough man had just discovered a survival instinct.

Singapore looked more severe if you were not American, and it looked very bad indeed if you were, as Hoyt was now, a citizen of the Third World. Really the planet was so simple. There was America, and there was everywhere else. Singapore, for all its modernity, was not America, and not very snug. Hoyt seemed to understand – perhaps too late – that he had chosen this world, and he did not like it much.

For one thing, it was small. We had business all over Southeast Asia, but it involved only short trips to big cities, usually the same ones. There was something so swift and hectic about these trips that we had no idea of the weather or seasons – the winter in Hong Kong, the monsoon in Jakarta, the stifling heat in Bangkok. We had client business in Russia and China. On the map Russia was vast; in business terms it was tiny, just one city and a few streets. We did business in China all the time. 'China's a closet,' Hoyt said. 'Russia's a toilet.'

'Don't bring a coat to China,' I heard Hoyt telling someone on the phone one day. It was the dead of winter in Shanghai, there was snow in Beijing, Harbin was frozen as hard as a cryogenic corpse. 'You never need a coat in China. You're always in taxis or meetings.'

The time we spent in America was not billable, and so our vacations seemed unreal and a bit frivolous. But real travel, real space and freedom was available in the United States, which seemed, with all its possibilities, the biggest country in the world.

'That's why aliens want to come to the States,' I said to Hoyt once, 'because there's room for them and opportunity and money. And you can drink the water.'

Hoyt had set his jaw and looked away and said, 'Serve them right if I took up residence where these fruit pickers came from. One of them tropical toilets full of soldiers and shoeshine boys and tax breaks. I'll live on orange juice. I'll get a tan. My kids can go swimming.'

He must have been thinking about renunciation for years and now he had done it. He kept saying he felt free, but I suspected that he was confused and now understood the true size of his world. There was no Second World any more – Russia was a welfare scrounger, Eastern Europe was just another basket case like Kenya or the Philippines. Beyond America was the Third World, of which Guinea-Bissau and Singapore were members. Never mind the way they looked: their thinking was the same.

The Singapore justice system was as primitive, as unfair and arbitrary as that in any banana republic. Guinea-Bissau had no newspapers; the Singapore press was gutless and unreadable, no more than convenient bum fodder for a repressive nanny government that rigged the courts and advocated caning and hanging. I hated caning most of all because it was the only topic at Singapore dinner parties; Hoyt seemed to like it for that reason, until he became a Guinea-Bissau citizen, for then it was his caning, not theirs. He had opted to belong in this world, and that's what they did in countries like his.

He said, 'It makes me want to litter.'

The incident at the Johor Causeway showed him that he had no authority any more. He had caved in to the unimpressed cops – very uncharacteristic for Hoyt. He had lost a tangible thing, his American confidence in the shape of a US passport. He watched his mouth these days. He had no one to back him up.

The other partners noticed this change in him, how subdued he was, as though he was nursing a cold: not talking so much, a bit fragile. Hoyt! There was not much sympathy. They knew about his million-eight; they knew about his passport.

Elfman said, 'You gotta feel sorry for the guy. It was this impulsive thing, like the fairy tale where the guy gets three wishes and totally fucks them up.'

The words were compassionate, but this tone from one of the men who had first suggested Hoyt's renunciation was a bit too strident for sympathy. It was the sort of calculated sarcasm Hoyt himself often used when he was talking about the United States, and you did not know until a moment later that he was mocking. By then Elfman was back in his office.

That was in February, the week of the party at the US embassy to celebrate Presidents' Day. A typed sheet enclosed with the invitation stated that the party was also intended To Welcome the Secretary of Commerce, the Honourable Mr Ron Brown, and his Delegation.

We soon discovered that Hoyt had not been invited.

'You don't mean to tell me you're actually going,' he said.

'Brown's travelling with about twenty CEOs,' I said. 'There's definitely action there.'

'Who needs it?' Hoyt said.

'Some of us do,' Warfield said.

'Not me,' Elfman said. He was smiling. His sparse moustache made the smile worse. 'I'm going because it's Presidents' Day. To honour my country.'

In that moment I felt sorry for Hoyt, but as he went back to his office I saw the others exchanging glances and thinking the thought that had just occurred to me: Hoyt had recently become a multimillionaire.

'These wealthy foreigners,' Elfman said.

That evening Hoyt was working late again, and I saw that he was furious. 'I can't believe it. Those embassy bastards are actually discriminating against Vickie. My wife's an American!'

The fact that Hoyt had not been invited to the ambassador's residence made me view the whole evening with his eyes, and I saw the cruelty of it; it was an opportunity he would have relished. Ron Brown was in the receiving line, the ambassador next to him and, further down the line, a car-maker, a drink-bottler, the president of a network, a computer tycoon and a dozen more – fresh from China, with deals on their mind.

Watching from the side, his smooth face lit with concentration, was Kinglet Chee. He stood compactly, as though steadying himself by clasping an untouched glass of mango juice. He smiled uncomfortably when he saw me, or perhaps it was my name – saying the word Grillo makes people smile, or at least show their teeth.

'What do you think of our secretary of commerce?' I said.

Kinglet said, 'He works hard. He has a good face. I think he is a good man.'

It was not sarcasm, though my first reaction was that Kinglet was mocking – after all, I was listening to this unexpected praise with Hoyt's ears. I looked at Ron Brown before I said; 'I'm sure you're right.'

'I am so fortunate to be invited,' Kinglet said.

He meant it, the light in his face said that. There was also something so careful in the way he was dressed, as though the grand occasion merited his best silk suit, his most expensive tie, his handmade shoes.

'This is American soil,' Kinglet said. He spoke with the utmost seriousness. 'I am happy to be standing on it.'

Just then, Vic Scavola passed us, deep in conversation with one of the members of the Singapore Parliament. The last time I had seen Scavola I had been with Kinglet and Hoyt and I understood why, seeing Scavola, Kinglet then said, 'I don't see Hoyt Maybry here.'

'Hoyt's on the other list now,' I said, 'Of people they don't invite.'

'I heard that he renounced his American citizenship,' Kinglet said in a level tone, giving nothing away. And when I nodded he said, 'Very interesting.'

'But what do you really think?' I said.

'Strange that he did it for money,' Kinglet said, and faced me.

'Why is that so strange?'

'Because money is so easy,' Kinglet said. 'To gain it or lose it. But you Americans are the luckiest people in the world. China was once the Middle Kingdom – centre of the world. Now it is America.'

I said with enthusiasm, 'I agree.'

'To lose your country can be a curse,' Kinglet said.

But then, wincing in a kind of reflex, as though he had just realized he had said too much, he fell silent and became watchful. When he spoke again it was in a chastened tone.

'My opinion is of no value. I am a refugee. I have a Tongan passport,' Kinglet said. 'I have never had to face such a choice, because my citizenship was of no value. The British have betrayed Hong Kong.'

At this noisy gathering of bureaucrats and businessmen, the unlikeliest occasion for candor, the visceral passion of this man was touching. Through two previous deals I had done with Hoyt I thought I had known Kinglet. But until now I had not had any idea of his strength of feeling.

I said, 'I was kind of surprised that Hoyt went through with it.'

Kinglet smiled, perhaps doubting me: his eyes were flinty. He said, 'I was not surprised. When we rode together to the embassy that day I heard his real voice.'

'When he was talking about the States?'

The memory of Hoyt's ranting made me cringe.

'That was sarcasm,' Kinglet said.

He surprised me, using that accurate word to nail Hoyt's monologue. It was clear that he remembered everything Hoyt had said and he easily characterized it.

I said, 'Hoyt lays it on a little thick.'

Kinglet's face was impassive and rather frightening for the sudden blankness that revealed nothing of his feelings. He said, 'He thought I did not understand.'

Kinglet did not say any more than that, nor did he suggest that Hoyt had mocked him. Yet it was apparent in his voice and manner that he understood everything. On the short ride to the embassy, Hoyt had lost him.

I said, 'I'll tell you frankly that I would never give my American citizenship away. Never, ever.'

Kinglet stepped back, because of the force of my words, but he said nothing, and that made me feel worse. Afterwards I wondered why I had blurted that out and I regretted that I had shown my feelings. Oddest of all was that I had not known how I had felt until I had heard myself saying it. It disturbed me to realize that, without planning to, I had probably told him the truth.

Nor was Hoyt invited a few weeks later to a poetry reading given by the visiting Maya Angelou at the American Cultural Center. He said he was glad to be excluded. 'When I heard her recite her horrible poem at Clinton's inauguration I knew we were in for a bad four years. God, that was embarrassing.'

Someone – it had to be a partner, though it could have been a secretary – taped an item from the *Straits Times* on to Hoyt's door: CHOLERA EPIDEMIC SWEEPS GUINEA-BISSAU. It was a lame joke but it made Hoyt defiant. He began talking about the infant-mortality rate in Mississippi. On the bulletin board in the room where we kept the coffee machine and the photocopier, strange little newspaper stories began to appear, on one occasion a list of sugar-producing countries with Guinea-Bissau near the bottom, highlighted in yellow; another day, a list of hopeless debtor nations, Guinea-Bissau near the top. An item from a Rhode Island paper, the *Providence Journal*, concerned a serial rapist and murderer who had been convicted and given a sentence of four hundred and twenty years: ' . . . is of Guinea-Bissauan nationality' was underlined, and in the same ink was written, Send them all back!

'Just a joke,' I said.

'Sure, I miss the United States a lot,' Hoyt said, 'but my aim is getting better.'

It was another of Hoyt's sayings, but did he mean it? I saw more
of Hoyt than the others did, so I knew that these days, perhaps
as a result of his renunciation – and his new wealth – he took a
much greater interest in American politics, in the progress of the
stock market, even the weather. He had sworn off skiing this
year – our rowdy haunts at Telluride seemed quieter without
him – but he said that he was intending to go to the States fairly
soon. He did not mention this again. And before I left for this
ski trip he asked me to bring back his favourite peanut butter,
some new movies on video and a case of a particular type of
Mexican salsa that was unobtainable in Singapore.

Hoyt bought a Jaguar Vanden Plas, white with gilded trim
and spoke-wheels and blacked-out windows. When I compli-
mented him on it, he said, 'I was going to get a Roller, but they're
too conspicuous.'

After work one day all the partners met at the Mandarin to
discuss an outing to a resort in Malaysia. The idea was that we
would bring our families so that they would not feel so alienated
by our long hours.

While we were drinking and talking in the bar, a group
of men, Africans perhaps, were talking loudly at the next
table. Hoyt called the waiter over and told him to quiet the
table.

'It is the United Nations delegation,' the waiter said.

Elfman said to the waiter, 'Ask that guy in the blue suit, the
guy who looks like Louis Armstrong, if he's from Guinea-Bissau.'

In the end Hoyt did not take Vickie and the twins to Malaysia.
He said they had other plans, but I felt sure he feared being held
up by Singapore immigration on the return journey. Hoyt lived
the way many other non-American aliens in Singapore lived, especially the Third Worlders like the Filipinos and Indians and
Bangladeshis. He stayed put. He tried to be inconspicuous. He
joined the Singapore Swimming Club. He did not travel.

'I can cut down these days,' he said to me, though I had not
asked him for an explanation. 'I don't have to stay up all night

servicing clients like I used to. I don't have to chase business. Hey, I was asked to give a talk at a business lunch in Tokyo. I turned it down.'

Elfman put a different spin on this. He said, 'How many visas do you suppose the Japanese hand out to Africans?'

This sort of remark reached Hoyt. He responded by spending money, buying clothes, buying jewelry for Vickie and talking about his new investments. The others said: Exactly what a real Guinea-Bissauan would do – when these simple people get rich they just blow it. Elfman said, 'Know the expression "nigger rich"?'

'Back off,' I said. 'You're disgusting.'

Hoyt was not bothered. He said, 'It's ironic. Now that I've given up my US passport I can at last afford a really good house in the States.'

It was about that time that he said casually – but knowing that it would be repeated – that Vickie had gone to the States, to Florida, the little town of Boca Grande on Gasparilla Island, just off the south-west coast, and not far from the Dupont Mansion, and had bought an ocean-front house for just under three million dollars. It was a select and sunlit island of second homes, connected to the mainland by a narrow bridge.

'Little island, a causeway, great fishing, no crime, no litter.'

'Sounds like Singapore.'

'No Chinese,' he said. 'It's a white-bread community.' He raised his eyebrows and looked down the corridor. 'Elfman could have a problem there.'

He showed me pictures of the house, a pretty white-frame mansion on seaside stilts, with porches and a cupola. He told me about the hotel in the town, the tennis courts, the restaurants, the marina, the Intra-Coastal Waterway, the ospreys that nested near it, the pelicans that roosted on the mangroves, the dolphins – even manatees.

'George Bush went marlin fishing there after he lost the election,' Hoyt said. He must have seen me smiling, because he added quickly, 'But I'm going there because I have a lovely home on the Gulf. And I didn't lose anything.'

The 'Elfman could have a problem there' remark must have got back to Elfman. Soon after, at a partners' meeting, Elfman looked up from *US News and World Report* and said, 'It says here that there are a large number of Guinea-Bissauans in the United States employed in the offshore commercial fishing industry in the north-east.'

'Grillo will back me on this, Burton,' Hoyt said to Elfman, and he stared at him and silenced the table. 'You bring this subject up a lot. I am not particularly interested in these references. It can't be a joke – no one's laughing. Are you laughing, Warfield?'

Warfield was stony-faced; Loong looked disgusted.

Hoyt said, 'When you look at me, I don't want you to see a Guinea-Bissauan. My passport is a detail. It helped me through a personal crisis. Do me the courtesy of seeing me as I really am, a colleague and a fellow human being.'

Lectured to in this way, in front of the partners, Elfman was furious, his eyes were dancing in anger. He smiled a wild carnivorous smile. He said, 'And reciprocation will be highly appreciated.'

Hoyt laughed and looked away. 'When someone gets as pompous as that, you know they're in the wrong.'

But Hoyt knew that he was a subject of gossip. He had more money than any of us now, but he was also aware that we were curious to know how strong that money had made him. He was restless too. In this way he was like the local Filipinos and the Thais and the Malays and the Indians who longed to go to the States but never brought the subject up. Because it was their most profound desire, it was the thing they never mentioned. Elfman explained all this to me, hoping that I would goad Hoyt by telling him.

At last Hoyt did what many Guinea-Bissauans did – though

no one risked his anger by reminding him. He applied for a United States visa. And like many other Guinea-Bissauans, he was turned down.

4

Hoyt had said, 'Don't bother, Jim,' when I said that I would go along with him the day he applied for his US visa. I wanted to reassure him of my loyalty to him – too many bad jokes had made the office seem negative and contentious.

I tried to hug him and insist on going to the embassy with him, and he quivered and then exploded. It took three distinct forms, like a beach toy blowing up. There was first my insistence, my pushing just too hard at the wrong time, murmuring 'Hoyt.' Then his howl, like the thing breaking with a bang, my name spoken in rage, 'Grillo!' Finally, a funny whimper of self-pity, not words, but a rubbery hiss of deflation.

'I have to do this alone,' he said after a while.

It seemed dangerous for me to say anything more.

'I am too ashamed to do it any other way,' he explained.

He was still breathing hard from his first outburst. I knew there was more to come.

'This isn't my first time,' he said.

I gave him a little space and then asked, 'Want to tell me what happened the first time?'

He smiled at me, his old Hoyt smile of utter contempt. He smiled like this whenever he said I was a lucky sperm. This time he said, 'They turned me down. Scavola, that scumbag.'

'On what grounds?'

'See, you're asking all the wrong questions, Grillo. They turned me down twice.'

He looked sad when he saw the disbelieving expression on my face. He had no answers. He was angry and incoherent. Twice?

'Scavola's got his own agenda,' Hoyt said. 'I'm in a lot of pain.'

He walked past me, kicked his office door shut and then stood in a tragic posture, talking to a picture of his late father.

'I never had enemies before. Strong men don't have enemies,' he said. 'Now I have enemies. Does it mean I am getting weak?'

He needed to tell me the story, but I let him take his time, and he did so, as though grieving.

It had started badly. Elfman had offered to help deal with it, since the impending trip to the States concerned a client they shared. He had sent Elfman's messenger to the consulate with the forms and the photographs and his distinctive passport. Elfman had assured him that it would be no more than a formality since he had already secured a visa for his client, a Taiwanese named Lee. The messenger returned empty-handed, and it was for Elfman to tell Hoyt that he would have to appear in person.

'The line was down the driveway,' Hoyt said. 'I told them I had meetings.' That smile again. 'You'd think the American embassy might consider hiring English-speaking security officers.'

He went to the end of the long line and stood there an hour in the heat with all the other hopeful nationalities. As he stood, shading his head with his application form, the ambassador entered in his official car, his Malay chauffeur tooting the ambassadorial horn, the Marine guards at attention.

'You know how big the commercial section of the embassy is, Grillo. You know how much business we've generated here,' Hoyt said. 'I was going to say something, just "Hello!" Then I'm like, "Why give him the satisfaction of seeing me?"'

At last, inside, he got to the visa window and handed his application to the clerk and was given a number. He was told to wait.

'Why is it that people always sound so rude when English is their second language?'

Witnessing other applications being processed ahead of his,

he complained. Still his passport was not returned. Chinese? Thais? Filipinos? Indians? He stuck his head in the window again. The clerk said, 'They are Canadians.'

'What's the problem with my application?'

'Just wait.'

They weren't taught to say please?

'I want to see Mr Scavola.'

'He is in a meeting.'

'Who is the supervisor?'

'I am the supervisor.'

'I demand to know what the problem is,' Hoyt said.

'Maybe insufficient supporting documents. Did you submit a return air-ticket, and the names of three referees in the United States? In addition, a letter from your American company? And your birth certificate?'

As he experienced the shortness of breath and the tightness of his scalp that was like flammable vapor building in his brain, all of it indicating that he was about to scream at the woman, he saw Scavola walking past. He called out, and hearing his own voice was disturbed by its similarity to a cry of pain.

'You're an African,' Scavola said.

'Listen—'

'Those are the requirements for Africans.'

Scavola had not even slowed down and now he was out the door.

'Sit down, sir,' the clerk said. 'Your paperwork is—'

'No,' Hoyt said, and he left so suddenly he forgot to collect his passport and visa application and did not remember them until he was in the taxi, on his way to the office. Back at his desk, he realized he would have to go again and reapply. He had accomplished nothing. Much worse, this delay meant that he would not be able to do the joint negotiation with Elfman.

That was the first failure.

'So Elfman got the contract.'

'You don't need it.' I felt it was what he wanted me to say, and yet he looked morose.

'I was going to stay on so that I could speak at Alison's graduation. They asked me to be the commencement speaker.'

On his second try his papers were in order – the pictures, the application, the letters, the names, the birth certificate, the air ticket: a thick file. He stood near the counter, his flimsy numbered ticket wilting in his palm.

Scavola leaned on the counter, notarizing documents for a Chinese man.

Hoyt said, 'I see. If you're Chinese you get service.'

'This American citizen is ahead of you,' Scavola said.

Hoyt said, 'I know my rights.'

'You have no rights here.' Scavola stamped the document. He did not even look up. He signed and dated each document, taking his time.

'This is not a commercial matter,' Hoyt said. 'I am speaking at a college graduation. I was asked to do this. I am the commencement speaker at Willard College.' He was about to add that his daughter was in the graduating class, but then thought better of it. 'I must have this visa.'

Still notarizing the documents, still looking down, Scavola said, 'No one can be guaranteed a visa. They are dealt with on merit.'

'If I don't show up,' Hoyt began.

'They'll find an American speaker,' Scavola said.

It was clear to Hoyt that he had been singled out for persecution. It made him angry, but what could he do? He regretted renouncing his citizenship in that hot, over-familiar little island. That had made him a marked man. He was thinking: I have always felt these people were mindless and robotic bureaucrats, but really they are vindictive, shallow, envious and disgusting human beings.

That was the second failure. Was it any wonder that he had not wanted me to go along with him the third time?

I left him to his bitterness and avoided him for the rest of the day. Going home that evening, passing his office, I was surprised when he called me in and told me that he had been granted an American visa. Yet he was sour.

'They gave me ten days,' he said. 'I own a three-million-dollar home in the United States – and I get ten days. "British businessmen get three months," I told them.'

Even with all his papers in order, Scavola had said, 'I'll need to see three forms of identification.'

'Look at me, Vic,' Hoyt had said.

'And when you produce them I will record the relevant numbers in your file.'

'It's me, Vic. Remember me?'

Under Scavola's fishy and disbelieving gaze, Hoyt took out a California driver's license, a pistol permit and his American Express Card.

'Credit cards are not a valid form of ID, I'm afraid,' Scavola said. And it annoyed Hoyt that the consular officer did not look squarely at him. 'Perhaps a bill or receipt with your name on it?'

Hoyt snatched in his briefcase and brought out a tax file. He showed Scavola his most recent tax return. It delighted him to be shoving this into Scavola's face. 'And you'll see what I've paid to the US government.'

Scavola blew his nose. He was looking at his soiled handkerchief as he said, 'Is that your signature, Mr Maybry?'

Scavola photocopied the documents and stapled them. He told Hoyt that he would be granted a ten-day visa and that he could pick it up at the visa window at a specified time the next day.

'Ten days is not enough.'

Scavola smiled at Hoyt's futile protest. He said, 'The consulate determines the time period.'

'I have a home in Florida. I am giving a speech in Oregon.'

Scavola said, 'Over the years we have found that certain nationalities overstay. Guinea-Bissauans are serious offenders.'

*

Hoyt flew to the United States, his first trip as a Guinea-Bissau citizen. Vickie had gone the week before with the twins and was waiting in the small Oregon town that was home to Willard College. On his arrival at what he always called Tom Bradley Airport in Los Angeles, Hoyt found himself directed to the non-US citizens line, 'And there I waited for two hours with half the population of Asia.' The immigration officer, a Hispanic woman, reminded him in barely comprehensible English (he said) that his visa was non-renewable, and then it was another three-hour flight to Portland.

An honorary Doctor of Law degree was conferred upon Hoyt the next day on the green lawn of Willard College while his family cheered; he delivered his commencement address; and afterwards, at a lunch at the president's house, he was asked in a fairly direct way, by the president himself, for a substantial amount of money to endow a scholarship in his name. So that was what it was all about: they gave you an honorary doctorate, and you gave them money. It was like the old wicked Vatican that had outraged Luther by its sale of indulgences.

Hoyt said, 'You can't have paid much attention to my speech.'

He had called it 'Unsung Heroes,' and the example set by each of these heroes – a particular policeman, teacher, scoutmaster, as well as his own father – was one of self-reliance. His father was a proud, stubborn man who was entirely unsentimental, and his stories gave color to the speech. The concluding story concerned a dog his father had owned.

'It was called a basenji, a strange little sharp-faced and short-haired dog that had been bred by the ancient Egyptians,' Hoyt told the audience. 'It had two unusual characteristics. The first was that it didn't bark – couldn't bark. It is the most silent dog in the world – the most it does is grunt. And its second odd feature was that whenever it saw a cut or a sore on a person's leg or ankle, it crouched and began licking. It licked any wound it saw – kept at it with its rough tongue. It was happiest when it was around injured people – it needed their wounds, even though for all its attention the dog made no difference to them.'

Hoyt described the barkless behaviour and the wound-licking, and he quoted his father as saying, 'Don't be a dog like that.'

'That lesson made me a lawyer,' Hoyt told the audience at Willard College. 'And when I see a basenji I often think, "I'd like to own half that dog." Because if I did I'd shoot my half. Thank you very much, ladies and gentlemen.'

'Given the message of my speech,' Hoyt told the president of Willard, 'you sure asked me a funny question.'

The president, not certain he had been rebuffed, went on to ask Hoyt whether he was able to attend a seminar on US trade that the college was sponsoring for the summer session.

'I'll have to get back to you on that,' Hoyt said.

Hoyt wondered if the man was mocking him, for the fact was that although he wanted to be part of the seminar – there were always potential clients at such gatherings – Hoyt had no idea whether he would be granted a visa for another visit. A request for money, a request to return. All this awkwardness. Did the president know something?

At the lunch itself Hoyt was seated between a student from South Africa – a young black woman who had just-visible freckles – and an elderly trustee, still wearing her robes and her purple Willard hood.

'I read that story in Mark Twain,' the young woman said. '*Pudd'nhead Wilson*. It's a good novel about racial paradoxes. "I'd shoot my half." Pudd'nhead says that.'

'My father taught me that,' Hoyt said.

'He must have read the novel,' the young woman said.

'Or perhaps Mark Twain got the story from my father.'

The young woman stared at him. Yes, they were freckles, mostly on the bridge of her nose, but also on her cheeks.

'We did a lot of work in South Africa in the seventies,' Hoyt said, but thinking: I need a lesson in American literature from a Hottentot?

'My country was not free then,' the student said. 'We were

suffering the twin evils of apartheid and political oppression.'

'What exactly does that mean?' Hoyt asked, smiling at her, though she could not have known the meaning of his smile.

The elderly trustee leaned over and said, 'Nelson Mandela was in jail then, is what she means.'

'My background is mainly Asia,' Hoyt said, hating both women. 'I wonder whether you realize that China is an economic giant.'

The student said, 'Africa's colonial past kept her from realizing her potential. Not just South Africa, but all over.'

'So Africa is a sort of unwed single mother on welfare with too many children, is that it?' Hoyt said. 'And we're paying the bills.'

As he spoke, he remembered his tax position and his Guinea-Bissau passport and felt light-headed, not angry any more. He was in the mood to tease and laugh, like an escape artist who has just freed himself of the handcuffs and the chains and the coffin.

The South African student was trying to reply, as Hoyt interrupted and said, chewing his food, 'What will you do when you go back to South Africa?'

'I am going to grad school here. After that, I might stay.'

'Just like that. "America's kind of a neat place. Think I'll just stay."'

Sensing the dark heat of Hoyt's hostility, the student frowned and became silent.

He left the next day with Vickie and the children to go to Florida, to the house in Boca Grande. It took a whole day to fly to Tampa, and by the time they had rented a car and driven it the hundred miles to Boca it was dark. Four days in this splendid house, then a meeting in Seattle, and his visa days were used up. He flew to Vancouver.

'I've never seen one of those before,' the Canadian immigration officer said. The green passport again. Why did they all say that? 'But your English is excellent.'

Hoyt tried to drive back to Seattle to see whether he would be allowed over the border. On the American side he showed his driver's license. The officer ran a computer check. Hoyt was escorted to a secure room, where he waited, with a woman from Pakistan. Hoyt knew from the way she was dressed that she was Pakistani: white veil, purple gown, yellow pantaloons; no dot on her forehead. She held a US passport in her skinny fingers.

'But why won't they let you through?'

'Sorry.'

She fanned him away with her passport to indicate that she did not speak English. She looked anxious. Then she smiled, seeing her husband appear in the room. The bearded and sandal-wearing man in a grubby gown gave Hoyt a malevolent look and helped his wife from the room and into the United States.

Soon after, Hoyt was turned away. 'I'm in the computer!' He called Vickie in Florida and flew to Singapore, where he told me this. He was limping. 'Somewhere along the way I pulled a hamstring.'

## 5

You know that an American is truly rich when he tells you how poor he is. Hoyt could not say that any longer, and I think it bothered him. When he said these days, 'I've got money,' it always sounded as though he had a problem, for the fact was that he had very little else. He had no hobbies, didn't collect things, didn't read. His golf game was too amateurish to be regarded as anything but a humiliation. In a working life of servicing clients and taking business trips he had developed no other skills and no pleasures. Hoyt's preoccupation with the Asian market had cast a spell on him, making him believe that he did not need a US passport. He soon realized that he could not be an effective lawyer without it. He said he didn't mind. He had money.

But without the passport it was almost impossible to use the money. He could of course buy anything he wanted. There was a brisk trade in Singapore and Hong Kong in Chinese porcelain and carved wood furniture and jade and Japanese prints and netsukes. Hoyt had worked so hard he had had no time to study the nuances of such collecting. He bought an expensive sound system and a video camera and had a wet bar installed in his Singapore house.

The Boca Grande house was shut much of the time, but still Vickie went there with the children and they played on the beach. She seemed to enjoy it and to manage without Hoyt. But he could not go to the States impulsively, as he once had, and he was an impulsive man – it was his most American quality.

Once, at a party for some Japanese automotive clients, an elderly Japanese with thick glasses and a hearing aid was introduced to Hoyt. They talked about cars. Hoyt mentioned his Jaguar.

'That's patriotism,' the Japanese man said. 'Because you are English man!'

A bad joke but a harmless one. Hoyt was livid. 'I'm not English – I'm American!'

Still feeling insulted the next day, he brought the subject up again, saying, 'Only a deaf and blind Jap would take Hoyt Maybry for an Englishman.'

It was true: no one was more American than Hoyt Maybry. It was not just the cowboy boots and the silver belt buckle and the aviator glasses and the turquoise stones in the silver bracelet that served as a watch band; it was his whole manner, his way of saying, 'I'm currently busy' and 'Thank you very kindly' and 'At this juncture.' It was the unhesitating way he shook hands – in his grip you felt your hand had disappeared. It was his generosity towards friends, his ruthlessness towards enemies, his blue shirts, his big feet, his obsessional cleanliness, his appetite for work. His very name was American, probably a corruption of a picturesque English name, for 'Maybry' grunted out of the side of an illiterate immigrant's toothless mouth was probably 'Mayberry.'

I have mentioned that Hoyt was accident-prone – probably as a result of his hurrying and divided mind, always seeming to hold two conversations, no matter what the topic, one for the defence and one for the prosecution. It was an occupational hazard but it was also related to his being an American. Was it also related to fatigue? That hamstring business after the Willard speech was typical. Hoyt often returned from a trip with a sore back or a sprained ankle. 'It's a strain,' 'It's some kind of rash that's going around,' 'Pulled a muscle in my groin.' As a lawyer who had worked on personal injury cases Hoyt knew the names of any muscle he injured. He was a scrupulous litigator, and yet settling into his desk he had a tendency to flip open the lid of his laptop at the same time he set down his coffee cup. As he fumbled the coffee cup and tried to right it he would knock his laptop to the floor.

'Stress weakens the immune system,' I said one day to my secretary, and I laughed when I realized I was quoting Hoyt again, who always said that when he caught a cold.

At one time he had been preoccupied with thinking of ways to save money on taxes. Having solved that with different citizenship he became preoccupied with ways to get into the United States. Being sent back to Vancouver had stung him.

'Imagine being sent back to Canada. Think what that does to a person.'

I said, 'There must be lots of countries that welcome Guinea-Bissauan citizens.'

'Probably,' he said. 'But I wouldn't go to any country that did.'

He did not say that he regretted giving up his US citizenship. He did not question the wisdom of having become a Guinea-Bissau citizen. He had not imagined how valueless that passport was as a travel document. It was questioned, or smiled at, or held up to ridicule at many airports in Southeast Asia.

Hoyt said, 'I was under a lot of stress over Kinglet's memory-chip deal. If I had to do it again I probably wouldn't choose Bissau.' And he made a point of saying that he knew nothing about Guinea-Bissau – had no idea where this place was.

He said to Elfman, 'Does every passenger on a Liberian-registered ship know where Liberia is?'

Elfman annoyed him by replying, 'Liberia is near Guinea-Bissau.'

So he schemed. He arranged for Vickie to be a director in a company that needed her to vote at semi-annual board meetings. Rather than find a willing company, he gave her the money to start one. I knew this because I was also a partner in New World Investments. We even held a meeting in Honolulu – Vickie and Elfman and me, though all we discussed was Hoyt's rage, because he could not be there. The meeting had an odd effect on Vickie, but in any case Hoyt was not granted a visa.

'My spouse has a business meeting in Hawaii!' he had told Scavola.

But all the consul said was, 'It doesn't follow that you need to go. She has the meeting, not you.'

'I am married to this woman!'

Scavola said, 'When you're doing business in Shanghai, do the Chinese recognize this as a valid reason to grant a visa to your wife?'

'I thought I was dealing with the United States government.'

'You are an African,' Scavola said, seeming to take pleasure in saying it, 'and therefore subject to all visa requirements governing Africans.'

'Guinea-Bissau is an independent republic.'

'And a member of the Organization of African Unity,' Scavola said. 'My last post was Senegal. It's next door.'

The directorship didn't work. A moment ago I used the expression 'had an odd effect on Vickie.' What happened was that Vickie invited me to her room at the Kahala Hilton and gave me a drink. We sat on the *lanai* looking at the moon on the water. I was talking – about Hoyt, of course – when I noticed she was crying. When I tried to console her and hugged her, she said in a throaty way, 'God, it's been so long since I've been held by a man.' And she was smiling.

Then she said, 'Jim, do you know how many women in Singapore wonder whether you're gay?'

There is a grinning Hindu goddess with about thirty arms. At that moment I felt I was being embraced by her. It took all the strength I could muster to disengage myself.

Hoyt had another scheme. He had noticed ('a bit late in the day,' Elfman said) that our British and European clients visited the United States with relative ease. Inspired by that freedom, Hoyt decided to apply for a second passport, one from a country in the European Union. Ireland granted passports to individuals who invested one hundred and sixty thousand dollars. The money was handed over in instalments, and after five years could be withdrawn. Hoyt put down forty thousand dollars and was put on a waiting list.

'If I get an Irish passport, I'm fine,' he told me. 'I'll have access to the whole of Europe, and it'll be easier to get into the States.'

He regretted that he had no Irish relatives, which would have made it easier. An Irish grandfather would have done the trick. Yet he knew that an Irish passport was available, at a price. In the meantime, because he could not see Vickie and the children in the States, they met in Mexico, stayed for a week at a time at hotels in Acapulco, got sick with stomach upsets, and he ranted over the hotel bills.

It was expensive to travel on the periphery of the United States, involving rental cars and two hotel suites and restaurants. Formerly he had broken his journeys in Honolulu. This was not possible any more. He got to know Vancouver well, which seemed to him a shabbier, less fireproof version of its sister city, Seattle.

There was an edgy and irritable atmosphere at partners' meetings these days. Warfield felt it too. 'It's our foreign colleague,' he said.

Then, 'No, not Ernie Loong.' One typical meeting concerned our effort in organizing a Chinese-American joint venture by a large American pharmaceutical company (which had a division in Singapore) to market an asthma medicine. Hoyt had done his homework. He found a Rand report stating that because of the bad air produced by China's successful manufacturing industry, China was full of asthmatics, almost a tenth of the country gagging. It was the sort of image that Hoyt loved presenting to clients: a hundred million Chinese gasping for breath, and we own the inhaler!

'It's like owning air,' he said. 'So let's do the deal.'

'It means meeting the principals,' Elfman said.

'It could be a conference call.'

'You call that service? Hey, I've lined up three days of discussions in San Francisco.'

'Why not Seattle?' Hoyt said. And I guessed what he was hinting: 'Why not Vancouver?'

'The Chinese want to see the sort of plant our people have,' Elfman said.

'And they like going to the States,' Warfield said. 'We'll probably fly them down to Disneyland on their free day.'

'This has to be next week?'

'Snooze, you lose,' Elfman said.

'You have this gift for phrase-making,' Hoyt said. 'Listen, I can't go next week. I think you know that.'

'Grillo can take your place.'

Afterwards, when he did not ask me about the deal, nor inquire how much my cut was, nor mention Elfman's commission, I realized how much it mattered to him and how it had hurt.

'I have plenty of money,' he said one day at lunch. He was chewing, taking his time, knowing that a statement like that got my attention. 'So I don't have to chase every deal that comes up.'

'You can stop and smell the flowers,' I said.

'Ever notice, Grillo? Flowers in the tropics have no aroma,'

Hoyt said. It was indignation rather than remorse. 'These Singapore orchids look gorgeous but they smell like potting soil.'

Hoyt was pleasantly surprised to find that he had no serious problem going to Europe. This discovery came about during a business trip to Hong Kong. He had taken the jetfoil across to Macau and had easily gotten a visa to Portugal. From there he could travel anywhere in Europe. He called Vickie from Paris to say that they might consider meeting there, but when he saw that his hotel bill for three days was more than four thousand dollars, he said it was out of the question.

Vickie said, 'I thought the whole point of your citizenship thing was to make us rich.'

'Cut me some slack!' he shouted and flew to Dublin. Once again an immigration officer smiled at his passport. He rented a car and drove to Cork in the rain and tried to imagine himself living in a house there, looking out of the window at the drizzle. He went to an agency in Cork, he looked at some houses and he marveled at how clammy they were. This country existed in another century: a cold damp century of stinking woollens and rotting plaster and toothless old men.

Travelling back to Singapore by way of Lisbon he had a giddy thought of stopping in Guinea-Bissau. Why not? He had the passport. He knew the place was not expensive. What if it happened to be palm trees and white sand beaches and outdoor cafés? He saw himself with a drink in his hand, at a café table, writing something. He heard himself on the phone. *I'm doing a book.*

The woman at the TAP Airlines counter at Lisbon printed an itinerary for him. Hoyt examined it. He said, 'Why do I have to come all the way back here? Can't I just go from Guinea-Bissau to – anywhere else?'

'You can go to Africa,' the clerk said. 'But this is the most direct route.'

'It's about two thousand miles out of my way,' Hoyt said. 'Where else can I go from Guinea-Bissau?'

'Just Lisbon,' she said, 'or Africa.'

Nowhere, he mumbled to himself, and he thought of that arrogant student he had met at the lunch at Willard College. I might stay.

And yet Hoyt still had a desperate curiosity to see what Guinea-Bissau looked like. The fact might be crucial. He imagined it as looking like a West Indian island. He said so to the clerk, who smiled, just the way strangers smiled at his passport. She said it was a terrible place, of deforestation and drought and bad soil. Now he imagined cindery beaches and isolation and hunger. They all want to leave. They are a problem here. You see?

What was she talking about? She had lifted her eyes to the people behind him in the line, perhaps a family, and yet there was just the merest resemblance, not in their features but in their coarse skin, a kind of acne Hoyt had never seen before except on the skin of certain blighted fruit. The women's hair was in plastic curlers, the men wore stained baseball caps and rags, their luggage was sewn in bales and bundles. Entering the ticket area half an hour ago, Hoyt had seen these people stretched out on the floor. He stepped aside and listened, and he gathered that only one of them was travelling, a young man in a shiny nylon tracksuit and torn shoes.

The ticket agent was shaking her head and saying, No, no, and showing them a circled paragraph on a printed piece of paper. The young man had a problem. He waved his ticket irritably while the clerk indicated that his passport was blank – no visa. The word was the same in Portuguese and English.

He knew what the woman was saying. He heard certain familiar words – 'JFK,' 'New York,' 'Lishboa,' 'visa.' He understood the gestures.

The clerk, who would not accept his ticket, was probably saying, 'Yes, you have a ticket to New York, but when you get to JFK airport they will not admit you. You have no visa. You will be put on the next plane and sent back to Lisbon.'

The language of rejection and humiliation was easy for Hoyt to follow.

The ragged family complained. They took turns whining. They muttered. They crowded the counter. The young man was the shrillest, his eyes shining in a fever of misery. But this was just futile noise, a kind of squawking: they knew they were beaten.

The young man's green passport was familiar to Hoyt, and just seeing it in their skinny fingers demoralized him and ended his desire to go to the place of his citizenship.

His European trip was an expensive one, no billable hours, no client meetings. It was a journey into frustration. 'There's so much emotion in airports,' he told me. 'People crying, people holding hands and hugging. People looking petrified, as though they're going to crash. That's taken its toll on me.'

Back in his office he calculated that eight months after his renunciation of citizenship his income dropped to a third of what it had been. He had been granted one US visa – the commencement speech. Alison now had an internship at the *Wall Street Journal*.

'I can't even see my own kid!' he said to me.

He said he could not trust anyone else in the office. They were stealing his clients, he said; they had muscled in on his accounts. Losing the pharmaceutical deal had been crucial; it was the first of many such losses for Hoyt. He was not imagining the attitude of the other partners. They had begun to treat him with the mixture of off-hand courtesy and evasiveness that they reserved for foreign partners who were not involved in our deals. Maybe it was better to tell them nothing, we thought, and because we were keeping them at a distance we were polite to them in a formal and unconvincing way.

'I've got a beautiful home in Boca! I never go there!'

These days Vickie was living in it with the twins and taking tennis lessons; but that was not the way Hoyt saw it.

This house, in his odd, resentful description, lay on the Gulf of Mexico, on a barrier island of multimillionaires. The rooms were in darkness, the shades drawn, the sun visible in knife-like slashes in the blinds. The tiles were white, the beams varnished, the furniture covered with sheets. 'Vickie chose all the accessories' – a giant paper parasol from Bangkok, some Mexican pots, a rocking chair. Empty rooms. The microwave clock blinked green, the burglar alarm blinked red. Dusty hibiscus bushes had been planted among woodchips. Many deserted houses were like that, but this was slightly different. This house had its own sound – the loud drone of air-conditioners, audible from their shelf just outside a rear window, cooling the house, month after month, cooling the Mexican pots, cooling the rocking chair, cooling the empty rooms.

The grinding sound was the same an office shredder made when it was chewing on something that offered no resistance, like hundred-dollar bills. That air-conditioner on that hot American island made the sound of money being shredded.

'So it's settled,' Elfman was saying. More and more he was taking charge of the partners' meetings. 'Lake Tahoe for the holidays. Something for the swimmers, something for the skiers.'

Woe had turned Hoyt's face a bloodless, corpse-like gray. We discussed the annual meeting in a circumspect way, knowing how keenly Hoyt was watching. He had become more intimidating as a listener than he had been as a talker.

'I know I can get ten days,' he said to me the next morning. 'I might get a month. But that's not the point. It's when my time's up – that hurts. When I have to go.'

'But you can always go back.'

'I like to do things in my own time, when I want.' That was another of his American qualities – impatience.

'Think of all the money you've saved.'

He did not reply to that. Wealthy people talked about being poor because they concentrated on what they spent rather than what they saved.

He said, 'When this Irish passport comes through I think I'll be in the clear.'

Alone of the partners, I knew that his reason for not going to Lake Tahoe was that Vickie had left him and decided to stay in Boca Grande. Their separation had proved to her that she did not need him, and she told me frankly that she resented his giving up his American passport. The lawyer I found for her was a shark. I hated his method, I admired the result.

Even the marital crisis was no help in his securing an American visa, and the Irish passport was so long in coming that Hoyt developed a set of Mexican clients. He seriously thought of becoming a Mexican citizen. 'After all, they seem to have free access to all parts of the United States.'

But no, he could not do it. 'I can't bring myself to become a fruit picker.'

Not long after the news of Hoyt's divorce, I received a call from Kinglet Chee, asking me to come to his office. He seemed relaxed; he showed me the panelling he had removed from our Harborfront Tower offices. It was a superb example of colonial workmanship, he said, but all I could think of was Hoyt's crack, 'You might have to sue me,' and the rest of the rant. I squirmed at the memory of Kinglet's telling me, at the Ron Brown party, how Hoyt had mocked him. I could not recall the exact words, only my feeling of discomfort, his eyes on me, his face impassive. And I had blurted out how I had felt.

But today, Kinglet was talking about my negotiating the terms of this new generation of memory chips. The great thing about this world was the way technology became so quickly dated. The typewriter hardly changed for a hundred years, but computers and chips became obsolete and worthless every year or so. This was another very big deal.

I said, 'Hoyt should be in on this.'

'He is not an American,' Kinglet said.

'He'll never speak to me again.'

'If so, then he is not your friend and never was.'

He chose me over all the other partners because of what I had said to him at the ambassador's house, that I would never renounce my citizenship, never, ever. Odd that a businessman should be such a sentimentalist, but he explained that it was his dream to become an American, and Hoyt was a liability there. Perhaps I might help with that? The profit for me was a million-two.

Hoyt stopped speaking to me. It was the money – so far, that was all he knew about, and just as well. The talk in the office was that he had begun to refer to me as a 'cheese-ball,' and to how Elfman had set him up.

All this I got second-hand. I was no longer in Singapore. At last I heard through Warfield that Hoyt, who was almost broken by the Irish passport he finally got, was applying for a Green Card.

I hope that he is turned down. Vickie and I are very happy in Boca Grande. 'I'm doing a book,' I say. 'Words for sale!' she calls out. Just a joke, but it disconcerts me that she uses so many of Hoyt's expressions. And I do too. I have begun to understand the meaning of the expression, 'not a lot of money in my tax bracket.' With all the assets in her name Vickie was now regarded as a very wealthy woman, but as a married couple living in America the fact is we don't have that much money.

1996

# The Rat Room

# 1. *Palm Sunday*

Sometimes, for no apparent reason, Linzi Palfrey thought of people moments before she saw them. It made her think she might have powers, or did they have powers, the other people? She had been thinking of the priest just before she saw him on this Palm Sunday in front of the Chapel of Hope, where she was dropping off her daughter, Venus. The priest was new, and yet he seemed familiar.

Approaching the chapel, Linzi had looked closely and seen that the palms the people carried were fresh, broken from the top of the living tree, as though it was not a made-up story but the truth.

'They're real,' she said – another pretty thing about living in Hawaii. The palms looked succulent and edible. Then she saw the priest.

Venus did not hear her. She was already out of the car, calling to a girl who also carried a palm frond. The new priest, in his dazzling white cassock, was waiting at the chapel door, looking at Venus then at Linzi, and he reacted swaying slightly, as though he had heard an echo. He was a handsome man, she thought, and she wondered whether he found her attractive too. He was smoking a cigarette.

He went over to her, seeming to glide because his legs were covered, and offered her a palm frond, and he laughed and blew smoke when she began looking in her purse for a five dollar bill. Did he suspect anything when he saw all those singles?

Linzi drove home to her apartment and with the bright slashes of blinds cutting across her body she slept until four, when she got up again. This time she dressed with great care, and afterwards she drove to a club called the Rat Room on Keeaumoku Street, where she worked as a dancer. On stage she danced with negligent attention to the music and removed her clothes until she stood naked on a lighted mirror before the hopeful men, who looked so horny they were pop-eyed, nearly thyroidal. They never said anything.

A man with his face averted reached out with his pale hurrying hand and slipped five dollars under her garter. The bashful ones were happier looking between her legs rather than at her face.

Except for the palms and the business of dropping Venus at the chapel and the swift attention of the priest, it was a normal day. Every afternoon, Linzi got out of bed and dressed very slowly, knowing that when she arrived at the club she would be taking those same clothes off in full view of the room, the other dancers and all those men. She concentrated hard on her choice of clothes, her underwear especially, like a priestess preparing for a ritual. And when she put on her make-up she gave herself a different face – a mask. Tonight, as always in the lights of the Rat Room, she would be naked.

Everything she wore was seen under the flashing lights of the stage, from the sleeveless jacket and silk blouse and skirt to the high-heeled shoes she had just slipped on, to the panties and bra that lay next to her skin. The other girls wore bikinis, and tugged them off quickly, but Linzi was, at thirty-two, ten years older than most of them. Her idea was to use her maturity, believing that a well-dressed secretary stripping was as exciting to a man as a girl stepping out of a bathing suit.

At last her skin itself would be revealed and the men staring at it, every area of her body, her tattoo, that cobra on her shoulder, a mistake. She said she was a dancer – the dance did not last long; there was no word for the rest of her routine. They called it a hostess bar but she was never a hostess.

Big reckless faces, only men had faces like this, urgent with hunger and concentration – she smiled at them but her thoughts

were elsewhere. The men seldom looked at her face, the men did
not have names, lined up at the edge of the mirrored dance floor
like pigs at a trough, anonymous and animal, and she was
anonymous too. It saved you, it was merciful, this namelessness.

Taking Venus to the Chapel of Hope at ten she had worn a scarf
on her head and sunglasses. She had been so tired – just five
hours before she had had to fight off a demanding and drunken
Japanese man, sucking his teeth and pinching her until the
Samoan bouncer Taufila had intervened. There had been
screaming and swearing. Moon, the owner, an old Korean woman
whose make-up gave her a monkey face, had hissed at them
all.

Venus was twelve but looked older, almost as tall as Linzi now,
rather skinny, still without much of a shape, but funny and
flippant; and with Linzi's cheekbones and full lips and slightly
prominent teeth, a pretty face on a body like the stem of a flower.

'Drop me here,' Venus said, seeing her friends.

Only then Linzi saw her daughter was wearing lipstick, a
vampire color, as blackish as day-old blood that darkens and
hardens like lacquer. The Rat Room was the sort of place where
some nights you saw fresh blood, on the floor or on a broken
bottle. Nowadays blood in the club was a horror, like poison,
lurid with the virus.

'What's this all about?'

It was not her own shade, which was lighter, pinky, deliberately
so, to catch the reflection of the overhead lights so that her lips
were luminous, like a doll's.

'It's Amber's.'

'That's not right for church.'

'Everyone wears it.' The girl shrugged, giving her bony shoulders skinny emphasis. 'It's no big deal.'

'It looks slutty,' Linzi said. 'Were you in Waikiki yesterday?'

'No,' Venus said.

'Cupcake said so.' Amber's mom Cupcake danced in a

notorious club called the Limit. Cupcake said: *Honolulu's full of rats.* It was.

'Hey, that's the new priest, Father Creech. He smokes.'

But Linzi had by then already thought of him and seen him. She said, 'If I had been caught wearing lipstick, my father would have hit me with his belt.'

'He did catch you. He did beat you. You said so.'

Venus was looking at her with pity that the black lipstick made severe.

The lipstick was the prize that Venus had won from Amber the day before in Waikiki. They had been playing what they called the Touching Game. They played it differently according to their mood, or the time of day, or the opportunity. One of them, seeing a stranger, would challenge the other to touch a stranger in the street – a tourist, a prostitute, a child, a policeman. The idea was to touch the person's body, and if the person realized that he or she had been touched it was no good. Venus and Amber gave each other points for difficulty or position – who the person was, the place on the body. Another version of the game was for one girl to walk the length of a block and touch everyone in sight, while the other girl watched. There was celebrity touching: Amber had touched the governor, Venus had touched Kevin Costner. There were many ways of touching, and none of them had names – Venus was looking the priest up and down.

'Come straight home after the picnic, you hear?' Linzi said. Venus was getting out of the car when Linzi added, 'I'll see you later.'

'Later' meant tomorrow – it usually did. They both knew what these expressions implied. Beneath this conversation was another truer one that was too harsh to be uttered out loud.

All this time, drawing nearer to the Chapel of Hope, Linzi had been noticing the palms in the people's hands, green springy fronds, picked for the day.

'They're real,' she said.

Venus did not hear that. When she hurried to the sidewalk to greet her friend, Linzi had a pang, something twisting in her heart, an intimation of her daughter's vulnerability, the danger such a young girl was in. With her restlessness and size and her flippancy she called attention to herself. She was active yet so weak – bony arms, thin ankles, the skinny neck and small head. When Linzi saw her from behind, passing the priest, swiftly touching his hand, she thought, *I would kill for her, I would die for her.*

And so Linzi was reassured when the young priest with the bright eyes and the cigarette walked over to the car and passed a sprig of palm to her and laughed as Linzi dug in her purse for money to give him.

That helped because this was a worse than usual good-bye. When Linzi went to the club at six, leaving Venus in the apartment doing her homework or watching T V, it was not as bad as seeing the young girl leave her and become lost in a crowd of larger and older people. Never mind that they were going to church and that the picnic was supervised – and Linzi who was not religious knew there were dangers everywhere, girls raped in church, priests fiddling with little boys, she knew men.

Yet the priest, his sudden appearance, his little gift, even the cigarette, had consoled her. Linzi understood the meaning in men's eyes. They searched for skin but went no deeper, they could look desperate, goggling upwards between her legs with the studious solemnity of gynecologists, as though they were examining for a subtle illness. At last, when they were satisfied, their eyes lost their light. Another man would take their place on the stool by the mirrored platform, and Linzi and the other girls went on dancing and stretching. But she could see that the priest was strong and that his eyes penetrated to her heart.

The Rat Room at six was almost empty, two men at the bar, one at the edge of the platform, goggling through thick glasses. Moon was saying something in Korean, yelling. She was sixty with orangey hennaed hair and a monkey jut in her jaw. The black girl Jessica smiled and wagged her tongue – it was pierced with a ball, another ball just below her lip. She winked at Linzi, she was young too, but tough. Another girl was waiting to speak with Moon. Seeing her, Linzi felt nothing. It was a sisterhood but that didn't mean you had to stick your neck out. There was always some kind of squawking and sometimes a fight when she walked through the door. But she asked no questions. Moon was a bitch. Getting involved was a mistake.

No one watched her dance, no one saw her until she began to remove her clothes. She did this suddenly, without grace, dropped her skirt, lifted her blouse, shrugged and unhooked her bra, knowing that a woman taking her clothes off struck postures of submission, bowing, making herself vulnerable, compact and small.

She smiled at the thought of the priest, Father Creech, the way he had stared, as though in hope. Turning to face the mirror, she saw only her flaws, despairing of her body and her weak flesh at the same moment as it aroused the staring men. In the depths of the mirror something dark jerked on the floor, then hesitated – a rat?

She folded each item of clothing and made a little stack by the side of the platform, near the stairs, where no one ever sat. 'Throw them off like the other girls,' Moon had said. And Linzi replied: 'You buy the clothes and I'll fling them. These are mine. I paid for them, so I'm folding them.' Nor did Moon see, as Linzi suspected, that there was something erotic, perhaps more so, in the way she knelt and stacked the clothes, getting down and up, then squatting naked again. From this lower angle she could see that the thing on the floor was a rat and that it had not moved.

Naked, still in her high heels, she held on to the upright bars on the platform and leaned and swung and canted herself backwards, and finally seeing men tapping dollar bills on the floor mirror she went over to them on her spikes and tipped herself and opened her legs. The rat was watching from the edge of a booth.

The men did not smile. They were solemn, intense, greedy, watchful. You could predict where they would look, you knew what they wanted, which was why a slight delay made them eager. They were dressed, among their friends, and she was naked, alone on the mirror. You needed Taufila and the other Samoans, the confidence that there were strong boys nearby to break up the fights. If a man touched any of the girls he was warned. The second time, he was thrown out, usually with such intentional roughness he would never try it again.

Now Linzi was on all fours, facing a man so that he could whisper to her, then facing away, reaching between her legs to part her vulva with splayed fingers, and she could feel the murmur of his grateful voice flutter on her vulva making the labia tremble like petals as he spoke in a filthy way, talking to himself. For allowing that she was rewarded, the man tucking the folded bill – usually a dollar, sometimes five – into the garter on her shin.

For lifting her leg like a dog at a hydrant and then placing her foot on the man's shoulder, letting the man stare up as she looked away, there was usually something extra. It was joyless and mechanical, just a ritual, but somehow it worked, because the men were hungry and their hunger made them stupid. Men liked the dancers in the dumbest and most obvious postures, which was fine, because posed that way she never saw the men's faces. She saw only the floor. The rat was gone.

When her set on the platform was over – four songs were enough – she carried her stack of folded clothes to the dressing-room and put on a see-through robe. She then lingered by the back booths until a man invited her to sit with him.

'A glass of champagne,' she said. It was just plain table wine but it was the price of sitting with him, twenty dollars for the bottle with tortilla chips, and she touched the men, just her hand in their lap, while they begged for more. Moon kept the booths deliberately dark, though the darkness seemed to make them smellier.

The men went on talking, but whispered, they made no sense.

They were not talking to her, they were talking to a woman, a particular one in their mind, not her. They did not know her, it was all ritual, and ritual made the whole business bearable.

Even when she knew they did not mean it – were too drunk, or had other women with them, or were on their way to catch a late flight, or saying it just to make their friends laugh – the men asked her to leave with them: always, as though it were expected of them. The girls were forbidden, not that Linzi was ever tempted to go, not once, not even for the large amounts of money the Japanese sometimes promised. She insisted they buy more champagne and for this she touched them again, until it was time for her next dance.

After work, almost at dawn, she was escorted to her car by one of the big Samoan boys and she went home, took a hot bath, and shampooed the cigarette smoke out of her hair. On week-nights often there was just time to wake Venus for school. Then Linzi went to bed and slept until early afternoon. She liked to be awake and up when Venus returned home. That was their time together, those several hours, until six, when she dressed again for work.

The work did not shame her. It was hard, Moon was a bitch, the other girls were tough or else pretended to be, the hours were long, the men were demanding yet awkward. Some men did not know what they wanted or else were too shy to ask, clumsy but greedy. Or she had to do all the work. She was willing to make all the moves, pretend to care, breathe as though she were aroused. All those staring men, all the music and noise, made her tired. And she felt nothing. There were other dancers who hated the men and some were outright dykes.

One was Lana. She was Vietnamese. 'I know I am not pretty,' she told Linzi. 'So I need something else. I practise shooting table tennis balls out of my hole. I sit on my kitchen floor for two months, maybe more. I teach myself. I am making money now.'

The naked Lana concentrating on the kitchen floor, her legs open, was to Linzi an image of desperation.

A Chinese girl, Mee-Ho, had just arrived from Hong Kong, had no money and lived in a curtained-off cubicle with Jessica (who told Linzi the story). She was continually bullied for sex by a particular Japanese man, but said no to him, and to every other man. The girl who was strangely virtuous was regarded as inverted and troublesome since, as Jessica said, it was easier and it was certainly more profitable to say yes. Linzi thought: That's how they feel about me. Mee-Ho danced naked and got the men going by dripping hot candle wax on her thighs. Mee-Ho said she felt nothing, nothing for the men either, and longed for the day when she might have her own hair salon.

Linzi understood – the money was good, a salary plus tips – and she too looked at the men with dull eyes. She was gazing inward, at what she treasured, the image of her daughter. Venus was a good girl at a dangerous age. Linzi did not look very far into the future. She imagined Venus graduating from high school and then junior college – already she could use a school computer. In six or seven years she would be on her way. She was an unusually bright girl who knew how to look after herself. Venus's father – Linzi's only boyfriend – had left when Venus was six. He was violent and lazy, it was better with him gone. He had come to Hawaii for the surf, had become involved in drugs – not just taking them but in a serious and stupid way boasting about their benefits. She gave herself credit for not remembering anything he had said about drugs. He had named Venus, he was on the mainland now.

There had been no other men in Linzi's life. The little apartment in Kalihi was a preserve – safe, clean, tidy; food in the refrigerator, books on the shelves, a VCR and a stack of tapes. The apartment had never been violated by a man. It was Venus's home and Venus was precious.

In order to remain sane and content Linzi found herself pleading and haranguing and defending herself against men, and so she had remained the same. No matter how her life appeared, no matter what she did at work, or what the men thought, she could only keep herself whole if there was a part of her that no one knew. That place deep within her was where she lived.

Like the other girls except the crazy ones, and there were too many of them, she refused on principal to kiss a customer. She touched the men, she did more, she took hold and massaged them until they gasped and were gone. But that was a mechanical act, like squeezing an orange. She did not give a name to it, she did not want to know any of the words, and not knowing them made it all easier.

Even at the height of a man's frenzy, when he was saying, 'Baby, harder, yes,' or muttering the name of a woman – girlfriend or wife, not her – she watched from within this space in her heart which was to be possessed by no one. Except when she was with her daughter, she kept to this space, which was her secret and her consolation.

She did not give a name to this void. She did not give a name to the work she did, except to say, 'I am a dancer.' It was crucial not to have words for any of it. Words would have made it unbearable. The idea that had sustained her was that what mattered most in her life, good or bad, had to be nameless.

She went through those motions. She did not consider the men, hardly looked at them, only the money – counted it afterwards, put it in her safety deposit box. She was not disgusted. It was work.

'I am a dancer.' And she imagined Venus saying, 'My Mom's a dancer.'

She did not care what the men thought of her, because she despised the ones she knew and mistrusted the ones she did not know. Men to her were the men who came to the Rat Room. The club changed them – they entered and became sweaty animals. She did not want to know them, nor did she allow them to know her, for fear they would corrupt the special area in her heart. Once a man had said to her, 'Got any kids?' and she was horrified by just the stranger's mention of her child in this place. Venus would never see the club. The very idea of Venus's name spoken here had seemed insulting.

The greatest deception of nakedness was the idea that a naked woman had no secrets; that a man knew a woman because she was naked. Not true: being naked had saved her. Men here never saw beyond bare skin – they saw flesh and no more. You were never safer in your anonymity than when you were naked. Men did not look a naked woman in the eye.

That men were animals inside here was awful, but helpful too since animals were more predictable than men outside. The men in the Rat Room wanted to watch and then be touched and when they were done they lost all interest, as though their vitality had leaked away. Women were so different. The busy active girls in the club were the hardest to know, the greatest riddle, sometimes so sweet, at other times crazy vicious sluts. Moon was tougher and more ruthless than any man Linzi had ever known, and that went for what's-his-name, gone now.

'Okay, go!' Moon said. You knew what she was saying even when she was speaking Korean, she was so mean.

Every night Linzi returned home to her daughter. On so many week-nights, Venus lay asleep in her school clothes so that when she woke she would hurry away, all wrinkles and haste, her hair ratty. The idea of the young girl's nervousness, her hope, her childish heart, made Linzi sad. Venus's innocence, her purity that of a flower coming into bloom.

As for herself, the thought that she had always cherished, that have given her hope was: My life has not yet begun.

But why tonight, which was like every other night, did Linzi crouch by her daughter's bed and weep? In her own bed, she still whimpered a bit. Nothing in the day or at the club had seemed unusual, yet something had changed and she wondered what. Then, as she had imagined the priest an instant before seeing him, she thought of a rat in the darkness and moments later she heard the thin ceiling being scratched from the attic, and an impatient gnawing – more than one rat. She lay awake, helpless, her face upturned to the sounds of yellow claws, yellow teeth.

## 2. *The Rat Sermon*

Venus stood and sang, she knelt, she said prayers, she sat and tried to listen. Had Father Creech known he had been touched? Even her shallow attention allowed her to notice everything, yet she thought only of yesterday, as she waited for the mass to end, all the while enjoying the taste of her lip-gloss.

Amber had walked beside Venus down Kalakaua, daring her. Venus had touched a man on his tattooed wrist, a chess player on his elbow, a Japanese man on his foot, a Japanese woman on one breast – 'if you call that a breast.' She made Amber giggle when she wagged her skinny finger and touched a tourist's hairy shoulder.

'That lady's so fat she's got dimples on her thighs.'

Without the woman suspecting, Venus touched a dimple on a thigh as sallow and soft as a sack of warm cheese.

The Palm Sunday service was longer than usual, and the yellow school bus parked outside distracted her too. It was the bus that had been rented for the day to take them all to the picnic at Mokuleia on the north shore of the island. The reading from the Bible was about Jesus entering Jerusalem in triumph, all the people cheering and waving palms, and the next week the same people would crucify him. She knew from last year that the sermon would be about not remembering and getting ready, and needing to be saved, and maybe about hypocrisy too: you could always predict the long boring lesson from the short vivid reading.

But the priest Father Creech was new to Hawaii and the Chapel of Hope. He stepped to the pulpit and smiled and reached into his white robe and took out a rat trap. The Filipinos in the front row recognized the thing and laughed softly and muttered to each other, as though dangling the rat trap this priest had shown them a token of friendship.

'I guess you know what this is,' he said, and set the trap with his thumbs and sprung it – it twanged loudly, making most of the people in the chapel jerk back and laugh.

The big Filipino woman Lerma cried out, 'Snap trap!' and that got them going again.

'First day in Honolulu,' Father Creech said, 'I saw a rat in the church. I looked under the pew and there it was, nibbling a candle. "I can give him a better meal than that," I said to myself, and spread some peanut butter on the trap, for bait.'

'Can use one cuttlefish.'

'Who said that?'

'Hilbert.'

Venus knew Hilbert Swinney's son Ryan, who was just as bad in his outbursts.

The priest did not seem to mind the interruptions. He said, 'I put the trap back under the pew. Next day the peanut butter was gone but the trap wasn't sprung. Almost took my thumb off baiting it with peanut butter again – snapped it myself! But the rat didn't make that mistake. Three days in a row he got the peanut butter without springing the trap. He was one happy little rat, getting his meals. Never thought there'd be rats in paradise.'

'Lotta rats – it's the fruit!' Hilbert again. And everyone laughed at the thought of this rat outsmarting the priest.

'I was frustrated, but I shouldn't have been. Without realizing it, I had been encouraging the rat to come up to my trap and eat. I hadn't failed. I had trained the rat to use my trap. Four or five days later I put a piece of meat in the trap. Couldn't lick that off. Had to tug it – which he was willing to do. I had one confident rat there. He tugged – didn't know it was a trap. Thought it was a feeder tray. Nice feeder tray! Snapped his head off–'

All this time, Venus listened, seeing the rat returning again, trusting the trap to give him food. She easily imagined. She had seen a large brown rat in a drawer once in her bathroom. She was eager to hear more.

But the lesson was next, and it bored her. The priest explained the meaning of the trap, the rat, and the mistake the rat had made, and said why, but by then Venus's mind had gone blank, she went deaf until she heard the word 'forgiveness' and heard, 'no matter what you do will be forgiven if you are truly sorry.' She listened then. Because you could be forgiven, sins did not seem so black and deadly – the soul was washable, and that made the soul stronger than the sin. No sin was fatal. Such a promise gave her hope and made her happy.

Venus knew how to be sorry and she knew about secrets. She had learned from her mother the way to say nothing, to give no name to the thing you did or the thought in your mind, and Venus had an aptitude for understanding what older people were thinking. She knew she was free and that she had greater freedom by never mentioning it. Her rebellion took the form of saying nothing of what she did. She was careful because she did not want to be called a sneak. And this thing about being forgiven. If you meant it you could make mistakes. Afterwards you had to be sorry. Also, if there was no name for the thing you did, how could it be wrong? The thing with no name was nothing at all. The touching game was just a game; it wasn't 'tag,' there was no word for it.

Older boys were more trusting, the younger ones mocked, because they were so awkward, not knowing what they wanted. They were afraid, and fear turned them into bullies. Big people kept to the rules. Even when they were rough they could be generous. She was happiest with them and hated the younger girls and the boys most of all. For one thing, they always complained when they were touched.

Venus's best friend Amber Delgado, who was not as good as Venus at the touching game, and knew the grossest jokes and the worst words and had a porno picture in her plastic wallet – Amber never got into trouble. She was so careful. Her mother

Cupcake was a dancer too except that Amber called her waitress. She worked at a different club but the same job, the same night hours, and Amber also went home to an empty house. No one asked where their mothers worked because everyone knew.

Last year Amber became famous at the school when she got the stud in her tongue and Miss Ishikawa demanded to see Amber's mother. Amber said, 'My mom opens her mouth. Don't say nothing. Sticks out her tongue. A stud!'

They were friends, Venus and Amber. They both played school soccer, they were learning to use the roller blades their mothers had bought them, they always sat together at the chapel, they hated the same boys. They hated Ashley Miranda. They wished that they were sisters.

Father Creech was saying, 'So get ready. Prepare yourself for the risen Lord.'

'I touched him,' Venus said.

'Where?'

'A whole bunch of times. Everywhere.'

Amber began to smile. Kneeling, while everyone else prayed, she said, 'Why don't priests ever get married?'

'They don't need to.'

'I don't get why.'

'They have us instead.'

'As wives or as kids?'

'Both.'

'You're sick, Venus.'

'Was that rat trap neat or what?' Venus said. She saw it snapping again and remembered the Filipinos screeching.

'Now I would like to make a few announcements,' the priest said.

That was the signal that the long service was almost over. Venus yawned, wanting to leave. Bored and distracted, she looked around the Chapel of Hope. She knew every bit of the room, the pillars, the painted ceiling, the altar, the electric fan. Balbino and the other Filipinos sometimes played guitars and ukeleles, and it seemed like a club. The flowers changed from Sunday to Sunday but smelled the same. In the colored glass windows there were angels. Angels always looked like women. In another window was a saint with a cracked cheek. A split in the cross looked like a smile, the velvet cushions were faded, and except for the angels every holy person had a beard.

The congregation was restless now, rattling their palms. Babies were crying, and the men in T-shirts and rubber slippers had stopped paying attention. Some people seemed to hide in the pews. The priest was still talking.

It was the same every Sunday. As soon as Venus entered the Chapel of Hope she began to wait for the service to end, and afterwards did not talk about it. What was there to talk about? It was something you did every week at a certain time, and then it was over.

The people were standing up, and they seemed patient the way they shuffled, plucking their sweaty clothes that were stuck to their bodies, and looking vague and flustered, like people on a bus who sway and stumble to the door as the bus is slowing down to stop.

Father Creech was smiling and holding his hands up and saying, 'Go, the mass is ended.'

Instead of cream pie and cookies and fruit punch in the chapel hall they crowded into two yellow school buses, Father Creech in the front seat of the first bus, Venus and Amber sitting together in the back, boys all around them giggling loudly and swearing under their breath. Hilbert was sitting in the front with the priest, Ryan in the back, his baseball hat on backwards and leaning over the seat and saying, 'Hey, suck on this.'

Amber said, 'Oh, shut up, dirty mouth,' so loudly that Ryan ducked down in shame.

His friend Kalani was saying, 'He take some hana batta from his nose and toss it in the fishbowl and the fish eating it.'

'My mom took me to *Basic Instinct*,' Amber said. 'It was

gross.' She laughed excitedly. 'Like dykes and stuff! Plus, she strangles this guy and gets off on it.'

'My mom would never take me to an R,' Venus said. 'But I saw *Indecent Proposal* on video. Demi Moore had this incredible dress and lingerie to die for.'

Amber was looking into space, at bright clothes.

'Hey, you think they get to keep those clothes they wear in movies?'

'Like they need them, huh!'

'I know. They have tons of money. Actors can buy anything they want. Plus, people give them stuff.'

'So if Robert Redford gave you like a million dollars would you like sleep with him?'

Amber wrinkled her nose. 'He's old as the hills. All those wrinkles.'

Venus was laughing. 'That's why it like costs a million dollars.'

'I'd do it with Brad Pitt, though.'

'He's so cute. He's got such great eyes. But he wouldn't be as kind as Redford.' Venus smiled again. 'And you sure wouldn't get a million.'

'Like which other guys would you do it with?' Amber was whispering, she was near, her breath was hot.

'Mel Gibson.'

'He's old too! He's got like fifty kids.'

'That's why he'd be real nice to you. He'd give you stuff – all kinds of neat stuff.'

'Plus he's got crazy hair,' Amber said. 'It killed me when River Phoenix died. I used to think about doing it with him.'

'Doing what?' Venus asked, wanting to hear more.

'Bump-bump,' Amber said, then howled softly.

Venus was excited and breathless, hugging herself, her hands tucked into her armpits the way she always did in a place that was air-conditioned.

She said, 'Like River Phoenix would have checked you out if he hadn't of died. Sure.'

'He might have come to Honolulu. My mom says a lot of big actors do come. Remember you touched Costner? And I might have been at the beach that day in my bikini.'

'And you'd just throw yourself at him like real slutty, huh.'

'Try it some time. How do you know it don't work?'

But Venus could not say and she went silent. Already this talk was getting out of hand and making her feel reckless – something about the other people talking loud in the bouncing bus and the fact that the church service was over.

Kalani was looking out of the bus window at a wreck by the side of the freeway and saying, 'That car rolled over two other more cars!'

'Geeks like Ryan and Kalani it doesn't work with them,' Amber said.

Only Ryan heard. He said, 'Shut up, bitch! What are you saying about me?' He sounded vicious yet the girl knew him to be harmless.

'Shut up yourself, you lolo.' Amber turned her back on him and made a face. 'My mom makes me nuts.'

'Same here. "Why don't you clean your room?" Hey, why doesn't she?'

'Plus, "Where have you been?" Like she can't come right out and say, "Were you with some boys?" Like it's so insulting. These geeky guys. That dweeb Kalani.'

And as they turned aside to see whether the boy had heard they saw Father Creech.

'Have you noticed what a lovely day it is?' he said.

Where had he come from? One moment the girls were whispering, the next moment this big white-robed man was standing next to them, folding his hands into the robe and smiling. He wore sandals. His hair was light, too – sun streaked, as though it had been tipped.

He moved aside and when they looked again the sun dazzled behind him, making it impossible for them to see him plainly – his face was a shadow, his body like a big dark cut-out.

Yet he had a friendly voice. The silly question he asked was the question that *malihinis* from the mainland always asked, except that he was saying it to be friendly, the way some of them did. He had come to Hawaii just after Christmas. This was the first picnic.

'May I join you?' he said, sitting and blocking the row of boys behind them. The boys stopped talking and behaved themselves and seemed to sulk because the priest had sat down.

Father Creech had interrupted the girls' talk, yet there was something reassuring about him. He was like a heavy weight which had settled into the back of the bus, steadying it and making it peaceful. That was another thing about adults, the way they brought balance just by being there.

'Have you been down this road before?'

The bus was rising on the road past Wahiawa and the first pineapple fields had come into view, the deep green of the spiky plants, the rust-colored clay showing through, the red roads.

'Like billions of times,' Amber said, and looked at him, having to screw up one eye because of the glare behind him.

'What about you, Venus?'

'Me, too.' He knew her name. That made her smile. It seemed such a different name when other people spoke it.

'Did you come with your parents?'

'My mother.'

Venus resented having to say this and was angry with this man who had asked the question, as well as at the man who was not there – for an instant they were both the same man. Venus did not know her father's face, had only heard her mother's description of him, how he was a pig, and, *I'll never let him touch you again.* So, any man's face might have been her father's face. She had no memory of the man, either as a brute or as a father. She was not fond enough of her mother to believe her and hate the man. Yet where was he?

'Pineapples,' the priest was saying, but Helemano slipped past and great leafy stalks, fields of them, like giant grass blades, appeared beyond the straight rows of low sharp plants. Green and sloping and untidy, the raw stalks of this other crop grew so high it formed a wall, a ragged wall of stiff tassels.

'Cane fields,' the priest said, telling them again that he knew the name of what it was – something everyone knew, but he was trying to be friendly again.

The girls smiled because it was almost silly, being so obvious. They said nothing. *Lost in a cane field*, people said. A cane field was like a forest, like a swamp. *The body was dumped in a cane field.* Because of the thickness of the crop it was the most hidden place. *Stabbed in a cane field and left to bleed to death.* A cane field was a place where corpses were found, where people were slashed and where murders were committed. *She was brought to a cane field and raped repeatedly.* People were left for dead. Old wrecked cars and pick-ups turned up in cane fields after the harvest, and once – they knew, it was only a year ago – a dead baby, among bagasse and hacked stalks and withered cane trash. The rats gathered in the cane fields and gnawed the stalks and squealed and fought over the ripest canes. A cane field was a haunted and dangerous place.

'So pretty,' the priest said. He probably looked at it and saw sugar.

That proved he was a *malihini*. He did not know it was a bad place, that over there in Waialua where the cane fires were burning it was dangerous, like a bad neighborhood, all those tall stalks, that it swallowed you up.

'Don't you think it's pretty?'

In the wind that blew up from Hale'iwa the ragged stalks thrashed like giant weeds – they had the same rough shape, the same odd toppling look. They grew fast and were too thick to see through, no roads, no trails, not even any paths. That darkness was another reason. When they were cut and stacked on trucks the cane stalks trailed on the road, dropping off and scraping, leaving the trash of the crushed cane and torn leaves and half-burned stalks and stubble.

Amber said nothing. Venus knew she was thinking the same thing. A cane field!

'Over there, that's the sugar mill,' Amber said, to avoid answering. She pointed to the far-off chimneys and rusty towers and the dirt-reddened storage cylinders.

'Really?'

Venus said, 'I think it's real pretty.'

'Good for you,' the priest said.

Under the palms of the beach park the children helped the older people set out the food – macaroni salad and a tub of poi and a stack of Spam musubi and lau-laus and boiled hot dogs and a tray of huli-huli chicken and manini fish and a pot of rice. There was a cooler of soft drinks and platters of cakes and some red Jello in large glass bowls for dessert and plastic buckets of potato chips.

'Bless us, O Lord,' the priest said, pronouncing grace in a voice of such authority and conviction that everyone stopped talking and became motionless and interested. There was no muttering – the priest believed and so the people did. In the past prayers made people impatient but this was something else.

'Is this codfish?' Father Screech asked, poking at the manini, and it sounded to Venus like 'godfish,' though she said nothing. Had Amber heard it that way too?

Venus and Amber got plates but did not take much food, a Spam musubi apiece, some macaroni and chips, and drinks. They went to the grass at the edge of the sand, away from the boys and the chapel people, and ate. Near them in the grass a pale dove was pecking at a dead rat.

'Touch him, I dare you,' Amber said.

Still chewing the Spam musubi, Venus poked the rat with her finger and said, 'Hey, I forgot my Walkman.'

'Mine needs new batteries.'

They chewed and swallowed and breathed in sniffs as they watched the dove return to the rat.

'It's the Holy Ghost.'

'It's a flying rat.'

The dove was frantic, tearing at the rat's flesh. Venus smiled and went on eating.

'What are you thinking about?'

'Have you noticed what a lovely day it is?'

'Give him a break.'

'Yuck. He's a mainland *haole*.'

'He was just trying to be friendly.'

It annoyed Amber that Venus was so understanding and serious when she wanted to mock. She said, 'I think you like him.'

'Who?'

'Godfish.'

'He's okay,' Venus said. Hearing insistent voices she looked up and saw that some children were calling to the priest.

Amber made a face and shrugged – Venus was her friend, so why argue? And the priest seemed popular. A game had started on the grass near the picnic tables, the priest leading it. He was not like a priest at all in the way he played the game. It was bunting and running, the priest pitching, urging each hitter to sprint to the base. He was running himself – seeing Venus and Amber going nearer for a look – and he ran to take them by the hand. He got them a turn at bat ahead of the other boys.

His pale soft hand in Venus's was clammy from his playing, his face was pink, his cassock dusty. He was a new priest, of a sort Venus had never seen before at the chapel, yet one she understood, because he was a man. Her fascination made her shy with him.

In the middle of the softball game, just as Father Screech was delivering a pitch, a scream went up near the shore – the words weren't clear yet they knew a kid was drowning. The priest rushed across the sand, past the people, into the shore break where some women were pointing, and he snatched a frightened boy – it was Julio Pagaragan – out of the surf. The boy squalled and gasped, choking on water as the priest said, 'I could let this little rat go–'

'No!' the women screamed, and so did the frightened boy, who looked like a rat.

The others laughed, and Venus looked at Amber and said, 'See?' because the priest had surprised them all. He was a hero and a tease. He was strong. None of the others had risked stepping into the shore break.

The lower part of Father Creech's white cassock was wet and dark, and when the softball bunting game resumed, he perspired and his face reddened. He was like the other men, yet it was so odd for them to see the priest as someone who sweated and was so breathless and giggly; and who had also plunged into the sea. Saying mass and leading the others in grace, and even giving his rat sermon, he was the sort of pale odorless person that all priests seemed to be. And yet, away from church – outdoors here on the north shore, he had become a man.

After the game he beckoned Venus and Amber to a bench in the beach park and he sat between them, with his arms around the two girls. His hands were warm, he smelled of sweat and sea water. No longer was he concealed in his white robes. He was a man, he was laughing, he was hot. When the people sang, he sang. He ate again. Venus watched him fill his mouth with a hot dog, licking his fingers, his cheeks puffed out, a dab of mustard on his lip.

'How about Julio?'

'That was a ten,' Venus said.

Again someone began to yell, the pinched-nose wail of a Filipino.

'It's his back! Mr Llacuna! Agostino hurt his back!'

A bent-over Filipino man was helped to the bench, where Father Screech remained seated with Venus and Amber.

'How did that happen?' Father Screech asked.

Venus was impressed that the priest did not get off the bench – just went on sitting there between her and Amber. She knew that he had not even moved, because she could feel his body and it seemed that he touched her, his fingertip like a timid request.

'He coughed and it just happened,' Hilbert said. 'He threw his back out when he coughed.'

'Lie down on the hot sand and get comfortable,' the priest said.

'If it happened at the yard he'd get Workers' Comp.'

'He's a welder at Pearl Harbor,' another man said.

Agostino, bent over, breathing hard, had not said anything, which made him seem pathetic.

Without any gestures, simply speaking, the priest said, 'Dig a shallow hole in the sand and help him into it. Then cover him with warm sand, his whole body, except his head–'

After the priest had given his explicit instructions, the man Agostino was taken moaning softly to the high part of the beach where the sand was hot. The men seemed glad for something to do, and the priest smiled as he saw Agostino covered with sand. Venus smiled too, feeling proud and proprietorial – she had seen all along that the priest was someone special, a priest, a man, a healer. He knew how to laugh and he liked her.

All this time he had kept to the bench with the two girls, not moving.

Venus moved aside as he clutched her shoulder and when he tightened his grip he said, 'What did I do?'

Everyone could see him with the girls. Venus said, 'Nothing,' and the people laughed, Venus too, who was glad for the way that Father Screech drew her closer. She realized it was what she had wanted all along.

'Agostino says he feels better,' Hilbert said.

An old woman said, 'All my life I live here and I never dig one hole for my sore back. Thank you so much.'

'I couldn't have done it without my two helpers.'

They watched Agostino being dug up like a corpse disinterred from a grave, and then he was led away limping – but not so badly as before – to the parking lot. Father Creech still smelled of the food he had eaten – the hot dog, the poi, the mustard. Yellow flakes and crumbs of potato chips still clung to his damp-stained cassock. He asked for a can of beer and was given one.

'I knew it was dangerous for me to come here to Hawaii,' he said. 'I resisted, you know. If I came I'd never go home. My friends warned me.'

'Maybe they were right.'

The priest was still sipping his beer.

'I hope so.' He looked at their anxious faces. 'What's wrong?'

The men and women watching laughed because they were so embarrassed.

Amber said, 'You're not supposed to drink here. It's a park, like.'

'But I'm a priest.'

They laughed again, all of them, this time with approval, and watched him finish his beer, smiling with pride, as though it were a privilege to witness it.

'Look at that sunset,' he said.

It was fire settling slowly into the sea and the nearer the water the hotter it seemed.

'There's going to be a green flash,' Venus said.

'Let's say a prayer.'

Father Creech took Venus by the hand again tightly. She felt so secure sitting next to him, she was smiling. Then when the priest stood up and let go she did not seem to know him as well. They knelt on the hard sandy grass and he led them in a prayer that he seemed to make up as he went along. He spoke of seeing the sunset, and the brilliant light on the sea, and a shark's black fin moving through the light. As he was saying it, Venus thought with annoyance that it was one of those made-up prayers that are impossible to remember.

At dusk they boarded the yellow bus. It was dark when they passed the pineapple fields, though the sour syrupy smell of the old fruit came through the open windows. Venus sat in the darkness, thinking nothing, looking at the lights, feeling frightened and insubstantial as she always did when she was alone.

## 3. *The Rat Room*

On the Monday following Palm Sunday Linzi felt something was wrong, an uncertainty loose in her mind that also sapped strength in her body. Was it the thought of the rats? They were silent, but she knew they were there, in a rat-hole in her attic, and her premonition that this thought would provoke their appearance made her fearful, and lonely. Yet, as the mother of a lovely daughter, she had never really been lonely. Perhaps part of an afternoon spent with Venus would ease the pain. She set her alarm so that she would be awake when Venus got home from school.

'You're up,' the girl said, surprised to see her mother dressed – not for work but in a T-shirt and blue jeans.

'Let's go shopping, sweetie.'

'Tons of homework,' Venus said, and let her books tumble onto the table. 'We'll have to come back early.'

'How was your picnic?'

'Okay – yeah, it was fun,' Venus said. 'A guy threw up. And a kid almost drowned. One of the Filipino kids.'

Venus had gone to the refrigerator and poured herself a drink of juice as she spoke. Linzi was proud of the fact that she kept no soft drinks in the house, only fruit juice and bottled water. No alcohol, no junk food. She liked seeing Venus gulping the fresh juice.

In the car, on the way to Ala Moana, Venus said, 'The new priest drank a beer.'

'He seems nice.'

'I guess so,' Venus said. 'He talked to me and Amber. He ate lots of the food. He even played games. He saved the kid that almost drowned. The kid's parents were going nuts.'

Linzi could not see the priest clearly in Venus's innocent description. She could not fit any of it to the face of the man she had seen yesterday in front of the church.

'What's his name?'

'Who? The priest? Father Creech.'

The name helped a little, but still Linzi wanted more.

'Another old guy hurt his back by coughing. That was the other thing that happened. But the priest didn't freak out. He told them to bury him in the sand. And they did. And he got better. Weird, huh?'

In Linzi's imagination the priest was now standing, calmly giving directions to people who needed them. Near him were a wet boy and a bent-over man. A moment ago he was just the blank outline of a man; he now seemed a strong and reassuring figure.

'I really like him,' Venus said. She looked down the sidewalk and, remembering the touching game, it seemed wrong to be here with her mother.

Linzi was smiling at her daughter. She was impressed that Venus liked him and 'really' meant something, because he was a priest, because he was a man. Venus knew more than she realized and her interest mattered because it was the interest of a twelve-year-old.

The next day, having left deliberately early for work, Linzi called the priest from a pay-phone at a gas station on the way. A woman, probably the housekeeper at the rectory, asked Linzi her name, and when Linzi said it and spelled it the priest quickly came on the line. He must have been listening on another phone, but you could not blame a priest for filtering his calls.

'This is a wonderful week for you to call me,' he said. His voice glittered with confidence. 'Holy week.'

'I'd like to see you.'

'Why not come right on over?'

It was what she wanted. She drove quickly to the Chapel of Hope and found the rectory. It was four, she was expected at the club at six. A Filipino housekeeper opened the door. The priest stood in a doorway at the end of the corridor, young, in his white robe, welcoming her to the darkness behind him.

'I saw the palms last Sunday – so pretty,' she said, and wanted to remark again, *They were real*, but felt awkward. She was wearing a new dress, yet she was convinced that the more she said the more the priest's suspicions would be aroused. It was a settled belief of the girls in the clubs that everyone else sneered at them. *They snob us*, Cupcake had said to Linzi. *They know.*

'I'm glad you came here.'

'I don't know why I did.'

She was wearing her most severe dress, her lowest hemline, but even so it seemed wrong – not just the dress but her being there at all, and she was at once ashamed in this tidy room with its crucifix and a large bright portrait of Mary. In this mood of feeling unworthy she no longer wondered why you never saw Mary's hair.

'In here, you don't know.' Father Creech tapped his head. Then he touched his heart. 'In here, you do.'

No, not even there. She said, 'Venus said she had a good time at the picnic.'

It was, she believed, her whole motive for having come here – that Venus liked him. To find a man her daughter liked – she always said how much she hated them – that was probably the reason. It was because of Venus.

He was young, polite and, she dared to think, even good-looking. He made her feel welcome, and although he was smart he did not make her feel stupid, though she suspected she was. He was not a man like any she had known, and she knew so many, all her work was dealing with men – the worst. The priest looked at her closely in that peering near-sighted way, as other men did, but he was kind. He did not judge her. Whatever he knew of her he accepted. There was a look she got in the street, in stores, in all the places outside the Rat Room. This was not the look. It was helpful, appreciative, not a sorry look of forgiveness – he was looking inside her, into her heart.

Then he said that same word: 'Your heart and the will of God. That's what brought you here.'

414

She shook her head, trying to deny it. She said, 'My daughter's very positive about you.'

The priest closed his eyes, as though saying another prayer, yet he was smiling – Linzi liked him for that.

'She looks like you.'

It made her uneasy, as when he had mentioned her heart and the will of God in the same breath, seeming to her another bad comparison. Linzi knew that Venus was prettier, politer, more intelligent; that she was everything her mother was not. That she had a future. Purer, too. But it was so hard to raise a girl alone, without a father.

The priest had not stopped looking silently prayerful.

'I guess I was curious,' Linzi said. 'So I came.'

'Jesus welcomed women,' Father Creech said. 'He had as many women friends as men. We know them by name, from the gospels – all sorts of women. He defied convention in his relations with them. He mingled with them on equal terms. He liked being with them, and they knew it. They followed him.'

'You make him sound like a man.'

'He was a man,' the priest said in a familiar way, as though speaking of someone he knew well. 'He might even have been married. It would have been very strange for him not to have been – the New Testament never says he wasn't married.' Smiling again as though recalling a harmless eccentricity, the priest said, 'And he was always a bit irritable with his mother. "Woman, what have I to do with thee." And in John he says flat out to his Mom, "That's not my problem."'

'Sounds like Venus.' Realizing that the priest was talking about Jesus, Linzi covered her face and apologized.

Father Creech laughed. 'Right! In Luke he is twelve and in the temple he snaps at her. "Did you not know that I must be in my father's house?"'

'I remember that part.'

'It is because he was a man that he was able to save us. He became flesh. He understood the flesh.'

Father Creech's words gave Linzi hope. She sensed hope like an uncertain bird within her spread its wings and launch itself and lift her spirit as it soared. She was glad she had come.

She understood why Venus liked the priest – volunteered it, Linzi hadn't asked – and again seeing such a man she lamented that she had no man in the house for Venus to know and be guided by.

'I worry about my daughter,' she said.

'Perhaps that means you're worried about yourself.'

'I was thinking of all the temptation.'

'That's what I mean,' the priest said.

'Kids grow up fast here. They're exposed to all this strange stuff.'

The priest again seemed to peer into her soul, like someone looking over the rim of a small cup.

'Perhaps you're talking about yourself?'

These questions stopped her – she did not know the answers. If I say I am worried about my daughter am I worried about myself? She wanted to say, *I can handle it, but then I'm not twelve years old.*

The priest was so sure of himself, and she was so uncertain. Linzi stammered and said she had to go.

'But I'll be back.'

That seemed to surprise Father Creech, who took her hand and enclosed it with both of his hands as though trapping a fluttering bird. There was no pressure from his hands, only warmth, as he whispered some words she took to mean 'Goodbye.'

After this Linzi went and danced naked at the Rat Room, alone on the mirror, under the lights, stroking herself, lifting her breasts and parting her legs. Turn down the loud music and it was not a dance at all, but rather the sequence of exaggerated and deliberate movements any woman might make in the course of a physical, or as the subject of a search of body cavities. She wondered what the priest knew of her. She was deaf to the music, and though she moved sinuously it was no more than habit. She had heard of priests coming into the clubs, wearing ordinary clothes – sandals, shorts, an aloha shirt, a baseball cap. She understood that. She believed that all men came into the clubs, for relief. They behaved differently outside, yet it was only inside the club that she ever really spoke to a man. She did not blame them for what they said, but it made her wary, the way the sight of a strange dog makes you alert.

Something about Father Creech's eyes told her that he might know more than he let on. He stared with such intensity – looked at her eyes, and into them; at her body, and beneath it. She knew that look, she was an authority on the way men stared, what they wanted without even asking. She knew his look, those eyes, even the way his mouth moved, how his lips went dry, how he breathed, and held his breath. He saw everything, he knew everything.

As these thoughts went through her mind the music stopped, more girls got on-stage, Linzi shook her head and picked up her clothes and slipped on her flimsy robe. She was so used to being naked here she did not even tie it and so it flapped and showed her body.

'Over there,' Moon said, then muttered in Korean to a dog-faced man in a suit. Still muttering impatiently to the man, she directed Linzi to a booth. Linzi hesitated. It was the booth where she had seen the rat; and the rat had seemed to watch her.

'He ask for you!'

Linzi slid into the darkness, towards the man. His shirt was white but in the shadows she could not see his face.

'God is love,' the man said.

She was startled, she drew away, she wanted to say, *He's wacko – get him out*.

'Christ could see to a woman's heart,' he said. 'Mary Magdalene, for example.'

It was him, the priest, in a shirt and dark trousers, holding his white hands clasped, not touching her.

417

He was still speaking. The men she knew never said such things, except when they were raving. Her surprise subsided. She was grateful that he did not accuse her, that he did not plead – that he treated her as someone with a mind and a heart. Yet still he was unexpected; and she was naked.

'He was a man of mercy,' the priest was saying, speaking from the darkness in the corner of the booth. 'Remember the woman who was a sinner, who wet his feet with her tears, and wiped them with the hair of her head and anointed them with precious oils? That was in Simon's house, and Simon rebuked Jesus. But Jesus said, "Thou gavest me no kiss, but she hath not ceased to kiss my feet."'

Linzi could see it all, the tears, the feet, the kisses, the hair – especially the hair.

'"Her sins, which are many, are forgiven, for she loved much."'

When the priest spoke Linzi felt tears welling in her eyes.

'Or the woman taken in adultery. "He that is without sin among you, let him cast the first stone at her." And what did Jesus do? He turned his back and doodled in the dust with his finger. It's there – you can read it.'

'I know it,' Linzi said.

Christ standing up to the other men and waiting until they went away – then alone with the woman. It was something only a strong man would do. She remembered it all.

'I asked your daughter what you did.'

Linzi smiled sadly as the innocent face appeared in her mind. And she realized that Venus was present in this conversation, in everything she had to do with this priest. Linzi here was both mother and daughter – the priest was seeing them both when he was looking at her; she felt that.

'She told me you're a dancer.'

Linzi nodded. Dancer was a word like mother or husband or waitress or policeman or manager – just a word that explained nothing. You had to know the person to understand the word. You had to see.

'You've seen me dance.'

The priest said, 'It is said that Mary the mother of Jesus was one of seven temple virgins, kept by the High Priest in Jerusalem. She would have danced.'

The word 'temple' she had heard in the Rat Room though she could not call up the face of the man who spoke it.

'I have never heard that,' she said.

'The Book of James tells us.'

Linzi smiled because she thought she was mis-hearing again, another garbled voice. It was not a Bible book that she had ever read or heard of.

'James was Jesus's brother,' the priest said. 'One of Joseph's other children. You see, Joseph had probably been married before. Mark tells us that Jesus had four brothers and some sisters too.'

Looking out of the booth, Linzi saw the men's faces and the lights and the beer signs and the girls dancing on the mirror. The men were horrible – only ugly people came to the club. The lights were wrong – too bright and yet they lit nothing but the naked bodies; everything else was in shadow. She saw the girls dancing and thought of what the priest had said. She smiled because she was confused. She said, 'But Mary, in a temple, dancing.'

'She was sixteen and six months pregnant when Joseph met her.'

'So what kind of temple virgin was she, then?' Linzi said, and saw Mary clearly.

'Not a very successful one.'

'Like one of these teen-aged pregnancies,' Linzi said, thinking of herself again.

'Like any girl in trouble,' the priest said. He was smiling – his voice was casual. 'And Jesus did not get on with her, or his family. He saw no sense in that kind of family. "Follow me – leave your mother and father and wife and brother and home–" He said that. The Apostles were his family. He never said, "The family is sacred – stay together."'

She turned to him, in gratitude, yet not able to say why she was so reassured by what the priest had told her. She would have been glad for him to touch her, and it bewildered her that he kept his distance.

'Jesus said, "God is love." That can also mean "Love is God."'

'God is everywhere,' Linzi said, remembering and reciting, trying to think of something to say that would please this passionate priest. She had learned those words long ago.

'God is within you,' the priest said. 'Love is within you.'

'Even me?'

But she was convinced of the truth of it as she said it, and it seemed marvelous, the way she was protected here in this strange shrill place, where everyone was so ugly, not just the hungry men but the girls who squatted and hung from bars like monkeys.

'Especially you. Everyone is equal. There is no first or last. Jesus mixed them up, and he wanted us to do the same. But you see he often got things wrong. He was a magician, a prophet, a wizard. Jesus was not a practical man. His parables usually have inaccurate information about farming or fishing or how high a mustard tree is.'

Linzi said, 'How do you know all this?'

'There isn't much to know. Jesus didn't write. He preached and people listening to him sometimes didn't hear him correctly, so the gospels are full of contradictions. It's noisy in here. Maybe you don't hear everything that I am saying. Never mind. The true words of Jesus are, "I came not to destroy but to fulfill."'

She had begun to see the face of Jesus shining in the words of Father Creech, who spoke about the Lord as though he was someone they both knew well – a friend they were recalling. This intimacy made Linzi confident, but self-conscious too. The only conversations she had ever had in the club were about her body, or the men's hunger, and they were never satisfied.

'They'll be calling me in a minute for a set. Unfortunately.'

Father Creech said, 'With the love of God in your heart you can never do wrong.'

It was what she had felt but could never explain: God existed in that secret place within her – that was why she was strong.

The priest was still speaking. He seemed to speak easily, without listening to himself, the way men did, talking as they stared. He was looking at her the way men did – fantasizing perhaps, holding himself back, his mouth never quite closing, as though his mind were crowded and steaming.

'Perhaps you'll come back.'

Did she say this, or did he? It was something she wanted to hear so badly, she did not know who said it. He was a man, Christ was a man, the woman with the long hair was a woman, but Mary was hardly a woman, a girl really, no more.

'I think you will come to accept Christ as your savior.'

The music was very loud now and someone was laughing, someone had fallen over.

'I know him now,' Linzi said. 'He was a man you could trust – not many of them around.'

'You said it.' The priest drew near her – his white face, his dark eyes. 'Remember that the kingdom of God is within you.'

Then he touched her, and though it was gentle, just grazing her with his fingers, he seemed to scorch her naked skin. Her wrist burned, her hand was on fire, but she knew it was a sign of strength. She was not ashamed. She knew that inside she was pure. She sensed that she had been touched by God.

## 4. Nakedness

She was naked in the greasy light of the revolving mirror ball with its small winking spangles. As she danced the faces of the men sitting at the edge of the stage seemed worse than just green and ugly – they were disgusting and dangerous. She had taken her clothes off quickly because she found herself hesitating. Now she simply wanted to get through this, and she felt trembly and out of breath, as though from a greater exertion.

Was it her sense – a fear, really – that the priest was still among the men in the club? Not that he was watching her in the way the other men were, but that he pitied her. It helped that there were other girls on stage – reckless ones, pierced ones, a drugged one rolling over and over. She could not have done this alone tonight.

Squatting, parting her legs by tugging her knees apart with her fingertips, she looked up, all the while searching the faces of the men. Some were familiar, the older men especially, but none was the priest. That did not calm her: she had a horrible feeling that Venus was watching her. She was ashamed and sad and she danced badly.

It was all so difficult tonight. The words of the priest stayed with her. Because he had spoken to her in the club, that whole conversation was part of the club's atmosphere. She felt clumsy and unsure of herself. She had lost that secret place within her. The priest had found it and filled it with his preaching and now he seemed to inhabit it. *God is within you*, he had said. She could not believe that, only that the priest was there. Her expression was severe and a little fearful. Men gestured for her to come over to them. She turned away. She did not want their money, did not want to be touched, nor to go near them. Men in the club seldom looked into her face, but today they did and she wondered why.

A man said to her in a hot impatient voice, 'Touch yourself and I'll give you five bucks,' and he hitched himself forward to see better.

I wouldn't do it for a hundred, she thought. It was dark and the music was so loud she pretended not to hear the man.

The other dancers were performing with such energy that Linzi knew she would not be noticed if she slipped offstage and collected her clothes and hid for a while – just sit out a few numbers. It was all so strange now – the darkness, the smoke, the music, the muttering of the men, almost hellish, because of what the priest had said.

There were so many men crowding the bar and the exit she ducked into the last booth and sat there. It was the same booth the priest had beckoned her into, near where she had seen the rat. She felt more naked sitting here naked than she had standing on the mirror of the catwalk naked. All her nerves were alive, crackling against the surface of her skin. She felt as fragile as wax, as easily injured.

Just then, at her most fragile, imagining that a rat had brushed past her ankle and sniffed at her leg, a man sat heavily next to her and shoved himself sideways against her. 'Move over.'

It might have been possible for her to sit there alone and think of herself as pure, overworked, just a dancer – but this man made her feel weak and foolish.

Sitting precisely where the priest had sat, the man said, 'Go on, touch it – take it.'

He stank of his unzipped pants and unwashed body and it was as though he held a dead rat in his lap for her to stroke and bring to life.

'No one's watching,' he said. 'What's your problem?'

He was louder than the others, and not drunk, but strong and sober, and that was worse because of the way he demanded that she listen and do as he said. Drunks were never so persistent or intense. They got bored, they forgot, they dozed.

'I am going to get dressed,' Linzi said.

The man reached between her legs and got a grip on her as though he were holding a bowling ball. She hurt where his fingers were jammed into her and she whimpered, 'No.'

'Yeah,' the man said, excited by her fear.

And he placed his free hand on the back of her neck and twisted her head towards his lap.

'Please – no,' she was saying, and she began to weep with helplessness, feeling too feeble to protest, believing she should be suffering and that there was justice in this, the way she was being treated. She was being punished, as she deserved to be.

'You love it,' the man said, enjoying her distress.

His horrible hunger made her panic and she began to object and to struggle against the way he was pushing her head. She knew that a man aroused was determined but often not strong, and was seldom agile, usually toppling, like someone balancing on tiptoe. He was top-heavy and tender. A man in this condition – she knew – needed help.

'Suck it,' he said. 'You know you want it.'

He was denying that he wanted it, the way they always did. She hated them for that – they wanted you to tell them that you were the one who desired them, who wanted to expose yourself, touch yourself, or touch them, or taste them, tempt them, or fumble with them. That was how they always wanted it, for the blame to be yours, always; the desire always – it was supposed to be your idea. Yet she was never in the least aroused, and she was often disgusted.

She breathed hard, a low furious howl that made the man sit back suddenly and relax his grip on her.

With her face close to his in the darkness Linzi said, 'I have a knife in my bag. Let me out of here or I swear to God I'll cut your cock off.'

She sensed air leave the man's body, as though he had actually been cut and punctured. He seemed to shrivel and become smaller. She felt stifled and angry and ashamed, and the man did not understand that she was ready now to leave the club entirely – to go and never return.

How could he know? He was not a man, he was an animal, just a creature with a cock like a miserably gnawing rat, and he was foolish enough to see this pathetic thing as a weapon.

Seeing him that way gave her strength and she felt as though she was rising as she pushed past him – he grunted, he was apprehensive, fearful of being stabbed – and still she ascended as she stood and pulled her clothes on, feeling hopeful and buoyant as she hurried to the door. The man was just behind her, complaining, whining like a child to Moon, because Linzi had truly frightened him.

She straightened her clothes; she left. It was not necessary for her to say anything at all. Moon called out, probably 'Come back!' but it was just another monkey shriek. Linzi knew she would never go back.

Something as easily torn and as fragile as tissue had begun to exist and slowly grow within her body. It was still small, trembling and tentative, like a pale bud with small blue veins. She had only ever experienced this feeling once before and that was when she had been pregnant with Venus. The sense that she was the protector of this new thing made her careful.

She was watchful, with a sense of awe at the change inside her, and so as not to disturb that sense, for two days following her quitting the club she did nothing at all except spend those days pretending that nothing had changed. She kept the same odd hours, as ever, but hid herself. She drove the length of the island; she parked by the sea. And she was interested in the look of surf in the moonlight, the softness and delicacy of it, the way it erupted in the middle distance, and rolled towards shore, then hesitated and collapsed on the beach. She recognized the whiteness of its froth, and sometimes walking the beach she had seen frail creatures of a sort she imagined growing within her, but these were dead things, flattened on the sand, like flowers made of jelly.

On the third evening she passed the Chapel of Hope and saw a service in progress, the chapel filled with people listening to a priest. The signboard on the lawn announced it as the Holy Thursday Mass.

Linzi deliberated and did not enter the chapel until she was sure the priest at the altar was Father Creech. He was holding a tall gold staff with a cross at the top. The prayer he was saying was incomprehensible to her at first – perhaps it was not English. And yet in her fervor of concentration, she understood it, as though this gabbling language was one which she had been taught a long time ago and which she now remembered.

The priest's words echoed in a small murmuring in her own throat, urging her forward, reassuring her, saying in her own voice, 'Come closer–'

She at once saw what she was being asked to do. Her own voice had been speaking to her from the first, from way back at the Rat Room, when she had threatened the man. The reminder that she possessed something small and new within her, something as insubstantial as a flame, and as easily snuffed, gave her the alertness to hear the words and remember their meaning.

That beckoning voice had directed her here – her voice, God's words. The other people in the chapel were so intent they did not notice her. She liked that, being one among many, unseen at the chapel, just another person praying in the prayerful mob.

The priest and his cross became a holy presence, the priest as upright and as dappled with glittering light as his golden cross, the cross itself as sympathetic as flesh; as fragrant and merciful, understanding suffering, forgiving those who were truly sorry.

So grateful was she for this mercy that still with tears streaming down her cheeks she left her pew and walked up the aisle, and with such conviction that it must have seemed to the people there that she was part of the service. All this while she heard her own beckoning voice, and she knew it was the power of God, glowing within her.

The priest was speaking, too. As Linzi approached, he held the cross out and lowered it. Linzi knelt and put her lips against it and kissed it. Her lips were damp with tears.

Blessing her, the priest lifted the cross, and like a child Linzi returned to her pew at the back of the chapel. The rest of the mass, seen through her tears, was a blur of blobby lights.

While Linzi lay awake that night at her apartment on her hot noisy street in Kalihi, the Lord spoke to her. His voice came with others – the neighbors, someone's television set, some boys under the streetlight. The Lord knew her in the same way as the priest, and the Lord's voice resembled the priest's, the same kindly words.

'Now you are free to be the woman you are meant to be,' the Lord said to her. 'You are no longer tied to your old habits and patterns and addictions.'

She shut her eyes and listened to the Lord's goodness.

'I will protect you for one year. After that, it is up to you.'

She covered her face with her hands. No more tears – she gave thanks, she was happy.

Less than a week after that Father Creech called her. She had expected the call. She was thinking of him, and was not surprised an instant later when the phone rang. He asked her to visit him. Linzi went to the Chapel of Hope. This time she was not met by a housekeeper. Father Creech opened the rectory door, and when they were seated she told him what she had heard.

'That is the word of the Lord,' he said. 'I know it was the Lord speaking to you. No one could make that up, in those words. He is all-knowing, all-seeing.'

'Now he sends me pictures,' Linzi said.

In them, in these clear mental images, she saw herself resisting temptation, treading a narrow path, guided by a shining light ahead in the distance.

'He doesn't speak to me any more,' she said. 'It was just that night. But I know the pictures come from him. I don't know what causes them. Sometimes I get them when I'm praying. Sometimes at work.'

'The Lord is giving them to you on a need-to-know basis.'

'I guess so.'

'Has he shown you a man?'

'I feel I have a husband and that he is the Lord.'

'What work are you doing?'

'Waitressing – but a real waitress. It's a day job at Junior's. That's mainly a lunch place.'

'We have an opening at the chapel for a housekeeper,' the priest said. 'There are benefits. Your medical would be taken care of. Venus would have her school fees paid, if she passed the school's entrance exam. And a small apartment comes with the job.'

Linzi was murmuring yes, yes, almost in shock, because it was more than she had hoped for.

'Why did you choose me?'

'Because you are strong.'

'You made me strong. Don't laugh,' Linzi said, 'but last week I had the spookiest feeling – like I was pregnant, not with a baby inside me but something alive, not human.'

'That is your soul,' the priest said. 'It is a real thing. You were able to feel it because you believe.'

'And it's my life. I am not that other person any more. I've been released. I have more strength than ever. And it's because of what I've seen that I am strong in my faith.'

Father Creech went over to her and embraced her, held her head again as he had done in the baptism.

'I am different from someone who never left home. Who doesn't know sin or who was never tempted. I have seen people at their worst, and I have been a sinner. Because of that I have knowledge. I have greater strength.'

She raised her eyes to Father Creech. He nodded at her and she knew he was proud of her and that she was possessed by a spirit he had rarely seen. He had struck a match and put it to dry tinder and she was so starved of spirit and so ready to receive it her soul had exploded into flame. She had known the darker side of its passion, the grossest urgency of sex, which had a single object, of men lusting after that one thing.

'You brought me to the Lord and helped me see his face.'

'Kneel with me,' Father Creech said. 'Let us pray together.'

That week she moved with Venus to the small apartment on Wilder in a block near the Chapel of Hope. She began work as a housekeeper, in a green uniform, mopping the floors, dusting the chapel, washing the windows, giving thanks.

## 5. *The Chapel of Hope*

'Where is your lovely mother?' Father Creech asked, as he closed the door, shutting out the last of the daylight. The candle-flame bulbs had not been turned on and so only the dim windows and the bearded figures of the saints lit the chapel. The priest slowly slid the scraping bolt, with such care it was as though he were doing it for the first time, learning how.

Venus kept sweeping the aisle so as to seem busy and attentive.

'Mom's shopping,' Venus said. 'She won't be back until eight.'

'She might come back early.'

'Never,' Venus said. 'The thing about my mom is that when she gives you a particular time she means it. She's real well organized, and I guess she hates surprising people.'

'That's very thoughtful,' the priest said. 'But you were late today.'

Venus's white legs and arms, slightly too long for her new school uniform, made her seem clumsy, and in the half-dark she was more like a small skinny adult than a tall child.

'On account of a dead guy at Zippy's, the parking lot, he somehow killed himself in his car, like, and they only found him after about ten hours, when he'd, like, been there all day,' Venus said, growing excited at the memory of the man they had seen after school.

'A man died?' the priest asked.

'Amber and I were getting smoothies and we saw it. We were the first ones, even before the police. We told the Zippy's manager!'

'That you saw the dead man?'

'Yeah.' In her eagerness to tell the story she had stopped sweeping. She was smiling, her eyes shining. 'It was almost like we were responsible.'

'How did you feel?'

'Stoked.'

'Some little girls would have been frightened.'

'I'm not little,' Venus said. 'And anyway he did it to himself. His eyes were wide open and his mouth was too. That's what made us look inside the car.'

'His open mouth?'

'And his eyes. It was so sunny – the sun shining into his eyes. That was the freaky part, that it was so sunny.'

The priest was nodding. He said, 'It was a lovely day. He killed himself in the parking lot, in the sunshine.'

'Some guys came and said it was wrong to do it there, in public, where people were eating.'

'What do you think?'

'If he would have done it somewhere else like how would we of seen it?'

Venus did not say that on a dare from Amber she had touched the dead man on his thick arm as he was dragged from the stinking car. His stiff hair and clay-like flesh had reminded her of the rat.

'What will your mother say when you tell her?'

'I wouldn't tell her. She'd freak.'

The priest sighed. It was so dark in the chapel she could not see any expression on his face but he seemed friendly when he asked, 'Are you a good girl?'

'I guess so.'

'It's so hard to prove that you're a good girl, isn't it?'

'Not really,' Venus said.

'That's nice. If you say that you must be very good,' the priest said. 'Come with me. You can put the broom down.'

Venus rested the broom against the end of a pew, and Father Creech took her hand. He held it in a firm familiar grip, as though he knew her well and did not have to explain where he was taking her or why. His grip gave Venus confidence – she wanted to be led by him, because she knew it was what he wanted. She did not want him to ask her any more questions. The silence was better. They were walking down the main aisle and now the stained-glass windows were almost indistinct. You would never have known there were pictures of saints on them.

'Is this whole thing yours?' she asked, surprising herself with her question.

They were near the altar and Venus could smell the flowers and the brass polish and the beeswax and the varnish.

'I'm in charge,' Father Creech said, and from his tone she could tell he liked her asking it.

Venus said, 'That is so cool.'

It was the size of the chapel and its shadows and the fact that they were alone that made it so strange – not a mass or a service or choir practice, but a huge empty room where they were sheltering from the seven o'clock dusk. Even the lights on outside did not clarify the stained-glass windows and the chapel itself was in shadow. It could have been a club with the lights off, one of those dangerous places like the Rat Room, before it opened with music and men.

'See?' Father Creech was holding a key. He locked the double doors at the side. 'Now no one can come in.'

Venus smiled at his power to do this, and at his conviction too, the way he had slid the bolt on the front door, keeping everyone out, being in charge.

'It's just us,' he said. He tugged her hand. He had not let go of it, even when he had been fumbling with the door key. 'You don't mind that, do you?'

He knew everything except what was in her mind, and she smiled thinking that something he thought was so important was the one thing he did not know. Why should she tell him?

'My mother's in here all the time,' Venus said. 'She sure can pray.'

The priest was facing her, probably staring with his dark eyes. All she could see were his white robes, the shadow of his face.

'What about you, Venus?'

She felt reckless. She said, 'I don't get it.'

'You're so truthful with me,' the priest said.

431

She said, 'I thought you'd care.'

'I like the way you tell the truth,' he said. 'You're not afraid.'

He was still leading her, drawing her to a corner of the chapel, where there was a bench covered with thick cushions. He moved without hesitating, as though the chapel were lighted, though it was all darkness. He had appeared just at dusk and in the short space of this conversation night had fallen.

Father Creech sat her down saying nothing, guiding her with his certain fingers, and then he sat next to her.

'Are you?'

Venus shook her head before she remembered the first part of the question, that he had asked, *You're not afraid*. It was when she denied it that the memory of the question made her fearful.

'Only if you hurt me,' she said.

'I'm going to do the opposite,' he said. 'Okay?'

'Whatever,' she said, and smiled nervously, glad that he could not see her face. 'Um, remember that rat you told us you tried to catch?'

'The one I caught?'

'I guess,' Venus said. 'Was it here?'

'Near here.'

'That's wild.' Venus was smiling, thinking of the sniffing rat.

'I brought you a present,' he said. With his free hand he took something out of his pocket and flicked it – a flame. He was holding a cigarette lighter. 'But that's not the present,' he said, and let go of her hand. 'This is.'

It was a shiny black and gold tube of lipstick and he pressed her fingers over it.

'You like lipstick, don't you?'

Venus nodded in the dark and then made a friendly yes-like sound in her throat.

'When I see you wearing it I know you're thinking about me. That will be our little game. But it's a secret.'

'Thanks,' Venus said.

He said, 'Will you play that game with me?'

432

She nodded in the light of the flame.

He said, 'I gave you a present. Now you have to give me one.'

Venus sniffed. She was confused, she laughed a little, she had nothing.

'Yes, you have one,' he said. He understood, as though she had spoken. 'Here it is.'

He took her hand and held it near the flame, as though to admire it, and then he clicked off the lighter and brought her hand to his lap and pressed it hard.

She was glad he asked for no more than this, she was grateful that he showed her what to do. She felt important that he needed her and after a few moments the priest seemed weak and appreciative.

'That's very nice,' he said, his voice changing as he chafed himself with her hand. Then he let go and he murmured eagerly in a whisper, as she continued in the same way, the same motion, lightly and then with more confidence.

She almost giggled hearing him breathe differently, gagging like a man dying. Then he held her tightly, almost too tightly. After a moment he moved her hand into a pocket in his white robe. He helped her again, showing her how to move her hand. He was big and bent over, and as Venus continued jerking her hand the priest seemed to weaken. It was as though she were throttling a small animal, choking a rat. The strength she pumped out of him surged through her hand and into her body. Soon, the priest whimpered and clapped his knees together and, like someone touched too hard, he snatched her small stiff hand away with his pale one.

He did not speak for quite a long time and Venus could hear his breath scraping the hairs in his nose.

'If anyone asks,' the priest started to say. His words were labored and uncertain. His tongue was thick, his mouth was dry. He did not finish.

Venus said, 'I won't tell anyone, don't worry.'

She was proud. She felt strong at last, he had made her so just a moment ago. It was as though she were reassuring a fearful child, a dear little friend, whom she had unintentionally frightened. She had power over him – over life and death. No one would ask, but if they did, and even if she did tell, no one would blame her. They would blame this frightened man – Godfish.

On Low Sunday, Linzi was baptized at the Chapel of Hope, which was empty this afternoon of sunshine. She wore a long white dress she had made herself. It had a pattern of blue flowers and it covered her body. She had cut her hair. Venus stood to one side watching her mother at the baptismal font, smirking at the uncomfortable bent-over posture, her mother's head lowered as though being shampooed at a hairdresser's sink.

When Linzi raised her dripping head she was smiling at the priest. But he looked at her closely, and fixed his gaze on her and at once she lost her smile.

'I know what happened to you as a child,' he said in a confiding way.

Venus watched from where she knelt with resentment on sore knees. She could not hear. She was glad there were no other people in the chapel. It was so stupid and meaningless. She smiled at the priest, feeling powerful. That pew was where she and the priest had sat, where she had touched him, and won.

'You were covered with a sheet,' the priest went on. 'And someone you knew well entered your room. A man. A near relation.'

The foot of the bed was a wooden plank, the curtains were gauzy, and the shadow of the figure at the door made him seem like a rumpled blanket. Linzi saw it all. Her body showed through the sheet, her narrow figure simplified by the thin cloth, and even stretched out like this she seemed so small and breakable.

Linzi began to cry – the answer was yes, she knew, she saw it clearly. But how did the priest know?

'Someone you trusted,' the priest said. 'He uncovered your nakedness.'

Linzi sobbed harder in fear and joy because the knowledge was miraculous. She saw too that he had to reveal this before he could baptize her. She was terrified again, and she felt faint, so exposed was she, as though it were about to happen, the re-enactment of her shame. The terror was of the fragile thing within her bursting and bleeding. Yet a moment later she understood that God was protecting her and she was strong again and knew that whatever was within her was safe.

'The Lord wants you to know that it was not your fault,' Father Creech said. 'The Lord will not shame you.'

Grasping her drenched head, holding his fingers on the back of her neck, he glanced at Venus, who was frowning – but this frown meant she was watching.

'I am the Lord,' Father Creech said.

As the holy water mingled with Linzi's tears and gave her life, Venus saw a thick shadow suddenly narrow, like a blade turning sideways, something alive and moving beneath the pew, quickly then stopping cold and sniffing, a rat. He hadn't caught it, Venus thought. She laughed to herself and once again saw the priest as weak in his unnecessary lie.

Afterwards, Venus asked her mother, 'What was he talking about?'

'He told me the truth.'

'So why were you crying?'

'Because I was so happy,' and she thought: Some day soon I will tell her the truth.

1998